Festival Season

TS Davis

For the odd ones, and especially, for Faeryn.

Festival Season

Part 1 - Revel

Chapter 1

"YEEEEAAAAUUUUGGGHHH!" I shrieked, diving out of the way of the mast of an enormous tall ship, as it toppled to the ground, snapping guylines in its path. It landed with a mighty crash beside me.

"Sorry 'bout that!" yelled a big man in a frilly white shirt. He grinned apologetically, then turned to chase after a child who had just run by him, both trailed by colorful scarves tied to their belts. I sat down hard on a big wooden chest and took a few deep breaths, at the center of the swirling chaos. This was all anyone had been talking about for weeks, and now I was finally here, at the Pirate Carnival, the first big revel of the festival season.

"This is wild," I said under my breath, surveying the scene around me.

The War Game had been on since this morning, and I had tied a colorful scarf onto my belt without any real idea of what to expect. Now, I watched as an extraordinarily striking redhead engaged a gray-skinned, ghoulish sort of creature in a fierce bout of swordplay. She held her voluminous skirts in one hand, wielding a foam cutlass in the other. My gaze must have lingered on her otherworldly beauty a little too long because she caught my eye and winked at me before dashing away.

Everyone in this crowd was strange, in one way or another. Some were tall, and some were small. Others were craggy and wizened, or hairy, or horned. All of these peculiarities came from their magical ancestry. From the particular mix of humanity and terrestrial magic that made them an intermagical. People who told the original folktales weren't pretending, you know? They were looking out at the world around them, and when they described elves and giants and faeries, they were talking about us.

I look more or less human, myself, although growing up in the Hollywood homogeneity of California, with an adopted mom who was always so critical of my curvy frame and my sensitive, scatter-brained temperament, had left me with a pretty low opinion of myself. My psychology degree had given me labels that helped me understand myself better, like ADHD, and the broader autism phenotype. Still, it wasn't until I moved up here to Oregon and met my birth mother, two months ago, that I really started to accept my own idiosyncrasies and understand them as a part of my magical faerie nature.

If I had been even stranger, like some of these folks here at the Pirate Carnival, maybe I would have figured it out sooner, I mused, watching an enormous bovine snatch the scarf from the waist of a tiny pixie. Or, maybe I wouldn't. If a completely ordinary human walked into the middle of the festival right now, would they see what I saw? Probably not. People see what they expect to see, and it is the nature of the hidden folk to stay hidden. Only those of us with magic running through our veins have the ability to see what's really in front of us, and even then, only if we know what we're looking for.

A tug at my belt alerted me to present danger. I whirled, but it was too late. A curly-haired little girl with mischief in her large, dark eyes waggled the scrap of yellow plaid that she had snatched off my belt and grinned, before turning and kicking up her skirt around her ankles. She dashed away with her prize.

The girl slipped underneath some decorative pennants and dodged between two round canvas tents. I followed more slowly, picking my way over the tight ropes that kept the walls of the big structures upright. Once I had navigated the tripwires, I was surprised to see that she was still in sight, waiting on the road ahead of me. She pushed over a big wooden barrel and sent it rolling toward me with a high tinkling laugh before dashing off down the laneway.

I pursued doggedly, trying hard not to turn my head toward the shining rows of colorful glass bottles, decorative swords, and oiled leather that filled the tinkers' shops lining the thoroughfare. Shoppers, seemingly unbothered by the chaos around them, stepped out of the way to let me pass when they saw my expression and realized I meant business. Eventually, I slowed, puffing with the effort of my pursuit, and lost sight of the girl again. Rounding the corner, I found her leaning against the hull of a large black pirate ship, waiting. When she saw me, she grinned and ducked through a low hatch, disappearing underneath the ship.

I followed her, bending nearly in half to clear the low entrance of the hideaway. As I began to uncurl into the large, dim space, something dropped on me from above.

"Aaah!" I shouted in surprise. I tried to raise my hands to protect my face, but they met a strange resistance. "What the—" I exclaimed as I crashed to the ground, tangling myself even further in the soft rope netting.

"Got ya!" said a high-pitched voice with a giggle. The smiling face of the child I had been chasing appeared above me, as I sprawled in a tangle on the floor.

I sighed, then flopped dramatically with a mighty 'humph,' and let my limbs relax. "Yeah, I guess you did," I said, smiling up at my captor. "But why? You already took my flag. What do you want with me, now?"

"Ransom!" she crowed, throwing her head back and cackling with glee. As she laughed, she stomped around in a circle, punching the air in a dance of celebration.

"Ransom," echoed another small voice from the shadows. "She'll sell you your freedom," it said. "For money."

"Money, money, money!" chanted my captor gleefully.

A second child stepped into the pale light of the doorway. She was taller than the other girl by almost a head, and she wore an expression of dour intelligence as she surveyed me, tangled there on the floor.

"Not real money, of course," she clarified. "Just carnival dubloons, but—"

"Dubloons, dubloons, dubloons!" chorused the other child, who must be her sister. They had matching poufs of dark curly hair and the same small, pointed chins, but the expressions in their large, round eyes set them starkly apart.

I sat up, awkwardly. The taller girl stooped to pick up a corner of the net and helped me get untangled.

"Nooo! She'll get away!" keened her sister

"No, she won't, Aylie. You caught her fair and square," my helper assured her sister. "She'll just sit here and drink our grog until the war's over, and then we'll sell her back. Pirate's code."

"You will?" The girl, who was apparently called Aylie, eyed me suspiciously.

"Yep!" I agreed hastily, holding up my palms in surrender. "Sure will, pirates' code!"

"Hmph," she grumped, disappointed. "Shouldn't we tie her hands behind her back, at least?"

"If her hands were tied, how would she drink the grog?" replied her sister, helping me off the floor and handing me a wooden cup. The grog was some sort of red-flavored drink mix, and I drank it gratefully. It was a warm summer day, and playing war was thirsty work.

From the sounds of shouting and crashing outside, it was clear that the battle still raged, and I sat on a low box to wait out my sentence of captivity.

"I can turn this back on now, right?" asked the taller girl. She flicked on a hanging lantern and pulled a thick paperback out from somewhere. Settling back into her corner to read, she ignored her sister, who hopped from one foot to the other, glancing at the door anxiously.

"Hey Zin, I'm just gonna head out and find some more captives, real quick. You can watch her for me, for a second, right?" the smaller sister asked, tone wheedling.

"Azalea," her sister replied, closing the book with a sharp snap. "If you step one toe out that door, I'm setting her free immediately, and you know it. I don't want to play the game, and I'm not playing. Your captive, your problem."

"Zinnia," whimpered her sister, letting the last vowel stretch into a plaintive whine. "What is the point of having a twin if you can't even help me out once in a while?"

"You're kidding me, right? Help you out once in a while? Like just this morning when I—" Zinnia started.

"Twins?" I blurted, interrupting her. "But you're so much…" I caught myself and trailed off, not wanting to be rude.

"Taller?" finished Zinnia. "Yeah, it's all the extra maturity."

Azalea glowered.

"And what do you want with more captives anyway? You already have one, and unless someone comes to rescue her in the next ten—"

As though summoned by her words, the bright doorway darkened, and a familiar face appeared. The well of magical power, the one that I could always feel inside myself now, pulsed warmly in recognition. My face split into a grin, echoing the bright white smile that I had been waking up next to every morning for the last two months. Or, every morning until last week, when he had gotten a call from his sister, and driven halfway across the country to go help her with something.

How could he have known to look for me here? I shrugged off the thought. I lived in a world of magic now, after all, and our connection was just like that. With his dark skin and short, pointed beard, Jaah didn't look like anybody else I had ever dated, but I felt closer to him than I'd ever felt to anyone. Except maybe my first love, back in high school, but there's really no competing with teenage hormones.

"Hey you," I said, spreading my arms and rising to greet him. Before I could, Azalea pushed by me, knocking me off balance. Zinnia followed close on her heels.

"Daddy! Daddy!" both girls cried, leaping into the man's arms and knocking him back. He caught them and swung them around, making them giggle.

"Hello there, little ones. Yes, I'm glad to see you, too," he said, his deep voice booming.

My chest clenched, and the words that had been about to bubble out of me caught in my throat, turning into a nasty squelching sound. The warm glow in my chest cooled and sank into my stomach, becoming an icy pit.

I stooped to pass through the low entrance and squinted against the sunlight, painfully bright after the ship's dim interior. On his next swinging turn, Jaah noticed me. Seeing my haunted expression, his own face fell, and he set the laughing girls back onto the ground.

"Fiona," he said, wide-eyed, reaching toward me in supplication. "It's not—"

I didn't wait to hear more, and whirled, disappearing into the throng of pirates.

Of course it would be something like this, I thought, chastising myself, as I flowed along with the crowd, feeling powerfully alone in the hot press of bodies. I had been fantasizing about a beautiful future and starting something new and special with Jaah. It had all been too good to be true. Of course it was. And now here was the terrible truth. He was already a father. He had a family already. Those two beautiful girls. My face heated with embarrassment at having allowed my imagination to run away with me, and my eyes pricked with tears.

There was no future for me with him. I was just someone interesting to talk to at the bar. Just a nice girl to warm his bed at night. Not someone important, or someone to start a family with. He had already done that with somebody else. And, who was their mother, anyway? Did he have a wife somewhere? My breath came faster, as I considered the implications of that. These past few months, had I been the other woman?

"Umph." I bumped into the wide back of the man in front of me, interrupting my spiraling thoughts. The throng stopped its forward motion and erupted in a roar as the closing ceremonies of the War Game began.

A booming voice rang out over the gathering. "Ladies and Gentlepirates, the first day of the War Game is officially over. Let the evening's revelry begin!" The crowd roared again in answer.

"Bring your prisoners to the tent to be ransomed!" cried a second voice to my left, and nearly half the group surged toward him, knocking me off balance, and sending me careening into the broad chest of a large, bearded man. He smiled and set me neatly back on my feet, before tipping his feathered hat and moving along.

He had been perfectly polite, but the encounter still set my heart racing. When I first came to Oregon, the men of this valley had been magicked into a state of dangerous aggression. After that spell was resolved, I had found all the men that I had met in this community to be considerate and respectful, but those first experiences had left me with some residual panic.

"Enough of this," I muttered, cutting through the crowd in the opposite direction. I took some deep breaths to calm the pounding in my chest, and in a few minutes, I was back at my own encampment.

I ducked through a curtain made of colorful tapestries and into our makeshift outdoor living room. As I stepped through the screen, the camp's illusion took effect, and the scene around me was of a French pirate villa, a picturesque courtyard complete with crawling ivy and a trickling fountain.

Evita, my faerie birthmother, was the only one in the camp. She stood in front of an outdoor stove made out of large stone pavers. It was actually an ordinary propane camp stove. I knew, having helped set it up yesterday, but my intermagical nature helped me see the illusion as it was intended to be, instead of the mundane reality behind it.

Tiny faeries flitted around my mother's shoulders, tucking strands of her waist-length hair back into the bun coiled on top of her head. The halo of little fluttering faeries suited her, I thought, since most folks called her the Little Queen. The diminutive moniker wasn't a reference to the size of her subjects, though. It was meant to differentiate her from her sister Vivienne, Queen of the Faeries of Portal Land and the Twin River Valleys. Evita had refused to bow to her sister's sovereignty, and so she was a Queen also, but only of her own little hill, and that was all. Thus, she was the Little Queen.

My mother's kingdom was like a tiny island in the ocean of her sister's realm, but she ruled it with seriousness and dignity, and her position did technically make me a sort of princess in this strange community. Not like my cousin Faeryn, though. She was the real faerie princess, growing up in the seat of her mother's power, revered by the Queen's many subjects. Right now, though, she was staying with Evita to get some space from her mother's overbearing nature. She had been planning to come with us to the Pirate Carnival, but decided to stay home at the last moment. My cousin's defective heart left her weak and fragile, but revels like this were what she lived for.

I could smell the mushrooms that Evita was frying, and my stomach rumbled. They were probably the chanterelles we had stopped to forage on our drive down to the festival. She had promised to show me how she had done the magic that told her where to pull off the road and find them.

One of her faeries alerted her to my presence, and she turned around. When she saw the expression on my face, she dropped her spatula and strode across to me.

"Fiona, what's wrong? What happened?"

"He, um. I, uh—" I stammered, unable to find the words to explain.

"Come, come, sit," Evita said, gesturing to a chair and bustling around with caring concern. "Let me get you some water. It'll be alright."

I accepted the mug she handed me, drinking deeply, and sat down in the ring of chairs around the fire.

"He has kids," I told Evita, voice carefully flat and emotionless. "Two of them. Girls."

"Who? Oh, the Gullah, you mean?" she asked, calling him by the title he used in public. Jaah was a private name that he gave to me to use, and I wasn't supposed to share it. I was proud of myself that I hadn't ever slipped up and called him Jaah in front of Evita. Especially impressive, considering how much I managed to bring him up in conversation.

"Yep," I answered, staring into the fire with the mug clutched in my hands.

"You know what, honey, let me grab you something stronger than water."

At my nod, Evita poured me a cup of strong mead, then moved to stand behind me, squeezing my shoulders comfortingly. I gazed into the fire, feeling the burn of the drink in my throat, and watching the shadows of the dancing flames.

"It's wonderful that you've found someone you are so compatible with, my dear, but please be cautious. I can't know everything the future holds for you because you still have to make your own decisions, but I've done quite a bit of divination about your life, you know," she said, moving to sit beside me and taking my hand in hers. She turned the palm upright and stroked the lines contemplatively. "There are several different ways that our story might be written. Some take longer to get where they're going, and some are quite quick. This path that you're on feels like one of the faster ones. In fact, we're moving so quickly that I don't quite understand how everything is supposed to work out, in the end." Her brow furrowed, then she smiled tightly and gave my hand a squeeze. "But, I trust in our family's magic and have faith that it will all turn out as it should."

"How what all works out?" I asked, confused.

"The turning of the wheel of life, dear," she replied esoterically, then continued, "Please take some time to get to know yourself, this summer, Fiona. Figure out who you are and what you really want for yourself. It's never too late to find oneself, of course, but it's certainly nicer to do it when you're young, without attachments and responsibilities to weigh on you."

I nodded, thinking about all the ways that my adopted mom's critical judgment had shaped me, growing up. She had commanded me to be 'normal' and I had done my best, shrinking and contorting myself into a shape she approved of. Away at college, I had started to untangle myself from those constrictive expectations, and I'd come quite a bit farther in these past two months with my birth family, but I still had a lot to unlearn.

"You'll be spending your summer at festivals like this, though, and there's really no better place to find yourself than at our fae revels," said Evita proudly. "Take your time and explore. Let curiosity be your guide, and try everything that our magical world has to offer. Intermagicals who stick to the straight and narrow end up missing so much of their own truth, and I want you to stand proudly in your own authenticity. When your little brother Zelai first told me that he thought he might be a boy, I told him to try it out at a revel just like this one, and see what it was like."

"Oh yeah?" I said, but I wasn't particularly surprised. I could imagine that a lot of folk figured out that they were trans at these kinds of festivals, where they got to dress up and try out new personas without worrying that anyone was going to punish them for it. That's when you know a community is really safe, when they encourage one another to embrace their full selves without judgment or condemnation.

I had seen several bearded pirates in brightly colored skirts here at the Pirate Carnival, but I hadn't seen anyone who was actually trans, other than my little brother. Maybe I had seen them and hadn't even noticed.

Jaah was actually non-binary themselves, I reminded myself. They didn't feel like they fit into the box of either man or woman, but found it easier and safer to let people assume that they were a man. They entrusted me with that secret at the same time they gave me their name, and I felt a small welling of pride at the memory.

The curtains split open, and we turned to see who had arrived. It was my little brother Zelai, as though summoned by our conversation. He was followed by a giant of a person, who stooped through the doorway, then stood up to reveal a frilly white pirate shirt. I recognized them.

"Hey!" I said, pointing a finger at the large man accusingly.

"Oh! Hello again. Sorry about nearly skewering you earlier!" he said, smiling sheepishly. "I picked the wrong pole to lean against. But, of course, I did," he shrugged apologetically. "My luck's just like that."

"Oh, you know Urb already, Fiona?" Evita asked, gesturing to our new guest.

"Kind of. We had a bit of a near miss, earlier," I answered, with a laugh, telling Evita the story.

"Well, it's fortunate that Fiona has the natural luck of the faeries to counteract whatever it is that you've got going on, Urb," said Evita with a chuckle.

"Faerie luck?" I repeated, wonderingly. "That explains some things, actually."

The curtain split, again, and this time it was the Gullah's harried face that came into view.

"Fiona, there you are. I just got here, and I didn't know where you were camped, so it took me a minute to find you." He brushed through the curtain of fabric, palms outstretched in supplication. "Can we talk, please?"

"Yeah," I said, picking up a cloak from the back of the chair I had been sitting in, and wrapping it closely around my shoulders. "Let's talk."

We walked in silence for a few minutes, getting clear of the crowds on the main thoroughfare. Finally, he spoke.

"I wanted to tell you before you met them, but I didn't have the chance."

I whirled on him, eyes flashing. "You didn't have the chance? We've been spending every night together, for weeks! And you didn't have the chance to tell me that you have children? That you already have a family?"

"That I-Fiona, wait," he said, pulling at my sleeve so that I would turn and face him.

I yanked my arm out of his grasp and took two quick steps away from him, down the path.

"Don't. It's fine, okay? I was obviously taking this thing between us too seriously. If you didn't even think that I should know that you had children…" I paused, shaking my head in disbelief. "And, you know what? It's fine, really. They seem lovely. Very sweet." I walked ahead of him and kept my eyes forward. "And I love kids, you know? I've always thought about having kids. A baby that was mine, after being adopted, like I was? But it's fine, really. I get it. I was making this something more than it was, in my head, that's all. I just—"

"Making this more than it is? Fiona, please, just let me explain. They're not my daughters okay. They're not my kids."

"They're," I stopped, turning back to face him. "They're not? But—"

"I know," he said, hanging his head apologetically. "And I should have told you. They are an important part of my life, and…" He stepped toward me, taking my hands in his. " You are also becoming a very important part of my life."

"I am?" I asked, feeling that familiar glow of warmth in my chest.

"You are," he said. "I apologize for upsetting you. Your face, when you came out from below decks like that." He chuckled gently. "They're my nieces, Zinnia and Azalea. I should have told you about them before now, but it's…" He sighed, shaking his head. "Complicated. They've been in the South with my sister all winter. I was going to tell you before they came back to Oregon, but Pythia had some emergency, and she wanted me to come out early. I'm sorry." He looked deeply into my eyes, showing me that he meant it. "I should have told you everything then, but you were at work, and she asked me to come right away, so…" He shrugged, and dropped my hands, stepping back to give me space to reply.

"But…" I paused, rubbing my eyes and trying to make sense of all of this new information. "They called you Daddy."

"Network security," he said, with a crooked smile. "Just like how people call me the Gullah in public. It's simpler for the girls if they call me Daddy. Less suspicious. Nobody thinks to ask questions or wonder who their parents are."

We rounded another corner, and I realized that we had come all the way back to the black-walled ship where I had been held captive earlier today.

"But you said they were your nieces. Aren't they your sister's kids, then?"

"What's that now?" The question came from above us. I looked up in time to see a pair of dark, athletic legs swinging over the side of the black ship, and stepped out of the way so as not to be trampled. A lithe young woman slithered her way down smooth black shipboards that matched her short, tattered-hem romper and the springy locs of her hair.

"Not my babies, thank you very much. Being Auntie is good enough for me."

"Fiona," said Jaah, taking my hand possessively. "This is Pythia. We share custody of our older sister's two daughters."

At the mention, the two girls emerged from their hideaway, and stood on either side of Pythia.

"And…" Jaah continued, indicating the two big-eyed girls looking up at me. "I believe you've already met Zinnia and Azalea."

Chapter 2

It was late by the time we went to bed. I could hear the sound of drums still beating in the distance, as I lay in my tent with Jaah snoring gently beside me, unable to fall asleep in the chill of the early summer night. Every now and then, the laughing voices of revelers would float in through the darkness, then drift away again.

I could understand why the fae folk loved these gatherings so much. The energy of the Pirate Carnival was palpable. I could feel it all around me. I smiled, thinking about how much I would enjoy spending this summer getting to know myself and my strange new community at festivals like this.

The drumming stopped abruptly, replaced by loud, angry shouting. It was far enough away that I couldn't make out any of the words, but the violent sound of it sliced through the sudden quiet like a knife.

CRACK! A gunshot rang out, then a moment of silence, and a chorus of even louder shouting.

At the sound of the gunshot, the Gullah sprang awake and scrambled out of bed, dressing hastily. He grabbed his cloak and sword belt and ducked out of the tent off into the night.

I followed, a few beats behind him, wrapping my own cloak around my shoulders, then paused at the entrance, peering out into the darkness. Evita was there, standing across from me, in the entrance to her own tent. I caught her eye, and she shook her head. *Not our weeds, not our garden.* I heard the words in my mother's voice, in my mind.

I nodded in agreement and pulled my head back inside, like a turtle into its shell. What good could I possibly do by getting involved with whatever was going on out there? I kept my cloak wrapped around me and crawled back into bed, hoping that the additional warmth would finally allow me to fall asleep. Whatever happened tonight, Jaah could fill me in, in the morning.

Chapter 3

Bright light filtered through the walls of the pale canvas tent. Something woke me up, but whatever it was had stopped, for now. I blinked, squinting against the morning sun.

"Ahoy and attention, fellow pirates," sounded a megaphone-amplified voice, a few moments later. "The rest of the carnival is canceled, effective immediately. The police will be here at noon, so get packing. You're gonna want to be out of here before they show up."

"Okay, now I'm really curious about what happened last night," I said aloud. Jaah was still asleep. He was lying next to me, on top of the blankets, still fully dressed. I gave his shoulder a shake.

"Bwah-huh?" he remarked sleepily. I told him what I had just heard, and his expression hardened.

"Well, if we're trying to be out of here before noon, we'd better get started," he said, turning and grabbing a piece of discarded clothing from the floor and stuffing it into a mostly full bag. "Kind of nice that most of it didn't even get unpacked."

As we gathered our things, he told me what he knew. There had been an altercation. The shouting I heard. Jaah didn't know the men who were fighting, and no one he had spoken to knew them either. He thought they might have been local townies who snuck into the festival after hours to steal things and make trouble. And to use and sell illegal drugs, which was apparently what they were doing when the fight broke out.

"Really?" I asked. "Are there a lot of drugs at these things?"

The Gullah chuckled darkly. "Oh sure. But what do you expect? We have to figure out how to get by in a world that's not built for people like us. It's easy to end up angry or depressed. Some intermagicals end up turning to drugs to take the edge off."

Festivals like this were an environment where folk who wanted to imbibe in such things could do so in good company and relative safety, Jaah explained. Ordinarily, at least. Last night, though, things had certainly gotten out of hand. He told me what happened after he left the tent.

When the Gullah arrived on the scene, he found a group of intermagicals restraining two townies. The gun that was fired was confiscated and would be handed over to the police. In addition to being dangerous, having a gun in public like this was illegal. The new legislation completely banning personal firearms was new, but the penalties were significant, and the fact that there had been gunfire was a serious thing.

"Someone fires a gun, and they cancel the whole festival? That seems like a pretty strong reaction. I know there are some new rules about guns, but—"

"They might not have, if that was the only bad thing that happened last night," Jaah interjected. Apparently, the men with the gun were selling drugs, and some had gone missing. And, while the other two men were waving the gun at each other, a third man had quietly overdosed, presumably on the missing supply. This place was about to be the location of a homicide investigation, and that wasn't the right sort of atmosphere for revelry at all.

Carrying our first load of packed bags, Jaah and I headed toward the front gate of the fair. It was such a shame, I thought, walking down the main thoroughfare, past the elaborate displays of mast and riggings that had been constructed for the festival just yesterday and were now being hastily torn down.

We followed a line of pirates on foot, hauling bags and pulling carts. Cars passed by us, going the other direction, and as I started to overheat in the mid-morning sun, my load felt heavier and heavier with each step, and I found myself regretting that we hadn't just gone to get the van. I trudged on, putting one foot in front of the other.

Beside me, Jaah stiffened, and I looked up, following his gaze. Three pickup trucks had just turned into the lane heading toward the fair. If you could even call them that. They looked like their ancestors might once have been pickup trucks, but these grotesque behemoths were swollen to an enormous size, almost beyond recognition, jacked up on mega-huge wheels with treads like tractor tires, and topped with bars of bright halogen lamps.

"Look at those douche mobiles," said a voice from over my shoulder. It was Urb, and he stepped away from the road with us, to watch as the trucks drove underneath a banner emblazoned with an iconic skull and crossbones and the words *Beware All Ye Who Enter Here*. They turned diagonally, blocking both lanes of traffic, and revved their engines.

Since discovering that I was an intermagical, I had been working on tapping into my magical intuition, but I didn't need any preternatural perception to tell me that something interesting was about to happen.

Chapter 4

Once all three trucks passed under the banner and into the carnival, the first revved its engine while the other two behemoths nosed their way into the crowd, pushing pedestrians back and blocking both lanes diagonally. Once they had maneuvered into place, the men packed in the oversized cabs piled out and climbed into the back. The front truck hoisted an enormous flag and a lucky gust of wind blew it open.

"Christ's Heart," I spat, recognizing the emblem.

"That's an interesting way to blaspheme," said Urb with a chuckle, misunderstanding me. On my other side, though, Jaah stiffened.

"Do you recognize anyone?" he hissed under his breath.

I'd had my first run-in with the Christ's Heart Church when I first moved to town, when my faerie luck had put me in the right place at the right time to thwart their big money-making scheme and save my poor, sick cousin Faeryn. In the end, the leader of the local Christ's Heart Church was in jail, and I was a local hero among the intermagicals, but I certainly hadn't made any friends in the church. I didn't think any of them would recognize me, though, other than the Deacon and his son, and with his father in jail, I didn't know whether Brandon would have stuck around. I scanned the group of men, looking from face-to-face.

"I don't see anyone I know," I told him with a sigh of relief. Looking forward to spending the summer following Evita's advice and connecting more deeply with my magical community, I was more than ready to put all this nastiness with the church behind me.

"Guess they found their new blowhard, after you got rid of the last guy," said the Gullah, gesturing with his chin at the man with the megaphone in the center truck. His short-cropped gray hair made him look older, but his shoulders were still powerful and broad, and his biceps bulged under his neatly tucked polo, as he held a large bullhorn aloft.

"Heathens and sinners," he intoned. "It's time to clean up this valley, starting with dens of iniquity like this one. Allow me to introduce you to the Morality Police, who will be helping me to put an end to these little sin fests, these pop-up Sodom and Gomorrahs."

"Aw hell," said Jaah, somewhat ironically.

"You people think it's alright to just do and be whatever you want. What you've got to understand is that there is a natural order to things in this world. A hierarchy. There's the nice, normal people and then there's the freaks. The lowlife misfits. Your kind used to be outcasts and loners, but you've all gotten entirely too comfortable and frankly, too numerous for comfort. I mean, look at you," the man said to a bearded pirate in a long wrap skirt. "Look at what you're wearing. Don't you have any shame, man?"

"Not a man, man," the skirted pirate shouted back, before turning and continuing to walk toward the parking lot, clearly having had enough of this.

"That's right, hang your head and leave. You should feel ashamed about what happened here. You all should. A man died here last night! This is always the way it goes when you punks and stoners try to build anything. People get confused, and they get hurt. Good, godly people."

"Yeah!" shouted one of the men next to him, pumping his fist in agreement.

"I've been living overseas for almost a decade, while this valley has sunk into the depths of depravity, and when my church leadership told me what happened here, I knew that God was calling me to bring his rule of law back to this place, and set some things right. Because God knows that you're all sinners, but Jesus died so you can be forgiven. So, if you felt that little pang of shame in your chest, just now, I want you to come see me at the Christ's Heart Celebration of Spirit, tomorrow, and take that first step on the path back to salvation and righteousness."

On cue, the men in the truck hopped down. They distributed brightly colored flyers to the crowd, tucking them under all the available windshields.

"So, come on down tomorrow, and let us show you what a real, wholesome good time feels like." He gave a theatrical shrug and a wink. "Maybe even save your immortal soul, how about that?"

With that, the men all climbed back into the trucks and peeled off, heading deeper into the festival to harass more unsuspecting pirates.

"What the truck was that?" asked Urb, as we continued on toward the parking lot.

"Trouble," Jaah answered soberly, then he told us what he knew. These kinds of groups had popped up all over the country in recent months. Local religious extremist groups were forming militias and using some new CCC regulations to enforce rules on their communities for the 'greater public good.'

He was talking about the Calamity Control Council, a group who had recently taken control of the global political scene. They were given the power to set international law, promising to help ease the general global unrest. I first encountered the Calamity Control Council when I was in college, where students protested both for and against various CCC regulations, but when I moved to Oregon and discovered this secret world of magic, I learned that intermagicals started using the abbreviation CCC a very long time ago. They used it to talk about the forces of darkness that robbed humanity of so much of its wonder and goodness. To the intermagicals, CCC stood for the evils of Capitalism, Conformity, and Climate corruption. And, as far as most intermagicals were concerned, the Calamity Control Council and the old CCC were one and the same.

"This is not good," said Jaah with a shake of his head. "Not good at all."

"No, it's not," Urb agreed. "Man, if my bad luck goes and ruins an entire festival season for everyone just so it can mess me up one more good time, I swear. A summer with no festivals would be bad for everybody, but it would be really bad for me and my family in particular, you know?"

"No," I answered. "I don't know. Why?"

"Oh," said Urb. "Sorry, I just assumed you would. Most people around here know me. My grandmother is the Shrew of the Shrewsborough Renaissance Faire."

"The Shrew, of—" I repeated, confused, but the Gullah's face lit up, beside me.

"Oh, sure, I know who you are. Just didn't recognize you," he said, enthusiastically. "I've never managed to make it to Shrewsborough, but from what I hear, you basically run that fair."

"Me and Mom," said Urb, shrugging sheepishly. "It's the family business."

"You think they'll really be able to do it?" I asked.

"I don't know," Jaah answered thoughtfully. "But it's possible, especially considering what happened here last night. With the overdose and the gunshots, they'll be able to make a decent case that these kinds of festivals are dangerous. The new CCC regulations could give them the license to shut our revels down, if that's their plan."

"Not if I can help it," said Urb with a shake of his head. "My family needs the fair this year. I mean, we need it every year, but this year," he said, clenching his jaw. "We need it more than usual."

"What do you have in mind?" I asked, seeing the cogs turning behind Urb's eyes.

"Well, for starters, I want to check out this 'Celebration of Spirit' thing tomorrow," said Urb, gesturing with one of the flyers that we were handed. "My mom says that people like that always tell on themselves, and I want to be close enough to hear them when they do it."

"That's an interesting thought," I told him, then turned and followed Jaah, who resumed walking toward the parking lot. Before we got there, we happened upon a spectacle. Not surprising, since we were at a fae revel after all, even if it had been canceled. Distractions were everywhere. This spectacle took the form of an orating pirate on top of an old-fashioned steamer trunk. He wore a dark orange coat that perfectly matched his flaming red hair, and he sloshed coffee out of his pewter beer flagon as he gesticulated.

"That's Fredbeard the Red, one of the Carnival's organizers," Jaah told me quietly, and we stopped to listen to the man speak.

"We don't want to underestimate what kind of things these Morality Police people will try to cook up, with the law on their side," he said, voice heavy with concern, and the crowd muttered worriedly. "But that's why we're glad I went to law school!" The man's face spread in a confident grin. "Whatever nonsense they come up with, I'll be able to find ways to poke holes in it."

The crowd's murmurs brightened at this, but not everyone was convinced by the man's bravado.

"You're not a miracle worker, Fred," called a skeptical voice from the crowd.

"No," Fred agreed. "I'm not a miracle worker, but bureaucracy makes the world go round, especially in matters of the law, and I'm the best Bureaumancer we've got. Underestimate our skills at your own peril."

"What about the Little Queen's new girl?" shouted an unseen voice.

"Yeah, talk about miracles! Look what she did for the princess. I bet she can fix this!" called another.

"Isn't that you?" Urb asked me, with a voice loud enough to carry.

"That's her!" said a squat little gnome standing next to us. "She's right here!"

"Fiona, the Little Queen's lost daughter! Let's hear what she has to say about it," said an insistent voice, as hands pushed me toward the front of the crowd.

From on top of the steamer trunk that was serving as a stage, the sea of faces looked alarmingly large. Urb stood a head and shoulders taller than the crowd of gathered fae. We locked eyes, and he mouthed the word 'sorry' with a look of concern on his face. What was done was done. I was just going to have to make the best of it.

"Fiona," shouted a burly dwarf from the front row. "Tell us what we should do."

"Save our revels, just like you saved the princess!" implored the beautiful siren beside him.

I was going to have to make a speech, apparently. Not my favorite thing to do. I swallowed and said the first thing that came to mind.

"I'm sorry this is happening," I told the crowd. "I was having a lot of fun this weekend, and I was looking forward to the rest of the festivals this summer. I don't have any idea what to do about any of this, but, uh, if I think of anything, I'll try it, okay?" The disappointed faces of the crowd before me made my stomach sink.

"No notion at all?" the dwarf shouted. He sounded more accusatory than seemed fair, I thought, considering the circumstances.

"Of course not," I replied hotly. "None of us do. All I know is what the men in those ridiculous trucks just told us." I noticed a row of fliers tucked under the parked cars' windshields. "Actually, you know what? I'll tell you one thing I'm going to do. I'm checking out that Celebration of Spirit thing tomorrow to find out who it is we're dealing with."

The small audience gave a cheer. My chest swelled with pride until I caught Urb's eye, and the sensation was replaced by a pang of worry. I didn't actually have any clue how our amateur investigation was supposed to help fix anything, but I swallowed hard and reminded myself to smile as I stepped back down into the crowd.

"You've decided to involve yourself, then," said Evita, stepping out from the throng to meet me as soon as I got down from the podium. I hadn't even realized she was there.

"It doesn't feel like I have much of a choice," I said, thinking about the many hands that had pushed me up to the front of the crowd.

"You always have a choice," said Evita, giving me a shrewd look. "And not making a choice is still choosing. But I'm proud of you for wanting to help. And, it makes sense that you like to meddle," she said, her expression teasing. "Our kind tends to be that way. Just don't get so distracted chasing your curiosities that you forget to come over tomorrow. The festival may be canceled, but our family dinner isn't."

"Yeah," I answered. "Sure. Of course. I'll come by after my, uh, investigation," The flyers said the celebration started at noon. We'd be done in plenty of time.

"You should come to dinner tomorrow, too, Urb," said Evita to the tall man who had just come to join us.

"I guess I might as well, if we're checking out that church thing together," answered Urb, turning toward me. "Those evangelicals make me nervous. It'll be nice not to have to go alone."

Part 2 - Disturbance

Chapter 5

"Oh, I know what this is. It's a Tent Revival! I saw these all the time, growing up down South," said Jaah, as we rounded a corner and a field full of white tents came into view.

"What's that?" I asked.

"It's a conversion party, basically," Urb replied. "Probably gonna give us the hard sell."

"Should I be worried about being, uh, convinced of anything?" I asked nervously. I had tried my best to imagine what kind of place we were about to walk into, but my limited church experience hadn't given me much of a frame of reference.

"Not particularly," Jaah answered with a dismissive shrug. "The church I grew up in did a lot of proselytizing, and even as a little kid, it was pretty obvious to me that they weren't convincing anyone."

"Well, yeah," said Urb with a chuckle. "They're not supposed to. The fact that it doesn't work is a key part of the strategy."

"Say what now?" Jaah replied with an inquisitive raise of his eyebrow.

The hard sell, Urb explained, has never been an effective way of getting people to join a religion. Missionaries with bibles knock on unsuspecting doors thinking they're supposed to be sharing God's word. But, the church leaders who sent them hope they come home rejected and demoralized into the loving arms of their church family who will comfort them and praise their strength for braving the cruel outside world.

"And they train them to be obnoxious," Urb added enthusiastically. "The more abrasive their tactics are, the better the results. It's a classic pain-reward cycle. Incredibly effective for brainwashing."

"Are you serious?" I asked, eyeing Urb in the rear-view mirror. "That's wild. The way you talk makes it sound like a cult."

"Well, if it walks like a cult and talks like a cult," said Urb with a shrug. He knew quite a bit about cults, apparently, and by the time we got out of the car, I was even more nervous.

The unsettling smiles of the greeters at the front gate did nothing to soothe my nerves. As we got closer to the entrance, an uncomfortable feeling washed over me, and I reached out to take Jaah's hand, for the steady flow of calming energy I knew his touch would provide. As I did, I watched one woman's smile flicker. By the time we reached her, it was plastered across her face again.

"Welcome!" said the perfectly coiffed church lady, taking my other hand and giving it a little tug to separate me from Jaah. "First time?" I nodded, and somehow her grin widened even further. It looked painful. "Oh, wonderful. Come with me and I'll introduce you to our Women's Ministry. They'll be just thrilled to meet you."

I looked back at Jaah, who shrugged as though to say, 'that's what we're here for, isn't it?'

As I followed my guide through the event, I found myself remembering what Urb had told me about cults, back in the van.

You are One of God's Own Special Children one sign read, and *Nothing is More Important than Your Salvation.*

"A cult convinces its members that they're part of a special group of sacred people with an all-important spiritual mission, where the ends justify the means," Urb had explained. "And then the leaders exploit the members for their money and free labor."

Give Generously of Yourself and Be Blessed, read another sign, next to a full-size whirligig ride, a professional-grade popcorn machine, and then, *Be a Faithful Servant of the Lord.*

"I can see what he's talking about," I muttered under my breath. The Pirate Carnival was run by volunteers, too, but it hadn't been plastered with propaganda like this. It hadn't had any actual carnival rides, either.

"Hmm?" answered my guide, turning back toward me. "Oh, did you want to walk the *Path to Salvation*? Please do! Go right ahead!"

She turned toward an expensive-looking fake boardwalk and smiled expectantly, waving me onward. I paused at the first set of footprints to read.

Step one: Realize that you are a sinner and you stand in the judgment of God.

"Is that so?" I replied, glad my keen-eared guide had stayed on the main road.

Step Two: Accept that Jesus made the ultimate sacrifice to save our immortal souls.

"Guilt trip, much?" I muttered, walking on past the rest of the stations without stopping to read any more.

"What do you think?" asked my guide when I rejoined her. "Are you ready to make the Salvation Prayer?" She must have seen something in my expression, because she continued on, saying, "How about I just pray for the both of us?" She took my hands and screwed up her face, then said "Amen!" and gave me another one of her simpering smiles. I was glad when she turned back down the path and continued her quick march toward our destination. Finally, I followed her helmet of hair into one of the large tents. Inside was a group of women who looked almost identical to each other, and my guide disappeared into the gaggle, calling. "Temperance! Where are you, Temperance?"

"What is it, Eugenia?" replied a tall, thin woman who stepped out of the throng, looking irritated. "Bertrand is just about to get on stage." My guide stood on her tiptoes and whispered to the woman, who gave me a level look, and then called over her shoulder. "Nora, I have another little job for you. Can you take this young lady over to the Youth Ministry tent and, er…" She shot an irritated look at my guide, whom she had called Eugenia. "Introduce her to some of our nice Christian boys?"

"Yes, Auntie," said a small voice, and a blond girl stepped forward, scanning the tent until her eyes met mine. They were bright blue and sent a shock of recognition through me. I knew her! Or, I thought I did. After a moment, I realized that I had never seen her before, but something about her did look incredibly familiar. I plastered on a fake smile of my own and returned her wave of greeting. I was glad to follow her back out of the tent. Those identical women were eerie.

"Sorry about that," the girl, Nora, said over her shoulder. "My uncle is about to give his big speech, and everybody's feeling a little tense right now. The Youth Ministry tent is right over here. Oh!" Nora had pointed at the same moment that my big friend had stepped back out of the tent flaps. "Hey, I recognize you. It's Herb, right?"

"Yeah," Urb agreed. "It's been a while."

A dark-haired youth appeared from around a corner. "Lena, it's almost time," he called, gesticulating at my new blond guide. "Come on, they're looking for you."

"Well, I guess I can leave you here with Herb. He's just about as nice a Christian boy as you could want to meet, I'd think." She smiled at me and winked at Urb. "You two might want to go find a good spot in the audience. It sounds like the big show's about to start!"

"You know her?" I asked, as Urb and I drifted along with the mass of people headed for the big stage.

"Ellie? Yeah, sure I do. I went to this church with Mom for a while, back when it was up in the mountains, closer to us. We quit going because they moved into a building downtown, and for a few other reasons. I remember Ellie from Sunday school. She's a real sweetheart."

We found a place at the edge of the crowd, close to the front, and I looked up to see the blond girl climb the stairs to the stage. Her aunt called her Nora, Urb knew her as Ellie and she had also answered to Lena. I found myself wondering what she called herself as she took her place next to her Aunt Temperance, off to one side of the platform.

Feeling his presence behind my shoulder, I looked up and caught Jaah's eye. He made a little grimace of acknowledgment. We'd all discuss what we had seen once we were safely away from here.

The lights dimmed, and the crowd began to murmur, as a fog machine spat puffs of vapor onto the stage. The lights flashed back on and spun chaotically as a voice over a loudspeaker intoned, "Please join me in welcoming the honorable Reverend Bertrand Rex."

Spotlights lit center stage, and the mists parted as the Reverend strode into view and the crowd erupted in applause. It was the man from the Pirate Carnival, of course.

"Thank you, Brothers and Sisters, thank you," the man said, reaching down to touch the hands of the people in the front row. "It is so good to be back here with you again. It has been far too long since I last set foot in this valley I call home. But God has called me back here to help in this time of need. And I am here to answer your call, oh Lord." He pumped his fist skyward. "I am here!" The audience applauded again, including Nora and her Aunt, who wore frozen smiles and stood perfectly still, except for their soundly clapping hands.

"And cult leaders always have a skinny white woman standing next to them," Urb had told me on the drive here. "Some people think it's a coincidence, but it's not. She has a very important role to play. She humanizes him, you know? He can't be all that bad, if he's got a woman like that by his side, can he? And she distracts the men and sets a standard for women to try to live up to, which keeps them hungry and at each other's throats. Pretty handy, if you ask me."

"This valley has lost its way," the Reverend admonished. "The forces of darkness used to stay where they belong, in the cracks and the crevices, but now they have crept their way into civilized society. The perverts, the weirdos, and the no-good-niks. Dark and dangerous strangers poisoning the minds of our youths and leading them down a dangerous path."

"That's me," said Jaah, in a barely audible whisper. "Dark and dangerous."

"Pretty sure he's talking about all of us," replied Urb, just as quietly.

"I have been called by God to set the moral standard and show this community the power of Christ's Heart. Our love for the Lord is stronger than our human weakness. We are obedient to God's Laws and trust him above all…" he paused to kiss his fingers and raise them up toward the heavens. "But, you can't trust a sinner to know what's best for them, so our Morality Officers will use whatever force is necessary to make God's kingdom here on Earth. It'll be an uphill battle but by the time we're done, all you good Christians will be safe from the perversions of the queers and the cross-dressers, and all the darkness that—"

SKREEEEEEEE!

The Reverend was interrupted by a violent squeal of feedback from his microphone. Moments later, the high-tech light board exploded with a loud *POP! POP!* A shower of glass rained down and made the folks onstage cower and shield their heads with their arms.

"Meet you at the car," Jaah muttered in my ear. I turned to follow, but he was already gone.

"Well, that was awful," I said, tossing the keys to Jaah, who swung into the driver's seat and turned the engine over. An enormous sense of relief washed over me as we drove out the front gate and away from the Tent Revival. "I don't get it. There were so many cheering people there. Is that really the kind of spiritual experience they're looking for?"

"Of course not. Evangelicals like that aren't spiritual," corrected Urb from the seat behind me. "They're religious."

"What do you mean?"

"Well, in a religion, God is separate from you, and you worship him, and follow his rules, because you're afraid of ending up in hell." I nodded. That had definitely been the messaging back there. "Versus spirituality, which is about finding divinity in everything, including ourselves, and creating our own Heaven on Earth." He chuckled and shook his head. "Man, it sure was hard to keep quiet in that Youth Ministry tent. There were so many things I wanted to say!"

"You were in that youth tent for a while, huh?" I asked with a laugh.

"Yeah," he said. "Ellie wasn't the only one to recognize me from back in the day. I've got a pretty distinctive look. Always have."

I glanced back at the big man in the back seat. I hadn't really registered it before, with the number of unusual fae folk that I encountered these days, but he was a little strange-looking now that I really thought about it, especially for a fae that spent his time around humans. His nose was a little flat, and his eyes were a bit too wide-set to look entirely human. His pale eyes, which I had assumed were green, were in fact a greenish-yellow, which was not, typically, an eye color that humans ended up with.

"What kind of fae are you, anyway, Urb? Do you know?" I asked. His face took on a twisted expression I couldn't read, so I added, "My cousin Faeryn will be at the hill tonight. If you don't know, she can probably tell you."

"Oh, no, I know. We're Firbolg. Giant kin. It's one of the reasons Mom likes to live so far outside of town. Firbolg like it better out in the wilds."

"Firbolg?" exclaimed the Gullah. "Really? I thought Firbolg men all had big, bushy beards."

"Yeah," said Urb, shrugging. "Oh man, Fiona, did you see what they were working on in that Youth Ministry tent?"

"No, what?"

"Drawing new logos for the church. Marketing stuff. Trying to come up with something that would appeal to the youths, you know," he caught my eye, smiling.

"And all that valley of the heart iconography? I swear they all just looked like butts and boobs."

"Hah," said Jaah, without much humor. "Sounds like you had a better time there than I did."

"Oh yeah?" I asked. "Do tell."

"Well, after y'all were whisked away so quickly, I was…" He took his eyes off the road to raise his eyebrows at me in emphasis. "Completely ignored. Absolutely nobody talked to me. Quite a few sideways glances, though."

"Really? Because you're—"

"The darkness, yeah," the Gullah sighed. "Seems like it. It was pretty blatant. Every time I walked up to one of those carnival games— whoops! It would need to close for a break. Every session I poked my head into was at capacity, or, I heard this one a lot, for 'select participants.' Yeah, I picked up pretty quickly what that meant."

"Wow," I said, with a heavy sigh. "In Oregon? That's wild. I thought, the West Coast, you know?"

"Oh yeah," said Urb. "We live way out in the country, and it's real bad out there. All kinds of prejudices against anybody different, anyone whose skin isn't white, and all kinds of LGBT folk," he shook his head. "As soon as you get twenty, thirty miles outside of any of the big cities, around here, it seems like."

"Yeah," said Jaah, shaking his head. "But it's weird up here. Back in the South, it was just good old capital R Racism. You knew where people stood. Up here, I don't know. It's all underhanded. Nobody will say anything right to your face, but they'll tell you clearly enough. It feels…worse, almost? I don't know. I got close to the buffet, at this thing, and somebody stepped in front of me and suggested that the food might not be to my taste. Like I would have eaten their food anyway. It was all stuff like that, the whole time."

I reached across to his hand that was clenched in his lap and held it in mine. Our fingers intertwined and I squeezed comfortingly.

"But," he said, more cheerfully. "Being left to my own devices to wander around, with everyone doing their best to ignore me, let me casually lean on quite a few of their generators. Which reminds me—"

He pulled off to the side of the road, turning to look back down at the event's festivities spread in the field below us, lit by thousands of twinkling lights in the church's signature pale blue.

He let go of my hand and picked up his phone, tapping quickly.

A few seconds later there was a sharp electrical crack, and the twinkle lights all went dark. The gently glowing tents fell dim, too.

"They're going to have to replace quite a few fuses if they want to keep going after dark tonight," said the Gullah with a chuckle. "And they were just getting started with those speeches, too, weren't they? Pity!"

Chapter 6

We made it to Evita's house by early afternoon. We were early for dinner, but I didn't think anyone would mind. Zelai was the first one to notice us, as usual. He was perched high in a tree above the steep driveway that wound its way up to my mother's hilltop abode. Urb grinned when he saw the young faerie boy. Zelai's expression matched Urb's, and he swung down from the branch and chased the car the rest of the way up the drive.

"Oh yeah, Zee and I are good buddies," said Urb, in answer to my questioning look. "We go way back." He stepped out of the car and bowed theatrically to my brother. "Come visiting with great *Zeal*, do *I*, old friend."

"I thought I felt a *disturbance* in the force," Zelai replied, puffing slightly from his run up the hill.

The two young men chatted together as I surveyed the scene around me. An enormous garden surrounded the round house that served as my mother's home and the seat of her court, and today it was full to bursting. I hadn't seen it this busy since she had summoned all the neighboring fae folk to a protest rally this spring.

"Hey Fiona," said Zelai, turning to me. "Did you guys actually go to that church thing? Mom said you were going, but then she said how she didn't understand why anyone would want to go to a thing like that, so I wasn't sure."

"Yeah, we did. It was really, uh, interesting."

"Fiona? Did he say Fiona?" exclaimed a nearby fae woman to another. "The Fiona who saved the princess?"

"Must be!" said another. "She's the Queen's daughter, after all."

"Fiona, is it?" asked the first, turning to me.

"Uh huh," I agreed, slightly reluctantly.

"Can you tell me whether you expect to have all this nastiness resolved before the Country Fair? I've heard they're thinking about canceling. I haven't missed a single fair in forty-two years, and I'd be devastated if we can't have one this year."

"I'm not sure," I told her. "But, um, I'll try."

"Ah, good. You've got it all figured out then, have you?" said a wizened old fae who sat by the door whittling wood with a long, curved blade. He set down the knife and peered at me curiously. "So, what do we do? What's the plan, girl?"

Thankfully, at that moment, the front door opened, and a tall blond faerie emerged.

"Oh, Fiona, it's you," she said. It was Arlee, my cousin Faeryn's closest companion. She looked a bit frazzled. "You're here a bit early, aren't you?"

"I am," I agreed, noticing her harried look but too eager to get away from my own conversation to pause in the doorway and inquire. "Mind if we go inside?"

"I'm going to take a walk and clear my head," she said, holding the door for us.

Inside, I headed for the downstairs bedroom where I usually slept when visiting the hill. The door seemed to be locked and I wiggled the knob to see if it was just stuck. The door opened with a sudden snap, and a face appeared. It was sharply angular, with bright blue eyes under a cloud of airy auburn curls, and I stared at the striking woman. I had never seen anyone quite like her before.

"The princess is resting," the stranger hissed. "And she is not to be disturbed." The door clicked shut again, quickly, but so gently that it barely made a sound.

"Huh, that's odd," I remarked to Jaah. "I thought Faeryn slept upstairs."

"Was that Fiona I just heard out there?" Faeryn exclaimed weakly. "Calliope! Did you just slam my door on Fiona?"

"But, my lady, you told me to turn away anybody who—"

"Not Fiona, Calliope!" I heard Faeryn snap. "Never Fiona. Obviously. Especially when I'm tired."

The door opened again, and this time Faeryn herself emerged, looking haggard, with dark circles under her eyes. She reached thin arms up to hug me, and I squeezed her tightly, thinking warm, happy thoughts.

It had never been as effective as the first time I did it, at the very moment I learned that everything had turned out alright, and my plan worked, saving myself and Faeryn also. I hugged her, magically 'powering her up' and filling her fragile body with some of my own abundant energy. Now, whenever I saw her, I gave her as much energy as I could, but it was only a fraction of what I'd been able to send that first time.

"Thanks," she said, stepping back and smiling up at me. She looked a little less exhausted, at least. "Sorry about stealing your bedroom. It's darker down here, and the light's been bothering my eyes lately."

"No problem," I replied. "Does that mean the room upstairs is free?"

"Mm hmm," she agreed, nodding sleepily. "All yours. Alright, I've got to lie back down now. Calliope just got back with fresh spring water for me, so I should be feeling better soon." She sighed. "It just takes such a long time, with only this tiny bit of water going around me."

"We could try to make it bigger again?" Jaah mused speculatively, leaning in to peer at the device she wore around her chest. It was a marvel of intermagical engineering that allowed Faeryn to live outside of the magical spring that kept her broken heart beating. The artifact wasn't perfect, though, and Jaah and his engineering friends kept making improvements and dropping off new versions.

"Bigger?" Faeryn raised her hands to cup the soft casing that let the water flow around her body in an artificial current. "Visc is already whining about how much it makes us look like a drag Queen."

Jaah snorted with laughter. It was true that the latest iteration did give Faeryn an impressively busty silhouette. "I'll see what I can do," he agreed.

"Well, I'll see you two in a bit, alright? Fresh water and that boost from Fiona will have me feeling alright by dinner, I expect. Help me back into bed now, Calliope," she said, letting the door swing closed between us. "No, ow! I told you. Listen when I tell you things! Not like that. Slow, like Arlee does it."

Feeling unwell can make anyone a little prickly, I reminded myself, as we climbed the spiraling stairs to the second level of the layer cake-shaped house. I could excuse my sick cousin's caustic attitude, but I was grateful that it wasn't me at the spearpoint of her ire, like Calliope seemed to be. I was glad I had been able to help her, in that one small way, but it was incredibly frustrating how little I knew about my own magic, I thought with a sigh.

Upstairs, Evita was watering her plants and listening to two lumpy little fae arguing in high-pitched voices. The fae folk were no taller than my waist, and Evita's houseplants towered over them. They were enormous, easily three or four times the size they were a few months ago, when I first arrived. Evita was finding all sorts of ways to recycle the reduced-potency spring water Faeryn's device was constantly producing.

"Give it back to him, now, please," my mother pronounced calmly, once the little folk were done arguing. "I know you think you won it, but cheating isn't really winning, is it?" she asked, chastising one of the squat fae. He made several indignant squeaks in reply. "No, it's not alright because you got away with it. You didn't get away with it. That's why you're standing in front of me. Now, give it back." The indignant fae handed a lumpy earthenware mug reluctantly to his fellow, who keened with glee, and dashed off. The defeated fae slumped out of the room, shoulders hunched.

I made a little noise to draw Evita's attention to me. She turned and smiled, a little too widely. "Oh, look! You're early! What a pleasant surprise. Another unexpected houseguest. Well, you're not exactly unexpected, but you know what I mean." She wrung her hands, looking flustered. "There are just so many folk running about right now. And it's fine, really it is. They needed a place to gather after all that unpleasantness this weekend. I could hardly tell them to just go home, could I? When we don't even know when we'll be able to gather again? I couldn't. I just couldn't," Evita paused and gasped, not having stopped to breathe since she started talking. "It's all just a little much to handle sometimes, you know?"

"Yeah," I agreed. "There sure are a lot of fae folk around here, today." And they were feeling pretty confident in my ability to fix things, especially considering how little I knew about my own magical abilities. I would have to fix that, and soon. It didn't really matter where I started, as long as I started somewhere, I thought, remembering the last bit of interesting magic I saw my mother do. "Can you teach me how you found those chanterelles the other day?"

Evita sighed deeply and sank into a chair. "The chanterelles. You want to know about the chanterelles? Alright." She shook her head, tiredly. "You know, if it's not one thing, with these subjects of mine, it's another. Constantly, with the silly requests and petty squabbles. I really must put some boundaries on my time. Egan's been saying so for years."

"Oh, okay," I said, backing away from her. "I hear you. No worries. Just forget about it." I felt my face redden with embarrassment. It had been a silly request. I didn't actually care about the mushrooms, I just wanted her to teach me some magic, and that seemed like a good enough place to start. "Maybe I'll just go rest for a little while and keep out of your hair until dinner. Faeryn said this bedroom was free, so…" I opened the door and stepped inside, gesturing for Jaah to follow me.

Chapter 7

Once the door clicked shut, I launched myself onto the large bed with an almighty flop. As I sank into the thick downy cloud, I let out a long and mighty sigh, and when I opened my eyes, Jaah was standing above me.

"That's how you feel about it, huh?" he asked, before launching himself onto the mattress.

"What am I supposed to do, Jaah? You heard those fae outside. I probably heard from a dozen more of them at the Pirate Carnival, who all said the same thing. They expect me to fix everything, but I have no idea how. Do you?" He shook his head. "And it's not like I'm above asking for help, you know? But Faeryn and Evita are busy. They have their own concerns, and they don't have the time or the energy to help me with mine."

"I don't know about any of that," he said, taking my hand comfortingly. "But, I do know that this bed is way more comfortable than the one downstairs." I nodded in agreement, snuggling deeper into the plush covers. "Yesterday was exhausting, and this morning was exhausting, too, and we have three hours before dinner. I think we should set an alarm and just take a nap."

I love that idea, I thought, drowsily. Thank you.

"I love you, too."

I sat up, startled out of my comfortable daze. "Wait, what?"

"I, uh, love you, too?" Jaah repeated, head cocked and expression concerned. "You said you loved me, and I said it back. What's wrong?"

I let myself fall back to the bed with a muffled *fumpf,* and shook the mattress with subterranean giggles. I definitely had not meant to say that. But, apparently he loved me. And, I realized, I did love him, too.

"I love you," I said, rolling to face him on the bed.

"Yeah," he agreed, with a slow smile, and leaned in to kiss me.

"Hey," he said, some time later. "We didn't really get to talk last night, and I just want to tell you, again, how sorry I am that I didn't say anything about the girls. It was stupid of me. Cowardly. But, you're so smart, and I knew that when I told you, you'd start asking smart questions about my sister and what happened, and…" They rolled away from me, looking up at the ceiling. "It's just hard to talk about, I guess. It's hard to explain."

"It's okay," I told him, laying my head on his chest. "We don't have to talk about it, if you don't want to, but I'm here if you ever do."

"I appreciate that. And I get it, but man, the way you stormed off, I really wasn't sure if you were ever going to talk to me again. I would have told you if they were my own flesh and blood, though, Fiona. Well, they are, but you know what I mean. I would have, I swear."

"Yeah, I was, uh, pretty surprised by my own reaction, actually. I learned some things about myself that I hadn't realized before," I told him, turning to look down toward his feet, which felt safer than looking up at his face.

"Oh yeah?" prompted Jaah after a few moments of silence.

"Yeah. It made me realize how much I'm looking forward to being a parent. Being a mom." Unexpectedly, I felt tears prick in the corners of my eyes. "Now that I'm an adult, you know, out of school, on my own, looking at the rest of my life ahead of me? That's what I really want. A kid. One of my own, that's a part of me. I want to start a family."

He was quiet, listening, so I continued, "It's the adoption thing, partly. Never having anyone around who looked like me? But it's more than that. You know, when I was a kid, I really wanted a pet monkey. I wanted to raise it and play with it, and teach it things. I was pretty serious about it. I did a bunch of research."

Jaah chuckled, and the subterranean rumble of it made my head bounce on his chest. "Of course you did. I bet you learned everything there was to know about it."

"Yes, of course I did the research! And the main problem with pet monkeys is that they get kind of mean when they grow up, because they're, you know—" I shrugged. "They're wild animals. They don't want to be in captivity. And that's not the experience I wanted. I'm realizing that what I actually wanted was a baby that would grow up into a kid."

"You do?" Jaah asked, stiffening slightly.

"Yeah," I answered, turning back over to look into his eyes again. "I think I do. And I'm not saying I'm trying to make one right now, or anything, but yeah. Seeing you with Azalea and Zinnia and hearing them call you Daddy, it made me feel some things, and they were…" I drummed my fingers on his chest, looking for the right words. "Unexpectedly intense. I think subconsciously, maybe I thought I'd found the man to make that baby with, and I let my imagination run away with me." Seeing a shadowy expression cross his face, I added, "It's stupid, though. Really."

"Fiona, I love you, but if that's what you want, I don't know that I'm the person you need."

"Not the person——" I realized what I had just said, and felt my breath catch in my throat. "I'm sorry I called you a man, just now. I know that's not true." But, I admitted to myself, it was easy to make those kinds of slip-ups when Jaah existed as a man in my head, and I resolved to do better. "What is it, exactly? Is it the idea of being a father that's a problem? Your nieces call you Daddy, right?"

"Not at all. I would love to be a father, actually. To be able to be there for my child in the way my own dad never was for me. I'm just not sure if I can. Like, physically, I mean. My kind has a pretty tough time reproducing. That's one part of my father's legacy that he passed down to me."

"But your father made you," I reminded them.

"Yes, he did," agreed Jaah. "And that gives me hope. My girls are amazing, my sister's girls, I mean. I'm so grateful to have them in my life, despite the circumstances. But to have a child of my own, that I could pass my father's legacy down to, and teach in the way my father never taught me, that would really be something else," they said with a sigh.

"That's right," I reminded myself. "I'm frustrated because Evita isn't teaching me faerie magic fast enough, but you didn't have any of that, did you? You've just been stumbling around in the dark, this whole time! How did you manage to——"

"Lots of research," they replied. "That's how I've been keeping myself busy, investigating my own culture and my father's legacy. And I've learned a lot, but there's not too much out there in terms of primary sources. It's all incomplete. Secondhand, word of mouth. Or, it's safeguarded, hidden in places that even I can't crack into."

"Behind super high-tech firewalls?" I guessed.

"Inside people's brains," they answered, running their fingers through my hair, then moving to lie back against the fluffy pillows.

"Oh, yeah. That makes sense." I followed them back down onto the bed again, listening with interest.

"I'm not even sure what the steps are. Just that the ritual is difficult to manage and the timing is really specific. A certain time of year, or point in the moon cycle, or something. Nobody I've talked to knows more than that. Or, at least, they wouldn't tell me anything more specific. It's been incredibly frustrating. I've considered asking my mother about it, but…" They shook their head. "That's not the kind of thing we talk about."

"So what I'm hearing is that we won't accidentally get pregnant?"

"That's my understanding."

"Well." I caught their eye. "That might have certain side benefits, in the meantime, I suppose." I crawled up their chest and kissed them, suggesting that we end the conversation there.

"Wait," they said. "Hang on. There's one more thing I have to say before there is total truth and understanding between us."

My stomach dropped, and I rolled back down onto their chest, turning away.

"What is it?"

"Fiona, I love you," they started, and I interrupted them.

"Yeah, we already did that," I teased petulantly.

"I love you, and I want to be with you," they continued, "Maybe forever, I don't know. But, the fact is that I am what I am, Fiona." I felt his chest rise with his deep intake of breath.

"I'm as much my father's child as you are your mother's." As much an African fertility deity as I am a faerie, was what they meant, but where they were going with this, I wasn't sure. "These last few months, at the Fair Isle, I've been spending all my time, all my nights, with you. And that's because I find you so engaging and so fascinating, and you—" they interrupted themselves. "I could go on, but that's not the point. The point is, I can't be with just one partner for the rest of my life. I know that about myself, and I want to be honest with you. My heart is mine to give, and it's yours if you want it, but my body…" They sighed, and I felt their muscles tense, waiting for my reply.

"Oh," I said, speaking slowly and parsing the words as I said them. "So, what you're saying is that you can commit to me, emotionally, but you still need the freedom to be with other people, physically?"

"Yes. I'm really sorry, Fiona."

"Don't be," I said. "Hang on, I'm still processing." I sat up again as I considered, crossing my legs underneath me, and staring out the window at Evita's colorful flower garden.

One of my roommates in college tried polyamory once. She told me all about it as she read books and learned the best ways to do things, before carefully broaching the subject with her boyfriend. Then, ultimately, she broke all the promises she made, betraying his trust and exploding her relationship in a spectacularly disastrous fashion. A cautionary tale for the ages. But, I decided, not a warning about polyamory, but about polyamory done wrong.

"I don't think I want that," I answered them, finally.

I heard their breath catch when they said, "Okay."

"I'm young, Jaah. Younger than you. You've had some time to be an adult and explore the world on your own. To figure out who you are and what you want in a relationship. I've only ever had two real boyfriends before this, and both of them were back in high school. Now I've got this whole new intermagical community to get to know, and I've barely even scratched the surface." I gave them a tight-lipped smile. "I know one thing that I want, though, and that's you. but if you can't commit to be wholly and completely with me and only me—"

"I understand, Fiona," Jaah interrupted. "It's alright, I—"

"Then I want to do it right, Jaah," I continued, talking over them. "Real, ethical non-monogamy, where we both have the freedom to make actual, meaningful connections with other people."

"Y- you what? You do?"

"Yeah, I do," I said, turning my face up to them and looking deeply into their eyes. "Do you?"

"Yeah," they said, their wide mouth spreading into an enormous grin. "Absolutely, I do."

"I wish solving this festival problem was as easy as that," I said, as we lay entwined in each other's arms on top of the fluffy covers.

"Well," said Jaah, speculatively. "If you could use your magic and do whatever you wanted, what would you actually want to do?"

I considered this. I knew that it was important to be careful with magic, so I tried to answer mindfully. "I'd like to strengthen my intuition. Evita is always listening to hers, but I don't feel like I'm very good at tuning into mine. I'd just like to know what to do, sometimes, you know?"

"You mean like when there's a problem?"

"Yeah," I agreed, hedging. "Sure, when there's a problem, but also, just, like, anytime, you know? So that I know I'm moving in the right direction."

Do you yearn for a Master, child? I heard the echo of my ancestor's voice in my memory. No, I argued, this is different. I don't want some outside force telling me what to do, I want this sense of direction to come from inside me.

"What would that look like, do you think?" Jaah mused.

"Well, you know how when you're a kid you assume that adults know everything, and then you grow up and realize they don't? And sometimes, even though you're technically an adult, you just want an *adultier* adult to help you?"

"Definitely," Jaah agreed with a laugh.

"Well, I kind of feel like that's how the intermagical community sees me, because of what happened with Faeryn's spring. They expect me to swoop in and be the adultier adult when I still feel like a kid myself." I shook my head. "But, the truth is, I'd love it if I could be that person for them. If there is some magical way to become more mature and grow up a little, I'd want to do it."

Jaah raised an eyebrow at me. "You sure about that? People always say you shouldn't be in a hurry to grow up too fast."

"Well, I sure feel like I grew up a little when those big trucks rolled into the fair."

"Yeah," they said with a sigh. "I feel you. This part of the world has a dark history I have no interest in revisiting. If I could use my magic to do whatever I want, I'd give those backwards people a glimpse at what the real future looks like."

"Me too," I agreed, sighing with regret. "But instead, we've got all this power and nothing we can do with it." I drummed my fingers on Jaah's lower belly, where I felt my power in a gently glowing ball, at the center of my own body. "Although Faeryn says I've been doing magic my whole life, without realizing it," I continued. "Manifesting, influencing, and creating, and everything."

"That's true," said Jaah. "We could always just focus our intentions and try."

"We could," I agreed. "And if we raise enough energy and have enough focus, maybe something will happen. Do you think we should?"

"We've been getting pretty good at raising energy using my favorite method," Jaah said, with a grin. They pulled me up for a kiss. "You want to try that?"

"Sure, yeah, okay," I agreed. "Just give me a minute to really set my intentions," I said, closing my eyes so I could concentrate.

Jaah was right, I thought, some time later, as their power crashed over me like a wave and I matched their energy with my own, sending it back to them, we were getting good at this. In that moment, there was no masculine or feminine, we were simply two forces of nature. Two magical beings, exalted in our union, directing our raised energies toward our sacred, powerful intention.

Chapter 8

I woke to the gentle beeping of Jaah's phone and smiled at the bright sunlight that streamed through the gauzy curtains of the cheerful upstairs bedroom. We had been asleep for the better part of an hour, and there was still plenty of daylight left. Midsummer, with its long days and gentle nights, was my favorite time of year. We had fallen asleep with our limbs entangled. Jaah stirred, next to me, and I smiled at them, too.

"That was something, huh?" I said, stretching my arms and beginning to unwind myself from the bedclothes.

"Yeah," they said. "With all that energy we had flying around, we definitely made some kind of magic."

I nodded, remembering the gusting wind, like a storm in the still room. It swirled around my body, stirring up my emotions into a tumultuous crescendo, not so much of physical pleasure but of resonant, intense energetic power. I had never felt anything like it.

"I set the alarm a little early," said Jaah, nestling sleepily into the covers. "We can lie around for a few more minutes before we head back out there, if you want to."

zrp zrp
no now

"Ack!" I gripped my stomach in surprise. Something just shocked me from the inside! It was as though my ordinary well of energetic power suddenly came to life and shocked me with a jolt of electricity.

"What the…?" I said, peering down at my abdomen with concern.

zrp zrp
come on

Again, that strange zinging feeling. That time, I wasn't quite as surprised, and I noticed that the sensation had come along with the cadence of words, in my mind.

Once more, that strange feeling.
zrp zrp

And along with it, the words, *let's go.*

"I think I'd better get back out there, actually," I said, and put my hand on my stomach, preparing for more of those unnerving little shocks and messages.

I opened the bedroom door just as Evita rounded the corner from the kitchen. She eyed my pose suspiciously, and I let my hand drop from my midsection. I didn't want to worry her, especially since she had so much on her plate already. A moment later, a door on the lower level slammed open, and Faeryn stomped up the stairs toward us.

"Calliope is tired of all of the traveling she has to do, apparently," she told us, tone sharp and eyes blazing. "She brought me thirty-two jugs, all at once. Thirty-two! What a clever idea," she said sarcastically. "Bringing me a month's supply all at once, when she knows it loses potency every day." She turned to shout over her shoulder. "I'm sorry to be so much trouble, with all my issues and problems," she spat harshly. "You can just go back up to the city if you don't want to deal with all of this. We'll be just fine without you, you know."

Calliope slunk out of the open doorway of the bedroom. She shook her head, keeping her eyes downcast. "It is no trouble, my princess."

"Ugh!" Faeryn threw up her hands in exasperated frustration. "Why do you have to snivel and squirm like that? I'm hardly even royalty here. You realize I'm not even a princess in this court, right? So, stop already," she said, stamping her tiny foot. "Just stop!"

"You will always be my princess, lady, and it truly is no trouble. I can fetch fresh water for you every day, if you ask me to. I just thought, with how tired you've been and with how much energy you have to spend, to maintain the Queen's city, from so far away…" She wrung her thin hands and snuck a glance up at Faeryn, then quickly looked away again. "I thought you might like to have a bath."

Faeryn opened her mouth, as though to reply, then shut it with a snap. She strode quickly around the corner, into the kitchen, and out of sight. From the stairway, we heard a high, keening cry, followed by the sound of racking sobs, then a slamming door, and silence.

I had never seen Faeryn like that before. I felt bad for Calliope, who really did seem to be trying to help. Faeryn grew up spending most of her time in the water of a magical spring that ran through her mother's city. The magic kept her deformed heart beating and helped maintain her delicate system. Like me, she was almost exactly half-human, and she needed to take care of her human body in order to survive.

When Jaah had presented her with the first model of a portable, wearable, 'techno-spring' that could circulate the magical current around her, while allowing her to walk around outside the water, she had decided to leave her mother's court and live life on her own terms. Evita had agreed to help, and the whole of my mother's little court had been working to help keep Faeryn healthy and comfortable, but it continued to be a struggle.

One of the first things we learned was that the spring water loses potency quickly. Always a devoted maid servant, Calliope had followed her princess down from the city a few days after she left, and had been making the journey to the spring and back, a few times a week, ever since. In fact, I hadn't met her before today, because every time I had visited the hill, she had been away, fetching water. Her help had been invaluable, but it didn't seem like Faeryn appreciated her efforts overly much.

Hesitantly, Calliope followed her lady up the stairs and paused awkwardly at the top landing, unsure of what to do with herself. Evita came to stand beside her, and put a comforting hand on the taller woman's narrow back.

"Did I do something wrong?" Calliope asked quietly.

"No, dear, you did well," said Evita, patting her shoulder. "You know how she gets when she's exhausted, and she's been feeling so unwell lately. It's understandable that her emotions get the better of her sometimes. A long soak will be just what she needs."

I gave Evita a tight smile, glad that she had known what to say to her at that moment. But, this was just one more thing that the Queen had to deal with right now, on top of everything else. I heaved a heavy sigh and headed in the opposite direction Faeryn had gone, ducking through the jungle of plants and into the living room. The large dining space where Evita usually held court had been draped with an elegant canopy of fabrics and adorned with a natural chandelier of fresh flowers, vines, and other dripping greenery.

A moment later, Evita followed after me. "Fiona, what's going on?" she asked, with a hint of accusation in her tone that reminded me of my other mother.

"Nothing," I responded automatically, not meeting her gaze. "Do you need any help before dinner?"

"The little faeries have everything handled," she said, waving away the notion. She came toward me, as I did my best to casually drift in the opposite direction. "Fiona, stop, please. Will you at least look at me?" I glanced up quickly, then away. Her eyes were scrutinizing and intense. "Fiona, what did you do?" Evita asked, seeing something in my eyes that told her all she needed to know.

"Nothing!" I said, doubling down.

"You're telling me that you don't know anything about the tempest of magical energy gusting through this house, about an hour ago?"

"Oh, that. Um." I swallowed hard, reminding myself that the fae weren't prudish about things like sexuality and pressing onward through my own awkwardness. "I mean, sure. The Gullah and I were borrowing the upstairs bedroom to take a nap. I didn't realize anyone else would notice anything."

"I'd be surprised if my human neighbors couldn't feel it. Wait." She eyed me with speculation. "Hang on. Are you telling me that you two weren't intending to raise energy? You just sent all that power out into the universe undirected?"

"No!" I answered more defensively than I intended. "I mean, yes. We meant to raise some energy, and we did put intention behind it."

"Well, that certainly doesn't sound like nothing," Evita retorted. She was turned away from me, but I could hear the smirk in her voice.

"It's nothing new!" I said, hearing the defensiveness in my voice, but unable to help myself. "Faeryn says I've been manifesting my whole life. We just added a little oomph to it."

"A little oomph!" Evita repeated. "Is that what you call it, flinging that much wild energy around? You've got power, dear, but you're still so new to all this. Why didn't you ask me for help before trying to—"

"I tried to ask!" I interrupted, my temper flaring. "Earlier today I asked if you would teach me, and you told me that you needed to 'set more boundaries with your time,' so I took the hint, okay? You're a Queen with important things to do, and I get that. But everyone keeps on asking me what I'm going to do to fix all this, so I just did something, alright? I gave it a try."

Evita's expression fell, and she sat down heavily at the table.

"Oh, honey, I'm sorry," she said, leaning forward to rest her forehead in her hands. "Yes, I can see how you could have—but, no." She shook her head. "I didn't mean that. I meant that I need to stop letting all of my time be nibbled away so that I can focus on the truly important things," she said, looking up to meet my eyes. "Like your magical education."

"Oh," I said, my anger dissipating, and leaving me feeling a little deflated. "Do you really think we did something that we shouldn't have? I feel like we did a pretty good job with setting our intentions, and I don't really know, but it seems like it kind of worked."

"It did, hmm?" Evita pressed. When I didn't elaborate, she reached onto a high bookshelf and pulled down a small black box. "Well, let's see what the cards say about that." She began to mix a large gilded deck. "And whether they think it 'worked.'"

She handed me the deck and told me to cut, then she flipped the first card.

"The Sun. Life itself," she said, smiling down at the image of a sunflower. "Happiness, optimism, fulfillment of your goals. Well, look at that." She turned her face up to look into my eyes. "It might just have worked." The next two cards were a magnolia and then a peony. "The Empress and the Lovers," said Evita, tapping the cards thoughtfully.

"You two have made a very powerful union together, I think," Evita said, looking over my shoulder, and I realized that Jaah had come to stand behind me, silently, as was their habit.

"These cards don't indicate anything worrisome or sinister," Evita concluded. "But when you're throwing that much power around in the dark, with only your intentions as a guide, it's likely you'll spark things you didn't entirely intend to."

"Was that what I felt earlier?" asked Faeryn. She stepped around the corner from the kitchen, looking much calmer and more collected than she had earlier. "I was wondering what was making all the energy fly around like a hurricane."

"Yes, it was those two," agreed Evita, shooting us a bemused sort of look.

"Sorry," said Jaah and I together, looking sheepish.

"They don't seem to have done any serious damage, but we're going to need to give our dear Fiona some instruction in magical fundamentals, immediately, in hopes that she won't try scrawling pentagrams on the ceiling and summoning spectral strangers, in her next round of esoteric experimentation," Evita said with a roll of her eyes that told me she was teasing.

"Hey!" I replied. "Not fair. You just said that it doesn't seem like I did any actual damage. And, I was really careful with my intentions." I told them what I intended the magic to do, but I didn't mention the little voice or the messages I had been receiving since waking up.

Evita sighed deeply, and Faeryn laughed. Recovering herself quickly, the younger faerie said, "There's nothing the universe finds more satisfying than giving us exactly what we ask it for in the way we least expect."

"Well, what should I have done, then?" I asked indignantly.

"Oh, we're not saying you did anything wrong, exactly," said Evita, shooting a pointed look at Faeryn. "But the way our family does magic is a little more balanced, and perhaps somewhat safer than generating enormous amounts of power with your bodies alone and throwing it out into the universe with only your intentions to guide it. You might get distracted and your attention might slip, especially if your body is, er…" She smirked. "Otherwise engaged."

"Did you call any of the elements at all?" Faeryn asked. "It sure seems like you got the wind's attention, with the way the curtains flew around like that!"

"Call the elements?" I asked my two faerie relatives. "What does that mean?"

"That will be one of your first lessons in our family's magic," said Evita, standing up from the table. "But right now, I need to go see about this meal. In the meantime, Faeryn, why don't you teach Fiona the secret to finding chanterelles? Because," my faerie mother said, with a pointed look at me. "Apparently, it's urgent."

"Oh sure," agreed Faeryn, launching into a long explanation that I did my best to follow. She told me how the prized mushrooms grow at the base of a few specific types of trees, in old-growth forests, where the trees have burned and re-grown and burned again, giving the mycelium the kind of deep, complex root structure that chanterelles require. My eyes glazed over, just like they did when my college roommate, the botany major, would go on about plants for too long.

"That's cool," I said, interrupting Faeryn as she listed the different types of local evergreens. "But that's not really what I was trying to ask about. I'm talking about the magic that Evita did. The spell she used to find the chanterelles."

"Oh that?" said Evita, coming back around the corner as though summoned by her name. "It was just a simple blessing to give gratitude to the land spirits and the mycelial network for the mushrooms I was about to take from the forest."

"But we found them right after that!" I protested.

"Yes," said Evita with an apologetic smile. "In an old-growth forest, at the base of a red hemlock, just like I expected them to be. Esoteric knowledge isn't always flashy, but it's still very powerful magic," she assured me.

Faeryn waved her finger like a wand and leaned forward to boop me on the shoulder. "Bippity boppity boo! Now you have the power to find chanterelles!"

Chapter 9

"Thank you so much for dinner, Aunt. It was absolutely delicious," said Faeryn, setting down her fork decisively. She couldn't have eaten more than two bites.

"Really, darling?" asked Arlee, shooting an unimpressed look at the amount of uneaten food on Faeryn's plate, as my cousin disappeared down the stairs.

"It's alright," Evita said, smiling with kind understanding. "I expect she'll be in the bathtub for the rest of the evening. We can go downstairs and visit her later."

Arlee picked up Faeryn's full plate and muttered something about preparing a nice illusion for our visit before following her lady.

"This all looks amazing, Your Majesty, thank you," said Urb, selecting another fresh strawberry from the display of summer bounty that Evita's faerie subjects constructed to serve as both our centerpiece and our feast.

"No need for all that formality," said Evita with a wave of dismissal. "We're all family here."

Calliope, who sat to my right, flushed prettily at this comment. Was it truly a preoccupation with royalty and station that was making her fidget so uncomfortably in her seat, I wondered, curious about the nervous girl.

"So, how'd it go, sister?" asked my brother Egan, catching my eye across the laden table. "Did you learn anything about these festival ruining zealots?"

The Gullah gave a humorless laugh beside me.

"A few things," I answered. "For one, they're incredibly well funded and they're definitely serious about this crusade they're on, against…" I raised my hands and made quotes in the air. "The forces of darkness."

"It's me," said Jaah, waving and pulling a sarcastic smile. "I'm the darkness."

Urb and I nodded our agreement, as the rest of the table erupted in horrified exclamations.

"But they're not just racist," Urb interjected, interrupting the appalled spluttering. "They've got it out for queer people, too. Gay, trans, everybody. You heard the kind of vile things they were saying at the carnival. They want to make sure everyone is as controlled, conservative, and Caucasian as they are."

"Controlled, Conservative, and Caucasian?" repeated Egan. "Classic CCC, huh?"

"I thought CCC was supposed to stand for Capitalism, Conformity and Climate corruption," I said, raising a quizzical eyebrow at my brother.

"Well sure, usually it does, but if the shoe fits, you know?"

I chuckled, appreciating my brother's play on words.

"Yep, you nailed it," said Jaah. "This is all happening because of the new CCC policies that just went into effect. There are new local militias cropping up all over the place, and apparently, the local branch is branding themselves the 'Morality Police' and putting themselves in charge of our communities' morals."

"Gross," said Zelai, wrinkling his nose in disgust.

"Totally," Jaah agreed.

"But, global policy applies to everybody, right?" Egan asked. "Is there some way we can use the new rules against them?" His eyebrows furrowed as his tactical mind latched onto the idea. "Can we form our own militia?"

Conversation buzzed around the table at that suggestion, but Jaah waved a hand, dismissing the notion. "Well, for one, there's all sorts of stuff we're doing they're offended by, apparently, but there really isn't anything we would want to forbid them from doing, is there? And for another, we don't have the manpower. We've got enough bodies, sure, but it's almost impossible to convince fae folk to pick up arms and fight against humans. It's not their nature."

"I know plenty of intermagicals who wouldn't hesitate to defend themselves," Egan muttered, but Urb interrupted him.

"I read the new CCC statute last night, actually," he said. "And there was one thing that stood out to me. The militias can set whatever rules they want, but they have to follow the standards they set. If they get caught breaking their own rules, they lose all legal standing. That's how the law makes sure they're being 'just and equitable,' apparently."

"Interesting," said Jaah, stroking his pointed beard.

zrp zrp
go see

"Which is a pretty good reason to get closer to the Christ's Heart organization and see what they're up to," Urb concluded, echoing the message I had just received from my now surprisingly vocal sense of intuition.

I gasped involuntarily, when I opened the steamy bathroom door. Arlee had done an incredible job with her illusion, and when the door clicked shut behind me, I couldn't even tell that I was indoors at all. To all appearances, I had just stepped into a misty forest in the early evening, with lightning bugs, or perhaps tiny faeries, glinting between leafy trees. Curling ferns beckoned from beneath a royal blue sky that was just beginning to dim with the suggestion of evening.

At the center of the glade Faeryn leaned against a backrest made of smooth rock, in a crystal-clear pool that sparkled with bubbles like a natural hot spring. If I squinted, I could just barely make out the modern lines of the jetted soaking tub that I would expect to find in this particular guest bathroom.

"I can't believe I missed the Pirate Carnival," Faeryn lamented. "If I'd known it was my only chance for a revel this summer, I would have found the strength."

"You needed your rest, dear," Evita said, squeezing the girl's thin shoulder. "Were you able to use the peace and quiet to learn anything useful?"

"Not really," said Faeryn, shaking her head. "I'm positive that there's someone or something attacking me, but it's so distracting to feel so unwell all the time, and…" she paused and a shadowy expression clouded her face. "Visc and I have both been so infernally irritated by our maidservant lately."

I wasn't entirely sure how it worked, but I knew that Faeryn and Visc lived inside the same body. I had only met Visc once before, but I thought I might recognize his fierce expression on my cousin's face, just now, and I found myself wondering whether I was about to encounter him again.

"I've been meaning to ask," Evita, settling down next to Faeryn and stroking her deep red hair. "What is it about Calliope that sets you off like that? You do tend to be a bit hard on the girl, if you don't mind my saying so."

Faeryn pursed her lips, in control once more. "It wasn't so bad when we were in the city, with so many other fae coming and going all the time, but in such close quarters, with our history, it's like every single thing she does makes me want to scream."

"Your history," Evita repeated. "You know, Faeryn dear, I asked Arlee, like you told me to, and she told me quite plainly that it was simply not her tale to tell."

"Please don't make me talk about it, Aunt," wailed Faeryn, sinking low in the water and threatening to go under. Just before she submerged, her eyes met mine, and lit with interest. She popped back out of the pool, looking much more cheerful. "And anyway, there are more interesting things to talk about than ancient history, like whatever it was that Fiona got up to this afternoon, that made all the curtains blow around like that."

My shoulders hunched, uncomfortable at the focal point of her twinkling gaze. My cheeks heated when I remembered everyone in the household felt the energy that Jaah and I had raised together earlier.

"You and the young concubus did raise a bit of a tempest," said Evita, seeing my reddened face. "But sex magic is nothing to be ashamed of, dear. Especially with a partner like that. But, I'll admit, feeling that much wild power flying around was a bit alarming, especially on a night like tonight."

"What's so special about tonight?" I asked, confused.

"You do know that it's the summer solstice tonight, don't you, dear?" Evita asked.

The kind concern in Evita's voice made my hackles rise. I hadn't known that, and this conversation was beginning to make me feel stupid. I took a deep breath to try to get a hold of myself before I answered.

"No, I didn't realize. I don't really pay attention to that kind of stuff."

"Well, if you want to learn how to use your magic, you're gonna want to start," said Faeryn. "The moon is full tonight as well. And there's a meteor shower," she added as an afterthought. "Which means that there's a whole bunch of energy available from the sun and from the moon, and from the whole rest of the cosmos, right now, so whatever magic you work is going to be supercharged."

"Oh," I said. "No kidding."

"Exactly," Evita agreed. "And there's nothing wrong with strong magic. But, I assume…" she paused and considered, then shook her head. "No, best not do that. Why don't you tell us a little bit about your ritual, Fiona dear? Please?"

"Oh, um…" My face reddened again. The question transported me back to this afternoon and the feeling of crisp cotton sheets clutched in my sweaty palm. Waves of passionate energy crashing over us, our bodies intertwined.

"Not that bit, love. I think we both understand that well enough," my strange faerie of a birth mother said with a chuckle and a wink at Faeryn. "I'd like to know how you told all that powerful energy what to do."

"Oh, that part," I said, letting out a sigh of relief. "Sure. We just talked about what we wanted, and I took a minute to focus on my intentions, and, uh, that was it," I finished, somewhat lamely.

"Mmm," said Evita thoughtfully, while Faeryn cackled, sending droplets of water flying out of the tub.

"And you're certain that you kept your intentions solidly in your mind the entire time, and didn't let your focus wander even for a second, right?" Faeryn asked, in between peals of laughter. "There wasn't anything to distract you, surely!"

"What Faeryn is trying to say," said Evita, shooting a stern look at my cheerfully thrashing cousin. "Is that we would recommend using some sort of tangible ritual to anchor your intentions to your energy, rather than relying on focus alone. And, like I mentioned earlier, we typically like to call on all four elements as a part of that anchor, which helps send our intentions out into the world in a balanced, grounded way that yields the best possible results."

"And you want to try not to use wish magic, even accidentally," added Faeryn, reigning in her giggles. "Make sure your preferred outcome is nice and general. When you're too specific about exactly what you want, you're probably gonna get it, just not in the way you hoped."

"Well, Evita did a reading upstairs, and it said that the spell worked fine," I said, trying to keep my tone from sounding too defensive.

"It didn't indicate anything sinister," Evita corrected, sharing a meaningful glance with Faeryn.

"Which reminds me, there's a type of divination I'd like to try, to learn more about this curse I've been struggling with, but it fails when I do it for myself," said Faeryn, saving me from further frustration by changing the topic. "Would you help me with it, Fiona?" I agreed enthusiastically, excited to see another example of that sort of magic.

"What have you learned about the curse so far, dear?" Evita asked.

"Not a whole lot," Faeryn admitted. "It feels like a black cloud inside me, or maybe like ink dropped into water, worming its way into my muscles and bones, making them ache. My brain is in a constant fog. I can barely think. I know some of it is my broken heart, and my human body compensating for it, but I know myself. I know my body. This isn't just a consequence of living outside my spring. It's something more than that. Something sinister."

A shiver ran down my spine at her words. In the same way that I knew it when something was true because it rang like a golden gong in my chest, this feeling of icy dread was just as clear of a confirmation. Faeryn explained what she wanted me to do, and I got into position.

"Right into the middle, here?" I asked, and she nodded, forming her arms into a ring at the center of the pool. I poured a stream of inky liquid into the water, where it ballooned into a black cloud, just like the one Faeryn described, dark tendrils snaking outward as it dispersed into the churning water of the tub.

"Now, concentrate," said Evita, placing her hands on my shoulders, as I bent over the pool, watching the ink bloom and swirl in the water. I focused on revealing the identity of the curse's sender, and as I did, I watched the ink blot morph and change, expanding into a many-pointed starburst, then contracting into the shape of a Latin cross.

"Fascinating," said Faeryn, dragging one arm through the center of the design so that the ink mixed and dissipated. "A Christian cross. You don't think it has anything to do with that group you went to investigate today, do you?"

zrp zrp
of course

"Somehow I feel like it might," I said, then asked. "Are you ready for the second pour?" Faeryn nodded and resumed her position at the center of the pool. I picked up the vessel Evita refilled. To my eyes, it looked like an elegant jeweled samovar, but to my touch, it felt exactly like a large measuring glass. "Alright," I said aloud, as the dark stream hit the water's surface. "If that's the source of the negative energy, what can we do to counteract it?"

Flowing with the power of my intention, the ink swirled again, then formed into three spiraling whorls.

"That's a triskelion," Evita whispered. "The sign of the triple goddess. Maiden, mother, and crone. But, what does it mean?"

zrp zrp
you three

"Maybe it means the three of us," I answered. "But I don't know how it could. You and I are both maidens, right Faeryn? And Evita certainly isn't a crone."

"Yes, I am an eternal maiden," agreed Faeryn. "This body will never bear children. But what about you?" She raised an eyebrow at me. "With everything you've been getting up to, who knows what you might spark?"

"What, and make me the youngest and fairest crone Queen in all of faerieland?" Evita asked, teasing.

I shook my head, cheeks reddening, but I couldn't help but smile at the idea. I had been telling the truth earlier, when I told Jaah how much I was looking forward to being a mother. Not yet, though, I reminded myself. There was no need for any of that, just yet.

A knock at the door made us turn.

"Hey Fiona, are you gonna be ready to go soon?" Jaah said, voice muffled by the closed door.
It must be later than I realized, I thought, as I rose to leave. We needed to get back to Portal Land tonight. Jaah had an important work meeting in the morning.

Evita followed me out of the steamy bathroom. "Take these with you when you go," she told me, placing the beautiful deck of gilded cards in my hands. "Use them to guide you, until you can come back for some proper lessons."

"Your beautiful cards? I couldn't," I said, clutching the opulent object.

"You can and you have," she said, placing her hands over mine. "They were never truly mine, anyway. There's a reason I pulled these particular cards down from the shelf today. I think they were always meant to be yours."

"Thank you," I told her, making the effort to meet her eyes in genuine gratitude.

"I know the reading from earlier was positive, but I still worry. I have the sense that tonight has set your life on a particular course, daughter. One that was, perhaps, inevitable, but…" She touched her forehead, as though pained by what she saw in her mind's eye. "There are other timelines where our lives move much more slowly, but that is not the reality we're living in. This night in particular feels like it might have accelerated things by years. A decade, even."

"And, that's a bad thing?" I asked, her worried expression making me nervous.

"No," she answered, forcing a smile and touching my shoulder reassuringly. "It is what it is. But, I want you to pay particular attention to living in the moment this summer. Have as many new experiences as you can. Young people always want to grow up so fast."

I remembered the intentions I'd set about stepping into my own maturity and becoming a more responsible adult, and looked away from her piercing gaze.

"Oh hey," said Urb as he bounded down the spiral stairs toward us, two at a time. "I'm glad I caught you before you left. I was thinking I'd check out the Christ's Heart service next Sunday. Do you want to come?"

"Absolutely," I told him, smiling up at the big man. "Count me in."

"Well, if you're already going all that way, why not come here first, on Saturday, and make a weekend of it? That would be a fine opportunity to begin your magical education."

"Sure, Mom," I agreed. "Sounds like a plan." Evita beamed and hugged me tightly before waving me off through the door that Jaah was holding open. They closed it behind us, following me out into the night-dark garden.

"Hey, sis," called a voice from the shadows. "What'd you do to make Mom mad?" I wasn't sure what to think, but when he stepped into the glow of the porch light, I saw that my brother Egan was smiling.

"Make her mad?" I echoed. "What do you mean? She didn't seem mad. She was perfectly happy when I left just now. She even gave me these cards." I held up the gilded box, which glinted in the low light.

"Well, she cools off fast, but she was pretty steamed up earlier. Slamming around the kitchen, muttering something about you and mushrooms."

"Oh, the chanterelles, really?" I asked, my brow furrowing. "Why would she be mad? I just asked her how to find them, and it's not like it's a big faerie secret."

"Oh, you asked her to do something for you, huh? Yeah, that'll do it." Egan replied, as though explaining something obvious. And, it probably was, to him. He was raised by Evita and had known her his whole life.

"And that's not an okay thing to do?"

"I mean, you're the lost daughter, so if anybody could get away with it, it'd probably be you, but I wouldn't recommend it. She really doesn't like it."

"Really? She doesn't like to do things for people?" I asked, confused. I hadn't known her for very long, but Evita always seemed selflessly giving, to me.

"No, she loves it. It's what she lives for, but only if it's her idea. She doesn't like it when other people make demands. Gets real imperious about it, as Queen."

"Huh," I replied, considering that as we walked through the garden to my van. "So, what should I do, then?"

"Make her think it's her idea!" Jaah answered with a chuckle, reaching past me to open the car door.

"Yep, that's the idea," Egan agreed. "She's a faerie godmother, after all. They love to solve problems. So, just tell her what your problem is, and let her decide how she wants to help fix it."

I looked down at the box of cards I held. I certainly hadn't asked her for them, even though I had been admiring them since she had first pulled them down off the shelf. I never would have dared to ask her to give me something so beautiful. And, I was certainly glad that I hadn't, since apparently that would have been exactly the wrong thing to do.

"Well, alright then," I said, pulling myself up into the van's high seat. "Thanks, brother. I appreciate the insight. I hope I didn't upset her too badly."

"Nah, she's already over it," he told me with a reassuring smile. "She burns hot, but she cools off real quick. That's part of her faerie nature, too."

"Fascinating," I said, as I put the car in reverse and headed back down the steep driveway. "You know what," I said to Jaah, as we pulled out onto the dark road. "That sounds like what my psychology professors would call 'persistent demand avoidance,' but I guess that makes sense. Somebody once told me that humans love to pathologize the fae."

Jaah nodded. "Intermagicals who live among humans tend to end up with a lot of mental health diagnoses."

I drove on through the dark, considering this. There are a lot of intermagicals who have no idea that they're magic. They just live life feeling strange and different, and struggling to cope with a human world that doesn't meet their needs or understand them. When I studied abnormal psychology in college, had I actually been learning about intermagicals the whole time, without realizing it?

Part 3 - Ritual

Chapter 10

I opened the back door to the Fair Isle late Monday afternoon and breathed in the familiar scent of cedar and whiskey. Coming here after work was a nice weekday routine, I thought as I nodded to a few familiar faces in passing, heading toward the raised bar at the center of the mostly empty pub.

"Hey there, hon!" came a hail from the small store-room behind the bar. To my surprise, the smiling face of Jaah's sister Pythia slid into view a moment later.

"Hey, what, uh…you work here?" I asked, startled to see her there, with a bar rag slung over a shoulder.

"Yeah, I pick up a few shifts when I'm in town. Just some quiet weeknights, you know, to give Isla a break?" She shrugged, picking up a bottle and giving it a twirl. "It's a good time. You want me to make you something fun?"

"It's a Monday," I hedged. If I accepted every drink I was offered at the Fair Isle, my liver would be pickled before I was twenty-five.

"Non-alcoholic, I got you," she said, grabbing ingredients from under the bar.

I hopped onto a bar stool to watch her work and noticed Zinnia and Azalea, tucked into a dark corner of the pub. Their faces were lit by the glow of the small screens they held. I was glad to have left my own computer screen at my office downtown, where I worked at the entry-level tech job Jaah helped me find. He'd taught me a few clever technomagic tricks, and that, plus my utilitarian bachelor's, was enough to land me a sweet little gig that paid more than enough to cover my bills.

"You didn't want to do computer stuff like your brother, huh?" I asked, watching Pythia mix and strain.

"No, not me. Computers'll steal your soul if you're not careful," she said, flashing me a bright, white grin. "I prefer to deal in reality. Real human connection, not that fake stuff you find online. And anyway, good customer service gets the good tips, you know?"

"Mmm," I said, making a noise that sounded almost like agreement. But I remembered the hard work and the small paycheck of my old coffee shop job, and personally, I thought her brother had the better idea.

"Here ya go, whaddaya think?" she asked, handing me a tall glass swimming with mint. It was fresh, herbal, and delicious.

"Thank you!" I exclaimed. "This is exactly what I didn't know I wanted."

"Pythia's specialty," said Jaah, sliding up beside me and neatly snatching the drink from my grasp. "Nice," they said, nodding their approval. "I'll take one, with rum in it."

"How was your presentation?" I asked, as Pythia rummaged under the bar for the ingredients she'd just put away.

"Terrifying," they said, with a maniacal gleam in their dark eye. "They loved it."

"That was the goal, huh?" I asked, skeptical.

"Oh sure, they hired me to audit their network and make sure their data is secure. If I didn't scare them a little by telling them all the ways they were in imminent danger before I got there, I wouldn't really be doing my job, would I?" they asked, turning to greet Zinnia and Azalea, who emerged from their technological cocoons at Jaah's arrival and came to join us.

"Hello, little ones. Having a nice day?"

"Hardly," Zinnia started, before being overrun by her sister.

"Those mean bullies keep stealing our territories in WyldSight," Azalea shouted, stamping her feet for emphasis. "Can you help us, Daddy?"

"Stealing your territory?" Jaah echoed. "In that new alternate reality game you guys were showing me? That means they must be right here in the neighborhood."

"Yeah!" Azalea agreed, as fired up as she had been at the pirate festival. "They're right here in the neighborhood!"

"I really don't know what this area is coming to, Gullah," Pythia said with a long, theatrical sigh as she slid a short glass across the bar to them. "I was talking to one of my friends and she says it's been getting real dangerous for the, uh, working girls of the neighborhood." She shot a glance at Azalea and Zinnia, who were distracted by their games again.

Oh yeah? Jaah asked, taking a sip of their drink.

"Mm hmm. One of 'em got beat up real bad last night. Little trans girl named Sylvie. She's in the hospital. Can't even tell us what happened, and I'm hearing through the grapevine that she might not be the first one, either, but you know how the rumor mill is. Nobody knows anything for sure, and everybody's scared. I was thinking maybe, on your day off, you could come with me and help them out with some of your tech stuff. Surveillance or something."

Jaah gave a tense little laugh and pushed away from the bar. "Really, Pythia? You've been in town for a few days, and you've already slithered your way into enough people's business that you have my whole next weekend planned out? Seriously?"

"What? Come on, Gullah. You know me. I get along with everybody. And I know you, too. Unless your new girlfriend has you too distracted to look out for your community?"

I put my hands up and leaned back, not wanting to get in the middle of this interesting new sibling dynamic. "Your brother won't be busy with me next weekend. I'll be down in the valley. Mom wants me at the hill on Saturday, so we can start magic school, and then I'm gonna go check out the church on Sunday."

"Church?" echoed Pythia with a grimace.

"Magic school?" asked Zinnia, with a very different expression in her bright, curious eyes.

Chapter 11

"What are they gonna teach us?" Zinnia asked, bespectacled and bouncing excitedly in the middle seat of my old minivan.

"I'm honestly not sure," I answered, looking at her in the rear-view mirror. We pulled off the road and up the gravel drive to the hill. I was grateful to see that it was emptier than it was last time, with only a few scattered fae in the garden. "I haven't done this before, either."

After Zinnia's enthusiastic interest in Evita's magic lessons, I asked Azalea if she would like to come, too.

"School?" she had scoffed. "No way, it's summer break."

Out of the car, Zinnia gamboled along beside me, teetering on stones and chasing after butterflies as we made our way up the sunny garden path to the kitchen door. She seemed younger and lighter without her sister, whether by lack of comparison or because she could let her guard down and take a break from being the serious, sensible twin.

As we came around the curve of the house, I saw Evita through the open kitchen window, waving tiny flying faeries out of her way as she bustled busily.

"Ah, Fiona, there you are," she said, stepping out of the kitchen door to greet me. "And who is this?" She smiled at the girl beside me, as she re-tied a flowery apron around her waist.

"Zinnia," I answered. "One of the Gullah's girls. She wanted to tag along for the magic lesson. I hope that's alright."

There wasn't any real way to contact Evita and the hill, from up in the city, except by passing messages through the little faeries that always seemed to be flitting between Portal Land and the valley. But, faeries being what they are, that sort of communication felt more like a schoolyard game of telephone, than an actual phone call. Jaah had offered to set her up with a cell phone or a landline, but she told them firmly that faerie queens didn't have need of such things, preferring the peacefulness and serendipity of doing things her way.

"Of course," Evita said. "Welcome, little one. I am happy to share what I know." She took Zinnia's small hand in her own and led her across the threshold and into the unusual house.

"Why is your house a big circle?" Zinnia marveled, examining the funny way the cabinets joined together along the curved outer wall of the kitchen.

"I don't know," answered Evita, with a tinkling little laugh that the flying faeries echoed, sounding like a chorus of tiny silver bells. "But when I saw this round house up here on the hill, I just knew it had to be mine."

"I've never seen a house like this. It's kind of weird," said Zinnia, which made Evita and the faeries laugh again.

"Well, I am weird," Evita told her, eyes flashing playfully at the little girl. "Do you know what that word really means?" Zinnia shook her head. "It comes from an older word. Wyrd with a y, which means the ability to control fate, and use ways beyond ordinary comprehension," Evita explained. "It's where we get words like witch and wizard, too. I wear my weirdness proudly, and so should you, dear."

Zinnia gave Evita a wide-eyed look, then continued poking around my mother's cozy kitchen. She peered at the jars of herbs and spices, and the heavy iron pots hung on the wall, until another question bubbled up in her curious mind. She met my gaze, and I nodded, giving her permission to ask.

"Are you a witch?" she inquired, large eyes round with curiosity.

"Well, I'm a woman," Evita replied, smiling down at the girl. "And I don't always follow the rules, and I know a few things," she added, laying a finger along her nose conspiratorially. "And so there are men out there who would call me a witch. And, you're here so I can teach you about magic, so I suppose you could call me a witch, too. Witches are wise women, after all."

"What magic are you going to teach us?" Zinnia asked.

Evita's eyes twinkled and she smiled mysteriously, then she turned back to the flour-dusted counter, where a mixing bowl and ingredients lay ready. "We'll get to that. First, would you like to help me finish my baking?" she asked Zinnia, who nodded enthusiastically. "And Fiona, would you mind seeing if there are any eggs in the yard today?"

"Sure," I answered, heading back out into the garden toward a small-fenced paddock where Evita kept her only livestock, a trio of large white ducks.

As I stepped through the gate, all three of the hefty birds waddled toward me.

"Kwak," said the largest of the three, accusingly.

"…'scuse me," I said, sidestepping them and making my way to the latch-topped duck house, where three large white eggs lay nestled in the clean yellow straw. "And thank you!"

"Perfect," said Evita, as I stepped back into the kitchen with my bounty. "Go ahead and crack one into here, if you please." She indicated a perfectly egg-sized well in the flour mixture, and I cracked the large egg on the counter before carefully ripping the unusually rubbery shell and tipping the rich yellow yolk into the hole. The white of the egg was thicker and stickier than I was used to, and I shook the shell, trying to dislodge the viscous stuff.

"Duck eggs are wonderful for baking," Evita said, taking the bowl from the counter and mixing it vigorously with an old wooden spoon. She scooped the mixture into a loaf pan, and popped it into the oven with a practiced motion.

"The topic of our first magic lesson is Ritual," said Evita, turning to address her students. Our lesson had officially begun. "Ultimately," Evita explained, "the goal of any ritual is to align the energies of the universe with our goal. With this baking, we have taken the elements of flour, sugar, egg, butter, and heat, and used their energy to produce a specific delicious outcome. And, we have done so by following the steps laid out by our wise ancestors."

I smiled blankly at her, unsure of how baking related to magic, but willing to hear her out. Seeing my expression, Evita walked to the top of the stairs and took a long look down at the quiet, closed doors below us.

"I hoped that Faeryn would be awake by now, to help me explain. She has the words for this kind of thing, not me," Evita said, letting out a long sigh. She began to gather her waist-length hair in her hands, twisting it into a high bun. "But, she's not, so I think we'll just have to learn by doing. Are you ready to try crafting your own ritual?" I met Zinnia's eyes, and we both nodded, game for whatever Evita had in mind. "Good. What would you like your spell to do? One ought to have a reason for doing real magic."

"Well," I said, not entirely sure what it was she was asking for. "I'm a little nervous about going to that church service tomorrow, with Urb. Could we do something to help me with that?"

"Ah, some protection magic. Yes," Evita agreed. "In fact, I'd like to reinforce the whole kingdom's defenses after what happened with Velia this spring, but that's a bit of a bigger task than we're looking for today. The intention of protecting your energy from the church will be a fine example for us."

"Okay," I said. "What do we do?"

"You tell me," replied Evita. "What do you think we ought to do?"

"I assumed there would be some kind of family grimoire, or something?" But, I frowned, remembering the chanterelles, I was learning that it was better not to assume anything.

"Well," answered Evita. "There are any number of protection spells that have been written down, and each one of them has some amount of power, but they won't work as well for you as for the person who created them. It is much more effective to craft your own rituals for exactly what you need. Although," she tapped a finger thoughtfully on a large, well-worn notebook that sat on the counter next to her. "It can be helpful to revisit your own past work now and again. There's no point in reinventing the wheel every single time. But, this first time, just let your intuition be your guide." She smiled at me expectantly.

I waited to see whether my intuition had anything to say, but nothing happened. "I'm still not really sure what you're asking me to do," I told her.

"I'm asking you to…" she paused, then wrung her hands in frustration. "Ugh, it really should be Faeryn explaining things, but she's been so tired, and I don't want to wake her unless we absolutely have to." Evita shook her head. "No, we'll muddle through." She walked back to the butcher block counter where the bags of flour and sugar still sat. "When we make shortbread," she said slowly. "We use sugar to create the quality of sweetness, and milk to imbue the nature of creaminess, and flour to lend it breadiness, which are all qualities we want in a shortbread." She eyed me with speculation. "What kinds of things might represent the qualities of the protection that you desire?"

"I don't know," I said, still not feeling like I was quite understanding what she was trying to get at.

"Open your mind's eye," said Evita. "When you imagine the protection you need, what is it like?" She took my hands in hers, and the sensation of magical energy tingled.

I remembered the way I'd felt at the Tent Revival, with its rigid organization and impressive infrastructure. It felt cold and alien. So different from the comfortable chaos of the intermagical Pirate Carnival. I was actually quite nervous about the church service tomorrow, now that I stopped to consider it.

"I don't know," I said, struggling to put words to the feeling. "The church is so big, and I'm so small. It makes me feel powerless and alone."

"I'm sure it does, dear," said Evita. "But we don't want to focus on what we lack when we set our intentions for a spell. Not unless we want to give that feeling more power."

Zinnia pursed her lips and furrowed her brow, considering this.

"An example, then," said Evita, seeing the child's confused expression. "Some native tribes," Evita told us. "Such as your brother Egan's people, use rain dances as a ritual of manifestation. Have you ever seen one?"

Zinnia and I both shook our heads, no.

"They are a sight to behold," Evita said, her face lighting up at the memory. "Dancers in tribal finery, bedecked in beads that make a sound like raindrops, who dance like they are splashing through the waters they so desperately need. It's a joyful celebration, and it gets its power from that exultation. Positive energy will always power manifestations much more effectively than yearning, and are less likely to create hazardous flash floods or other disasters like they might, if they simply threw their energies into their desperation."

She squeezed my shoulder comfortingly. "Can you tell me what it would feel like if you were to step into the church tomorrow knowing that you were wholly and completely protected?"

"Um," I said, then closed my mouth, considering. I closed my eyes, too, and tried to sink into my body, envisioning a state of total safety. After a long moment, I opened them again. "I would feel warm and cozy, like I'm in a fuzzy blanket. And, all around me," I told her, reaching out my hands like a mime touching invisible walls. "There's a force field that keeps all their negativity out and hides me from the people who would want to hurt me, if they knew that I was there, and what I was doing."

"An excellent place to start," Evita said with a nod. She began to tidy up the baking supplies, reaching high to put the flour back on the shelf. "It's one of the great contradictions of Christianity, that they spend so much time on their knees begging to the powers that they worship for forgiveness and for favors, when it is so ineffective. But, of course, they want their followers to exist in a state of wanting, and not one of personal power. That would be threatening to their control." She shrugged and reached for the eggshell that I cracked to toss it away.

"Wait," I said, reaching out and taking the shell from her. "I think I'm starting to get it. If I want to be protected, I have to feel protected, and if I want to get protective energies from outside myself, I need to find things in the world that have the kind of energies that I want." I held the shell in my hands, fitting the two halves together like puzzle pieces, and fingering the strange rubbery texture of the duck egg.

"This shell is a pretty good representation of protection, don't you think? Especially since it's from your ducks." I held it up for Evita and Zinnia to see. "Would this be a good place to start?"

"Yes, I think it would. I've never thought of creating a protection quite like that, but…" Evita beamed at me. "That is precisely why each of us uses our own intuition for these sorts of things. Is there anything else that you can think of, here in the house, that would help complete the feeling?"

"Hmm," I considered, then turned and dashed off to the bathroom, returning with a handful of cotton balls.

"Mmm, yes," agreed Evita. "That should help you feel nice and warm and secure."

Back in the kitchen, Evita opened up a large cabinet that I hadn't noticed before. It was filled with an array of jars and containers full of all sorts of things, some of which I recognized and many of which I didn't.

"As I mentioned before, I'd recommend that we include something to represent each of the four natural elements: fire, water, earth, and air," she said. "Next week, we'll start talking about the elements in detail, beginning with fire, but for now, how about we just use these?"

She handed me an incense stick, a white candle, and two jars labeled 'salt' and 'moon water.' I carried them, along with the eggshell and cotton balls, to Evita's big square dining table.

"Oh, and a couple more things," said Evita, bustling back to the kitchen and returning with a silk scarf, a piece of chalk, and a small metal tin. She opened the tin and handed it to me, then lit the incense and began waving the now-smoking stick around the objects on the table.

Inside the tin were all sorts of things: natural tumbled stones, coins, beads, bits of broken jewelry. I ran my fingers through the collection and paused when I found a small, clear crystal point. It reminded me of the bit of earthly magic that a ghost of my ancestor had given me, in one of my darkest hours. That one sat on the windowsill of my room up in Portal Land. I held its fellow up to the light, enjoying the way it made the facets glint.

"Is that your signifier?" Evita asked, as I turned the small stone over in my fingers.

"My what?"

"Your signifier, for the ritual. The material object that you will use to represent your own body and spirit, in the magic."

"Um, yeah," I agreed, holding it out to her. She didn't take it, just waved the incense around the hand that held it, three times.

"Now, it's entirely up to you," said Evita, continuing her hypnotic motions with the fragrant stick. "But some people like to join themselves with the signifier in some way. Bleed on it, for example."

I eyed the sharp little thing, then, letting my intuition guide me, I gave it a lick. It felt smooth and cool on my tongue.

Out of the corner of my eye, I saw Zinnia wrinkle her nose in distaste.

"Perfect," said Evita, smiling. She spread out the silk scarf, forming a sort of work surface. "Now, Fiona dear, close your eyes, take a few deep breaths, and let your intuition tell us what we ought to do with these things."

"Well," I said, picking up the eggshell contemplatively. "First, I think I want to fill it full of cotton balls."

Some time later, I snuffed out the final candle, completing the ritual. Smoke still drifted from the glowing wick when Faeryn's bright red head appeared at the top of the stairs.

"Oh no, did I miss it?" she asked sleepily. "I'm sorry. I've just been so tired lately."

She walked over to the table where the duck egg sat in a puddle of salt and moon water, sealed with wax so that it was whole once again. The esoteric symbols I drew on the outside of the shell were barely visible in white chalk, but I hadn't been trying to make art, only magic. My signifier, charged with my energy, was nestled safely inside the cotton balls, protected from anything that might try to harm it, and especially from the machinations of the Christ's Heart Church.

"Very nice," Faeryn said, who leaned in close to peer at the artifact, but was careful not to touch it. "I wish I could have watched you make it. I love seeing other people's intuition at work." She looked up at me, beseeching. "Can I help you charge it, at least?"

"Oh, um, sure, okay," I agreed, stepping forward and taking her proffered hand.

"Evita!" she called, and my mother rounded the corner from the kitchen, completing the circle with our joined hands. A sensation of energy welled, and in my mind's eye, I saw the spiraling shape of the triskelion, glowing with an unearthly fire, in the empty space between us.

"Fire, earth, water, air, elements of the natural world. Spirits, beloved ancestors, lend Fiona your power so that she..." Faeryn paused, realizing that she didn't actually know what we had been trying to accomplish. "Can achieve her important and worthy goals." She finished, vaguely. With a final squeeze, Faeryn released our hands, and as our arms fell, I felt the energy we raised billowing out from us in all directions.

"Wow," said Zinnia from the doorway. "When do I get to learn how to do that?"

"I really am sorry I missed the magic lesson," said Faeryn again, some time later. "I know, I know, it's fine. But it's just so frustrating feeling so sick all the time. I'm always missing things, or so exhausted I bite people's heads off when they're only trying to be nice."

"I'm sorry, cousin," I told her, taking her small hand in mine and sending her some energy through the connection. "Is there anything I can do?"

"Could you tell me about the lesson?" she asked. "That would be almost as good as being there."

"Sure," I agreed, and told her about the way Evita helped us to understand how to develop ritual. "It's kind of like a craft project, and I've always liked those," I said, and told Faeryn how much I enjoyed the process of sealing the cotton-stuffed duck egg with wax. "And, I like how we call on all the elements. That seems like a very logical kind of mysticism."

"Logical mysticism, have I heard you say that before?" Faeryn asked.

"Yeah," I said. "It's what I've been calling the sort of magical philosophy that I've been learning from the intermagicals," I told her shyly. "But I know you're the 'namer' in our family, and—"

"Logical Mysticism," Faeryn repeated, tasting the phrase. "I like the sound of that. Well named, cousin," she said, bestowing me with a proud smile. "It's wonderful to have another intermagical naming things around here."

Chapter 12

Sunday morning, Urb picked me up from the hill in a big, rusty van with *Shrewsborough Renaissance Faire* painted on the side.

"Nice ride," I said, swinging up into the high front seat.

"It's my grandma's," he told me with an apologetic shrug. "Ready for this?"

"Sure am," I agreed. "Let's get going. We wouldn't want to be late to church!"

As we drove down from Evita's house and into the town proper, I counted the churches as we passed them.

"Six, seven, there's another one! Why does such a little town need so many churches?" I wondered aloud.

"Life without Jesus is like an unsharpened pencil," said Urb, reading from the letterboard on the lawn of the church we just passed. "Pointless!" He snickered at the joke, but I found the idea disturbing.

"I don't get it," I told him, as we drove on, leaving the sign behind us. "I mean, I understand the pun, but I just don't understand why anyone feels that way. Life without Jesus is pointless? Like, why?"

"It's a little heavy-handed, sure," said Urb, turning on his blinker to follow a sign reading 'detour,' "but his teachings speak to a lot of people."

"You think so?" I asked. I eyed the long line of cars in front of us irritably. We had left on time, but I hadn't been counting on this delay.

"Oh yeah," said Urb. "Christianity is a bit of a special interest of mine. Especially the controversial theories that make my mom throw her slippers at me."

"Well, you want to explain it to me, then? Seems like we've got plenty of time."

"Sure. You're into psychology, right? Well, the New Testament, Jesus and the disciples, and all of that? It's kind of like the first psychological case study. This collection of stories about this man, Jesus, and the things he said and did, but we only ever hear about him from other people's perspectives. We don't have any idea what was going on in his head, just the stories people told. And those stories were wild! He was acting totally differently from anyone else around him, and it got him a lot of attention. But," said Urb, with a sly glance at me, "if you dig a little, you can find a lot of parallels with Eastern philosophy."

"You mean like Hinduism and stuff?"

"Yeah," Urb agreed. "The Golden Rule is pretty similar to the Hindu concept of dharma, or 'right action.' And the Seven Deadly Sins are basically the same, too," he said. "Except for sloth, but that's part of dharma anyway."

Finally, it was our turn, and the big van rumbled to life.

wee-oh-wee-oh

The wail of sirens sounded behind us, and Urb rolled to a stop again. I gritted my teeth as one police car passed us, then another and another.

"That must be nearly every cop in town," I mused, as I watched them pass. "At this rate, we're never gonna get there."

We pulled back onto the road, and I glanced at the clock. There was still a little time, but we were cutting it close. I hoped there wouldn't be any more delays.

"This is the part that makes my mom throw her slipper, okay?" Urb said, continuing his lecture. "There are eighteen years of Jesus's life that are unaccounted for. Did you know that? And one theory is that he spent that time traveling in Egypt and India, and maybe even Tibet, studying with gurus there."

"Really? Just because some of the philosophies are the same?"

He took his eyes off the road and shot me a glance.

"Not just that. There are several ancient Buddhist memoirs that talk about a yogi named Issa who came from the West seeking knowledge, and we're all pretty sure it's the same guy."

"Pretty sure, huh?"

"Some important gurus have written books about it, but they keep getting 'mysteriously lost' or outright stolen by Christian missionaries, and when the church tries that hard to keep people from finding out about something, it sure makes it seem like there's probably something there, you know?"

"Why would the church care if people found out that Jesus traveled in India, or wherever?"

"Because they're distorting his teachings, for one thing. And when you look at the source material, that all falls apart pretty quickly."

"What do you mean?"

"An example? Alright, how about this. Jesus said, 'The kingdom of Heaven is within you,' or at least that's how it's sometimes translated. And if you look at that from an Eastern perspective, it means to look for the divine within yourself. But, that's way too empowering, so instead the message is re-translated and twisted to mean that you have to make a kingdom for God inside of you. And, presto change-o, Churchianity is in control again."

"Churchianity?" I asked with a chuckle.

"Yeah, I've heard some Eastern philosophers call it that. Ones with respect for Jesus Christ as a person, but not so much for the churches that use his name."

"Speaking of," I said, "this thing is starting in a few minutes. Are we close yet?"

"Actually, I think I'm a little lost," Urb admitted. "This isn't the part of town I thought it was. That detour really messed me up."

"Yeah, I don't think we're making it to church today."

zrp zrp
protect you

"I'm sorry," said Urb, hanging his head and slumping in his seat. "It's my fault. I have terrible luck. Always have. I shouldn't have offered to drive us."

"Actually," I said, putting a hand on my stomach contemplatively. "I think it might have been me," I told Urb about yesterday's magic lesson and the protection ritual I crafted. "I think I might have protected myself a little too powerfully. I'll have to ask Evita what to do about that before we try again next week."

Chapter 13

"Sunday was a total bust," I told Pythia, hanging my head. Tucked in close to the long wooden bar at the Fair Isle, I told her about the unlikely series of delays that kept us from getting to the church on time. It was demoralizing to report that I hadn't even made it through the front door, but she was interested in the idea that my own protection ritual kept us from getting there.

"Zinnia told me y'all were cooking up some pretty powerful stuff over there," she said, then held up a long finger and danced off down the bar to serve a hulking man with a long-braided beard who looked thirsty.

Hearing her name, Zinnia wandered toward us, trailed by Azalea.

"I wanna go to magic school next time!" said Azalea, stepping in front of her sister and making Zinnia catch herself to avoid stumbling. "Fire, fire, fire!"

"I keep telling you, I don't think you'll like it," said Zinnia, shooting me a pleading look over the shorter twin's shoulder. "I shouldn't have told her what the lesson was going to be."

"You want to go too, huh?" I asked her, stifling my urge to answer 'sure!' for Zinnia's sake. Pythia was back now, and I turned to her, changing the subject. "How did everything go, up here? Did you guys learn anything?"

"Not really," Pythia answered, with a roll of her large eyes. "Nothing new. But we spent a while there and heard some more about what happened last week."

"Oh yeah?"

"Yeah, that poor girl Sylvie is still in critical condition at the hospital. She's totally out of it. Can't tell us anything about what happened. Weirdest thing though. Another working girl, one of her friends? She up and disappeared that same night. Nobody's heard from her, since."

"Oh no!" I said, aghast. "That's awful. Nobody knows anything? How scary. Was your brother able to put up some cameras, or something, to help keep an eye out?"

"Nah," she answered. "They wouldn't let us. Not exactly legal, what they're doing.

Understandable that they wouldn't want a bunch of recording equipment set up, you know? But we hung around till late on Saturday, keeping watch."

"And they got us lots of new terrain in WyldSight!" said Azalea, waving her phone and jumping around.

"Cool!" I said, catching some of her energetic enthusiasm. I knew very little about WyldSight, the new alternate reality game it seemed like everybody was playing.

"Which reminds me," said Zinnia. "Auntie, can you come out to the park with us and claim the spot by the swings? We don't want anybody to poach it."

"No, child. I'm working right now. I can't go wandering off. Why don't you see if Fiona will go with you?"

The two girls turned imploring eyes on me.

"Sure," I agreed with a chuckle and only the smallest exasperated glance at Pythia. "I can download something new, I guess. What do you need me to do?"

Zinnia explained as we walked down the pretty, shop-lined street outside the Fair Isle. In WyldSight, players claim territory in teams of five. Since there were only two sisters, when Zinnia and Azalea claimed a territory, they left three open spots on their team.

"Players are supposed to respect each other, it says so on the website!" said Zinnia. But a group of teenagers in the neighborhood kept on taking the extra spots and using their majority to kick the girls out of their territories, over and over again.

When we reached the park, I touched the new WS icon on my screen, launching a stylized GPS map of the area.

"Here," said Azalea, waving her phone at me. "See? Just click here!" *Bing!* I claimed my first territory. The area filled in with color, and a blinking dot appeared. "Click on it!" Azalea crowed.

10,000 WP - New Wyld Sighted! I clicked *OK*, and a new window opened showing a very curious picture. It was an animal with four long legs, large tawny wings, and a pointed red face.

"What is this?" I asked Zinnia, turning the image toward her.

"Oh, it's just an Owl-Fox-Deer. They're everywhere around here. I was all excited about them a couple weeks ago, when we first got here, but they're like—"

"The most common Wyld ever!" interjected Azalea, and Zinnia agreed, nodding solemnly.

"When you claim a territory, you get points for all the Wylds that pass through it," Zinnia explained, clicking a red dot in the corner of her screen.

"See? These Wylds have all passed through here since we claimed it an hour ago." Zinnia scrolled through more of the strange amalgamation creatures. "Ooh, Azie, look! We got a new um—" She bent closer to her phone. "What do you think this one is?"

Azalea opened the notification on her own device, and cocked her head to the side, considering. "An iguana-parrot-monkey? Maybe they're here on vacation," she speculated.

"I'd rather be on vacation there!" said Zinnia, looking suspiciously at the sky, which was beginning to fill with thick gray clouds. There was always a chance of rain, even in the middle of the summer, here in Oregon.

"Who is on vacation? What do you mean?" I asked, peering at the interesting tropical creature. It was almost cute, with its little monkey face and colorful bird body, but the lizard tail was a little off-putting.

"Anybody who isn't playing is a Wyld," explained Zinnia, gesturing to a mother pushing her young son on the swingset. "She's the Owl-Fox-Deer. Those are all local animals from right around here."

The app, she explained, assigned non-players Wyld identities by taking three different native animals from the farthest places the cell phone traveled and mixing them together. Every six months or so, the Wylds were re-shuffled and re-generated, creating the mixed-up fantasy creatures on the screen in front of me. Someone with an iguana and a monkey in their Wyld must have been somewhere tropical recently.

"Wait, so all these weird creatures are actually people?" I asked as I watched Zinnia scroll through her inbox, collecting points. "Like, people playing the game who walked by?"

"No, other people playing the game don't count," Zinnia corrected me.

"The Wylds are everybody else. Anyone with a cell phone."

"Wyld creatures!" Azalea chimed in.

"Huh." I watched as a man crossed the small grassy area toward the pair on the swings. As he got closer, another blinking dot appeared on my screen. I clicked on it. Just another Owl-Fox-Deer. I looked left and right, checking to see if anyone else was heading in this direction. Yeah, I chucked to myself, I could see how this game might be fun.

"Daddy!" cried the little boy on the swings, reaching his arms toward the man.

That reminded me.

"Hey Zinnia, do you know when your dad is going to be getting home?"

"Oh, Daddy's there now," answered Zinnia breezily. "Went upstairs with a friend. Some lady. Said to make ourselves busy and give them an hour or so."

"Oh," I said, taken aback. Jaah was up in their room with some woman, huh? Well, that was what they told me they would be doing, right? What we'd discussed? I pocketed my phone, somewhat less interested in the game than I was a moment before.

A few minutes later, we walked through the front door of the Fair Isle. At the same moment, Jaah ducked in from the back. I looked away, not wanting to meet their eyes.

Pythia hadn't seen us, either. "Gullah! Welcome back," she called across the mostly empty pub. "I bet you're hungry, let me grab you some of this nice stew Isla made."

"No thanks," they said, leaning back to belch loudly, then thumping their chest. "I'll be good for a bit, after that." Zinnia and Azalea ran to greet them, with Azalea swinging up into their arms. They saw me and their face lit with a smile. Slinging the little girl over one shoulder, they headed toward me. "Hey," they said, then, seeing my expression, added, "Is everything okay?"

"Yeah," I said, still not meeting their eyes.

"Fiona," they said, looking worried. They reached out and grasped my arm.

Zap! The electric sensation of their touch made me lurch away from them.

They dropped my arm. "Fiona, what's wrong?"

"It's nothing," I told them, refusing to meet their eyes. "Just something to get used to, I guess. We did talk about it after all."

"Oh," they said, their expression sheepish. "Yeah, that makes sense. Uh, I'm sorry?"

"Don't be. It's okay. I'm fine," I said, not entirely sure who I was convincing.

Chapter 14

A slender pixie of a man eyed the Gullah up and down, as we sat side by side in a dark book at the Fair Isle, late Thursday night. "Hey, you," he said. "Haven't had the pleasure since our chance encounter last summer, honey. You know, they're starting those parties back up again, right? Next one's tomorrow night. Maybe I'll see you there?" He batted long eyelashes at the Gullah, beside me, before turning to mince away flirtatiously.

Jaah grinned, watching him walk away. Beside them, I stiffened.

"Oh, sorry," said Jaah, their expression dropping. They took their arm off my shoulders and turned to face me.

"It's fine," I said, looking straight ahead at the flickering candle that lit our table.

"No," they said, "clearly it's not. Can we talk about it, please? You're obviously uncomfortable. I love you, Fiona. I don't want you to feel that way."

zrp zrp
loves me

That's right, Jaah loves me, I remembered. Just me. Not all of them.

"Thanks," I said. "That does make me feel better, actually. Just knowing that it bothers you…" I looked up at them and smiled at the caring concern I saw in their large, dark eyes. "I've just never done this before, and I didn't think it would be so hard, seeing you with other people. Thinking about it was easier. But, it turns out that I really care about you."

"And I care about you, Fiona. A lot, like I said before, what I need from other people…it's just physical. I don't—"

The front door to the Fair Isle slammed open, interrupting us. It was Pythia, body language communicating her extreme distress.

"GULLAH!" she exclaimed, seeing us and striding purposefully toward our table. "It happened again, Brother! Tonight, I just heard," She gesticulated dramatically as she spoke. "A sweet little girl up in the North part of town was beaten with a belt, real bad. Said the guy was shouting Bible verses at her the whole time."

"Trans?" Jaah asked, already starting to rise from the table. She nodded. "Before or after?"

"After, of course." Pythia scowled, and my own brow furrowed with anger. It was one thing to judge these women for what were selling, but it was a whole other level of evil to use their services first, and then beat them up, after.

"And is anyone missing?" Jaah asked.

Pythia shook her head. "Not that I know of, but I've been asking around and—" Her phone buzzed to life, and she looked down at it. "Yep, look at that. There's a stripper who didn't show up for her shift tonight. Her friend went by her place, and it was all cleared out. Same part of town where the girl was working, too."

"I want to go check this out. Talk to people while their memories are fresh," said Jaah, reaching for their unseasonably long, dark overcoat, which hung on a hook nearby. "Fiona, would you mind staying at my place tonight? The girls are already asleep upstairs."

"Sure," I agreed, heart pounding. It was nice to have some way of helping in a situation like this.

It was nearly morning when Jaah got back. I sat on the low sofa wrapped in a blanket, lit only by the yellow light of the streetlamp outside the window.

"How did it go?" I asked, startling them.

"You're still up," they said, recovering themselves quickly. "I thought you'd be asleep by now."

"My mind's too full to sleep. What happened tonight? Did you find anything?"

They shook their head. "Nothing much. We talked to some people, but nobody saw anything useful. But hey, since you're up, can we talk about earlier? We were having an important conversation before my sister interrupted us."

"Okay," I agreed hesitantly. Admittedly, it hadn't only been thoughts of Jaah and Pythia's mission that kept me awake tonight.

"I'm sorry about that guy at the bar earlier. I try to keep it out of your face as much as I can, because I know it's upsetting to you. I didn't know he was going to come up to me, right in front of you, like that."

"Oh, uh," I started, then stopped again. That wasn't the way this conversation had gone in my head.

"But, I'm a concubus," Jaah said, raising their hands in a shrug. "That kind of thing's going to happen from time to time. There's not a lot I can do about it."

"I don't—" I tried again, still not quite sure how to say what was on my mind. "I don't want you to hide it from me. I think that's what bothered me the most, the other day. The fact that I didn't know where you were, or what was going on." My cheeks flushed in memory. "I found out from Zinnia! How embarrassing!"

"Oh," Jaah replied, shoulders slumping. "I didn't realize." They took a seat next to me and we sat together in silence for a long moment before they asked. "And, how about tonight?"

"Tonight?" I echoed, then felt my face heat again, as I voiced the thought I'd been pondering for hours. "Tonight, I think I was actually just jealous."

"Of that guy? He doesn't mean anything to me, I—"

"No, not of him, of you. I'm jealous that you've had all these adventures and done all these interesting things. You're so worldly and experienced, and I'm, well," I looked down at my blanket-covered lap. "I'm not."

"Oh," they said, considering this. "Well, we just got invited to a play party tomorrow. Do you want to check that out? I didn't think it would be your kind of thing, but if you're looking for new experiences, it's not a bad place to start."

"You got invited," I corrected testily, remembering the pretty young man's salacious wink.

"Well, you're with me," said Jaah with reassuring confidence. "So, we're invited."

I didn't need to leave for the valley until Saturday morning, I reasoned with myself, and I had said that I wanted to try new things.

"Sure," I agreed. "Why not? Sounds like an adventure."

Chapter 15

"You ready?" asked Jaah, with their hand on the door to the party. "Remember, don't do anything you're not comfortable with, and if you don't like something—"

"The two feet rule," I said, interrupting. "I remember. Use my two feet and walk away."

"Sounds like you're ready, to me," Jaah said, pushing open the door. To my surprise, inside was a surprisingly normal living room full of people socializing and holding cans of soda and seltzer.

A large, beautiful woman sat regally on an overstuffed sofa, chatting cheerfully with the man next to her. When she saw Jaah, though, she paused her conversation in mid-sentence.

"You," she said, voice deep and loud. "I've been hoping you might stop by. After the kind of week I've had, I could sure go for some of your energy."

"Oh, uh, do you mind?" Jaah asked. "I can stay with you till you're comfortable," they offered, but I eyed the expression on the powerful woman's face.

"No, it's okay," I told them. "I'll be alright." Jaah had warned me that they might be pulled away by someone or another. I wasn't expecting it to be quite so soon, but I had prepared myself for the possibility.

"I won't keep him long, I promise," the woman reassured me, hooking a finger in Jaah's shirt collar. "Make yourself at home," she called over her shoulder as she led my partner up the stairs. "The real fun's in the sunroom and the garage."

Now alone, I wandered into the kitchen where non-alcoholic drinks and a nice cheese platter sat on display. Through an open doorway to what must be the sunroom, I could see a man tied up with rope, suspended from the ceiling. He spun slowly in a circle, and I watched him twist there for a long moment, fascinated by the contorted shape of him and the way the ropes cut concentric circles into the flesh of his arms and thighs.

The door next to me swung open, and a tall man stepped through it. "Thanks again, hon," I heard a voice call after him, and he raised a hand in acknowledgment, letting the door swing closed behind him. This must be the garage, I thought, and slipped through the door before it could shut completely.

A pretty woman sat on a low black bench. "Hey there, darlin'," she said when she saw me, continuing to roll long stockings up her short, shapely legs. I blinked at her, mind momentarily blank. She smiled at my vacant expression. "Looking for someone, honey?"

"No," I answered, snapping back to myself. "Just looking around. Sorry."

"Don't be. You new here, sweetie? I don't think I've seen you around before."

"Uh huh. What were you doing out here?" I wondered aloud, then added, "Is that alright to ask?" I couldn't help glancing at the half-rolled stocking that still hugged her thigh. Something about her being half-dressed like that felt more scandalous than bare legs would have been.

"Oh, just getting my backside warmed up, and my mind straightened out," she said with a little laugh. "Got to have some way to work through big, powerful feelings, or else they run away with me, and I end up saying something I regret!" She gave me a wide-eyed grin, then added, "You ever feel like that?"

"Not really," I said with a shrug. "I could probably use some help getting in touch with my emotions, honestly." My adopted mom didn't appreciate big feelings, so I learned to detach as a survival technique. As I unlocked my intuition and my magic, though, I was getting more in tune with my emotions and my body, too.

"Is that so? A little too aloof and detached for comfort, are we?" she asked, eyes alight with playful teasing. "What are you? Some kind of stoic little gnome or something?" The question had a familiar ring to it. That double-crossing betrayer, Velia, had said something similar to me when she was trying to keep me away from my birth family. She called me 'A round little goblin or a gnome or something' and I was certain she hadn't meant it to be flattering. I felt my hackles rise.

"No," I told her. "I'm a faerie." My reply was far more intense than was warranted, and a familiar childhood shame rose up in me. I opened my mouth to apologize for my outburst, but before I could, she surprised me by meeting my passionate fire with some of her own.

"Oh really?" she retorted. "One of the hoity-toity High Sidhe, huh? What the almighty Queen likes to call Real Faeries? You know that we vila are Slavic faeries, right? Just because we don't fit into the Queen's precious little boxes—"

"But I'm not one of them," I blurted, interrupting her. "I'm not part of the Faerie Queen's court."

"No?" She cocked her head, considering. "But you still dare to call yourself faerie, right here in Portal Land? How can you—"

"I'm with the Little Queen's court," I interjected, interrupting again. "The one down in the valley."

"The Little Queen, hmm?" my new friend replied. "I do know of her, though not many will. She has been kind to my sisters, unlike some." Her eyes flashed with anger again, then she sighed, exasperated. "Ugh, look at me, all worked up again, and just when I had everything smoothed out so nicely. Would you mind helping me out, hon?"

"Mind helping with—" I asked. She picked up the paddle from the bench beside her and waggled it at me. "Um, sure, I guess I can do that."

She climbed onto the bench, on all fours, and wiggled, drawing my attention to the intended target. "Right here on the cheek," she told me, reaching back and rubbing a spot below her high-cut pantyline. "Ten good smacks ought to do it."

"Okay." I raised the paddle up and brought it down with a loud *crack!* She made a small noise, and my breath caught in my throat. "Did I hurt you?" I asked, worried, as I watched her pale skin redden at the point of impact.

"You're a natural, sweetie," she said. "Do it again, but rub it out this time, okay?" She reached behind herself and massaged the red spot for a second. "Other cheek now, though. Got to make me even!"

I raised the paddle again, this time aiming for her other side. *Crack!* I watched as her skin rebounded like a raindrop in a puddle, then remembering what she said, I reached out and rubbed my hand over the growing red welt. Her skin felt hot and very smooth.

"That's probably enough," she said after a minute. "I'm all better now."

Reddening with embarrassment, I pulled my hand back. "I'm sorry!"

"Don't worry about it, honey," she said. "That's two!"

"So, what did you think?" Jaah asked, as we walked together down the quiet neighborhood street where people slumbered, totally unaware of what was going on just a few houses down. It should have felt devious, I thought, going to a party like that and watching people being tied up with rope and hit with things, but it hadn't, really.

"It just all seems a little silly," I told them. "I'm not saying I didn't like it. I did. It's just, well…" I paused to decide how to say what I meant. "I thought it would be more dark or serious, but people just kept laughing, and I can understand why. It's just all kind of…" I paused, not knowing how to finish the thought.

"It's a play party," Jaah said, reaching out and squeezing my hand in the dark. "That's all it is, just play."

"I guess so. I always thought that was a euphemism or something."

"Not really," Jaah said with a shrug.

Then, why do the Morality Police have so much of a problem with it? I wondered, as we reached my van and climbed inside, ready to head home. What's so immoral about playing with sensation and having fun with our bodies?

My phone buzzed to life, and I smiled, seeing the message.

Thanks for the help tonight, sweetie. Here's my number.
Let me know if I can return the favor sometime.

Part 4 - Fire

Chapter 16

"Fiiiiyeuurrrr" said Azalea for the umpteenth time, from the backseat of my minivan, as we drove toward the hill and our weekly magic lesson.

"Can you please stop saying that?" asked an exasperated Zinnia. Her displeasure at being overruled and having to take her sister along had shown me an interesting new side of her personality.

"If she wants to go to school, then I'm gonna let her," Jaah had told Zinnia, again, giving the girl a pat on the head as they sent us off this morning. "You'll be fine."

Faeryn did not want to risk sleeping through our second magic class, so we scheduled this lesson for later in the day. When we rounded the final turn up to the hill, she was already out in the garden. I could see her at the top of the yard, with flaming red hair and a burnt orange dress whipping in the summer breeze. She stood next to a large bonfire whose flames licked the clear blue of the late afternoon sky.

My van rumbled to a stop at the top of the driveway, and I got out.

"Hello, cousin," said the pretty red-haired youth by the fire.

"Nice to see you, Visc," I replied. "What a pretty dress you have on." Now that I was close enough to see my cousin's expression, it was obvious that we would not be dealing with Faeryn today.

"Yes," said Visc with a bit of a hiss. "Isn't it?" He spun, a blocky masculine gesture, shaking out his long hair, which shone with sun and firelight. "I think we look just like a flame, don't you?"

I hadn't seen Visc since the night I watched him psychologically torture someone, on my orders. I liked him, but he made me a little nervous. Visc had enjoyed his role in our plan a little too much and hadn't been able to stop himself until Faeryn took control of their body and allowed us to make our escape.

"FIRE!" repeated Azalea, with enthusiasm.

She and her sister followed me out of the car, and immediately ran to the bonfire and started poking it with sticks. Even sensible Zinnia couldn't resist the temptation of the flames, I thought with a smile, and left them to it. It was the theme of the hour, after all.

I looked over Visc's shoulder and raised my chin in greeting to Calliope, who just opened a door to the garden. Visc gave his neck a sharp twist, turning to see what I was looking at, and Calliope shrieked and whirled, closing the door behind her with a snap.

"She really does scamper like a nervous little mouse, doesn't she?" Visc said with a cold laugh that made me want to take a step back from him. His gaze lingered on the closed door with an odd intensity.

"The girls are really excited about all this fire," I said, calling his attention back to the lesson.

"As am I," said Visc, bending close to the flames so that an orange glow danced on his pale, freckled cheeks. "Fire is our element. We are fire." I could see the flames reflected in his dark eyes. "We are vital and ever changing. Red, yet many colored. Flaming and infinitely faceted. And capable of burning those who get too close." He smiled, and the fire glinted off his shining white teeth, as well. "I like fire. That's why I made such a big one." He raised his hands, and the fire swelled, growing even larger, with Visc's intention. "It's also the season for fire. High summer. The sun burns bright in the sky."

By this time, the girls were paying attention. They moved to stand on either side of me, and we all watched Visc somewhat worriedly, edging a little further away from the roaring blaze. He didn't notice, entranced by the flames in front of him, and he smiled widely as they grew larger and larger.

"In Vedic wisdom, the spirit of fire is called Agni, and has three forms. Fire, sun, and lightning. It's dry enough. Maybe I'll whip us up a nice electrical storm, as a fun little demonstration." I felt both girls cling more tightly to my sides as the wind and Visc's enthusiasm made the fire swell even higher. "What are the characteristics of fire? That's what you're here to learn, isn't it? Assertiveness, passion, enthusiasm, and also impulsiveness and aggression. It's all fire energy!" Visc grabbed an old wooden chair that sat halfway hidden in a garden bed and broke it, throwing the pieces onto the bonfire.

"Fire is light and joy, and also hate. Creation and destruction. Purification in flame!" He poked the pieces of the chair with a long stick, sending showers of bright sparks up into the air and out toward me and the girls. I hurriedly brushed a stray ember off Azalea's shoulder. "In the Tarot, fire is passion, but, more interestingly, I think, it represents conversion. Fire changes whatever it touches, often irreversibly and beyond recognition."

The bonfire was lit in a wide, open area at the top of the yard, which seemed safe enough, when we arrived, but by this point, Visc coaxed the fire to such a large size that the flames now threatened to lick the branches of the towering pine tree above it.

The door to the house banged open, and Evita stalked out, toward us and the roaring blaze. I let out a sigh of relief, only then realizing that I had been holding my breath.

"Visc, I think you had better let Faeryn teach this lesson," she said, ice in her voice.

"Why Aunt? We're all having fun, aren't we?" His sweeping gesture included the raging bonfire, the girls, and me, who stood white-knuckled and wide-eyed beside him.

"Visc, please remember that you are my guest, and are required to follow the rules of hospitality while in my realm. My word here is law," she intoned with regal intensity. She took a deep breath and continued on with a more regulated voice, "As you might recall, I've had visions of this house going up in flames, and I'd appreciate it if you could demonstrate restraint, or, better yet, allow Faeryn to do so."

"You, of all people, are going to tell me I have to follow the rules?" Visc's pale face screwed up in an expression of anger that I couldn't imagine on Faeryn. "Fine!" he shouted and threw himself back into a bed of leafy green plants that erupted in a fragrant puff of mint. He lay there, in a dead faint, body limp.

"Ow," said Faeryn a moment later, sitting up and rubbing her elbow.

"Welcome back," said Evita with a tight smile, helping her to her feet.

"What's going on?" Faeryn asked, looking from me to Evita, and then to the raging bonfire. "Why is there such a big fire in the garden? I thought we agreed that we were just going to have a small—"

"Visc," said Evita curtly, picking crumpled leaves out of Faeryn's hair.

"Ah," she replied. "I see. I'm sorry."

"You don't have to be sorry, it's not your fault," I told her, meaning to be reassuring, then paused, considering. "Or, is it? I'm not really sure how any of this works, in your, er, relationship."

Faeryn shrugged. "Suffice it to say it's at least somewhat my fault."

Evita patted her shoulder comfortingly. "I could hear Visc from inside the house. He ranted and raved his way through most of your lesson plan," said Evita. "But there is still the protection ritual for us to do."

Faeryn nodded, looking chagrined. "This really wasn't how I'd planned for today to go, but sometimes I'm just more Visc than I am Faeryn, especially these days, and it just happens like that. I'm sure the big fire didn't help."

"It's alright, dear," said Evita, understandingly. "I'll go grab the ingredients for the gunpowder, shall I?"

"Gunpowder?" chorused the two girls, Azalea's voice excited, Zinnia's a little alarmed.

"No, I'll get it," said Faeryn, "and you explain. It was your idea after all."

This valley, Evita told us, could use some new layers of energetic protection after everything that had gone on this spring. Velia, formerly the Little Queen's right hand, had betrayed her by trying to prevent me from ever meeting my birth family. When she had been revealed to be a traitor, Velia had been banished far away. And, while it was certainly preferable to be free from the woman's nefarious influence, Evita had relied on Velia's powerful magic for much of her realm's defenses, and her absence meant that the valley was now quite a bit less secure.

"But it is no matter," said Evita, resolutely. "We will develop our own defenses. And..." She smiled, pleased with her own cleverness. "We can build them up together, week by week, and element by element."

"For the hill and the valley?" I asked her. The valley, I knew, was ruled by my Aunt, Queen Vivienne, and not by my mother.

"Yes," Evita agreed, understanding the meaning behind my question. "The hill and the valley both. It is my home, and it's the right thing to do. And," she added, with a glint in her bright eyes, "what my sister doesn't know won't hurt her."

My birth mother had a tendency to thwart rules that didn't suit her. Remembering what Visc said earlier, I wondered if it might be a more significant part of her nature than I realized.

Under Evita's instruction, we mixed sulfur, charcoal and saltpeter, making a smooth black powder that tickled my nose and made me want to sneeze. With some experimentation, we managed to craft clever paper funnels that poured the dark powder in a steady stream and allowed us to draw designs on a patch of smooth white sand.

"Now, the fun part," said Evita to the twin girls, motioning for them to stand behind her. She brought a lit twig from the now smaller bonfire and lit the corner of our carefully connected design. The evening had just started to dim when the sigils that held our intentions lit in a flash of bright fire. We all exclaimed in awe, and when I closed my eyes, the triskelion at the center of the design still glowed behind my eyelids.

When Pythia arrived to pick up the girls and spirit them back to the city and to their beds, Zinnia had already started to nod off at the table. With a smile, I imagined Jaah carrying them up from the car to their beds.

"Me and a couple of girlfriends are gonna check out this horror movie marathon tomorrow night. D'you wanna tag along?" Pythia asked me as we sat in the plant-filled living room, waiting for Azalea to find her shoes. "It's late, so it'd be after you get back."

"Um," I hedged. "I've never actually seen a horror movie. My parents were pretty strict about that stuff when I was young, and I guess I just never really got around to it."

That wasn't entirely true. I had snuck into one psychological thriller, and it scared me so badly that I wasn't eager to try to evade my parents' ban again.

"If you could please keep avoiding the horror movies," said Evita, poking her head in from the kitchen. "I'd appreciate it. The Ancestor Garden already takes enough tending, and there's no reason to give a bunch of new nasties license to wander around and muck things up."

She ducked back around the corner. I stood up to follow her, and Pythia came with me.

"Now wait just a minute, there, Evita. You can't say something like that and walk away. What is an Ancestor Garden, and um, what's the reason I can't watch horror movies, exactly?"

Evita sighed, then pulled a tall stool up to the counter and took a seat. "Well, you're going to do what you're going to do." She looked guarded and irritable. "You're an adult, and you can do what you want. Lots of people watch those kinds of things. I'm sure nothing I say will stop you, if that's what you want to do."

"Huh? What do you mean? I didn't-I don't..." I spluttered, taken aback by Evita's sudden change in attitude. "I just wanted to know why, okay? The truth is, I've never had much of a desire to watch those kinds of movies," I told her. Now that I was an adult with the freedom to make my own choices, anyway, I added silently to myself. "And now you're telling me that there's some magical reason why? I've gotten used to being weird, but that doesn't mean I like it. If you know something about why I am the way I am, I want to hear about it."

At my words, her hard expression softened, and I took a seat beside her, pulling out a third stool for Pythia. We sat in silence for a long moment while she twisted her lengthy hair into a high bun and collected her thoughts. Why had she reacted that way? I wondered. Seeing her contemplative expression I thought that Evita might be asking herself the same question. Probably because that's the way she would have responded herself, if she felt like someone was telling her what to do. My mother did not play well with authority. Even her own, apparently.

"Have you been plagued by many demons in your life?" Evita asked, finally.

"Demons?" The church called fae folk demons, I knew, but I didn't think that was what Evita meant. "You mean like mental demons? Like trauma?" She nodded, and so did Pythia. My mom was weird about food and made me self-conscious, thinking I was fat. That wasn't great. And I'd been an odd kid. Sure, a few people said mean things to me, but nothing too outrageous, and I'd always been able to find a few friends. Mostly, the people who didn't like me just treated me like I was invisible, and that wasn't too bad, usually. "Honestly, Mom, all that stuff that Velia did, sending all those aggressive men after me when I first came to town?" Pythia grimaced. I had told her story just the other day. "That was some of the worst that's ever happened to me, actually. And nothing really terrible happened, even then." I shrugged and shook my head. "Not many demons at all, really."

Evita beamed, wrinkling her small, pointed nose in pleasure. "Oh, I'm glad. I've been working hard to keep your part of the garden nice and tidy all these years, seeding it with only the best of my intentions."

"My, uh, garden?" I prompted, urging her to say more.

There were any number of ways, Evita explained, to interact with other people's energies. Since she was a gardener, she liked to tend to her ancestors alongside her garden, investing energy in her plants and also in her relationship with the spirits of the ancestors that came before her. Especially our mothers, and our mother's mothers, back through the generations. Her attention gave them power, and the ability to influence and guide our family. And, as her children's ancestor, she reserved parts of the garden for them, as well.

"You know," Pythia speculated, "that super-powered manifesting ability you were telling me about? I wouldn't be surprised if it was all those well-fed ancestors."

Evita nodded, looking pleased with herself. And, she reminded me, she had been the reigning Queen of a small, peaceful kingdom for a long time, before my arrival a few months ago shook things up. She spent her time on important projects, like ensuring that the family's worst demons didn't sneak into her children's gardens. Mine had been protected especially well, she said, since she could focus so clearly on wanting the best for me, without the additional complication of needing to raise me and know me personally.

"And that's why I'd recommend staying away from the horror movies," said Evita, reaching out and taking my hand. "They're full of toothless demons. Demons you can make friends with. They can help folk feel more comfortable with the demons in their own lives, and in their family's garden. And, in a place that's full of demons, what are a few more, especially if they're toothless?" She flashed her own pointed canines. "But, in a nice, tidy garden, introducing the toothless ones just makes it look inviting, and makes it easier for a few fanged ones to slip through the gates." She patted my hand. "It's all about the energy. Like attracts like."

"Well," said Pythia with a wry chuckle, "my family's little garden patch is teeming with toothy ones, so I'll take the toothless horror movies for company, if you don't mind!"

Evita dropped my hand, turning and taking Pythia's instead, looking her in the eyes. "Oh, my dear, yes. You have to walk among your ancestors' demons every day, don't you?"

Pythia gave her a tight smile and stood up quickly, calling, "Azie! Come on, child, it's getting late. Time to be getting home, with or without those shoes."

Chapter 17

"You know what's funny?" I said, poking my poached egg with my fork and letting the bright yellow yolk run out over my avocado benedict. "My cousin was joking about calling up an electrical storm yesterday. You don't think this weather could be because of that, do you?"

"Seems like the kind of thing a powerful faerie's intention could put into motion pretty easily," Urb said, eyeing the thick, roiling clouds gathering above us as we sat outside eating breakfast at a cute café just down the road from the Valley of Christ's Heart Church. "We might want to see if they have a table inside."

"Maybe," I replied, still not wanting to believe that it could actually rain on the Fourth of July, even here in Oregon. "Can we wait to do that until we feel raindrops on our head?"

Urb shrugged and took another bite of toast. He and I had met at the restaurant this morning, and I was relieved when we both arrived early, without any strange detours or accidents. It made sense, though. After the girls went home, I spent some time working with Evita to modify the eggshell protection so that I would be able to make it inside the building this week. Now, we had a leisurely forty-five minutes before it would be time to make the short walk to the church.

A bolt of lightning cut through the clouds making the gray morning burn white for a split second, followed moments later by a loud peal of thunder.

"I guess Zeus is up there shooting lightning bolts around, huh?" I joked to Urb, who leaned back in his chair, sipping his second refill of coffee.

Urb chuckled and said, "Speaking of Zeus, you want another slipper-throwing Bible theory while we wait? My mom really didn't like this one."

"Oh, definitely. Hit me."

"Okay," Urb leaned forward conspiratorially. "Try this on for size, what if the Christian Bible is just a retelling of the stories of the Greek gods, except it's Zeus pretending he did the whole thing all by himself?"

"What do you mean?"

"Well, take Genesis for example. You know how this big bearded, male God created the Heavens and the Earth," and then said, "Let there be light?" Urb shrugged. "Well, that sounds an awful lot like Zeus claiming the mythical feats of Chaos, Nyx, Hemera, and Gaea."

At my look of confusion, Urb clarified. "The primordial deities of air, darkness, and daytime, and Mother Earth, respectively. Men who want to feel important love taking credit for other people's achievements, you know?" He shrugged. "I mean, it took the whole Greek pantheon working together to defeat their giants, but the Biblical God destroyed the Nephilim with that big Noah's ark flood, all by himself, using Poseidon's powers? I doubt it. The Greeks' flood myth makes way more sense."

"There's a flood in Greek mythology, too?"

"Oh yeah, just about every culture has a great flood, if you go back far enough. In some accounts, Deucalion, that's the Greek Noah, even brought animals two-by-two into the boat that saved him."

"Seriously?"

"Uh huh, that's the thing about these stories, once you let go of the details and start looking at the themes, it's easy to see how one version got transformed into another and another." He shrugged, as though ceding the point to an internal debate partner. "Or at least that they were all inspired by the same source material."

"Source material like the real, actual Greek gods and their adventures?" I asked, curious, to find out what this intelligent, analytical man actually believed.

Urb laughed. "No, of course not. Source material like the world around us and all the miraculous things in it that inspire people to tell each other stories. The Greeks got their ideas from the people who came before them, and the people before that. Now, at least, we have the ability to write things down. In the past, everything had to be passed down by oral tradition."

Now it was my turn to laugh. "Like a giant, historical game of telephone?"

"Exactly like that," Urb agreed. "I mean, look at Zeus's name. It comes from the Indo-Eurpean root word Dyeus Pater. That's where we get the name Jupiter, too. Same root, but they put the emphasis on the end of it instead of the beginning. Day-YOOS-pater, you feel me? And, Dyeus Pater literally means 'sky daddy'. Our Father who art in Heaven? It's all right there." Urb shook his head, expression exasperated. "That's one of the things that annoys me about so many modern Pagans. They want things to be separate, but when you actually look at the source, it's obvious that it's all the same."

"Do you run into a lot of modern Pagans?" I asked, curious. "I don't."

"Oh sure," said Urb. "But you've got to seek them out."

"Not like the dozen churches full of Christians that I drove past on my way here," I commented wryly.

"No," he agreed. "Not as many as that. But, there are definitely people online who are rediscovering the old knowledge and the old ways. Reclaiming the pre-Christian magic. You don't think I'm coming up with all of these hot takes on my own, do you? And it just kills me to watch people leave Christianity and 'rediscover the truth' of these old gods and pantheons without stopping to realize that the Greek gods aren't 'real' either, they're just another limited interpretation of our magical world, that was controlled by the Roman State," he said, and shook his head, ruefully.

"So, you don't think that there were actual Greek gods who—"

"Of course not! But you've got to understand," Urb said, leaning forward and almost vibrating out of his chair in academic excitement. "The Greeks, and the Norse, and the Celts and the Hindus don't actually disagree. There isn't really any argument between them at all. They're just explaining the divinity of our world through their own cultural lenses, and giving it faces and names that people can connect with. If the primordial forces of those gods and goddesses are real, then they're real across all cultures, for everyone, everywhere. People just like to make them look like themselves because it's easier to talk to something when it has a name and a face."

"Huh," I said, considering. "So, you think that everybody's right, but also nobody's right, and the Christians have it especially wrong?"

"Oh, I don't know, I guess it's splitting hairs at that point," said Urb, with a bemused shake of his head. "But I do feel like assigning all of the incredible powers of creation to one big sky daddy is just about the most limited, cop-out of an explanation that I can think of to explain the magic of our world, you know?"

I laughed. "Well, that's certainly one way to think about it. Should we head over there and hear what Reverend Rex has to say?"

"Yeah, let's go," said Urb, pushing his chair back from the table as another peal of thunder rolled over us. "It'll be good to get inside."

In just a few minutes, we arrived at the Valley of Christ's Heart Church. The building had looked large, the last time I saw it, from across the street, but as we mounted the stairs to the front entrance, it loomed above us enormously.

As we walked down the block, I eyed Urb's casual jeans skeptically, but now that we were surrounded by other church-goers, he blended in better than I did, in my conservatively polite sundress. Even Rev. Rex, greeting people as they passed through the inner doors to the sanctuary, wore a pair of blue jeans under a comfortable plaid button-up.

"More coffee?" I asked Urb, gesturing toward a table set with carafes and paper cups. Nora, the pretty blond who had unnecessarily introduced us at the Tent Revival, was stationed next to the coffee, looking bored. Urb glanced toward the table and caught the girl's eye instead. Her face lit up, and she abandoned her post, heading toward us.

"Welcome!" she said enthusiastically. "I'm so glad to see you, Herb. It was such a nice surprise running into you at our picnic the other week. And you've brought someone with you. How wonderful!" She turned her attention to me and truly looked at me for the first time.

I always find eye contact a little intense, and I tend to use it sparingly, but I was trying to blend in, so I met her gaze squarely and looked into her eyes for a long moment. They sparkled with bright curiosity, and just the barest hint of well-concealed pain. The feeling of tension that rose between us, like a balloon inflating, made me hold my breath, and I only released it after she looked away with a shy smile.

"This is my friend, Ona," Urb said politely, remembering the alias we agreed on. I didn't want the church to have my real name, but after a childhood of being called a name that never felt like it fit, I wanted a pseudonym that was close enough to feel comfortable.

"Yes, of course, I remember you from the picnic. So glad you two are hitting it off so well!" She beamed, looking from me to Urb and back again. "Sorry, I was so distracted when we met. There was just so much going on that day." She extended a slender hand to me, and I squeezed it lightly, focusing on the bridge of her nose to avoid meeting her eyes again. Her touch was cool, and it sent a shiver down my spine. She whipped her hand back quickly. "Ope! Bit of a shock. There's electricity in the air today!"

"So, what's new with you, Ellie?" Urb asked, chatting politely.

"Oh, nobody really calls me Ellie anymore," the young woman said with a shake of her wispy, pale head. "It's Nora, now, or, um…" She hesitated for the barest second, and I saw her flick a glance over Urb's shoulder before she said, "Some people are starting to call me Lena?"

I was wondering what she preferred to be called. Noted.

"Alright then, Lena…" said Urb, then he paused to think and added, "I hope it doesn't rain-a!" He chuckled to himself while Lena and I looked at each other, confused.

"It's a mnemonic," Urb explained. "The rhyme'll help it stick in my brain better, so I remember what to call you."

"Time to go find our seats," said Lena, responding to some cue I hadn't noticed. "Do you guys want to sit with me?"

"Sure," said Urb, and we followed the slender girl as she weaved through the masses of bodies that had piled into the stadium-sized room.

Lena gestured us into seats in the first row. Urb took the seat on the aisle, and I sat next to him. She stood and looked around for a second, then, satisfied, sat down next to me. A moment later, she was joined by the dark-haired youth who had come to find her at Tent Revival. Or, as Lena called it, the picnic.

"Wow, Lena, these must be the best seats in the house. Thanks," said Urb companionably, thumbing through the paper program he was handed at the door. His booted toe tapped nervously, though, and I suspected he might not be as relaxed and sanguine as he looked on the surface. I didn't think he was looking forward to being nose to nose with the Reverend any more than I was.

Lena's boyfriend leaned in close and put an arm over her shoulder so he could whisper into her ear. I was close enough that I could hear him when he hissed. "Did I just hear what I think I heard? That's my special name for you. Why's that guy saying it?" I felt the girl rock against me, the motion punctuating his words.

"What? It's just starting to catch on, that's all," she lied smoothly. "I can't help what people call me." Catching me looking at her, she gave me a quick wink, then she turned to face her boyfriend, pulling her shoulder out of his grasp. "Byron, have you met Ona and Herb yet? They're new, from the picnic!"

Byron glowered at us, but we were saved from further conversation when the lights dimmed and enormous screens suddenly came to life. The words *Welcome Home* appeared then faded, and music swelled.

A puff of stage smoke tooted out of a nozzle by my feet, and a beam of light twisted through the fog, like at a rock concert. A drumset and guitarists rose out of the floor on hydraulics, and the crowd roared in appreciation. Urb and I rose to stand with the rest of the congregation, and I caught myself tapping my toe to the catchy beat of the music.

From our spot at the edge of the front row, I looked out at the crowd. Most were clapping and singing along, with heads bowed and hands raised. I could hear Lena's high soprano next to me, belting out the chorus.

I thank the Master, I thank the Savior, I thank God.

The Master, huh? That idea made me extremely uncomfortable, I thought as I looked out at the enormous sea of congregants. What was it that they all needed saving from, I wondered. What was so terrible that they were all willing to give up their own autonomy to live under the control of a Master?

The refrain repeated over and over. With the rhythmic clapping and stamping of the crowd, the energy swelled until it crackled like the lightning storm outside.

"And if he did it for me, he can do it for you!" An amplified voice boomed as the music surged to a final crescendo.

Reverend Rex stepped out of the shadows and into the spotlight of center stage, and the crowd cheered, then quieted. In their sudden silence, the energy raised by the singing and the stamping washed over us like a wave, with a palpable whoosh.

I raised my eyebrows, catching Urb's sideways glance. "They do this every Sunday?" I whispered, awed by the amount of energetic power that just crashed over me, toward the man standing at the podium.

"Today," Rev. Rex boomed, voice amplified so that it carried all the way to the back of the stadium. "We are gathered here to talk about trust." After this first stern pronouncement, he stepped out from behind the podium, tucking one hand into his pocket with practiced casualness.

"In our world today, we have trust issues with God. When we want something, we listen to our human desires and just take what we want, even when God says it's not for us." He reached out, grasping at the air in exaggerated longing. "Like we're saying, 'God, I know there's something so good, right over there, and you're holding me back from it. I know you tell me it's wrong, but it just looks so yummy, so delicious, so tempting. Maybe you're the one who's wrong. Maybe I know what's best. Maybe my desires are the most important thing, and not my faith and the love that I have for you.'"

Urb leaned close to me. "Think you can trust yourself?" He muttered, voice dripping with sarcasm. "Well, you're wrong." I stifled a giggle, all too aware that we were mere feet away from the man onstage.

The Reverend stepped behind the podium again, resuming his stern lecturer's air. "And at that moment, when you decide that God doesn't know best. When you trust your own instincts more than you trust God, that's when you can truly damage your relationship with him." He shook his head, disappointed. "Your trust in God is the most important thing, do you understand that? You have to show him that you are willing to do what he's asking you to do. You have to trust." His gaze, scanning the crowd, now landed on me, seated in the front row. I froze, and a chill ran down my spine. Luckily, he looked away almost immediately and fiddled with something on the podium, saying. "Now, let's all take our Bibles and turn to Romans 12:3."

The crowd rustled and resettled, and I exchanged a meaningful look with Urb. This service had certainly gotten off to an interesting start. The Reverend's message was contrary to everything the fae had taught me about magic. They told me to trust my own instincts above all else, and look inward to find my own inner truth. Reverend Rex was preaching the opposite, telling this enormous crowd that they should ignore their instincts and their own free will and listen to God instead. And, who was God's messenger on Earth? Well, that would be Reverend Rex himself, wouldn't it?

He held up a gilded black Bible, cleared his throat, and read aloud. "Do not think of yourself more highly than you ought, but rather think of yourself with sober judgment. Now, what do we think that means?" He closed his book with a snap and walked out from behind the podium again. "It means, don't think too highly or too lowly of yourself. Be realistic. You're not God, you're not Jesus. You're just a flawed human. A sinner, like all of us. But you're not a godless heathen. You've been saved because you accepted Jesus into your heart and committed your life to God, and you can help others find that same salvation."

"Don't forget that you're bad," Urb muttered to me under his breath. "But you're one of us, so at least you're not as awful as everyone else."

What an incredibly depressing outlook on life, I thought, as I watched the rapt faces of parishioners nod along with the Reverend on the enormous screen behind the stage. The video feed must be live, I realized, as a man holding a professional shoulder-mounted video camera stepped in front of me to get a better angle on the Reverend.

"Now, as we all know, today is the Fourth of July, and that's a day to celebrate," the Reverend said, tone brightening. He pumped a fist in the air, and the crowd cheered. "And we want to give glory to God and honor this great country by lighting up some big old fireworks, am I right, boys?"

The crowd cheered again, this time with a deeper, more masculine resonance.

"Alright! We've got some red-blooded American men right here, and that sure is a good thing to be. But…" he paused and held one finger in the air, and the room waited. In the silence, we could all hear the rumble of thunder. "That doesn't mean that you get to let your desires rule you. Not in the Kingdom of God. You know as well as I do that it's been dry as a bone all week, and Jesus told me, just last night, that it was my duty as a leader in this community to make a recommendation to my friend the fire marshal, and thankfully, he's a godly man and he agreed with the Lord. He took my advice and issued a burn ban for the entire county, just this morning."

The Reverend smiled proudly while the congregation erupted with disgruntled rumbling.

"See, there it is, that sinner nature in all of us, thinking that our good time is more important than the will of the Lord." The stained glass at the rear of the church flared with brilliant color. "Believing that our earthly pleasures are more important than…" he paused again and waited for a loud peal of thunder. "More important than the plan that Jesus has for us. And that's the Devil right there, speaking to us through our own base desires. And that's why…"

The Reverend motioned with his hand and a second spotlight turned on, lighting a choir loft, high up in the rafters, at the back of the church. There, sat the largest pile of fireworks that I had ever seen. The entire mound was spangled with red white and blue, and emblazoned with more hazard symbols and fire icons than I could count.

"I've arranged to have the rest of the county's fireworks stored right here, under the watchful eye of our own Morality Police, so that no one has to face the temptation of giving in to sin and lighting them up, tonight."

The spotlight clicked off, bringing our attention back to the Reverend, who had a lot to say about sin, and how we're all sinful by nature. As I listened, I found myself wondering if all this focus on having a 'sinful nature' might actually encourage people to sin more, especially since they're told it's inevitable that they will sin, and they'll be forgiven if they confess and be saved by Jesus anyway. I resisted the urge to lean over and whisper the thought to Urb.

CRACK!

A bright flash and a sound like a gunshot rang out over the crowd. The next moment, the sanctuary was plunged into darkness, and the stadium-sized room erupted in chaos as people screamed and scrambled in panic. The smell of ozone tickled my nose, making me want to sneeze. After a few seconds, our eyes adjusted, and once we realized that the mid-morning light filtering through the church's stained glass windows was bright enough to see by, even on a cloudy day like this one, the crowd began to calm.

"What happened?" I asked Urb. "Did we just get hit by lightning?"

He ignored me, facing toward the back of the room where the spotlight had recently been shining. "Look," he said, pointing. Thin tongues of flame were beginning to lap through a hole in the roof. As we watched, they started to creep down the wood of the high, drafty rafters.

"FIRE!" The cry rang out from someone in the audience, sending the crowd into mayhem. Parishioners at the back of the room piled through the double doors and out of the building, but most were stuck inside, crammed into the narrow aisles between the pews, unable to move. The flames continued to creep down the rafters toward the Reverend's confiscated fireworks. Seconds later, we could hear the tell-tale hiss of a lit fuse. I stood frozen, watching as the first of the fireworks ignited.

SNAP! FIZZ! POP!

At the very front of the crowd, there was no way we could make it through the crush of bodies cramming through the back doors. We would be the last ones to escape.

BANG! WHIZZ! SKREE!

"Come on, we've gotta get out of here," said Lena. She grabbed my hand and I grabbed Urb's, following her onto the stage. She led us away from the screams of the crowd, as more fireworks whistled and howled in the flaming choir loft behind us. We followed her through a maze of hallways and out into the alleyway behind the church, while the fire alarm blared in our ears.

Lena held the door open and gave me a tight smile as I stepped past her, out into the alley. "What a frightening and intense first impression of Christ's Heart," she said with a strangled little laugh. "I promise it's not usually like this!"

zrp zrp
be honest

"Yeah," I agreed. "You're right. The idea of giving up my free will and submitting to a 'Master' is a little frightening and intense."

She cocked her head, startled by my response, then furrowed her brow processing my answer. I took Urb's arm and turned, heading away from the sound of approaching sirens. We walked back down the alley, and the entire time, I could feel the sensation of her eyes on my back.

Chapter 18

"FIYEURRR!" cried Azalea gleefully. She leaped off her chair and pantomimed fireworks exploding.

"Sounds like you had enough adrenaline in your Sunday, even without that horror movie marathon," said Pythia, polishing a glass behind the quiet bar. It was a Monday, after all.

"Yeah," I agreed. "And hey, sorry about Evita being awkward the other night," I said, remembering how Pythia had left my birth mother's house so abruptly. "Faeries just say things, sometimes."

"It's alright. And, you know what?" she said with a shrug. "I'm glad for you. If your world is sunny enough that a couple slasher flicks are going to give you the ancestral heebie jeebies, well, I guess that's pretty nice, you know? Protect that delicate little flame, girl. Next time I'm going to a happy chick flick, I'll call you, alright?"

"Thanks," I said, looking past her to the open front windows that let in the warm evening breeze.

"And she's not wrong, you know. I do walk among my ancestors' demons every day. It hasn't been very many generations since this, right here, was a sundown town, you know that?"

I nodded. That was something Jaah and I had talked about. I was shocked to learn that, in the past, Black people hadn't been allowed to stay inside the city limits after dark, under threat of violence. A chill ran down my spine in the warm room, and I shuddered. There was so much I hadn't known about Oregon's troubling racial history.

"Which reminds me," she continued, "oh wait, do you want me to keep you out of the gory details of everything that's going on? Save your delicate sensibilities from the grittier side of life and all that? Just because my brother is helping doesn't mean you need to be involved."

zrp zrp
no way

"No way," I repeated. "Tell me, please. I don't need to play with make-believe demons in my spare time, but I want to know everything I can about the real ones on my street corner."

She nodded, satisfied, and filled me in on the latest.

Sylvie, the first girl who had been hurt, was awake and able to answer questions. She described her attacker as middle-aged, well-dressed, and charismatic. He paid upfront and didn't seem like he would be any trouble. Once they were alone, he started to tell her about a place he could take her where there were people who could help her get back on her feet. When she told him 'no thanks,' she thought her voice might have given her away, because he switched up his attitude, and got real loud, then beat her with his fists and feet until she couldn't remember anything else. He definitely shouted some trans-phobic slurs at her, she recalled, but whether or not he had quoted the Bible, she said she didn't know. She wasn't religious.

That description could fit any one of at least a hundred men, just at that church service yesterday, and who knew how many thousands more, in a city as big as this. There wasn't even any guarantee that the two attacks had been by the same man. The two violent episodes had been different enough that it was possible that there were two bad men in town.

"Not a lot to go on," I said, echoing Pythia's disappointment.

The twins sat at a table behind me, playing WyldSight on their phones. With Azalea, Zinnia, Pythia, Jaah, and I all playing, we now controlled most of the territory around the bar. One of their devices chirped, and I reached for my own phone in a Pavlovian response. Opening the app, my phone began to chime as new Wyld sightings hit my inbox. When I checked in after my weekend in the valley, the new sighting list was long enough to almost crash my phone, but today there were only three new Wylds.

"Hey, I got that iguana-parrot-monkey, too," I said, turning my screen toward Zinnia and Azalea.

"Oh yeah, I talked to that guy for quite a while this morning," said Pythia, leaning on the bar and twisting a loc around her finger. "He was kinda cute, actually. From Venezuela, just passing through. He gave the girls these sweet little worry dolls. Can y'all show Fiona?"

116

Zinnia produced a small yellow box and pulled off the tight oval lid to reveal matchstick-sized dolls in colorful thread costumes. "He told us to put them under our pillows when we sleep and they'd take our worries away," said Zinnia, skeptically.

"And where are yours, Miss Azalea?" Pythia asked. "Lost them already?"

"No," said Azalea, looking sheepish. She picked up a bright purple thread off the table in front of her. It looked like it might once have been a piece of a worry doll's dress.

"Well, you can't have mine," said Zinnia, pocketing the little case.

I tuned out the girls' bickering and stared into the face of the Venezuelan spider monkey.

"So, this bad guy," I said, talking slowly as I thought it through. "This John that we have no information on…Sylvie said that he was well-spoken and well-dressed, right?" I held up the phone, letting Pythia in on what I was thinking. "You think he might also be well-traveled?"

Pythia's eyes lit up, and her excitement exploded out of her in a few lively dance steps. "Now that's an idea."

"You think you could get all the working girls to play, if you told them it was for surveillance?"

"Oh girl, they're already playing it. They've got to do something to keep themselves entertained, hanging around on the street all night. Hey Gullah!" She called across to her brother, who had just opened the back door, heading toward us. "Can you come out and help again tonight? Fiona just thought of something."

"Tonight?" Jaah asked. "Really? There's another play party I was gonna take Fiona to. I already asked Isla to watch the girls."

"Oh really, brother? You want to blow off important work for play? That doesn't sound like you."

Jaah looked at me, expression miserable. They wanted to keep their promise to me, I knew, but Pythia had twisted their words in a way that only a sister can.

"I could go by myself?" I suggested, intentionally keeping my voice light.

"You'd feel safe doing that?" Pythia asked, her direct gaze demonstrating that she knew exactly what kind of play to expect at this party. Now that the idea had presented itself, I found that I actually liked the thought of going to the party alone. I wanted to find myself on my own terms, didn't I? Not as a nervous companion on Jaah's arm. Last time, I was alone, at least at the beginning, and it felt perfectly safe to me. I said as much, then looked to Jaah for confirmation.

"You won't be in any danger," Jaah agreed. "Consent is absolutely mandatory at those parties, and anybody who breaks that rule is gone, right away. In fact," Jaah said, looking thoughtful, "if you want to go by yourself, that's my biggest warning, Fiona. Make sure to ask before you do anything, and especially before you touch anyone, okay? You have to follow the rules, too. Women sometimes forget."

"Because of the way we girls are socialized," Pythia agreed. "Pretty girls think they can't possibly be predators, but the truth is, we've got sharp claws!" She mimed a cat swipe at me. "Mrar! And we can really hurt people, if we're not mindful."

An hour later, I climbed back onto my regular stool at the Fair Isle and slumped onto the bar, burying my head in my arms.

"Oh no, girl, what happened to you?" Pythia asked. Luckily for me, she and Jaah hadn't left yet.

"Migraine," I told her. "Can you call your brother and let him know I'm here?"

She nodded and turned to the set of tubes that ran from behind the bar to Jaah's upstairs apartment. "Gullah, your girl's back and she's looking rough. You're gonna wanna come back down." She turned back to me. "You able to tell me what happened?"

"Yeah," I said, the word a long, pitiful moan. Before I'd finished my first slow, painful sentence, Jaah bounded across the bar and wrapped their arm around me. The flow of energy between us helped ease my pain, and after a few minutes, I was able to sit up, although I still kept my eyes half closed, squinting against the low light of the pub.

"The trouble started as soon as I walked in," I told them. I had opened the door and immediately been hit with a thick cloud of incense smoke.

"Lavender?" Jaah asked, understanding. I nodded. They already knew about my sensitivity to the aromatic flower.

"It's so funny, whenever I smell it, I'm like, ooh, what's that strange, lovely scent?" I told them, with a small, careful chuckle. I do my best to avoid it, but sometimes it sneaks up on me. The realization of what happened hit me a moment before the pain did, and I sank into one of the plush couches, blinded by the stabbing behind my eyes.

Listening to the sounds of the room gave me something to focus on other than the throbbing in my head. There were three girls on the couch across from me. I saw their long, shiny black hair and sultry expressions when I first walked in, and I could imagine them now, as I heard them murmur and laugh quietly to each other. I couldn't hear the words but the tone was catty and mean-spirited. I wondered if they were talking about me.

"Sounds like demons," said Pythia, nodding sagely, "they're such mean girls. Pretty, though. Damn pretty, if you know what I mean."

Jaah shrugged. "Not my type. Too skinny. And I don't know about the whole 'mean girl' thing. That's just the way demons are. They can't help it."

"I didn't say they could help it, but it doesn't make me want to get too close to them, Brother," said Pythia. "That's such a 'man' thing to say." Jaah winced, and Pythia saw it. "What, did I offend you?"

Jaah shrugged. "I just don't really like being called a man, I guess," they admitted. "I haven't really felt like one for a while, now."

Pythia's eyebrows shot skyward. She gave me a look that said 'did you know about this?' and I nodded.

"Well, how am I supposed to know what I don't know?" she asked, shaking her head in exasperation. "I didn't mean to misgender you, brother. I mean," she corrected herself, "sibling."

"Brother's fine," Jaah said. "And so is Daddy, for the girls, but I guess I wouldn't mind being a they, every now and then, if you happen to think of it."

"You got it, them-brother," Pythia told them with a wide smile, then turned back to me. "So, there were some bitchy demons gossiping about you, and then what happened?"

I felt the looming presence of someone above me, and I opened my eyes a crack to see. The first thing I noticed was their long lavender hair cascading down dark-robed shoulders. Whether this was a man or a woman, I couldn't guess, but they were certainly striking, standing over me with an air of caring concern.

"The lavender incense gave me a migraine," I said, answering their question, my voice small through the pain.

"Oh no! My kin has wronged thee?" They tossed their purple mane over a shoulder. "Let me help, if I can. May I?" I nodded. They leaned down and touched my forehead with their lips, very softly. Ripples of soothing coolness radiated out from the kiss, and I was able to open my eyes and look up at them without pain.

"Thank you," I said. "That was incredible. I really appreciate it."

"It will not last forever. You should go now. Try to get home before the pain returns. But…" They smiled in a way that made a shiver run down my spine. "I hope to see you here again, some other time, lovely lady."

"It's a shame you didn't get to play at the party tonight," said Jaah as we lay in bed later that night. "I know you've been wanting to have some, uh, new experiences, and with all the festivals canceled, there aren't very many other places to meet like-minded intermagicals."

"Yeah," I agreed. "But, I don't really know how comfortable I feel, trying anything at a big party like that anyway. I think I'd feel better about something a little more private," I told them, thinking about the demon girls giggling on the couch. "If you know what I mean?"

"Sure, but the parties are where you meet people. Unless there's already someone who's caught your eye?"

"Um," I hedged, remembering the lavender-haired entity from earlier.

"Asmodeus?" Jaah asked, with a shocked expression, when I described the individual I encountered.

"Why? Is that a bad idea?" I asked, then added, "Wait, you said Asmodeus? Isn't that a demon name?"

"Yeah," Jaah agreed. "It's a demon name, but Asmodeus isn't a demon. They're a dragon. And it's not a bad idea, exactly. It would be jumping in the deep end, that's for sure. But dragons are trustworthy. You'll be safe with them. And, if it's an experience you want, you'll certainly get that."

"A dragon, huh?" I said. "That's interesting." I resolved to spend some time this week doing research on dragons. What I could find in library books and internet searches wouldn't be entirely accurate, of course, but there is a lot that can be learned from folklore and fiction when read with the right sort of metaphorical lens.

Part 5 - Water

Chapter 19

Faeryn greeted us at the base of the hill with a concerned expression. She wore a delicate floral bathing costume, and an airy translucent garment that drifted around her thin shoulders. Underneath this, a new, wider band circulated spring water around her chest, and she looked a little healthier, on this hot summer afternoon.

"Azalea didn't want to come with you, this time?" she asked. "Did Visc scare her off? I'm so sorry."

"No, she had a great time," Zinnia answered. "I think Visc is her new hero. She won't stop talking about him. She didn't want to come this time 'cause we're talking about water, and there wouldn't be any fire."

Evita asked us to wear our swimsuits, so Zinnia and I were prepared for whatever the faeries had planned for our lesson.

"That sister of yours sure is a firecracker," I said with a chuckle.

Zinnia nodded solemnly, in agreement. "She hasn't stopped talking about the fireworks in the church, either."

"About the what, in the where, now?" asked Faeryn, turning and motioning for us to follow. I filled her in on what had happened after our last magic lesson, as we wound our way through the garden.

"Do you really think it was our magic that made that whole church burn down?" Zinnia asked, wide-eyed. "Auntie Pythia said so, after I told her about the fire spell we all did."

"It didn't burn down," said Evita, stepping out from behind a bend in the path. "That church is still standing. It just caught fire, a bit. And, no, we didn't start that fire. It was lightning, and the giant pile of fireworks that foolish man stored in his wooden rafters."

"But—" Zinnia interrupted, but Evita continued, unperturbed.

"We set our intentions to protect the hill and the valley from the forces of evil, wherever they might be found. That's all. And anyway," she added, "chasing the preacher off stage in a rain of fire in the middle of his sermon is an unreasonably intense result to expect from this kind of magic, even if that man is the kind of evil we'd like protection from."

Evita clearly already knew all about what happened, which shouldn't surprise me. She made it her business to know what was going on in her community.

zrp zrp
the triskelion

I considered that. Zinnia and Azalea had been with us to set up the fire ritual, but just like the first time, it was Faeryn, Evita and myself who gave it power.

"But these rituals are powered by our three energies, all together," Faeryn mused, clearly thinking along the same lines as I was.

We reached the top of the hill, and I admired the towering pile of rocks that stood in the same place where last week's bonfire had burned. Water burbled from out of the top of the rock, and I skirted along the outside of the pile, peering up at it, when I tripped over something at the height of my ankles.

"Whoops!" said Faeryn, who reached out to steady me. The daily baths and her new spring water device must be doing her body good. The arm that supported me felt sturdy and strong.

Letting go of my arm, she bent and tossed a green garden hose out of the path. Her tug on the hose made the pile of stones sway in a way that a pile of stones should not, and the illusion lost its integrity for a moment, allowing me to see that the rocks were actually an old wooden step ladder covered with a sheet. The hose snaked up one side of it, with its stream directed at a waist-deep portable swimming pool. The ladder steadied, and the illusion reformed as we walked around the front of it and found ourselves, to all appearances, in a charming rocky grotto with a crystal-clear pool and a sparkling waterfall.

"Watuuurrr," said Zinnia, mocking her sister good-humoredly. We all laughed, but her eyes sparkled in the reflection of the pool, and she looked more excited than I had yet seen her.

Arlee was in the pool already, eyes closed, relaxing in the cool water. As we approached, her eyes opened, and she twitched her shimmering tail, coming to sit upright. Twitched her—I did a double-take, but it was true, Arlee did appear to have a glistening, icy blue tail. She pulsed it rhythmically, as though treading water.

"Arlee! I didn't realize that you were. Wait, are you a—" I spluttered, not sure what I was looking at.

"A mermaid?" asked Faeryn. "No, she's faerie, like we are, but water is her element, like mine is fire. In fact, she dampens my fire quite often," she said with a laugh. "And sometimes I need that. It's one of the reasons we're so well matched."

Arlee kicked her feet, and I saw her two legs separate momentarily, behind the mirage.

"So, it's just an illusion?" I asked, wanting to be sure that I understood.

"Yes," said Faeryn hesitantly. "But it's an, um, how should I say this, an incarnation of Arlee. An avatar," she explained. "Her own true expression of herself."

"So," I clarified. "If you or I get into the water, we're not going to have tails?"

"No," Faeryn laughed. "I wouldn't think so. I certainly won't, anyway. And, of course, Arlee would never have fox ears, like mine." Faeryn rumpled her own bright hair, and as she did, I noticed the tufted orange ears that looked perfectly natural atop her slightly vulpine face.

Zinnia, who was listening with wide eyes, now leaned in and whispered, rigid with barely-contained excitement, "I think I would have fox ears, and a tail, too."

A few minutes later, I was perched at the edge of the pool, legs dangling in the cool water, watching Zinnia dip and dive happily, the water beading off her pointed purple fox ears and her matching mermaid tail. Evita and Faeryn sat beside me, enjoying the water without submerging ourselves.

"What are the qualities of water?" Evita asked me, and from her tone, I could tell that the day's lesson had begun.

"Um, well," I kicked my feet, moving them through the silvery substance. Once, I spent an entire afternoon thinking about the natural magic of water and all of its different properties, but my mind was in a different state, and those expansive thoughts felt far away now.

"Water is cold, and it's um, wet?" I answered, somewhat lamely.

"Very good," she said, encouraging me, "Aristotle agrees with you. The Classical Greek elements do describe water as cold and wet. Fire, then, is hot and dry. Air is hot and wet, and earth is cold and dry."

"Huh," I said, trying to piece that together. "Fire makes sense, I guess. But, is air hot and wet? Oh, like evaporated water, okay. And, earth is what's left over after the water has run off and the fire has cooled." I nodded. "That's logical. I like it."

"After the water has run off, yes," Evita repeated, agreeing. "That is another important quality of water. It is the lowest point of matter. It trickles ever downward, working its way into any crack or crevice. It stops only when it has pooled at the lowest point possible, and it will rest there eternally unless disturbed."

Her words made me shiver, and I pulled my feet out of the water, wishing we weren't sitting in the shade.

"And water is relentless. It seems to flow and change to fit its environment, but water carves its own path, mercilessly and deep."

I remembered the feeling I'd had, one cold, clear winter night when I had looked out over a sea-carved cliff at the reflection of the full moon in the black ocean. That was the kind of water Evita was talking about.

"That makes water sound pretty scary, actually," I said.

"To an earth elemental like you, I suppose it might," said Evita, teasing. "We air folk just make like a bubble and rise above!" She shook out her sheet of soft waist-length hair, and for a moment I thought I saw the suggestion of tawny wings.

"Earth is my element?" I asked, considering the idea. "You think so?"

Faeryn and Evita both made affirmative noises, but I remained unconvinced.

"Well, what's your favorite animal?" asked Zinnia, with her new ears perked forward with interest.

I hated that question. People never liked my answer, so I usually just made something up, but I knew that, in my present company, I was going to have to be honest.

"Um, humans?" I said, making the answer an apology.

Evita and Faeryn both laughed.

"That doesn't count!" said Zinnia, putting her hands on her scaly hips. The motion unbalanced her, and she splashed around awkwardly as she righted herself, which made us all laugh some more.

"We shouldn't forget that humans are animals too," Faeryn said, when Zinnia recovered herself. "We lose a lot of our own truth when we separate ourselves from the rest of the animal kingdom."

"Well, yeah, but," argued Zinnia, "Humans aren't like other animals. We're different. More advanced."

"Humans certainly like to pride themselves on being so," said Evita. "But crows can use tools, just like humans can, and humans can't even fly! A crow might have reason to think that it was the most advanced species."

"Elephants have their own spiritual practices, did you know that?" Faeryn asked Zinnia, who shook her head. "It's true. They use branches to wave at the waxing moon, like they're saying goodbye, and they take ritual baths when the moon is full."

"Elephants appreciate the magical qualities of water, too," I mused.

Faeryn nodded. "Humans aren't the only animals to have mystical experiences. We all exist in the same natural, magical world."

Late that night, after the lesson was over and Pythia collected Zinnia, I sat with Evita in her vine-covered living room while she told me the latest about the Morality Police and their continued hostilities.

"They drove their trucks right through people's camps?"

"Right through," Evita told me. "Chasing people, elders, and children, threatening to hit them. It was chaos. Or, so I was told."

"Just because some folks showed up to the Country Fair anyway?"

Evita nodded solemnly. "Those folk have been gathering together on those fairgrounds for so many decades, I don't think they could help it. They didn't sell tickets or advertise, just gathered on the grounds, like they always do."

"But if it wasn't official and they didn't sell tickets, how could the Morality Police break it up?"

"Apparently their charter now includes, 'Gathering at the same time and location of a previously ticketed event of a prohibited type, with prohibited materials,'" Evita quoted, reading from the paper in front of her.

"And what's on the list of things that are 'prohibited' now?" I asked her. She handed me the paper, and I skimmed over the document that described the specific powers that the Christ's Heart Morality Police were granted by the CCC.

"Tie-dye clothing is the latest. They're calling it 'drug paraphernalia' apparently."

"Tie-dye? You've got to be kidding me." The Morality Police's charter had been constantly changing all summer. As soon as the fae folk found ways to work around the ridiculous restrictions banning their gatherings, a new version of the charter was submitted for approval, with even stricter limitations.

"I just don't get it," I reflected, as Faeryn rounded the corner from the kitchen and sat down to join us. I understood how they were doing it by manipulating the new CCC regulations. I just couldn't wrap my head around *why* they were doing it, and I said as much to Faeryn.

"Why can they run down elderly women and children in big trucks and still believe they're in the right? It's because they're being told that they're saving people from eternal torment," Faeryn answered, "and that it's their duty to God to do all these awful things. They're doing it under his authority. Just following orders."

"Authoritarianism," Evita spat. "Now that's real evil. I'm glad Zelai is safely away. I can only imagine how things will escalate by the end of the summer."

"I had been wondering why we hadn't introduced Zelai and Zinnia yet," I said, realizing that I hadn't seen either of my brothers since the night of the solstice.

"I asked Egan to take his brother south with him for a long visit with his father's people," answered Evita. "It's been too long since he's spent time with that side of his family. Just because his father is no longer with us doesn't mean he should lose his connection to his tribe."

Evita looked at a painting of a long-haired native man on the wall. From her expression, I suspected this portrait, one of several indigenous artifacts in the room, was of Egan's father.

"Zelai had never been there, and it will be a powerful experience for them both. And…" Evita smiled grimly. "It will keep him far away from these Morality Police. You remember what Urb told us about how they're treating trans people. He will not be safe while they patrol."

I nodded. Taking the drastic measure of sending her children away for the summer really drove home how seriously Evita took the threat of our current situation.

"Do you think our water ritual will end up being as intense as the fire spell was?" I asked, changing the subject.

"Water isn't as flashy as fire," Evita answered. "It destroys by finding the cracks in things, eroding their very foundation out from underneath them. But," she continued, flashing me a fierce smile, "that doesn't mean it lacks intensity."

"As a magical scientist, I must admit that last week's results exceeded my expectations considerably," Faeryn mused. "Assuming that our ritual actually helped start that fire. Correlation doesn't equal causation, after all. But, it does seem like an awfully large coincidence."

I looked from one faerie woman to the other, taking in their grim, serious expressions. What was going to happen at the church service tomorrow?

Chapter 20

This time, I picked up Urb, and when I rolled into the grassy driveway, he was already standing outside, hands stuffed into his pockets and shoulders hunched against the morning chill.

"I can't believe they're using that old church," Urb said, as he slid into the passenger seat of my van. "I kind of thought it would have been condemned by now."

The Mountain of Christ's Heart Church, the original home of the congregation, was just a little way down the road from Urb's family home. It had been abandoned more than a decade ago, when the church moved into town and took possession of the large, modern complex of buildings that recently caught fire.

"Not that the old church isn't large too," said Urb, clarifying. "It's plenty big. Drew farmers and ranchers from probably a hundred miles around. Now they drive even farther, to get to the church in town, I guess, but that's country living for you. It takes forever to get anywhere, and that's just a fact of life." I was surprised by how long it took us to drive from Urb's place to the old church. It might be 'just down the road' by the standards of the people who live way out here, but it seemed like quite a distance, to me.

Eventually, we rolled onto a gravel driveway and jounced over the potholes of the unmaintained parking lot. The old church's roof was covered in piles of pine needles from the towering trees above it, and the corners of the lintels were tinged with the greenish algae that is common to Oregon architecture, but other than that, the old building looked alright.

We made our way inside. The space was large, like Urb said, and the vaulted ceilings rose high above us, leaving plenty of space for a familiar portable light and sound system to be erected over the stage. An attempt to bring us the Christ's Heart experience without any electrical power to the building.

We found seats near the back. Lena was nowhere to be seen, and although I was glad not to be dragged to the front this time, I wondered where she was. As I looked around for her pale blond head, I noticed a strange cube at the center of the stage.

"Doesn't that kind of look like a hot tub?" I asked Urb, pointing at the incongruous box.

Music swelled out of the portable speakers, signaling the start of the proceedings, but it lacked the emotional punch of last week's live music. Reverend Rex walked out onto the sun-bleached red carpet of the old church without any hydraulics or smoke machines at all, and tapped his microphone to get the audience's attention.

"It's baptism day," he announced enthusiastically. "I know it doesn't look like it normally does. This isn't…" He opened the lid to the hot tub, and a small green frog hopped out. The Reverend jumped, startled, and dropped the lid, and several people in the audience tittered quietly. He tried again. "This isn't what we're used to. It's not the state-of-the-art baptism tank that we have at home. But God says, 'When two or three are gathered in my name, there am I among them,' and this here," he said, slapping the brown vinyl lid. "This is our history. It doesn't matter if we have the nicest, newest things. God just wants to know that we have him in our hearts and that we're listening to him and letting him guide us in our lives."

A line of people filed in to stand in front of the Reverend's podium and the less-than-optimal baptismal font. They all wore flowing white robes. The women's reached all the way to their ankles, and the men's were shorter, paired with simple white pants.

"No, Sir, we didn't let a little thing like the church catching fire stop us from letting these good people commit their lives to Jesus today." He gestured to the white-clad people before him. "Yes, Lord, we're gonna have us some baptisms!"

He lifted the lid again and paused. This time, nothing jumped out, so he opened it the rest of the way and climbed onto the rim.

"We got this old girl scrubbed up and had her on the generator all night, so the water should be nice and toasty." He dipped a foot inside. "Ope!" he exclaimed, pulling his wet foot back out of the water. "Tepid," he said resignedly, before plastering a superficial smile on his face and climbing down into the pool. It was surprisingly deep, reaching the middle of his chest when he stood at the bottom of it. It must be sunk below the floor of the dias, I realized, as I watched the Reverend shiver involuntarily. "It's not that bad," he said encouragingly to the line of people waiting to be baptized. "This will be the first test on your new path. The first challenge that God is asking you to overcome, for Him."

A muttering and rustling ran through the white-clad line, but everyone stayed on the dias.

"Nothing makes me more excited than this," the Reverend said, as music swelled from the speakers. "Than watching other people step into these waters and make the courageous choice to say, 'My life belongs to you, Jesus. I am your tool now, God. Do your good works through me.'"

A moment later, singers with microphones stepped onto the stage, and Lena was among them. That mystery was solved, at least.

"I guess that's why she didn't pull us up to the front again," I hissed to Urb. "She's busy."

"Who's going to be the first to say 'me too' to Jesus, today?" Reverend Rex asked.

The broad-shouldered youth at the front of the line bellowed a masculine "Huh!" and clambered into the pool without hesitation, coming to stand next to the Reverend. The older man dunked him under the water with a splash and the crowd cheered as the youth sprang up out of the water with a triumphant shout, and sprayed the first two rows with droplets.

Next up was an older woman, who accepted the Reverend's helping hand as she descended shakily into the pool. As she did, the first man made a wet procession down the center aisle of the church, peacocking proudly in his wet, clinging clothes.

"It's never too late to commit your life to Jesus!" the Reverend said, as the now-drenched old woman gasped for breath, shocked by the cold water. She climbed out of the pool awkwardly, tangled in her wet robe. Two young women ran up to the podium to help her and wrapped a blanket around her shoulders.

This was boring, I thought to myself, beginning to fidget. Quietly, I pulled my phone out of my pocket and tapped on the WyldSight icon. The game was kind of fun, I had to admit. Sometimes I would even leave it open at work so I could sight all the Wylds that walked by my office, downtown. I wondered how many new Wylds I would get in a crowd like this.

The map loaded. This territory was available to claim. No surprise, I thought, since this church had been abandoned for years before today. I clicked to claim it. Immediately, my screen was filled with hundreds of pulsing red dots. Urb looked over, distracted by the sudden burst of light from my lap, and I closed the app immediately, stuffing the phone back into my pocket and blushing.

I looked back up at the stage, feigning attentiveness. The next baptismal candidate was a very pretty young woman. When she resurfaced, the white robe clung to her chest, and the effect of the cold water was pointedly apparent. No one came up to hand her a blanket, and I was unable to tear my eyes away as she processed down the aisle, hips swaying. Her now translucent robe clung to her curves and left little to the imagination. My short, round little self could never look like that, I thought, mindfully remembering to shut my open jaw as I admired her long, sleek lines.

"How lucky we are. Such a fresh and juicy peach for God's orchard," said the Reverend, and to my surprise, the girl turned her head and gave him a coquettish smile. "And she's going to make one of you men a beautiful wife one day soon, boys, so before you go thinking about sin, remember, that's one of your brother's future wives, right there."

Chapter 21

We rumbled down the gravel driveway away from the old church. My hands gripped the steering wheel, knuckles white with anger.

"What made you so uncomfortable?" Urb asked.

"Well, for one thing, the fact that they obviously knew those robes were going to be see-through. Remember that one real pretty girl? Her nipples could have cut through that fabric, I swear. You could see everything. And I don't think it was a mistake, either. They weren't a new model of robe or anything. Urb, you saw what I saw, those women were basically naked, in front of everybody."

"I guess I didn't notice too much," said Urb with a shrug. "The men's pants were plenty clingy, too, though."

"What do you mean you didn't…wait, are you…" I paused, not wanting to offend him, but then remembered that the fae didn't typically have those sorts of hangups and plunged onward. "Urb, are you gay?"

"So gay," he agreed. "I'm a card-carrying member of the LGBT family whichever way you want to slice it." He laughed. "Sounds like you noticed plenty, though."

"Sure I did," I said. "How could I help it, especially with that first girl? Yeesh!"

"Fiona," he asked, eyeing me from the passenger's seat. "Are you gay?"

"No!" I exclaimed indignantly. "Come on, you know my boyfriend! People always ask me that, and I don't know why. I…" I paused, remembering watching that pretty girl's hips sway. Was that jealousy I was feeling? I thought so, but Urb's question made me wonder. I'd always assumed that people thought I was gay because I was bulky and awkward, like lesbians looked on TV when I was a kid, but maybe they were seeing something in me I hadn't been ready to acknowledge. I had been enjoying dating a nonbinary person for several months now, after all, even if they seemed plenty masculine to me. And, I repeated, reminding myself, the fae didn't have those sorts of hangups. "Urb," I asked hesitantly. "Am I gay?"

He threw his head back and gave a hearty laugh. "Yeah, Fiona, you might be."

I considered that for a moment. "Well, then it's even worse!"

"What is?"

"The way she was put on display like that, in that ridiculous religious wet t-shirt contest. It was impossible not to ogle her. I would know! 'Now don't assault her, ya hear,'" I said, mocking the Reverend's folksy speech. "'She's gonna be some man's wife someday.' Who cares that she's a person, right? All that matters is that she'll be some other man's property. And how he called her a juicy peach? So gross."

"She didn't seem to mind the attention," Urb said with a shrug. "I noticed that much."

"Yeah," I said, remembering the girl's coy smile. "I noticed that too."

I turned that idea over in my brain for a minute. Why were these young women choosing to join this church? I thought back to last week's sermon about following the will of the Master, and the weirdly predatory comments that the Reverend made today. Why would any of these women choose this? What was appealing to them?

"Hey Urb," I asked, a few minutes later. "Do you think it's kind of funny how good-looking all the women were, on that stage today?"

"I wasn't paying too much attention," Urb shrugged. "But yeah, they did kind of look like the women in magazine ads, I guess." He was right. Every one of the women who were preparing to be baptized could have been a catalog model. "Guess you're bummed more of them didn't end up getting wet, huh?" he teased good-naturedly.

"Nah," I teased back. "I'm just glad we got out of church early again!"

Halfway through the line of baptismal candidates, there was a commotion among the people onstage. They were muttering to each other and picking up their bare feet. Before long, we could see a dark circle forming on the carpet around the tub, increasing rapidly. A minute later, the circle of moisture had reached one of the amplifiers, and it shorted with a screech of feedback and a loud pop. The singing stopped abruptly, and the crowd started buzzing.

"We seem to have sprung a leak," said the Reverend, shouting to be heard over the murmuring crowd. "It'll be alright, but, we're all going to want to make our way to the exit, please. Now."

As we waited for the disorganized mass of people to press through the two small sets of doors, Lena ran up to me, still holding her dead microphone.

"I'm so glad you came back," she said. "I didn't think you would, after last week, but I've been thinking a lot about what you said." She reached out as though to touch me, then pulled her hand back at the last second. "I think you've gotten the wrong impression about us, and I really, um…" she paused, looking at her feet and scuffing one on the carpet before continuing. "I feel like Jesus really wants to know you. There's this Women's Group. We meet every Sunday night, and I'd really like it if you came. New people don't usually get invited," she said, averting her eyes and looking apprehensive. " But if you're with me, it'll be fine. And that will give us a chance to talk about what it really means to follow Jesus." She looked up at me, wide blue eyes beseeching. "Will you? Please?"

"Oh, uh,"

zrp zrp
get close

"Tonight is just a clean-up party. I wouldn't want to rope you into that," she said, continuing to chatter nervously. "You know what's crazy? It was the water that put out the fire that did the most damage. It flowed into every crack and cranny and got into everything. Ruined more than a thousand books." She picked a Bible out of the back of a pew next to us, fingering it nervously. "Luckily, the old church still had all these ones," she said with a shrug. "They're the old version, but Uncle says they're pretty similar, so they'll be okay." She set the book down and looked back up at me. "But next week will be the ladies' summer social. They're having it at our house, since the church is out of commission. Will you come?"

zrp zrp
flow in

"Yeah, okay. I can do that. Next Sunday, huh? Sure, I'll be there," I told her, not at all sure what I was getting myself into.

"Church again next week?" I asked, as we pulled into Urb's driveway. We would have to keep doing this, at least one more time, if I was planning to go to Lena's party.

"Sure," he agreed. "If Christ's Heart finds somewhere they can hold it!"

Chapter 22

"Where's your brother?" I asked Pythia. "They don't have a contract right now, so I figured they'd be around, but I can't find them."

"You know them, they're a leaf on the wind. They've drifted off somewhere, but I expect they'll drift back this way soon. But what's on your mind, hon? You look bothered."

I sat down at the bar and stared at the rows of shiny bottles. Nobody at the Fair Isle offered me alcohol anymore after I'd turned it down so many times. But, it's not like I didn't drink, I just didn't want to do it every day. Although now that I thought about it, I hadn't had a drop since that last night at the Pirate Carnival. Well, I could fix that easily enough. I opened my mouth, intending to ask for a drink, but instead I said, "Pythia, were you ever baptized?"

She looked at me critically, then shrugged and answered the question at face value. "Sure, when I was younger. Mom went through a real religious phase."

"She did? I…" I paused, trying to remember everything I could about Jaah and Pythia's mother. "I don't know much, other than the fact she's a nurse. Your brother hasn't really said anything about her."

"Yeah, they don't talk much these days. Her religious phase had a lot to do with that, actually."

"How did it feel?"

"To be baptized? Oh, I dunno. I was just a kid, I didn't really know what I was doing, just did what I was told." She looked off, contemplatively, and then said. "The cheering did feel real good, though."

I told her about the church service, the baptisms, and especially about the girl in the wet dress.

Pythia nodded sagely. "I bet she was real pretty, too, huh?"

"She was!" I exclaimed, glad that Pythia seemed to have some insight that I lacked. "She was stunning. Could have been a model. A lot of the girls were. Unusually good looking, I mean."

"I see it down south all the time," she said, shaking her head. "Hot property."

"What do you mean?"

"The religious, conservative trap these pretty women like to fall into. All that 'saved' stuff, it puts them above everybody. Morally, you know. Spiritually, or so they think. They buy into the idea that some people are just inherently superior to other people. And all the attention they get for their looks will back that up."

"Part of the whole white supremacy nonsense, right?" I asked.

She shrugged, looking grim. "Sure, there's some of that, but I've seen plenty of black folks get caught up in the same kind of thought trap. You start thinking that certain people are inherently superior to other people, and there's a short leap from that to believing that the inferior people deserve to be exploited."

A wizened old fae knocked his flagon of beer on the counter, getting Pythia's attention. "Now, I don't come here for all this politicking, young lady," he said testily.

"Then don't come here, Melvin. It's my bar tonight, don't test me. Anyway—" She turned to me and poured me a tall seltzer water as she talked. I didn't want to interrupt her flow to ask her to put a splash of something harder in it. "Now, in their ideology, women are inferior. We're property."

I glowered and quickly checked left and right to be sure that Zinnia and Azalea hadn't heard that.

"But," Pythia held up a finger. "Those women, they're hot property. Valuable property. The game is rigged, sure, but they're guaranteed to win, so why not play?"

A fae at the end of the bar made a gesture with one long-nailed finger, and a scene appeared. A team of barbie doll blonds in high-heeled baseball uniforms hit a home run in the direction of the liquor bottles. Apparently, he was enjoying the discussion enough to illustrate it.

"And of course, for her, winning means getting a powerful, superior man to choose her as his wife and whisk her off to a superior life, because she's what he's been told he's supposed to want."

"Supposed to want?" I repeated, making it a question.

"You know," she said, opening her eyes wide and pulling a face. "Thin, blond. They're not supposed to want me." She gestured down at her lythe, dark, dancer's body. "And they're not supposed to want you." This time she indicated my round, curvy frame, and winked. "But they do, though."

"Anyway," she continued, "it's not about what he actually wants, or what she actually wants, it's about possessing her, which makes other men impressed. And she's been trained to submit and obediently cater to his sexual and domestic needs, for the rest of her lonely, limited life, or, God forbid…" Pythia drew a dramatic sign of the cross on her chest before continuing, and the blond barbies traded their baseball bats for oven mitts and baby bottles. "She gets sick or disabled, or otherwise unhappy and therefore unpleasant enough for him to stray into the arms of the beautiful new young secretary or lonely neighbor. And she won't think twice about stealing our girl's husband, because that's her ticket to that same superior life."

"Why don't they warn the young ones?" I asked. "It seems like women could break women out of this cycle, couldn't they?"

"And realize that they've been flattered into spending their entire life in service to a man who only ever saw them as a commodity? That being hot property wasn't protection from being used up and discarded? Of course not. They're in too deep. That would mean admitting to themselves that they'd been had."

The blond barbies morphed into middle-aged women with sharp a-lines and botox, throwing shovelfuls of dirt over pantsuit-clad shoulders, as they dug themselves deeper underground.

"So that's why they do it, huh? They buy into a rigged game without realizing it's rigged against them, too?"

Pythia nodded. "Or it's the only game in town. A lot of women don't really have a choice except to play."

At that moment, the Gullah and the twins came through the front door of the Fair Isle with shopping bags and ice cream cones. Jaah's face split in a grin when they saw me, and they crossed the room to me in a few long strides.

"I missed you this weekend," they said, pulling me close and kissing me soundly, in a more public display of affection than I expected from them, especially in front of their sister. "One day a week is hard enough, but when I didn't get to see you last night either—"

They went out of town for a job. The weekend rate made the trip worthwhile, but it meant that they hadn't gotten back until this morning, and we spent an extra night apart.

"I didn't know you felt so strongly about it," I said, bringing my hands up to their chest, to put some space between us and give myself a little breathing room. That hug was fiercely tight.

"Brother, guess what?" Pythia said, interrupting this uncharacteristically romantic moment. "We were right, surprise surprise. I asked those two working girls who got beaten up to compare their Wyld sightings, and they both had the same one, from around the right time."

Pythia held up her phone and showed us an image of a pale, hooved creature with enormous curving horns.

"What kind of horns are those?" I asked, leaning in close.

"I've been trying to figure that out," Pythia said, squinting down at the image. "I think it might be an Ibex. With the face of a stork, maybe?"

I nodded. That sounded right to me. "You really think that's him?"

"It could be," said Pythia. "We can't be sure, obviously, but it's something. And it's more than we had to go on last week."

"Oh yeah, I forgot," I said, pulling out my own phone and opening the WyldSight app. "I actually claimed a territory at church on Sunday, when I got bored."

"That boring, huh?" Jaah asked with a snicker. "Not everything you hoped it would be? Does that mean you're ready to be done with this whole thing already?"

"Seriously? You think I'm going to that church because I'm enjoying it?" I asked, temper flaring. "I'm trying to learn about them, okay? Trying to understand why they're doing what they're doing. And if I can figure out a way to stop them, I'm going to do it. You're not the only one who wants to try to help people, okay? So no, I'm not ready to be done. I'm only just getting started."

"Did you see that girl again?" Jaah asked, gaze accusing.

"Yeah, I did, actually. She invited me to this Women's Group next Sunday, at her house, and I think I'm gonna go. She's my ticket into their inner circle."

"Yeah, sure. Keep telling yourself that."

"What's that supposed to mean?"

"It means that you can pretend all you want that you're investigating them, or whatever, but it's obvious what's really going on," they said, voice tight with emotion. "Do you have any idea how many times you've said that girl's name in the past few weeks?"

"What, are you jealous, Jaah?" I exclaimed, then clapped my hand over my mouth, realizing what I had just called them, right in the middle of the Fair Isle.

"Yah, you sound real jealous, Gullah," Pythia lilted, thinking quickly to cover up my mistake. "I thought you two had some kind of an arrangement."

I met Jaah's eyes, apologizing wordlessly for my slip-up. They shrugged, looking away.

"She's just a friend," I told them. "But, your sister has a point. It would be alright if I did like her like that, wouldn't it? Isn't that our deal?"

"Yeah, sure, whatever," they said, and shrugged again, not meeting my eyes. "It's fine."

"Clearly it's not," I replied, trying my best to keep my irritation out of my tone. "What's going on with you?"

"I just don't like it, okay? I don't like you getting close to those people. They're dangerous. I watched my sister get swept up in all that stuff. I thought she was smart, too. I thought she had a good head on her shoulders. She's my older sister, you know? She always knew better than me. And then she went and—"

Pythia interrupted, giving them a stern look from behind the bar. "And went away. She went away. And that's business that we don't need to talk about right now, do we?"

Jaah made a rumbling sound deep in their chest, but stayed silent. I knew that something had happened to Jaah's older sister, the twins' mom, I remembered, catching their wide-eyed expressions out of the corner of my eye, but I hadn't known it had anything to do with the church. Seeing Pythia's ferocious expression, I knew better than to ask questions right now.

Looking for any distraction, I picked up my phone from where it sat on the bar, checking the open WyldSight app. It showed me a mostly empty map with only a few scattered Wylds. There were several people in the pub, even on a quiet Monday, but there were hardly any patrons at the Fair Isle human enough to carry a cell phone, who hadn't already been caught up in the WyldSight craze.

A notification blinked in the corner of my screen with a surprisingly large three-digit number. "Hey girls, come check this out," I called to Zinnia and Azalea. "I've never had this many new Wylds before." The twins gathered around my screen and made impressed exclamations as I opened my inbox and scrolled through the hundreds of creatures that had crossed my territories since the last time I played.

"Where did you get all these?" asked Zinnia, eyes wide.

"I think they must be from the territory I claimed at the church the other day," I answered. "I had no idea there would be so many." We scrolled through page after page of strange animal amalgamations.

"That's Auntie's guy!" said Azalea, pointing at an image of a pale Wyld as it whizzed past.

"What?" I asked, scrolling back up to it. "What do you mean, Auntie's guy?"

"There, see?" said Azalea, pointing. "The Wyld that Auntie showed us, that she was so excited about."

She was right. There it was, that strange pale deer with the beaked face and the long curving horns.

I turned my phone toward Jaah and Pythia.

She gasped. "The Ibex!" she exclaimed, reaching out to take the phone from me. "He was at the church!"

Part 6 - Air

Chapter 23

"We don't know for sure that he was at the church," I told Evita, sitting in her sunny kitchen, Saturday morning. "I have a few WyldSight territories near my office, downtown, and it's possible he walked through one of those, at some point on Monday."

Evita nodded sagely. She struggled with human technology and concepts like cell phone apps, but once I explained how WyldSight was like birdwatching, she grasped the concept easily enough, even though I was the one who had to explain it to her. I drove down to the hill alone this week. Zinnia had a birthday party invitation that she just couldn't pass up.

"Just the two of us, then," Evita said when I came through the door, by myself. Faeryn and Arlee went to visit a friend for a few days, for a change of scenery, and Zelai and Egan wouldn't be back until next week.

We took a moment to enjoy the quiet morning before beginning our lesson. I sipped the brightly green herbal tea Evita made for me and gazed out the window at Calliope in the garden. She was picking blueberries in the midsummer sun, and the sight of her long, lean frame, in an airy white sundress, among Evita's overgrowth of flowers, looked like something out of a storybook.

"She didn't go with them, huh?" I asked, indicating Calliope, out the window.

Evita shook her head. "She's a large part of the reason they took some time away, I suspect."

"Huh," I said. "She's always seemed nice enough to me." Evita eyed me curiously, and I averted my gaze. Spying one of her colorful hula hoops leaning against the wall, I asked about it, changing the subject.

"I haven't been taking them out to the park lately," she told me. "I had a sizable group gathering with me for a while, but the 'Park Overlords'..." She leaned on the weighty title, her tone sarcastic. "Have informed me that I'm not allowed anymore."

"Park Overlords?" I repeated. "Are they part of the Morality Police? Are those guys shutting you down, too?"

"Oh," said Evita, now refusing to meet my eyes. "No, I don't think so. They called themselves the Parks Department, actually. They said I needed a permit. There's some form over there." She gestured dismissively at a desk in the corner of the kitchen, where stacks of papers were piled. I hadn't noticed it before, shielded by the illusion of Evita's idyllic kitchen.

"So, you just need to get a permit, and then you can have your hula hoop group again?" I asked. "That doesn't seem too hard."

"Human nonsense," she said, shaking her head. "Silly rules and ridiculous regulations. I won't take part in it."

It seemed to me like it would be pretty easy to solve this problem by following the proper procedure, but Evita's attitude toward human rules was an important part of her faerie nature, and I had the feeling that there was nothing I could say that would change her mind. Instead, I picked up a piece of shortbread from the plate in front of me and nibbled. It was perfect. Clearly measured and baked with precision.

"These are great, Mom," I told her, changing the subject again. "Mine never turn out as good as these."

"The secret is to follow the steps precisely, dear," she told me. "Baking follows the laws of nature, and those rules are absolute."

We chatted some more about the happenings in the valley and up in the city, until Evita set her cup down with finality, and said, "That's enough tea and sympathy for now, I think. Let's get started, shall we?"

She led me outside to where a ladder was propped on the side of the layer cake-shaped house, and beckoned me to climb up with her. On the roof, a beautiful, airy pavilion was erected. A trellis was draped with flowing white fabrics that whipped around in the strong summer breeze. The space was dotted with large round pillows, and I followed Evita's lead, taking off my shoes and settling myself onto one of the soft poufs, sitting cross-legged.

"There's something I would like to show you," said Evita, her voice taking on a dreamlike quality. "Something I want to share with you about our family. And after I do, I want you to take everything you've learned so far and craft your own air ritual to protect this valley. Does that sound alright to you?"

I agreed, and she nodded, satisfied, then leaned her head back.

Hoo hoo. Hoo hoo

She hooted loudly, and from high up in the trees, a tawny owl swooped down and landed gently on Evita's outstretched hand. I watched as the bird's menacing talons made deep divots but didn't pierce her skin.

"In the dark of the night and the light of the day, she brings that which is unknown into knowledge." Evita reached out and stroked the owl's smooth head. The animal pushed against her, obviously enjoying the attention. "She is wisdom," Evita continued, "She brings us new understandings about change and about death. She brings us warnings of things soon to come, so that we can make our peace."

"She's beautiful," I said. The owl used her sharply curved beak to preen her speckled chest feathers delicately before peering at me with intensely dark eyes.

"She is a particular friend, and a familiar of mine," said Evita, stroking the bird lovingly. "And the owl is a powerful totem of the women in our family."

She told me about a vision that came to her in a particularly dark moment of her life. An enormous golden owl swooped down upon her and swept her up in its wings. It flew with her to an island and transformed into a goddess that Evita recognized as her own. She embraced Evita, and gave her a message to carry in her heart.

Be at peace. It will all turn out alright.

This powerful message soothed Evita's aching heart and allowed her to move forward into the next part of her journey. She felt no shadow of a doubt that this goddess had spoken the truth, and that knowing was a powerful gift. And, she told me, if things were going to turn out alright for Evita, then it stood to reason that they would for me, as well, since I was her daughter and my well-being was as important to her as her own.

I smiled. Without the powerful experience of the vision, I didn't have the same unshakable faith that Evita did, but the comforting premonition that Evita relayed was certainly reassuring.

Evita raised her arm, and the foot-high bird stretched out her enormous wings and flew to a nearby perch. "To connect with the element of air, I have invited my friend to guide us in an experience of flight."

"Ooh," I exclaimed, delighted.

"Alright," said Evita in a calm, hypnotic voice, "let your body be still, and your mind go quiet."

I sat comfortably with my eyes closed and tried to clear my mind, focusing on the sensation of the breeze on my skin.

"When you're ready, open your mind's eye and come fly with me."

My mind's eye? What was that supposed to mean?

zrp zrp
just imagine

Well, that was one idea. I took another deep breath, pushing away the intrusive thoughts at the edges of my mind, and unsure of what to expect, I imagined opening my eyes.

"Wow," I said aloud, in wonderment. Behind my eyelids, I could now see a wide expanse of Earth and sky. I felt the sensation of wind rushing past my body and riffling through my feathers. I was flying, gliding high above the tall grass of a green field just beginning to yellow. It felt euphoric.

I circled, rising and falling on the invisible currents of the breeze. My crystal-clear gaze searched among the swaying stalks for any sign of life. There, a rustle. That was the sign! My body tensed, and I hurtled toward the earth, pulling upward at the last second seizing something warm and soft in my talons.

zrp zrp
eyes open

I followed this advice, and the vision of the owl's flight was replaced by mundane reality again. Across from me, I watched Evita's animated face as she described how the owl devoured her prey, rending and tearing. I was glad to be skipping the brutal scene.

Soon enough, though, I closed my eyes and I was flying again, across a river and over a valley stippled with the tops of thousands of pine trees. We swooped and dove, finally coming to rest in a hole high up in a tree. From there, I watched the sun rise over the pines until finally, I nestled my beak into my soft chest feathers and slept.

"Wow, Evita, that was extraordinary, thank you," I said, opening my eyes and coming back to myself.

"Thank her," my mother said, nodding to the bird on her perch.

I did, and she ruffled her feathers at me in pleased response.

"Alright," said Evita. "Now, look inside yourself and tell me. What should we do for an air ritual?"

I hadn't forgotten my part of the lesson, and I looked around at the space Evita had set up for us and the items she had gathered for inspiration. There was a good selection of objects that might be associated with the element. She had set out fans and bells, and feathers and flutes, and incense smoke curled around us, perfuming the warm summer air.

"Well," I answered thoughtfully. "What if it was a dance?" The way we flew with the owl reminded me of dancing, and a ritual that left no trace seemed like a good way to honor the incorporeal element. We could use some of the flowing fabric and dip and dive like birds, through the incense smoke. Channeling the spirit of the owl with some feathers in our hair, I thought we could ask the energies of air to protect the valley and stalk any dangers like an owl pursuing her prey. "Would that work?" I asked.

"I think it would do beautifully," said Evita with a proud smile, and I glowed with pride at her praise. "Shall we get started?"

"Sure," I agreed, rising awkwardly from the low cushion and shaking out my tingling legs.

zrp zrp
one more

From high up on the roof, I could see little winged faeries cavorting among the riotous blooms of the garden, and among them, with a basket full of ripe summer vegetables, was Calliope.

zrp zrp
the three

"Do you think Calliope should join us for the ritual?" I asked Evita, watching how breezily the waifish fae moved. She looked more at ease than I had ever seen her, and I wondered how much Faeryn's absence had to do with it.

"Calliope?" asked Evita with obvious surprise.

"Yeah," I answered. I didn't mention the pulsing messages that I had just received. In fact, I still hadn't mentioned them to Evita at all. I didn't want it to seem like I was taking instructions from something outside myself. And, I reminded myself, I wasn't. The messages were coming from inside of me. The whole idea of the spell had been to trust my own intuition, and my intuition was telling me to believe these little messages. They hadn't led me astray yet.

"I just feel like it would be more powerful with three of us, just like the rest of the rituals. And Calliope seems kind of airy to me, you know? I feel like I wouldn't need to teach her the dance steps."

"Well, it's your spell," Evita said skeptically. She leaned over the balcony and called for Calliope to join us on the roof.

With obvious surprise, the delicate fae set down her basket and climbed the ladder. I stepped forward, in front of Evita, and extended my hand to help Calliope up the last few rungs. Her bright blue eyes met mine. I hadn't ever really met her gaze before, I realized, and I forgot myself momentarily. She really was a striking-looking fae.

zrp zrp
explain now

Huh? Oh. Remembering myself, I smiled warmly. "Thank you for joining us," I said, releasing Calliope's long fingers as she straightened to stand. "I was hoping you might be able to help us with our ritual today. We need one more dancer." I explained, and watched her nervous expression transform into one of surprised delight.

"Like a bird on the breeze?" she asked, eyes alight with excitement. "Yeah, I think I can do that."

And so the three of us, scarves around our shoulders like wings, danced together and called to the spirit of the wind to lend its power to our cause. We moved like a windstorm, and like a gentle breeze, bounding and twirling, high above the ground.

With her long, graceful frame, Calliope's long leaps truly captured the spirit of wind in motion.

Eventually, we tired from our exertion, and spent, Evita and I flopped back down onto the cushions. Calliope's dance didn't falter, though, and she continued to leap and spin, like a leaf in the wind. She looked so full of joy that I didn't want to interrupt her, but she was dancing with her eyes closed, and the curved edge of the roof felt dangerously close. I didn't want her to fall.

"Calliope?" I called, timing my interruption so as not to startle her.

It didn't work. Calliope's head whipped around at my words. Thrown off balance, she tripped over her long, flowing skirts and tumbled off the side of the roof. Time seemed to slow, elongated by the adrenaline flooding my brain, and she appeared to hang there, like a cartoon coyote, for a long moment, before disappearing over the edge of the roof and out of sight.

I hopped off my pillow and ran to look. To my surprise, she was still falling, drifting like a leaf, with her white dress floating around her like a cloud. A moment later, she made landfall, coming to rest softly in the same springy patch of mint that Visc had thrown himself into, a few weeks before.

Evita stood beside me, looking down at the crumpled pile of limbs that was Calliope. She nodded, pleased. "Apparently, our ritual was a success. We've clearly made a powerful alliance with the spirit of air today."

"You know, I think I knew that was about to happen," I said, watching Calliope sit up and start to pick bits of leaf out of her pouf of hair. "I thought, 'I hope she doesn't fall off that roof,' just a second before she did."

Evita nodded. "Yes, I'm not surprised. You have been activating your intuition these past few weeks. All of the members of our family have at least a touch of pre-cognizance."

"Huh," I said. "That's cool, I guess." It seemed like most of the people I read about in stories were pretty tortured by that particular gift, and I wasn't sure that I wanted it for myself, but, I thought resignedly, I probably didn't get to pick and choose.

We climbed down and rejoined Calliope.

"Sorry about that!" I said, extending my hand to help her off the ground.

"It's nothing," she shrugged. "I didn't mess up the spell, did I?"

"Not at all," said Evita with a laugh. "Your dramatic flight was just the kind of finale that Fiona's air dance wanted."

I agreed and told Calliope so, and there in the garden, under the open sky, we joined hands, closing the ritual by sending the power of air out into the valley to safeguard us with its elemental power.

Releasing our joined hands, we turned up the garden path to head inside. I shook out my sore fingers and said, "Wow, Calliope! That's some grip you have there."

"Oh," she said, hunching and rubbing her upper arm self-consciously. "I'm sorry. Carrying all those jugs of water for my lady is giving me big muscles. It's not very feminine looking."

"And you don't like that?" I asked. With her delicate dresses and demure attitude, Calliope seemed like a perfect picture of femininity to my eyes, muscles or no.

Her expression clouded, suggesting a deep well of painful feelings. "I grew up in a different court, did you know that?" she asked. I nodded, remembering what Faeryn told me. "They weren't so tolerant about things like gender expression, there."

"They thought you ought to be more feminine?" I asked, taking in the pretty girl's thin, square shoulders and sharp jawline. I hadn't ever taken notice of the somewhat masculine features underneath the trembling femininity that so characterized Calliope.

"No," she said, looking puzzled, and then, a moment later, blushed a deep, delighted crimson. "Oh, you thought…you didn't know!"

Of course. It was obvious, now. Calliope must not have been raised as a girl. And, apparently, she hadn't been allowed to express her true self, in the court she had been raised.

"No," I said, with a chagrined shake of my head. "Sorry, I didn't realize."

"Oh, no! Don't apologize, please! That's…" she flapped her long hands delightedly, momentarily without words.

"That was a beautiful ritual today, Fiona. Thank you," said Evita, giving Calliope a chance to recover herself.

"Thank you!" I replied. "It feels like I'm starting to get it. Is that the kind of thing you would have done, for an air ritual?" I asked her, curious. Dance seemed like such an obvious choice.

"Not at all," she said, shaking her head with a bemused smile. "Which is why we each ought to use our own intuition for these kinds of things, rather than following someone else's rules."

"But not when baking shortbread," I clarified.

"Precisely," she agreed.

I thought about that for a second, then said, "I guess one of the tricks is going to be figuring out what sort of magic should be intuitive, and what sort of magic is shortbread."

She laughed with a tinkling like so many tiny bells.
"Yes, I suppose it will be."

Chapter 24

Evita waylaid me as I prepared to leave the hill Sunday morning and handed me a paper packet of the fresh focaccia bread she had served Calliope and me for our breakfast, and a large wooden box.

"What's this?" I asked, admiring the dark, oiled hinges and the intricate latch. "It's beautiful."

"Something I want you to have. A place for the things you need to work your magic, wherever you are. I've started by stocking it with a few basic supplies, but there's plenty of room for more."

"Oh, Evita…um, I mean, Mom. Thank you." I reached out and took the chest from her, gratefully. It was as though she had read my mind. After yesterday's lesson, I was feeling pretty confident in my ability to improvise, magically, in the way that she and Faeryn were teaching me to do. I was itching to try out this interesting new skill on my own, but I didn't want to jump ahead of the lesson plan and risk upsetting my teachers.

"You are ready to make your own magic," Evita told me, smiling proudly. "You have an incredible amount of power, daughter. Just remember to embody having what you want, instead of focusing on what you don't have. Magic works best from a place of fulfillment, not one of yearning."

"I do have what I want, Mom. This life, here with you, and up in Portal Land, full of folk who like me, who understand me, it's all I've ever wanted." My eyes pricked with tears, and Evita reached out, squeezing my arm.

"Then you will make powerful magic, my dear. Don't forget to ask for assistance from the elements and other natural sources of power. They will help you, if you ask them, and it's not necessary to do everything, even if you are strong enough to manage by yourself."

"I can do that," I told her. My childhood was a lonely one, and I had to be self-reliant, but I was slowly learning to let down my guard and accept help in this new life among the fae.

"Next week, we will explore the nature of earth, but I don't think there is anything much to teach you about that particular element, so there is no need for a proper lesson. You understand its nature, because it is your nature, grounded and steady. Realistic. It's something we flighty, fiery, flowing faeries struggle with, sometimes, but not you." She smiled at me kindly. I'd always assumed it was my human upbringing that made me different from my faerie family, but it made sense that it would be my elemental nature, also. "So, instead of a lesson, let's have a celebration of earth's bounty. My garden is full to bursting with the summer's harvest."

I drove away from the hill, and into the little town behind it, where Urb had asked me to meet him. "Lena called my landline last night," said Urb, swinging his large frame into the passenger seat next to me. "We were all pretty surprised when it rang, actually. Didn't realize it was still connected."

She found Urb's number in an old church roster, and called to let him know where the service was going to be held, today. Apparently, when they pulled up the soaked carpet after the baptism debacle, they found the whole subfloor covered in black mold and the entire building was condemned.

"Oh wow!" I exclaimed.

"Yeah," Urb agreed. "But apparently they'll be back in the church downtown, next week. The repairs from the fire damage are almost finished."

"So where are we headed, then?" I asked. Urb sent me a message telling me to meet him in the tiny town behind Evita's hill, but he hadn't told me where we were going.

"Marys Peak. Highest point in the Coast Range," said Urb. "The higher the sermon, the closer to God, I guess! Oh hey, can you pull in here, I want to grab something to eat."

I turned into the parking lot of a small country store that was the last outpost before the mountains. "I think you're out of luck," I said, rolling past dark windows and an unlit *open* sign.

"Are you kidding me?" he said, voice heavy with exasperation. "You're right. My luck just will not give me a break this morning."

Urb had cooked the last two eggs in the house for his breakfast, he told me, and when his back was turned, his naughty dog had nabbed them off his plate. So, he had gone out to the duck house looking for more. "They're better for baking than for frying, but they'll work in a pinch," he told me, shrugging. On his way out of the slimy duck yard with his clutch of three large eggs, he slipped and fell, smashing all three of them into a gooey puddle in his sweatshirt pocket.

That was when he had messaged me to meet him in town, and grabbed the keys to his grandma's van to drive to his favorite bakery. It was closed. "So, I just went through the McDriveThru," he said. "And I took my egg muffin over to that park where I met you, and I sat down on a bench to eat it, and…" he looked at me, pausing for dramatic effect. "I dropped it."

"You didn't!"

"I did. And there was this big crow that was cawing at me, up in an oak tree. He saw it happen, and he swooped down and snagged it."

"Would you have picked it up?"

"At that point, yeah, probably," Urb admitted. "I'm a breakfast guy," he clarified, with a self-deprecating shrug. "I know some people don't need it, but if I don't have breakfast, it starts my whole day off on the wrong foot."

"I get it," I said, remembering the delicious vegetable focaccia that had been my own breakfast. "I'm that way, too. Wait!" I reached behind me and handed him the large square of the fresh bread wrapped in parchment paper. "Here, Evita sent this with me this morning. I bet she meant it for you. She's always doing stuff like that."

"Amazing," said Urb, unwrapping the herb-scented package and inhaling deeply. "I love faerie godmothers."

"And, I just remembered, Evita wanted me to invite you to the hill for a little revel next Saturday. Egan and Zelai will be back, and so will Faeryn and Arlee."

"For sure," Urb answered enthusiastically, voice thick with crumbs. "I'll be there. But, don't let the Morality Police guys at church hear you using that word!"

I chuckled, but he had a point. With the current political climate, it was dangerous to call anything a revel.

"How far out is this place?" I asked, after we had been driving for some time.

"It's a little farther still," Urb answered. "Want another Bible theory to pass the time? I just heard this one, and I think it's pretty good. Remember that thing I said about how the Biblical God could be Zeus?"

"Yeah," I answered. "It was a pretty memorable day, with all the thunderbolts and everything."

"Well, it's a solid theory, but somebody on the forums challenged it with this one. What if God were Baldur?"

"Okay, hold on. I knew about Zeus, but now you've lost me. Who's Baldur?"

"Sorry," said Urb. "Let me back up, then. Baldur is a Norse god, the son of Odin. They call him the Light Bringer, and he was supposed to be invulnerable to anything except mistletoe," he said, glancing at me, "but don't worry about that, it's another story."

The death of Baldur, Urb explained, is one of the big events that will set off Ragnarok, the end of the Norse gods and the destruction of the world. But, after the pandemonium, legend says, Baldur will rise again, and a single man and a single woman will start the human race anew.

"You know what their names are supposed to be?" Urb asked. "Guess, just guess."

"Um, Adam and Eve?" I asked skeptically.

"No, Ash and Elm. Totally different."

"Ash and Elm, huh? Yeah, you're right, that's not similar at all," I joked back, "There aren't any apples in Norse mythology, are there?" I asked, my curiosity piqued.

"Funny you should mention it. Actually, the Norse gods were supposed to get their immortality by eating apples from the Goddess Idun's orchard."

"Eden's orchard?" I asked, incredulous.

"No," corrected Urb with a sarcastic grin. "Idun with an I. Totally different."

Chapter 25

Shivering uncontrollably, I clambered back into the van and slammed the door shut. A gust of wind helped it along, and the car shook with its force.

"Aw, heck," said Urb, body half-inside the car. He dropped his paper cup and splashed dark coffee all over the seat. "Sorry about that," he said, expression aghast. "There goes my luck again."

"It's okay," I said, shrugging and handing him a towel. At least it wasn't my mom's van anymore, I thought, as I watched him rub ineffectually at the dark stain. In the end, Urb decided to climb into the back seat to save his best pants from the spill, and we drove back down from the peak only ten minutes after we arrived.

"That was crazy," said Urb from behind my shoulder. "Didn't they check the weather forecast at all? Those must have been seventy-mile-an-hour winds up there, and I thought I felt a snowflake. Did you feel any?"

"I can't feel anything at all," I said, chilled numb by the onslaught of weather we just experienced. "But they managed to get all that equipment set up. Maybe the storm came up quickly. We, uh—" I glanced sheepishly at him. "We worked with air at Evita's family magic school yesterday."

"Ah, I see," said Urb, nodding sagely. "So, you're saying this might not be an entirely natural mid-July snowstorm."

"Sure, it's natural!" I argued indignantly. "The natural forces of the universe, protecting the valley from anything that would harm it. What's more natural than that?"

"The Kalapuya, the local native tribe?" he said, and I nodded. "They call this peak Tcha Timanwi. It means 'place of spiritual power'. Seems to me like those spirits might not take too kindly to the Reverend and his congregation, either."

"No," I said. "I can't imagine they would."

We drove back down the winding path, past a mossy rock wall, dripping with glittering droplets, and I slowed, rolling the window down to appreciate it.

"Beautiful," said Urb, from the seat behind me. When I pressed on the gas and picked up speed again, he added, "Since we're all the way out here, do you want to spend some time exploring? You're not leaving town until after that thing tonight, right?"

"Yeah," I agreed. "Might as well."

It certainly wasn't the whole congregation who made the ill-advised trek up to the peak this morning. There was only a small group huddled together in front of the church's portable scaffolding when Urb and I stepped out of the van and were immediately buffeted by wind. The Reverend's niece saw us arrive and hurried over to greet us. Her excited expression was the only thing that kept me from turning around and getting right back in the car.

"Well, I'm sure impressed that you two made it all the way up here! I'm sorry it's so awful today." Her teeth chattered, and she wrapped her light sweater closer around her thin shoulders. "But, I know you must really be serious about knowing Jesus if you went to all this trouble. Are you going to come tonight, Ona? I can put my address in your phone."

"Yeah," I said. "Sure."

Pulling out my device, I saw the WyldSight icon and remembered I had another job to do. I was supposed to be trying to figure out who the Ibex was. But then I noticed the 'X' on the top of my screen and sighed resignedly.

"I don't have any service up here, Lena," I told her, handing her my device. "But you can put your address in my notes app, okay?"

"Great," she said. "But, uh, could you go back to calling me Nora instead of Lena, please? Sorry. Gotta keep the peace, you know?"

"Yeah sure, Nora," I said, although I wasn't entirely sure that I did know. "You got it."

As we drove down the winding mountain roads, Urb told me more theories about Norse mythology.

"Now, you might be thinking, 'Wait—didn't you say that Baldur was called 'Lightbringer' and doesn't Lucifer also mean 'Lightbringer'?' And, well, you'd be right!"

"Huh," I said. I had not, in fact, been thinking that.

"But Baldur's brother Loki would have found stealing his brother's name and pretending to be a snake to undermine Baldur's godly authority to be pretty funny. Loki was supposed to be destroyed in Ragnarok, of course, but he's kind of like a cockroach, if you know what I mean. The theory is that he could have hidden out in hell. Helheim, I mean. Loki's daughter's kingdom."

"Norse mythology has a hell, too?" I asked. "I thought that was a Christian thing."

"It's not a place of eternal torment," Urb clarified. "It's just the realm of the dead."

"That sure is a lot of parallels to be a coincidence," I said, tapping the steering wheel thoughtfully. "They didn't have anyone named Jesus in Norse mythology, right?"

"Nope," said Urb with a laugh. "Although, since you mention it Freya's twin brother, Freyr, did walk on water, heal the sick, and turn water into wine. And, he was supposed to be resurrected too, so if you wanted to argue that the Bible is a version of post-apocalyptic Norse mythology, I'd say that you've got a pretty good—"

Creeaaaaakkk creeeeeeeeeaaakkk

A loud, eerie wail cut through the sound of the road-noise, interrupting our conversation.

PFUMPH!

A fluffy pine tree crashed down onto the road, twenty feet behind us.

"AAAH!" I screamed, pressing down on the gas pedal and speeding off.

"Woah there!" said Urb, from where he sat behind me. He reached forward and put a steadying hand on my shoulder. I clutched the wheel, knuckles white. "It's okay, Fiona. It missed us. We're safe. That was a pretty close call, though. It'll be fun for those church folks trying to get down the mountain later."

"Yeah," I agreed, pulling the car over to the side of the road. My heart was still pounding in my ears.

"You know," said Urb, chattering to try to calm me down. "That's not the only time I've almost had a tree fall on me. One fell into my house when I was a kid. You know me and my bad luck. Actually, I think that might be the earliest one that I remember, but…" he paused and considered, "I also remember feeling like it wasn't a big surprise that something unlucky happened to me, so I guess it must have started before then."

"Huh," I said, my breathing slowing as I focused on Urb's story. "Tell me more about your bad luck," I asked, calm enough to pull back onto the road and start to drive.

It was mostly just small stuff, Urb said, like the mishaps around his breakfast this morning. Food was a big problem, actually. If he wanted something special from the bakery, they were almost guaranteed to sell the last one to the person right in front of him.

"It's not so bad," he said with a wry grin. "It teaches you to have an open mind."

"A tree falling on your house isn't little stuff, is it?" I asked. "Are you sure it was your bad luck, that time? I mean, your parents were the ones who had to deal with it, right? Do they have bad luck too?"

"It didn't just fall onto my house," Urb clarified, "it fell into my room, in the middle of the night while we were sleeping."

"Oh no!" I exclaimed. "Were you hurt?"

"No," he said. "I wasn't in my room. I slept in the living room that night."

"Why?" I asked. "Did you often sleep in the living room?"

Mostly, I watched the road, but I glanced into the rear-view mirror occasionally. The dappled leaves cast interesting shadows on Urb's expressive face as he talked.

"No," he answered. "I didn't, but something told me that I should, that night. It's not like my parents didn't know that tree might fall. They'd been talking about it for weeks, how it might hit the garage or a car in the driveway. Nobody thought it would go through my window. It sure did, though! There were glass shards all over my bed the next morning. It might actually have killed me."

"Well, that sounds like some pretty good luck, to me," I said, glancing back at Urb in the mirror. I shivered. Those strange dappled shadows almost made it look like there was someone looming over Urb's left shoulder.

zrp zrp
same thing

"Yeah, I guess so," Urb agreed, then shook his head. "But it was the bad luck, I'm sure of it. I can't really explain it, but there's a feeling that goes along with it."

zrp zrp
a lesson

"Like it's some kind of lesson?" I asked.

"Yeah," Urb agreed, and the shadow figure behind his shoulder nodded, also. An icy chill ran down my spine.

zrp zrp
meet them

"Urb," I asked hesitantly, "do you feel like it might be, um, someone in particular that's doing it?"

In the mirror, I saw Urb glance up, reflexively, toward his left shoulder, and my breath caught in my throat.

"Yeah," he agreed. "Maybe."

Chapter 26

A minute or two down the road, Urb pointed out a good place, and we got out of the car at the edge of a small rocky creek, overgrown with ferns and the springy green moss that covered almost everything, here in Oregon. Tiny violet flowers erupted from the greenery, and birds chirped cheerfully in the trees.

"Nice spot," I said to Urb, closing my eyes and listening to the birds and the babbling of the brook. Away from the windy mountain peak, the day was balmy again. The sense of unease that gripped me in the van faded in the warmth of the summer sun.

"What's this?" Urb asked, holding the wooden chest that Evita gave me.

"It's for making magic," I told him, coming over and opening the lid to show him the kit that my mother had so lovingly prepared for me. She was awfully good at knowing exactly what someone was going to need.

"Nice," said Urb. "You want to try it out? We were looking for something to do, after all."

"That's true," I agreed. "But if we're going to make magic, we've got to come up with a good reason." I considered, then remembered the shadow behind Urb's shoulder. I told Urb what I saw in the rear-view mirror. His eyes went wide, and he nodded, glancing up and to his left, like he did in the car. I hadn't mentioned which side it was on.

"I think it might be causing the annoying bad luck, but it doesn't really feel malicious," I said, trusting my intuition. "I also think it saved you from being hit by that tree when you were a kid."

Urb agreed. We didn't want to charge blindly forward and banish this entity, whatever it was. At least, not before we had the chance to talk to it and figure out what was going on.

I carried my little chest over to the riverbank, where three stones made a convenient conversation circle. I pulled a candle and a stick of incense from the box and lit them both, sticking the incense into the damp earth at the edge of the stream so curls of smoke drifted around us. With all four elements represented, we were ready to begin.

"Which one's the best seat?" I asked Urb, eyeing the three river-smooth rocks. He pointed at one of them. "Sit somewhere else," I told him, taking the third seat for myself. Following my intuition, I picked up a chunk of amethyst and an amethyst point hanging on a single chain, appreciating the way they matched. Holding the two stones together, I took a deep breath, looked at the space behind Urb's shoulder, and said, "Please join us. We would like to have a conversation with you." Then I placed the amethyst chunk on the best rock seat and handed the pendulum to Urb. It hung straight for a moment, then began to swing forward and backward, a response that I understood to mean yes. "It's here and it's chatty!" I said, surprised at the effectiveness of my first solo magic working.

Urb furrowed his brow. "They don't like when you call them 'it'."

A tingle ran down my body from my top to my toes, and I took a deep, steadying breath before replying.

"I didn't realize. How rude of me. My sincerest apologies to them." I gave the empty stone a deep nod of my head and committed to remembering this entity's preferred pronoun. I didn't want to be disrespectful.

"They say, um…" Urb paused, then continued, looking uncomfortable. "They're saying that nobody has any sense of hospitality anymore?" The pendulum swung forward in a resolute 'yes' at their words.

"Oh, uh," I looked down at the case, not sure what to do. Seeing the answer immediately, I pulled out a small bottle of whisky and two tiny cups. I filled them and handed one to Urb, setting the other on the rock. Without a third glass to serve myself, I held onto the bottle and touched it to my lips when Urb raised his glass in a toast. The strong taste made me grimace and I capped it again, putting the bottle away.

"That's better," said Urb. "They'll talk to us, now. Do you have any cards in there, or anything?"

"Not in here, but, one sec," I said, hopping up to grab them from the car. I took the gilded cards out of their box and began to mix them. Across from me, the pendulum in Urb's hand swung from side to side.

"They don't like those ones. They're too flowery," said Urb.

"They're the only ones I've got," I said, continuing to mix. "Sorry." As I shuffled, a chunk of cards fell out onto the moss of the riverbank. "That's too many," I said, picking up the fallen cards and directing my comment to the amethyst on the rock. "Just one or two, please." A few seconds later, a single card fell out of the deck, followed by a second and a third. I laid them out on the rock, in front of the amethyst. The Queen of Cups, the Queen of Wands, and the Queen of Swords sat before me. "That's a lot of queens!" I said. I opened the booklet and began to read.

"What does it say?" asked Urb, as the pendulum he held swung idly in a circle.

"It could be three different people, I guess," I said, letting my intuition help my interpretation. "But I think it's a journey. The transformation from someone dreamy and emotional, into a person who is ingenious and creative, and finally into someone with great strength and personal fortitude."

"Looks like you're onto something," said Urb. The pendulum changed direction, swinging hesitantly forward and backward.

zrp zrp
toughen up

"Really?" I said. "Is that what it is? You're trying to turn a dreamer into a warrior by ruining their eggs and never letting them have their favorite donut? Seriously?"

"I think they're feeling…" Urb paused, closing his eyes and concentrating. "Sheepish, maybe?"

At the same moment, two more cards fell out of the deck, landing face up on the moss. I opened the book and flipped through it. "Three of Swords. Disappointment, emotional upset, broken heart," I read. "And the Wheel of Fortune, a stroke of good luck." I let out a little laugh and then said, "Urb, I think this is an apology."

"I think you're right," said Urb, as the pendulum swung forward in confirmation.

Urb finished his portion of spirit, and I poured the rest of the second dram onto the rock. Then I dunked the amethyst in the flowing water of the stream, severing the connection, and Urb felt the entity settle back into their place behind his shoulder.

"I wonder whether it's going to work," I said, once we were back in the car. "Going to change your luck, I mean." The conversation with the entity had been impactful, but every second that passed put more and more distance between my current reality and what we had just experienced, and already the power of it was fading.

"Yeah," said Urb. "Me too. I guess we'll see."

"And what was with all those queens?" I asked, turning back onto the main road, headed toward civilization. "Three out of four. That's just a whole lot of feminine energy, don't you think?"

In the rear-view mirror, Urb fidgeted awkwardly, his kind, intelligent face looking shiftily, everywhere but back at me. I cocked my head, sneaking another glance at Urb's soft, round jawline. All male Firbolg have beards, isn't that what Jaah said?

"But you're so big!" I exclaimed, exasperated with myself. "Am I just stupid, or what?"

Urb laughed, understanding. "You really didn't know I was trans? I thought Evita might have said something."

I shook my head and then told Urb what had happened with Calliope. I truly had not known, for the second time in as many days.

"Don't feel bad," he said, seeing my hangdog expression. "It's nice. You see people how they want to be seen. It's a gift, really. Don't change."

Chapter 27

The streets were filled with large, shiny SUVs packed tightly together, and I had to park several blocks away from the address Nora gave me. "Maybe I should have gotten here earlier," I mumbled to myself as I approached the large brick house.

Two blond women were talking on the front porch. I could hear them clearly in the still evening. "Take a couple of 'em before you go to bed, and another one if you need to relax a little bit, hon. It'll take the edge off. I get 'em from my doctor, and he's a friend of Bobbie's, so I can always get more if you need 'em, okay?"

I reached the front steps, and the women stopped talking, looking me up and down as I climbed the stairs to the landing. Their critical expressions made it clear that my appearance did not impress. I straightened the new crystal necklace Jaah had given me self-consciously, and wondered if I should have tried harder with the curling iron this afternoon.

"Anyway," said one of the women, turning away from me dismissively, and handing her companion a little yellow pill bottle. "Start with these and let me know when you're running low."

I pushed open the heavy front door, leaving the pill-sharing friends behind me as I stepped into a simple entryway decorated with a prominent Bible verse. I followed the sound of voices into a living room where Temperance Rex stood in front of a whiteboard.

"The most important thing, even more important than raising your future children in God's light, will be to support your husband's relationship with God by being his helpmate, and not another burden for him to shoulder."

The living room wasn't small, and it was packed full of women, listening attentively. The seat I found near the door was one of the few left available.

"Make sure to greet him with love and sweetness when he comes home for the day. Not with problems and complaints or a list of things for him to do around the house. Make home a place of ease and comfort, after the trials of the world, and make sure that you are beautiful, loving, and available to meet his needs. You are God's gift to him, after all. A reward for all his hard work."

The woman next to me nodded solemnly, fingering the edge of the expensive leather handbag in her lap. On her left hand, she wore an enormous, sparkling engagement ring.

"Which brings us to our next point," said Mrs. Rex, pointing at a line on the whiteboard. "*Number Four: Be Confident That God is Enough.* An important fact of married life is that your husband is not going to meet all your needs, and he is not supposed to. As a Christian woman, you must turn toward God to find your own happiness. Daily prayer can—"

"Hey," said a quiet voice next to me. It was Nora. I hadn't heard her sneak in. She gestured for me to follow, and I got up as quietly as I could. "You and Herb aren't engaged yet, are you?" Nora asked, when I joined her in the austere entryway, "that's Auntie's class for ladies preparing for marriage."

"No, we're not," I answered, then noticed a sparkling new ring on Nora's finger, "but how about you? Are you engaged now?"

"I've heard it already," she answered, tucking her hand under her arm with a grimace. "Let's find somewhere private to talk. The study should be free." I followed her to a set of double doors. She opened them and then shut them again. Not fast enough, though. I saw what she'd seen. A young woman, thighs bare and eyes swollen with tears, held a thick leather strap in one hand. Her red-rimmed eyes glared daggers at Nora in the brief moment the door was open. When it shut again, I heard the distinctive crack of leather hitting flesh, followed by an anguished cry. "Not in there," said Nora. "It'll have to be my room. Sorry."

I followed her into a small room with a desk and a chair, and a single bed against one wall. The other wall was piled high with moving boxes. I sat down on the chair, and Nora perched on the edge of the bed. She didn't say anything for a moment, wringing her hands nervously in her lap.

"So," I said finally. "Do you want to tell me about Jesus?"

"I don't know," said Nora, still looking down at her hands. "Do you actually want to hear about him? We're supposed to share the gospel, but I'm starting to realize that most people don't actually want to hear it."

I held back a smile, remembering what Urb had said about intentionally annoying conversion tactics at the Tent Revival.

"Well, you were right when you said it seems like I don't like the church much," I admitted, "but I came because I was curious about it, and I really would like to learn more. Truly," I told her. It wasn't a lie. The more I could learn from her about the church and the way it functioned, the more useful my time here would be.

"Well, it's a good thing you have a nice godly man like Urb, already," said Nora, twisting the ring on her finger. "That way, they won't have to find one for you."

"I get the feeling you're not very happy being engaged," I told her.

She shrugged. It happened this afternoon, apparently. Her boyfriend, Byron, had met with her father and her Uncle, and the three men had called her in to join them and told her the good news.

"He didn't even get down on one knee?" I asked.

"No, he did," she said. "And I told him I would. I know my duty."

"Because that's what Jesus would want you to do?" I asked. At this, her somber expression changed and her cool eyes flashed at me, full of emotion.

"Would he?" she asked. "Would he really? I've committed my soul to Jesus, and I hear him speak to me in my heart. People like to say they follow him and walk his path, but sometimes I don't think they even know him at all. Jesus never married, did you know that? And he had women he took as his disciples. But people don't want to act like Jesus, they just want to worship him like some false idol. His name wasn't even really Jesus, did you know? His name was Yeshua, and he didn't think women were property; he treated them with respect."

"Really?" I asked.

"Yeah," she said. "All that stuff about how men lead the family, and have dominion over their wives? That wasn't Jesus' teaching. It was all Paul. He wanted to make the church acceptable to the ancient Romans, so he included a bunch of their values. That's where the term paterfamilias comes from. Father family. It's Latin, see?"

"You sure know a lot about this stuff."

"I've had a lot of time to read," she told me. "Aunt Tempy's real protective. She doesn't like me leaving the house much. But we've always had Uncle's library, even when he was away overseas, and it's all Christian books, so she thought it was probably fine that I read them."

"But it wasn't?" I asked.

"It's certainly made me think about some things," she said, shrugging again, "especially now that I'm getting older."

"Like what?"

"Like how sometimes I feel like most of the people I know are hypocrites. They talk about loving Jesus, but then they turn around and gossip and lie and brag anyway. That's why I don't hang out with the other women at church much anymore. They'll take it from Aunt Tempy, but they don't want to hear about morality from me."

"It's a shame they don't listen to you," I said. "Seems like you're pretty smart, to me."

She smiled at that, meeting my eyes for the first time today. She didn't look like the other church women here. Her hair wasn't long and curled, and highlighted to be blond. It was straight, cut shorter than her shoulders, and there wouldn't have been any point in highlighting it, since it was already so pale as to be almost white.

She was pretty. Really pretty, actually, which was maybe why I hadn't noticed those differences before. Fine, snow-white skin set off her almond-shaped eyes and petal pink lips in a strikingly symmetrical face. She told me about her life, and I watched her, enjoying the way the story animated her expressions.

Nora hadn't always been a part of the church. Her mother had died when she was young, and she was taken in by her aunt and uncle. She only had a few memories of her mother, but her face positively glowed when she spoke about her.

"But," said Nora, her expression clouding, "Aunt Tempy says it's a good thing that I got to live with her, and be saved. She always says how great a tragedy it would be, if I ended up in hell, like…" she paused, then plastered on a strained smile and finished. "She's glad I got to be saved."

Aunt Tempy homeschooled her, raising her in the ways of the church, and receiving regular instruction from her husband, the honorable Reverend, even though he found himself called away by his work, most of the time. Nora's father lived with them, too. "He's not big on kids though," said Nora with a shrug. He hadn't been very involved until lately, when he met Byron and decided Nora needed a husband.

"And you don't want to marry Byron," I added, saying the quiet part out loud.

"I don't want to go to hell," she replied.

"But, what about everything you just said, about the paterfamilias stuff?"

"Yeah," she said. "Maybe. I don't know. It sure is good to have someone to talk about it with, though. I'm all alone, in my head, so often. If it weren't for Jesus, I think I'd be so lonely that I'd die, and then I'd definitely go to hell."

"For what? Dying of loneliness? I'm pretty sure suicide is supposed to be a sin, but that wouldn't actually count, would it?" I joked, trying to lighten the mood, and she smiled weakly, appreciating the attempt.

"That's not, uh…" she paused, glancing up at me shyly. "That's not really the sin I was thinking about, actually. And I'd sure like to think about something other than Byron for a minute. Do you, uh, want to see how I've been sinning lately?"

Part 7 - Earth

Chapter 28

"Hoo, girl! That Bible basher's got the hots for you!" said Pythia, shrieking and pounding the solid wood of the bar percussively, as I recounted the story at the Fair Isle on Monday night.

"That's what I've been saying," said Jaah, shaking their head.

"Guys!" I said, exasperated. "It's not like that. Hang on." I held up a hand and continued telling my story.

Nora walked over to the wall of boxes and pulled one off the top of the stack. "Uncle wanted to get rid of this stuff, but Auntie saw that there were books and papers in here and saved it for our family's genealogy. That's Aunt Tempy's hobby, doing genealogies. And then they just got stuck in here."

She set down the first box and reached for a second.

"They told me not to mess with any of it, and disobeying my elders is a sin, so every time I go in here, I'm technically sinning." She sat back down on the bed and took the lid off the first box. "This stuff was my grandmother's. My mom's mom."

"The Reverend's mother?"

She nodded, taking a piece of black cloth out of the box and revealing a much more interesting collection of items than I expected. I came to sit beside her on the bed to get a closer look at the curious contents.

"Is that a crystal ball?" I asked, pointing at a large, clear sphere nestled in a satin cushion.

"Mmhmm," she said, reaching into the box and pulling out a well-worn leather-bound book. "I've been learning a lot about my grandmother from her journals. She was a very interesting woman. Sinfully interesting, if you know what I mean."

She opened the journal, and I saw a familiar five-pointed star labeled with the alchemical symbols for the elements that Evita and Faeryn had taught me.

"Seems like it," I agreed. I reached out hesitantly, and at her nod, pulled out a bundle wrapped in a silk scarf with an image of the phases of the moon in the center. Unfolding it, I revealed a large, well-worn deck of cards.

zrp zrp
hands off

Using the scarf to avoid touching the cards, I held the deck out to Nora and asked. "Who was she?"

"She was a medium. That's what her journals call it, anyway. She used to talk to spirits and hold séances in her home." She took the deck from me and fanned through it. A single card fell out onto the bed between us.

"I keep getting this same one, over and over." She held it up, showing me. It was an image of a winged man with a crossed shield, blowing his horn for a group of chubby cherubs.

"Judgment," she read. "I really don't know what any of it is supposed to mean, but that's a clear enough message, isn't it? My sinful nature is tricking me into being so interested in all of this stuff, and thinking that Grandma's writing makes a lot of sense. 'The Devil doesn't walk around with red horns looking evil,' that's what Aunt Tempy always says. And clearly this is God judging me for my sins."

"Judgment, huh?" I said, peering at the card. "You know, my mom gave me a set of cards kind of like these. Mine came with a little booklet. These didn't?"

She shook her head.

"Well, I remember a little bit about that one, because I thought that's what it meant too, but it's not about anybody judging you. It's a spiritual awakening, or a rebirth. A resurrection," I said, then added helpfully, "Like Jesus!"

"Like Jesus!" Jaah repeated, throwing their head back with a loud laugh, as I recounted the tale.

Pythia shook her head. "Bible baby's got herself some Tarot cards, huh? Oh no, here we go!"

"You really don't think I'm sinning, for looking into all this stuff?" Nora asked, thumbing through the books.

"I don't think it can possibly be up to me, can it? It sounds like you know Jesus pretty well. Would he think you're sinning?"

She thought about it and said, "No, I don't think he would. But, Auntie would probably say that it's my sinful nature talking and making excuses for my human desires."

"Listening to your own gut feeling is a sin, now? Alright, that's something I just can't agree with. You're a good person, Nora, if you can't trust yourself, who can you trust?"

She set down the book she was holding and picked up another one. It was an art book, and it fell open to a middle page featuring a baroque oil painting of three voluptuous, nude women wrapped in a gauzy piece of fabric. I glanced at the title, 'The Three Graces,' before she flipped the page.

"I'm not entirely good," she said, looking at the next image, which showed tiny bodies plummeting into a dark pit of winged demons. 'The Hell Fall of the Damned,' the label read, 'Peter Paul Reubens c.AD 1620.'

"I guess I don't get it," I said, looking at the tiny bodies in the painting. "I thought the whole point was that you just have to accept Jesus into your heart, and then he forgives your sins and you go to Heaven anyway. Which seems pretty dangerous to me, by the way, telling people they have a sinful nature but they're going to be forgiven? Seems like that makes it pretty easy to excuse some pretty big sins, doesn't it? But, by that logic, you'd be good to go, no matter what, right? Because you've accepted Jesus?"

"That's how a lot of people treat it, yeah," said Nora. "But I don't think that's right. I think you should feel real remorse before you ask to be forgiven. That's why I don't just ask for forgiveness whenever I open these boxes, because I know I won't stop. I'm just going to do it again."

"Doesn't that seem like something that a good person who can trust herself would believe?" I asked.

She shrugged again, still staring at the painting.

zrp zrp
go now

This seemed like a good stopping point. Nora had a lot to think about tonight, and I could leave her to it.

"Anyway, thanks for inviting me," I said. "I'm glad we got to talk."

"Me too. Thank you. I get the feeling that you're not actually all that interested in joining the church," she said. "But, do you think you could come back next week anyway? I don't have anybody else, and it's so nice to have someone to talk to about this stuff."

zrp zrp
of course

"Sure," I said. "I can do that."

Chapter 29

"Ooh, girl, you are in, or she is out, or both!" Pythia crowed, kicking up her feet gleefully.

"Yeah, it does seem like Nora has some room for doubt," I agreed.

"And a taste for curvy women. You know that book didn't flop open to that page accidentally, it's getting opened there a lot, I guarantee it," said Jaah, taking a sip from their pint.

"Is that the new kombucha on tap?" I asked them, eyeing the frothy pink brew. "Pythia, can you pour me one?"

"Finally, I get to pull you a real drink, girl. You know I haven't served you hardly anything all summer? I was starting to get offended."

"N ow that you mention it, I don't think I've had a drink since the Pirate Carnival. I just haven't felt like it, I guess. But you know what? You're both invited down for a revel at Evita's next Saturday, and I feel like letting loose. That'll be my chance to make up for lost time, okay?"

Pythia danced off to pour a drink at the other end of the bar, and Jaah took the opportunity to lean in and whisper into my ear.

"There's another way you can let loose, if you'd like." They handed me a palm-sized crystal sphere. "I just got this from Asmodeus. They're free tomorrow night."

"What is this?" I asked, turning the ball around in my palm. It was satisfyingly heavy.

"Play," said Jaah, tapping it. An image appeared, warped by the curve of the sphere.

"I would be more than charmed to host you in my humble lair," said a voice that I recognized as Asmodeus. An image of a lushly furnished room all in shades of purple appeared, and panned to show a long wall of shelves, covered with the sorts of implements I'd seen people use at the play parties, and many other items whose purpose I couldn't begin to guess. "I hear you're interested in new experiences, and I am sure I can accommodate you in that desire. Dress for the occasion, dear. I'll be looking forward to it."

Dress for the occasion? I mentally reviewed the contents of my closet. There was time to go shopping before tomorrow. I thought about asking Pythia to go with me, but one look at her slim dancer's body convinced me not to. It would be nice to have another curvy girl around, for times like this.

All the stress about finding an outfit was helpful in one particular way, though. As I drove toward the address that Jaah had given me, in new lacy underwear and a silky wrap dress, I realized that I had been so worried about what to wear that I hadn't even started thinking about what the rest of the evening might have in store for me. Now that I was thinking about it, though, my skin prickled with tingles of anticipation.

"It's okay. You've got this," I told myself, steeling my nerves as I prepared to get out of the car and approach the door. It was a large house with dark gables that loomed over me, like their Master had done, that night at the play party.

I knocked and waited.

There was no answer, but deep from the bowels of the house I heard a keening cry. I knocked again. The neighborhood was dark and still, and I listened for any noise in the quiet night. Eventually, I heard the sound of footsteps approaching the door, and it swung open a crack.

"Oh," said Asmodeus. They looked haggard, with dark circles underneath their eyes. "Right, I had forgotten. My inner demons…" They looked up at me, and I could feel the torment in their pale gaze. "Have been relentless. It has been an extraordinarily difficult day. I am not fit to be good company tonight."

"Oh," I said. "Okay."

"Both of you have the right to withdraw consent at any time," Jaah had reminded me before I left. I hadn't imagined it would be like this, though.

"I apologize," Asmodeus told me, shutting the door with a click.

"All dressed up and nowhere to go," I said with a sigh, back inside my van. I picked up my phone to let Jaah know that I would be coming back earlier than expected, but before I did, an old text preview caught my eye.

Thanks for the help tonight, sweetie…

I clicked to open it. This was a night to be brave and try new things, I reminded myself. I took a deep breath and typed a message. To my surprise, my phone dinged with a reply, almost immediately.

Just hanging with my girls, honey. You should come by.

The address wasn't far away. I turned the engine over and drove off into the night.

"You look nice," said my friend, the girl from the first play party, eyeing me up and down. She stepped aside, letting me past her. "Come in and tell us about these plans that got canceled."

Stepping inside, I was momentarily overwhelmed by the sheer overload of femininity. There were pink velvet poufs and matching satin curtains. Rhinestones sparkled and lace dripped from every possible surface. One piece of the decor moved, and I realized that some of the sparkles and lace were adorning beautifully dressed women who blended seamlessly into the opulent scenery.

"Asmodeus, huh?" she replied, once I explained. "They do have a certain appeal, I suppose. And what exactly was it that you wanted to get up to with our friend the dragon?"

"Honestly, I'm not sure. I just wanted to, uh, try some of the stuff I've seen at the parties, you know? But, somewhere more private."

"This private enough for you?" my friend asked with a smirk. "It's just us girls, after all. That's Illuria," she pointed at one of the beautiful women nestled into the luxuriant space, who simpered and gave me a little wave. "And Elenia, and Ordelia, and I'm Atalia, but you knew that already, of course."

I hadn't known that, actually.

"I'm Fiona," I replied, my own lyrical name making me feel slightly more at home with this aggressively feminine group.

"Well, Fiona, what would you like to try first?" Her tone was light and playful and I blushed at her teasing wink.

"I have no idea," I told her, honestly.

"Well, how about I show you some things, and you see how you like them?" she said, then addressed the crowd. "That sound entertaining to you girls?" They tittered their assent. She pulled a chair into the center of the room and motioned for me to sit. I settled myself into the seat, and my satin wrap slipped off my shoulder, revealing the top of my new lacy underthings. "My my," Atalia said, clicking her tongue. "You sure did dress to be the center of attention tonight. May I touch you?" I nodded. "Verbal consent, please."

"Yes."

"Good girl." She ran her long fingernails down my arm, and the tiny hairs stood on end. "Would you like to try a blindfold?" Atalia asked. "Taking away one of your senses can really heighten the others."

One of the women caught my eye, and I looked away nervously. "Sure," I agreed. "Yeah." A blindfold meant I wouldn't have to worry about eye contact, at least.

She slipped a rose colored sleep mask over my eyes, and everything went dark. I was being a little reckless, coming here without telling anyone, and now this. But, I wanted to try new things, and this was certainly something new. Without warning, I felt her long nails trace their way down my other arm, and it felt like lightning on my skin. I shivered, unable to help it.

"Mmm, very good," she said, and I felt energy swell inside me at her words, as well as her touch. "Let's try a few different sensations, shall we? You don't have to tell me if you like something, but I need you to make sure you say so if you don't like something, okay?"

I nodded, and then, remembering her instruction, added, "Yeah, I can do that."

The anticipation of waiting for her next touch was almost as electric as the sensations themselves. Some of them were sharp, sharper than her fingernails. Some were soft, like rabbit's fur or downy feathers. It made my body warm and my breathing quicken.

"Let's try this one next," she said, and the sensation that followed was something very different from the ones before. It felt like little needles making pin pricks across my chest, next to my collarbone.

"No, nope. I don't like that," I said, and the uncomfortable sensation ceased immediately.

"Good girl," Atalia said again. "Now that you've demonstrated your very fine ability to say no, let's raise the stakes, shall we? Have you ever been tied up with rope?"

I'd seen people get tied up at the parties, and they had looked like they were having a good time. And, it was just a bunch of other women here, which made me feel safer. "No," I told her, "but I'd try it."

"Excellent," she said, and I could hear the smile in her voice. "I could use the practice." The pull of the rope against my skin raised as many goosebumps as her fingernails had done.

"You know who would really have enjoyed this little show?" I heard one of the other women say. "Poor Velia. Don't you think so, Elenia?"

"It's a shame, yes," said another woman who must be Elenia. "But that's what happens when you go and get yourself banished by the Queen."

"Her letter said she's making new friends, but there's no way they're as fun as we are," said another, cattily. "Or as pretty."

"If I ever got my hands on that princess girl, I'd show her what we vila are really made of. You can't do that to one of our sisters without consequences," said the first speaker, and the delicately feminine menace in her voice made me nervous.

My phone buzzed to life in my pocket.

"Getting a message, sweetie?" Atalia asked. I nodded, and she pulled off the blindfold and freed my arms for me.

It was a text from Jaah, checking in to see how I was doing.

"Oh no!" I exclaimed. "I've gotta go. I need to get home, right away." With my arms free it was easy to pull off the rest of the ropes, and I made some hasty goodbyes, before leaving Atalia and the rest of the vila sisters behind me.

Alone in the van, I breathed deeply, glad to be safely away before any of the women could discover my connection to Velia's banishment. My cousin Faeryn was the faerie princess the vila sisters had mentioned, but my own role in Velia's fall was considerable, and I couldn't imagine they would feel kindly towards me, if they found out who I was. I thanked my faerie luck for the well-timed text message and took stock of myself. My body still glowed with the feelings that Atalia raised in me, and I felt full to bursting with the energy of it.

Back at the Fair Isle, I headed straight up the back stairs to Jaah's rooms.

"What's wrong?" they asked, seeing the fierce expression on my face.

"Nothing's wrong, but," I said, pulling them toward the bedroom. "I need you. Now."

It was quite a while before either of us said anything further. "Wow," they said, flopping down onto their pillow, some time later. "You sure raised some energy with Asmodeus, huh?"

"What?" I asked, surprised. "No. Actually, I've got an interesting story to tell you. You'll never guess whose sisters I ended up meeting, tonight."

Chapter 30

We arrived at the hill early on Saturday morning, with the ingredients Evita asked me to bring for the feast.

"How do faeries manage to buy groceries anyway?" I asked nobody in particular, unloading a canvas sack onto the counter of Evita's sunny kitchen. "I thought mostly-magicals couldn't really shop at human stores, except for thrift shops and things. Is this all from the used food store," I teased, gesturing to include all of the dishes in mid-preparation, "or did it fall off the back of a truck, do you think?"

"I don't think I want second-hand milk," said Azalea, eyeing the jug she held suspiciously.

"It was freshly milked this morning," said Arlee, taking the jug from Azalea and pouring a measure into the bowl of eggs she was whisking. "The Little Queen's domain is mostly farmland, so she's made friends with quite a few of the local farmers."

Faeryn sat in the corner by the window, shelling peas. Her color was good, and she seemed energetic, but she snapped each pod with such force that the peas kept skittering away across the kitchen floor, then glowering after them as though they had personally offended her by flying off.

"It's like you forget that intermagicals like us even exist," said Faeryn, irritably. "Haven't you ever been to a Trader's Outpost? Every other grocery carries all the same brands, and then there's the Outpost, with their bright colors and storybook labels, and humans flock there and fill their carts with fae foods, pretending they don't even notice us hiding in plain sight."

"Trader's Outpost?" I asked, surprised. "I used to shop there in college. It's a fae place, really?" I'd mostly gone there for the suspiciously inexpensive fancy wines and cheeses, and the shiny produce that never seemed to spoil. It did seem obvious now that Faeryn had explained it. I guess I really had been missing the truth right in front of me.

"An intermagical place," Faeryn corrected testily, white knuckles squeezing another unlucky pod.

"Is everything alright, Faeryn? Did you have a nice time while you were away?" I asked.

"A week at a dwarf lodge, what could be nicer?" she said, her voice dripping with sarcasm. "Countless hours in front of the fire, all alone, or listening to old hunting stories I've heard a hundred times before."

"Huh," I said. "Not what you were hoping for?"

"Well, it's been a welcome break from this mockery of a kingdom, at least."

"Mockery of a—" I repeated.

Arlee spoke at the same time. "She's the Little Queen's daughter. Take care with what you say, lady."

"No, it's okay," I told her. "I want to know what's going on. I'm not going to be offended, I promise."

"That's exactly why she deserves to know the truth, Arlee," said Faeryn.

Evita wasn't supposed to be a Queen, Faeryn told me. A powerful faerie, certainly, but not ruler of her own kingdom.

"She should have been one of my mother's subjects," Faeryn explained, "but she refused to be ruled. As much as it is my mother's nature to give orders, it is Evita's nature to refuse to follow them."

"You know, I've been noticing that," I interjected.

She gave me a thin-lipped smile and continued, "'If my sister is a Queen, why shouldn't I be one, too?'" Faeryn said, pursing her lips in imitation of Evita's prideful expression. "And my mother knew her sister too well to try to argue. She made her Queen of this little hill, and all the land she sees. Of course, Evita treats the town in the valley like it's her own domain, also, but mother doesn't mind. I think she'd give Evita the valley outright if she thought she'd appreciate it. But, she knows that the Little Queen would declare herself exhausted by the burden of ruling the valley, even though she's doing it already. She simply won't be told what to do. So, mother leaves her to her own devices. Mostly, anyway."

There were some rules the Queen insisted that even her sister must obey, and it was one such rule that had kept Evita from granting her adviser Velia full membership in her court. Only the Faerie Queen could grant that status, and Velia's petition had been denied.

186

"Why?" I asked. I had met Velia and could certainly imagine why someone might dislike her, but she had been doing her best to stop me from rejoining my birth family at the time. I suspected that she could have been quite charming under different circumstances.

"Because she lies," Faeryn said, with a dismissive wave of her hand. "Vila like Velia have too much deviousness and deception to be faerie, even if we do share certain other qualities." She tossed her long red hair over her shoulder, haughtily. Faeryn really was very pretty, I thought, admiring the way her pale skin glowed in the mid-morning sun. "They claim to be so much like us, but then they go and lie, in a way that a faerie would never. Could never. Seems to me that they're almost as much like demons as they are like members of our court."

"Faeries can't lie?" I asked. "Is that really true?"

"Well, do you lie?" asked Faeryn.

"Not really," I admitted. Lying had always seemed like more trouble than it was worth. "But I bet I could if I wanted to." I picked up a knife from the sideboard. "This is a spoon," I said resolutely, brandishing the sharp thing.

"Well, you're only half-faerie," said Faeryn dismissively. "And you're not really trying to make me believe your lie, are you? But my point is that it isn't our nature to be deceitful. Faeries might enhance ourselves with illusion, but we are who we are, and it wouldn't occur to us to try to appear to be otherwise. Unlike the vila. Now an elf like that," she said, indicating Calliope, who we could see through the garden window. "She's so irritatingly straightforward, I don't think the possibility of lying has ever occurred to her."

"Calliope's an elf?" I asked, surprised.

"Obviously," said Faeryn. "What else would she be?"

It hadn't been obvious to me, but, noting Faeryn's fierce expression, I decided it would be wiser to keep my mouth shut. Instead, I exchanged a meaningful glance with Pythia. She was learning at least as much about my family as I was, in this interesting exchange.

At that moment, Evita returned, bustling through the kitchen door, arms laden with packages.

"Fiona, what are you still doing here? It's almost noon. You should be at your lesson!"

"Noon!" Faeryn exclaimed, bolting up and scattering the bowl of peas all over the floor. "My Knight will be here any minute, and I'm still sitting here shelling peas? I've got to get ready! Don't forget to set him a place at the table!" She scampered off down the spiral staircase, leaving Arlee behind her, gathering fallen pods.

Momentarily stunned by Faeryn's abrupt departure, I recovered myself, and turned to Evita. "What do you mean, my lesson? You said we weren't going to have one today because you two didn't have anything to teach me about earth."

"Oh," said Evita. "That's right." She considered this for a moment, then tried again. "Fiona, I've found someone with something to teach you about earth, and I've arranged a lesson for you."

"Oh," I replied. "I see."

"Yes. Good. And it's right now. You'd better be going, you're already late."

Chapter 31

"You're late," said an old woman. She was dressed in all black, and wore thick black sunglasses in the dim garage.

"I'm sorry," I answered, ducking my head submissively. "It was unavoidable." That was what I'd been told to say.

"She doesn't have time for stories and she isn't interested in excuses," Evita had told me, scribbling instructions on a slip of paper. "Just get there as quick as you can, don't argue with anything she says, and be polite!" Luckily the address she gave me was just a few houses down the road.

The old woman nodded, satisfied. "Your mother says that you want to learn a thing or two about metalsmithing."

"Um—" I started. That certainly wasn't something I had ever said, and it didn't exactly align with what I had been told we were doing, but remembering my mother's advice, I closed my mouth and nodded my agreement.

"Mmm," said the old woman, eyeing me suspiciously. "Alright. Grab a mandril. Today we're gonna make a ring." For all her gruffness, she was an excellent teacher. "Let the saw blade drag along the metal. Don't force it. The teeth'll do the work for you if you let 'em. Nice and easy."

Before long, I had a strip of silver ready to bend.

"Stand back now, girl. First time lighting the torch in the morning'll blow your eyebrows off if you're not careful." She lifted up her strip of dark glasses to show a bare, liver-spotted forehead. "And if you do it enough times they won't grow back!" She cackled, then flicked a switch. The torch bloomed into a small cloud of fire before condensing back into a cone of blue flame. "Heating the metal changes the cellular structure," she explained as I worked. I clanged my hammer down onto the anvil again, missing the ring I was supposed to be shaping. Now that I had heated the metal until it was red hot, it bent easily under my hammer. "Imagine the cells are like little building blocks. When they're all lined up, they're hard to move around. You move one, and they all move with it. But when they're hot, it's all a big, messy heap. More open-ended and flexible."

Clang!

This time I hit my mark, and the hammer dinged off the ring.

"When you hit it like that, you're lining the building blocks back up. Bringing order to chaos. The more you hit it, the stronger it'll be."

"That seems counterintuitive," I said.

"Well, it's true for metal, not people," she replied acerbically.

I considered that as I pounded the metal. My upbringing had given me a bit of a pounding, actually. My adopted mother was strict and unyielding, doing her best to shape me into someone socially acceptable and ordinary. Something my faerie nature made it impossible for me to be. Her efforts had made me stronger, though, I thought. More resilient than some of my intermagical peers, in certain ways. And it had also left me more brittle and fragile. In the warmth and the fire of my birth family, I could feel that rigidity beginning to ease. I was beginning to feel more comfortable in my own chaos.

"Neatly done," she told me, handing me the smooth, hammered silver ring. "Fine work for your first time."

"Thank you," I said, taking the ring and extending my other hand for her to shake. As she grasped my hand, her coat sleeve rode up and something caught my eye. "What's this on your wrist?" I asked.

"Oh, it's a dragon's tail. The rest of him snakes all around my body, from tits to tailbone. Got in a bad accident and got burned all over when I was young. Way of taking my body back. Making art out of pain."

As I walked back up to the hill, I felt the soft loamy earth under my feet, then rubbed the smooth, hard metal of the new ring on my finger. This hard, brittle strength was a new side to earth magic, and that excited me. I would have to thank Evita for expanding my thinking, and for the opportunity to study under that fascinating individual.

When I stepped back inside the kitchen, it was bustling chaos with so many chefs and helpers running over each other. I slipped through them and poured myself the last glass of white wine out of the bottle by the stove. It was now late afternoon, and I wanted a drink. I was ready to cut loose a little after an extraordinarily dry summer.

"Fiona, can you stir this for me?" Arlee asked.

"Sure," I answered, setting my glass down and taking the spoon she held. When I returned for my wine a few minutes later, it had already been added to the soup pot.

"Drat," I muttered. I hadn't even gotten a single sip. Deciding to seek my fortune outside the crowded kitchen, I headed out the door and into the garden.

"Sister!" my brother Egan hailed me, coming up the garden path. He looked darker and leaner after a summer in the desert.

"Good to see you, brother!"

"Good to be back." He reached me and clapped my shoulder in greeting.

"Want to have a drink by the fire and tell me about your travels?" I asked. Egan was still underage, it was true, but the faeries didn't put too much stock in human rules like that. Or, at least, Evita didn't, and I had drunk wine with Egan at dinner, and passed a bottle around the fire with him before.

"No, not for me," he said, looking solemn. "The drink, I mean. I got a good look at what it's done to a lot of the folk down there." He shook his head. "No thanks."

"Well, that's hardly the part I was interested in," I fudged. "I really just want to hear about your trip."

Chapter 32

"All season, we have tended tiny sprouts, encouraging them to blossom and fruit. Just as our Mother Earth nourishes and protects us, and as our family nourishes and protects each other." Evita looked at me, smiling tenderly. She took my hand on one side, and Faeryn's on the other. "Let our magic nourish and protect this valley, and everyone who lives within it." She released our clasped hands, and I felt a surge of power flow out from us, down into the valley below, and deep into the earth under our feet.

"Now, let's feast and celebrate the bounty of the season," said Evita, gesturing toward the impressively laden table set in the middle of the lushly overgrown garden. "Please, eat, drink and be faerie."

I chuckled the first time I'd heard Evita use that particular phrase. "It's 'eat, drink and be merry,'" I'd told the wizened old fae seated beside me.

"No," he corrected me. "It's eat, drink, and be faerie. If humans misheard and misinterpreted the saying, that's not our fault. Humans are always borrowing our best phrases, anyway. Fae are just clever, that's all."

I sat down next to Jaah. Faeryn's seat was farther down the table, and I eyed the empty place next to it. It seemed as though her Knight had not arrived yet. Her irritable mood seemed to have worsened, and she glowered at Calliope from across the table. The girl shrunk back, as though worried that Faeryn might throw something at her. Considering my cousin's fiery mood, I thought her response was probably a reasonable one.

Some of Evita's subjects served the food the family prepared this afternoon. "It's an honor!" squeaked a foot-high fae, setting a rustic earthenware plate down in front of me. The first course was a warm mushroom salad. In fact, most of the dishes prepared for this feast featured mushrooms. When the rich, earthy umami hit my tongue, I understood why. They positively burst with elemental power.

Azalea picked listlessly at the plate in front of her. I wasn't surprised. Not a big eater at the best of times, this vegetable-heavy fare was not her favorite. I watched as she slipped her phone out of her pocket, keeping it out of sight below the table. She noticed me, and gave me a winning smile, hoping to hypnotize me with her adorableness, so that I wouldn't alert the Gullah or Pythia.

I winked my complicity, but a moment later, she blew her own cover anyway. "What?" she exclaimed. "Why aren't there aren't any Wylds here? Are all of you already playing WyldSight or something?"

She held up her phone, showing a topographical map of the area. It was completely empty, which was admittedly a little eerie for an experienced WyldSight player looking at an entire dinner party's worth of potential Wylds to sight.

Confused mutters ran through the gathered crowd. "Wild sight? What is that? Do you know? Me neither."

"No, darlin'," said Pythia, leaning over and taking Azalea's phone out of her hand. "I think these folk are all a little too fae to have cell phones."

"Woah," said Azalea, looking down the table with interest.

Now the group's attention was piqued, and we explained WyldSight to the crowd. They might not have any concept of a cell phone game, but nature watching was a familiar idea, and the game appealed to the gathered fae.

"It's like a type of illusion," one interested fae said, as he watched the red dot on Azalea's screen. Jaah worked some technomagic to allow us to show the curious fae how the game worked. Their phone now appeared to as a Wyld with a chameleon head, and eight spindly legs on a panther's body.

"Where is this Wyld from, Daddy?" asked Zinnia, peering at the strange creature.

"It's from hacking," they replied with a smirk.

"Is that in South America?" she asked. Jaah opened their mouth to answer, but Pythia interrupted.

"Speaking of Wylds from far off places, we've actually been using this game to try to track down a big nasty who's been hurting some of our friends, up in the city." She explained about finding the Ibex in the game. "He keeps popping up in new spots, though, like he's worried about being recognized. Which…" She tapped her phone with one sharp nail. "He's right to be. But it means that we're always chasing him, and we need to be a step ahead of the guy for this app to be much help."

The fae next to her asked a question, and she shook her head. "It only works if you have the territory claimed already, and it doesn't tell you exactly when or where you saw something. You have to be watching your screen when you see it, to know for sure." The fae leaned in again, too quiet for me to hear. "He's beat up six working girls so far, from down in Salem and all the way up into Washington. And that's just the ones we know about," she answered. "He must be new to the area, but it seems like he knows all the popular spots."

"We know one other place he's been," said Jaah, sourly. "This church that Fiona keeps going to."

I rolled my eyes. Jaah was even more outspoken about the church since I came back from the Women's Group with my story about Nora. They said it hit too close to home but they still refused to talk about what happened with their sister.

"And that's a pretty good reason for me to keep on going, so I can figure out who he is," I insisted, not for the first time. I chose not to mention my doubts about whether the Ibex had even been at the church at all. It was still possible that he could have just walked by my building downtown.

"I just don't want you to be one of the girls that disappears, okay?" they said sternly, eyeing me.

"Which reminds me," said Pythia. "Brother, I just got this today." She held up an already-opened envelope. "It's from one of the girls who disappeared, postmarked from a little town a few hours east of here. Her friend gave it to me. It reads nice and cheerful, but her friend says she thinks it's a code. The memories and the people she's talking about are all made up. They never happened. Like she's trying to pass a secret message."

She handed the envelope to the Gullah, who pulled out the letter and started to read.

"Yeah, that would be a smart way to pass a coded message," they said, eyes flicking busily. "But whether or not we manage to figure out what she's talking about, I think I'll take some time off and make a trip to that little town."

"Seriously?" I said, words erupting out of me unexpectedly. "You're going to run straight into danger with no plan, just to see what you can find? Are you kidding me? After the hard time you've been giving me about going to the church?"

"Well I happen to know how dangerous and racist that church is. I saw it first hand, at that Tent Revival, remember?"

"There are racists in Eastern Oregon, too! You're the one who warned me about how it is when you get into the backcountry. You're worried about me, am I not allowed to be worried about you?"

"Look, I'm not going to get into any trouble. I'm just going to take a look around and see what I can find. This is the kind of thing I do, okay?"

"And I'm just supposed to sit idly by, while you put yourself in harm's way?"

"I'm willing to make certain personal sacrifices, Fiona. It's my own safety I'm risking."

"Oh yeah? Well, what if that's not something I'm comfortable risking?" I asked, my voice breaking as my emotions overwhelmed me, my eyes pricking with tears. I balled my fists in my lap, trying to get ahold of myself, and felt the sharp edge of the ring I had just made cutting into my palm. I couldn't bear the feeling of so many eyes on me. I pushed myself away from the table and fled to the safety of Evita's cozy kitchen, pulling the rough ring off, and stuffing it in my pocket as I fled.

I swung the door open wide with adrenaline from storming out of dinner.

"Oh!" I exclaimed, stopping suddenly to avoid stepping on Calliope. She was curled just inside the doorway, thin body racked with heavy sobs. The intensity of her distress pulled me away from my own upset immediately. "What are you doing down there?" I asked, extending a hand to the crumpled elf. Instead of taking it, she flinched back, scrambling to get off the floor and out of my way.

"I'm sorry, I'm so sorry. You're right. If I'm banished, I should leave. I should already be gone," she said through wet sobs. "I'll go now, and you'll never have to see me again. I'll just disappear into the wilds you're all talking about and I'll," she sniffed pitifully. "I'll make my own way. You don't need to worry about me."

"Into the wilds—" I echoed. "Calliope! Don't be silly."

At this, her cries intensified. "I'm sorry, I didn't realize that I was being silly. I won't do it again, I swear I won't." She wiped streaming eyes on the corner of her sleeve.

"No, Calliope! I didn't—"

At the word 'no' she crouched even lower, contorting into a rictus of sorrow, and, for a moment, I understood how one might become annoyed with the girl's 'sniveling and squirming,' as Faeryn had described it.

"Look," I said. Her large eyes opened even wider, and she turned them on me intently, seeming to take my meaning literally. "I just meant that you don't need to run off into the wilds, that's all. And I'm sorry Faeryn is so mean to you. It doesn't matter how irritated she is or how much you…" I paused. This was not the time for indelicate observations. "Or how much she might want to, banishing you…"

zrp zrp
banish how

"Wait, how did she banish you? Calliope, Faeryn isn't a princess of this court, but I am. I, uh—" I hadn't done this before, but I closed my eyes and let my intuition guide me. "I grant you full status as a member of the Little Queen's court, in my capacity as princess, and give you my protection, that no, ahem," I cleared my throat and steeled myself. "That no visiting or foreign royalty may question or deny."

I reached out and touched her, and to my surprise, my touch seemed to bestow something. Calliope shivered, then stilled and looked up at me with a slow, hopeful smile.

"Truly?"

"Yes," I said, returning the smile with interest. "You don't belong to Faeryn anymore. You're free."

Her face broke again, and she melted into a puddle of hot, fierce tears.

It's funny how anguish and joy can look so similar, I thought to myself, smiling down at the howling Calliope on the floor. After a few minutes, my smile faltered. Happy tears would, I would think, have died down by now, but Calliope's apparent grief only seemed to be mounting.

"Calliope, I thought you would be happy. What's wrong?"

"I don't—" Her breath caught. "Belong," she sniffed, punctuating the words. "To Faeryn anymore." She howled in agony, writhing on the floor.

"I don't understand. Calliope, can you at least get off the floor and talk with me?"

The obedient fae untwisted her tortured limbs and sprang to her feet, shoulders still shuddering with feeling, but managing to hold back further sobs. I led her to Evita's small sitting room, which was tucked away into a slice of the round house's lower level. The book-filled nook was dim, with late-evening light filtering in through the single small window. I flicked on a hanging lamp and directed Calliope to the chair that Evita kept for guests, settling myself into what was, effectively, Evita's throne. It was good to be princess, I thought, as I nestled into the comfortable, blanket-covered armchair.

"Now," I said, addressing my newest subject who sniffled quietly in the chair across from me. "it's up to you. You can tell me why Faeryn banished you, or you can tell me why being set free makes you wail like that." At this, she started crying again. There were tissues on the table, and I handed her one. This wasn't the first time someone had broken down in that particular chair.

"It was something he told her," Calliope managed, between gulps of air. "The Knight. She was—" Calliope hiccuped, but pressed on, choking the words out. "Complaining about me, and telling him how I—" She shook her head. "I don't know. How I make her uncomfortable, I guess. And he said that if I make her feel that way, she should just send me away and tell me not to come back." Her tears had soaked through the thin tissue, and I handed her another.

"So that's why she sent you away? Because this Knight of hers told her to?"

Calliope's fists were balled, knuckles white. She nodded tersely.

"Calliope," I said, watching the thin fae shudder miserably in the chair across from me. "I want to help you, but I don't understand. Faeryn is so cruel to you, but you cling to her so tightly. Why? Is it really just because she's royalty? You know, I'm a princess too, at least, technically. And I can tell you, it's not all that special, really. I promise."

"Oh, I know that well enough," said Calliope bitterly. "It certainly never did me any good to be royal."

"Huh? Calliope, what are you talking about?"

I didn't know anything about Calliope's origins, but her humble, subservient attitude certainly hadn't suggested a royal heritage. That was, apparently, a large part of the problem. She just didn't have the proper temperament for royalty.

"I was the second-born grandchild of the High Elf of my village. My grandfather raised me to be a fierce hunter like my brother, Leaf, but all I ever wanted to do was dance and play with the puppies."

One day, Calliope told me, the elven village received royal visitors from a distant court, the Faerie Queen and her young daughter. Calliope had joined the rest of her family in the audience hall, holding her favorite of her grandfather's prized hunting dogs, and that was when she first set eyes on Faeryn.

"She was so beautiful. I had never seen anyone like her before. I was shocked when my grandfather told me that they were sending me away to live with the faeries, but if it meant that I could be near her, I didn't mind. They told me that the princess had asked for me, and they let me take my favorite puppy with me."

Her new life with the faeries was unlike anything she had ever known before. She was completely free, allowed to do anything and be anyone she wished, and so, she became herself, shaking off her grandfather's uncomfortable expectations. Her only duty was to care for the puppy, and to bring the dog to visit the princess whenever she asked. Living inside Faeryn's sparkling creation, she became more and more enamored by the brilliant intermagical, and Calliope came to live for those moments when she could bring the dog to Faeryn and see the joy of it light the girl's somber face.

"All I wanted was to be near her," Calliope confessed. "So I asked the Queen for a favor, and she made me one of Faeryn's handmaidens."

"And it's been like this ever since?" I asked.

"No," she said. "I don't think Faeryn even noticed that I was serving her, at least not at first, but…" Her face reddened, and she looked down at her knees. "Visc did. He started doing things to me. Seeing what he could get away with. How much I could take. One time he used me as a footstool for an entire meeting…" Calliope trailed off, refusing to look at me.

"Oh, Calliope, I know Visc has a cruel streak. I'm so sorry that he—"

"No," said Calliope. She turned her eyes up to me, and they were blazing with emotion. "It's not like that. I didn't mind. I liked it, actually. Visc appreciated me. He enjoyed me. But after that meeting, Faeryn found out. She was so embarrassed by it. She blamed Visc, not me, but she was so cruel to me after that. It's been all I can do to keep her from sending me away, entirely." Her face cracked, and fresh tears welled at the corners of her eyes. "At least, until tonight."

She liked it? I contemplated that idea. It wasn't all that different from what some people got up to, at the play parties I had been attending, I realized, glad that I'd gotten to have those experiences, as a reference. Before I'd seen what people did there, I wouldn't have been able to understand what Calliope was telling me at all. And, even if I didn't entirely understand her reasons, Calliope was an adult, and it was my job to respect her choices.

"So, you still want to keep serving Faeryn, even after everything?"

Calliope nodded miserably. "I love her. She is so creative and beautiful, and brilliant. She burns so brightly, and she is so strong in spite of her weaknesses." Her face lit up, in admiration of the princess. "And, she chose me. She saved me. She turned my entire world upside down and made me who I am. I owe her everything. I owe her my life."

"I'll talk to her," I said, clasping the elf's bony shoulder comfortingly. "You can stay in here tonight, okay?" I told her, standing up to leave the cozy study. I wanted to do what I could for the sweet, sad girl, but first I needed to get my cousin's side of the story.

When I stepped back out into the bookcase-lined vestibule that made up the lower story of the round house, I came face-to-face with Arlee who had just closed the door to the bathroom.

"He never came," she told me, shaking her head sadly, "my lady's Knight. He said he would, but he didn't. I don't know why he keeps doing this to her."

I shrugged, thinking about what Calliope said, "Maybe it's because he's not here to see the fallout."

"Maybe," she agreed.

"May I?" I asked, gesturing to the closed bathroom door. She nodded.

Inside, the air was thick with steam, and Faeryn lay in the deep tub at the center of a twilit forest glade.

"Hey, cousin, it's me," I said, coming toward her through the mist.

"He didn't come to me," she moaned. She lay with her head back, eyes closed against the beauty of the scene.

"Yeah, that's what Arlee said. Is that who you were visiting when you went away?"

She nodded miserably.

"He told me he had to leave the city because of my mother. I wanted to believe him, but now I know I've been a fool. He promised me his life, and his fealty, but he hasn't visited me since I left my mother's court. Not even once! And when I went to him, he barely had any time for me at all."

"Your Knight?"

"Is he?" she bleated piteously. "It doesn't feel like it. But who can blame him? It's such a bother to care for me, with all my needs and difficulties. And it's not like I make it easier, being so irritable and agitated. I'm surprised anyone can stand to be around me at all. But, can you imagine how frustrating it must be to be me, stuck here, sick and miserable all the time, feeling like a burden to everyone?"

"Oh cousin, you're not a burden. We all love you and want to help you. In fact, just now, Calliope was telling me how much she—"

"Calliope?" she interjected harshly. "Am I supposed to be flattered by that foolish girl's obsession with royalty? It doesn't matter what I do, or who I actually am, she just goes on sniveling and serving anyway. That's not real admiration, it's just baseless fealty."

She didn't know.

"Faeryn, Calliope is an elf, right? How did she come to be part of your mother's court, do you remember?"

"Oh," she said, with a dismissive wave of her hand. "She was one of the refugees, I think. Sometimes folk will steal away with us when we visit foreign realms. My mother will sometimes let them join our court, if they have the proper temperament for a faerie."

"The proper temperament," I echoed. "Unlike the vila?"

"Mmhmm," Faeryn agreed. "She might be a confounding irritation, but she's not inclined to be a liar."

Then hopefully you'll believe what she tells you, I thought, as I said my goodbyes and left my cousin in the steamy bathroom. This was a story for Calliope to tell, for herself.

Chapter 33

I collapsed against the bathroom door, exhausted by the effort of handling other people's emotions. At that moment, the front door opened.

"Jaah," I sighed, stepping forward and letting myself fall into their arms. "Can you hold me for a minute?" They wrapped their arms around me, and I melted into them as the energy flowed between us, relaxing and revitalizing me.

"I'm sorry," they said after a long moment.

"Huh?" Buried in their arms, soaking in the warmth of their energy, I couldn't remember what they were apologizing for.

"I'm sorry I upset you earlier. You're right. If you told me you were going to do something risky like that, I wouldn't like it at all."

Oh, that's right. Remembering the scene I made earlier, at the dinner table, I released them and stepped back from their embrace, shoulders hunching in embarrassment at the memory.

"You want to take a walk and talk about it?" I nodded, and they opened the door for me. I stuffed my hands into my pockets and stepped out into the warm summer night. Inside my pocket, I found the ring I'd made earlier and rubbed the rough edge of it against my thumb.

"I don't know what's been going on with me lately, Fiona," Jaah confessed, walking beside me in Evita's darkening garden. "Where were you this afternoon? I couldn't find you."

"Oh, I went to meet a teacher that Evita found for me. By the time she told me about the lesson, I was already late. I made this." I pulled the ring out of my pocket and held it out to Jaah. They took it, twisting the shining circle in their hand. After a moment, they tried the fit and slid the ring onto one long finger.

"I was looking for you," they said. "I got so upset when I couldn't find you. I don't know why. Nobody else was worried. It's been like that all summer. Since I told you I loved you, it's like the flavor of your energy changed. I haven't been able to get enough of it. Almost like I'm addicted to you."

zrp zrp
my energy

"My energy," I started, echoing my internal voice. "Has a flavor? That makes it sound like you're eating me."

"I don't know why I said that. I shouldn't have. Don't tell your family, okay? I already know what they think of me and my magic."

"What do you mean, Jaah? My family loves you."

They shrugged, twisting the ring on their finger distractedly. "They don't love my magic. Do you think I didn't notice how fast they stepped in to teach you how to do it the right way? To use good, clean elemental power? Couldn't have you making evil magic like me."

"Jaah, what are you talking about? What magic…" I paused, remembering the gales of wind whipping the curtains of Evita's spare room. "Oh, you mean…"

They nodded, eyes smoldering with internal fire.

"Fiona, what do you know about vampires?"

"Jaah, I don't—"

They interrupted me. "Your mother called me a concubus. She's not wrong. I raise sexual energy, and I feed on it. What do you call someone who feeds on other people?"

"You're not a vampire, Jaah. Vampires drink blood."

"Semantics," Jaah spat. "People like to say that, but what is blood? It's life force, it's energy. It doesn't feel like I'm hurting people. Everyone always comes back for more. You wouldn't think they would, if I were hurting them. But, ever since that man called me 'the darkness' I haven't been able to shake the feeling of being bad. Of being evil."

"Why are you saying all this, Jaah?" I asked. "You're starting to scare me."

"I don't know. I don't know why I'm saying any of this," Jaah said, looking down at their hands. The silver ring glinted in the moonlight. "Fiona, where did you say you got this ring?"

"I made it," I told them. "Earlier today. I told you. Why?"

"That's some strong magic," they said, twisting the ring off their finger and pressing it firmly back into my palm. They made quick snapping motions in the air with their hands, catching thoughts like invisible bugs trying to fly away. "As soon as I put it on, it's like everything I've been thinking and keeping to myself just fell out my mouth."

I stared down at the little circle. "Yeah, I know what you mean. That's how I felt at dinner, when I got so upset and stormed off, like that. I worry about you every time you leave me at home to go investigate something dangerous, but logically, I know that you can handle yourself in those kinds of situations. I didn't mean to—"

"It's okay," they said, interrupting. "No worries, I get it. I don't think you could help it, considering."

I stuffed the ring back into my pocket. At the same moment, Jaah's phone blared to life with a noise I'd never heard before.

"What's that?" I asked as they pulled the device out of their pocket and silenced the alarm.

"It's a local disaster alert," they said, reading the message. "I'm a first responder. Woah, look at this."

They held the phone out for me to read.

"A sinkhole?"

"Sounds like it," Jaah said. "Wild. Want to go check it out?"

Letting Pythia know that we would be right back, we climbed into my van and headed down the darkening driveway. To our surprise, we found Urb at the base of the hill, carrying a bottle of mead.

"Sorry I'm late," he said, once we rolled down the window. "Did I miss the whole party?"

"No, we're just popping out for a second." I told him about the message Jaah just received. "Do you want to come?"

"Sure," said Urb, hopping in the back seat. "Sounds interesting."

Chapter 34

"So what made you so late to dinner?" Jaah asked.

"Bad luck?" I guessed.

"Not at all," Urb answered. "Good luck, actually. I, uh…" He smiled sheepishly. "I had a date."

"No kidding!" I said. "That's great! You didn't have to cut your date short to come here."

"No, that's alright," he said. "It didn't get cut short. It ran pretty long, actually. It was a lunch date."

"Turn left," said Jaah as we reached the bottom of the hill. "It looks like these coordinates are somewhere downtown."

"You don't think…" I said, meeting Urb's eyes in the rear-view mirror.

"That Evita had a garden party that made an evil church fall into a sinkhole?" he finished. "Nah, that's crazy."

"So," said Jaah, turning and waggling their eyebrows at Urb. "How'd you guys meet?"

"It's a pretty wild coincidence, actually," said Urb, leaning forward excitedly. "We met online, on that forum I've been telling you about, Fiona. Somebody with the screenname AlphaBSira, started an argument about how the serpent in the garden of Eden couldn't possibly be Loki, because it was obviously Lilith."

"Um, what now?" said Jaah. "You lost me. The serpent can't be what because of who?"

"Urb has been telling me his alternative theories about the Bible these past few weeks, while we've been going to church," I explained. "Loki is Lucifer and God is Baldur. Or possibly Zeus. If you're interested, I'll fill you in later." I flapped my hand dismissively. "But who is Lilith supposed to be, now?"

There's an interesting little text from the Middle Ages about Lilith, Urb explained. It says that she was actually the first wife of Adam. God created Adam first, but eventually he decided that it wasn't good for man to be alone, so he created woman from the same clay. That was Lilith.

"But when Adam said, 'You are fit only to lie below me' Lilith said, 'The heck I am! We're made from the same stuff. We're equals, and if you don't see it that way, I'm out of here."

"That sounds fair to me!" I said, reaching over to squeeze Jaah's hand. They smiled back at me.

"So, Lilith left, and God made Eve out of Adam's rib, in the hopes that she wouldn't get so uppity. But Lilith wasn't gone, she'd just left the garden. And, after the things God did to punish her, I'd be willing to bet she was angry. What if she snuck back inside to convince her ex's new boo to grow a backbone, and get one over on the big guy, as a bonus? Sounds pretty reasonable to me."

"Yeah," said Jaah, nodding. "I like that idea."

"But I thought Eve was the all-mother. If there were two original women, wouldn't that mean there were two original lines, one from Eve and one from Lilith?" I asked, considering the implications. "I wonder which one I came from?"

"Lilith," said Jaah and Urb, together, and our laughter spilled out the van's open windows as we drove through the warm summer night.

"So, then you two went on a date?" I prompted.

"Yeah," said Urb. "We started chatting about books, and they mentioned the flying buttresses of the university library. It's lucky that I'm into architecture, and happened to recognize the description. Otherwise, we might never have figured out that we live in the same place."

"Lucky, huh?" I said with a pleased smile. "How about that?" Maybe Urb's traveling companion was finally giving him a break, after our little chat. I sure hoped so.

Following Jaah's directions, I pulled off the main road and onto a familiar side street. I caught Urb's eye in the rear-view mirror and returned his wide-eyed expression. We were getting awfully close to where the grand re-opening of the church would be held tomorrow.

"It can't be," I said, as we turned the corner and saw the silent flashing lights of emergency vehicles. They illuminated a crowd of onlookers gathered to witness the extraordinary act of nature that had befallen…

"The Valley of Christ's Heart Church," said Jaah, shaking their head. "Well, well, well."

We got out of the van and joined the throng of onlookers. Jaah clearly wasn't needed as a first responder. It took us time to get down from the hill and the professionals had everything well in hand.

"What happened? What happened?" a red-faced man crowed, repeating himself until a uniformed officer gave in and answered him.

"Sir, please calm down. We don't have much information right now, but it looks like the church collapsed into an abandoned sub-basement. Could'a been all that water that soaked into the foundation after they put out the fire, or something. I don't know. Building's condemned, though, that's for sure. This one, and the little café behind it. Shame about that, they made a good sandwich."

"Well, I guess we're not going to church tomorrow," said Urb, as we climbed back in the van to drive back to the hill.

"Are you still trying to go to that Women's Group?" Jaah asked, with a look that said they hoped I wasn't.

"Yeah," I answered. "I think so. Nora asked me to come back. I'm worried about her."

Jaah nodded. "That's fair. Well, help her if you can, but make sure you wear that camera necklace again, okay? The videos you got last week were crystal clear."

"Wear the…" My jaw dropped, aghast. "The video necklace? What? Wait, is my new necklace a spy camera?"

"I told you that," they said, then paused and considered. "Or, I thought I did, anyway."

I met their eyes, and their look of sheepish innocence made me smile. I rolled my eyes at them and sighed, picking up the crystal on my chest to examine it. The necklace was beautiful, a large clear quartz point, with a pretty silver setting and a strange flat gemstone that could be a lens, I realized, now that I knew what I was looking for. I never would have guessed that it was a camera.

"Is it waterproof?" I asked, suddenly worried. "I haven't been taking it off to shower."

"Yeah," said Jaah with a chuckle. "I've noticed. I thought it was on purpose, but, uh, I think you should keep on doing it." They gave me a lecherous little wink. "The crystal powers it, so there's no electrical components. No reason it can't get wet. A little technomagic experiment some friends and I have been working on. Pretty neat, huh?"

"Oh yeah," Urb agreed. "That's really nice."

Back at the hill, some time later, I stood by the open window of the breezy upstairs bedroom, letting the summer night air cool my sweat-speckled skin. I felt tired and a little drained, and when I reached inside myself, I could feel that my energy store had been depleted. Behind me, in bed, Jaah had rolled over and gone to sleep like a well-fed cat. I took a few deep breaths of the sweet evening air, pulling the energy deep into my belly, filling myself back up.

zrp zrp
doesn't hurt

"No," I said into the silence of the night. "It doesn't."

Part 8 - Void

Chapter 35

"Into a sinkhole?" Evita asked. "Truly?" Her expression was a mix of horror and macabre fascination.

"Collapsed into the sub-basement, actually. Right, Fiona?" Faeryn corrected, and I nodded my agreement.

"At least you didn't have to get up early to go to church," Egan quipped.

"Always focused on the important things in life, huh?" I teased. I wasn't used to having a brother, but I realized how much I missed his energy while he was away.

"Yep!" he agreed, grabbing another piece of toast from the pile.

It was nice to have a lazy Sunday morning together on the hill.

Pythia stopped by the kitchen earlier and muttered something about being a coffee person, not a morning person, before disappearing out to the garden with a large, steaming mug. Jaah wasn't even awake yet, but the rest of us were gathered in Evita's sunny kitchen.

Zinnia and Azalea chased marshmallows around cups of hot chocolate, and Zelai was tucked into a window nook, sketching a spider who was making its web in a corner.

I sat at the table with Faeryn, Arlee, Urb and Egan, eating a breakfast of eggs and sautéed vegetables while Evita still bustled around at the counter behind us.

"Sit down and have some breakfast, Mom. All of us are taken care of," Egan called over his shoulder.

All of us, except Calliope, I realized, as the elf's wispy head appeared at the top of the stairs with wide anxious eyes.

"Come, join us," I said, catching her eye and beckoning her forward.

She made her way nervously across the kitchen and sat at the table, her thin back hunched.

"Queen Evita, allow me to introduce you to the newest member of our court," I said, standing up to muster as much formality as I could, considering the fact that we were all eating breakfast. "She found herself, er, unexpectedly unattached yesterday, and I gave her a place with us. What do you say, Mom?"

Evita shot Faeryn a look that made my cousin blush deeply pink. "Of course, Calliope, dear," Evita answered. "You are welcome here."

"I'm sorry," said Faeryn, hanging her head. "I shouldn't have done that. I wasn't feeling like myself yesterday, but I've managed to get it under control, I think."

"I'm glad, cousin," I told her, putting a hand on her thin shoulder. "It's hard being disappointed."

Her eyes flashed up at me. "You think that's all it is?" she shot back, with a fierce expression I didn't expect. She took a few slow breaths, getting her emotions back under control. "There it is again. Been getting stronger all summer. It's not just my illness that's been making me irritable."

"Faeryn, dear, what are you talking about?" asked Evita, handing a steaming cup of tea to Calliope, who quivered in the corner of the kitchen, making herself look small.

"It's this curse," said Faeryn matter-of-factly. "I figured out what was happening yesterday."

Faeryn spent most of last night in the bath, soaking in the magical spring water and lamenting her Knight's absence. In a particularly dark moment, she disassociated completely, turning control over to Visc.

"When I came back to myself," she told us. "He had written on the foggy mirror. It said, 'Look what she's done to you!' in his big, sloppy writing, and that got me thinking because, well, as far as I'm aware, he's never considered Faeryn before."

"Look what she's done to you?" I repeated. "Who is she?"

"It was something you mentioned yesterday morning that gave me the clue, actually," Faeryn said, turning her face up to me. "When you asked about the vilas."

"The vilas?" Evita asked,

Faeryn had been trying to find the source of her curse all summer, but the effort of trying to keep herself alive had left her with little energy, and any extra strength she drummed up was spent on my magical education. "It was such a welcome distraction," she assured me. "I didn't give a second thought to that Velia woman, after I banished her."

I was grateful to Faeryn for banishing Velia, after all the trouble she had made this spring. It wasn't only that she had chased me out of town, and tried to prevent me from meeting my birth family. Velia had also been helping the old Deacon of Christ's Heart with his plans to enrich himself and seize even more local power. Once her plot had been discovered, Faeryn had arranged to have her sent far away. If Velia dared to set foot in the Queen's kingdom again, she would face immediate imprisonment. Faeryn had trusted her mother's guards to enforce the sentence.

"Velia is back?" Evita asked. "Are my sister's minions as incompetent as that?" she added, smugly.

"No, of course not. But they were only watching for her physical body, weren't they?" Faeryn snapped. "I'm sorry," she said, and took another deep breath. "I feel like I'm constantly apologizing these days. Her curse is playing on my natural weaknesses and making me even more irritable and fatigued than usual. And, of course, my feeble body makes it all the more exhausting to fight against it."

After sending Velia away, Faeryn had chosen to put the vila out of her mind and focused on other matters.

"Sounds like she didn't forget you, though," Egan quipped.

"No," Faeryn agreed. "She didn't. She's been targeting me all summer, and I didn't even realize what was happening. And she's not doing it alone." Once she identified Velia as the curse's sender, it was easy for her to see where her own illness ended and the curse began. In the bath last night, Faeryn had scried in the spring water, learning all she could. "There's an enormous amount of human energy powering her spell. What I can't figure out is how she's channeling it."

"Oh," I said, in sudden realization. "I think I might know." I told Faeryn about the swirling, crashing energy that I had felt at my first Christ's Heart service. "She was with the church when she left, wasn't she? I bet she's still with them."

"Prayer energy," Evita said thoughtfully. "That's certainly one way to channel human power."

"Wait," I said, furrowing my brow. "What about me? I haven't been feeling irritable or exhausted. Why would Velia curse you, and leave me alone?"

"I was curious about that myself," said Faeryn. "Are you protected in some way that I'm not?"

"No," I told her. "I don't think so."

At the same moment, Evita answered. "Yes, she is."

"I am?"

"You'd think you'd remember magic you set on yourself," Evita admonished, and I considered, racking my brain.

"Oh! That first protection spell!" I exclaimed, remembering. I had set safeguards to protect myself against the energy of the Christ's Heart Church, during my very first magic lesson. "Did that really work?"

"Of course, dear," said Evita. "Why do you think we're doing all this?"

"I'm going to start making preparations to return to the city," said Faeryn, and every head in the kitchen turned toward her in surprise.

"Really?" I asked. Faeryn was hell-bent on staying out of her spring, and making her own way outside of her mother's dominion.

She nodded. "The most important thing, now, is to learn as much as possible about this curse, and figure out how to defeat it. Or turn it back on its sender," she added, with a hint of Visc's signature menace. She would have more resources at her disposal if she returned to the seat of her mother's power to make her investigation. "I'm glad that you have secured a place here," Faeryn said, addressing Calliope. "So, there is no reason for you to return to my mother's court with me. I'll have plenty of support there, and you won't have to worry about Visc anymore."

"Um, actually," I started, but my eyes met Calliope's, and she silenced me with a single shake of her head. "Actually, that'll be great. We'll be happy to have her." I finished. It wasn't my place to tell Faeryn what I had learned. It was Calliope's story, and I would let her tell it in her own time.

Chapter 36

Evita waylaid me as I prepared to leave for the Women's Group and then back to Portal Land.

"A little bird told me we won't be meeting next week," said Evita. "I planned to explore the fifth and final element that we call spirit, or aether or void, but…" She smiled sadly. "The universe has its own ways of teaching us important lessons." She placed a smooth black orb in my hand, wrapping my fingers around it. "This is for your mother. Give her my condolences, please. And my thanks."

"Okay," I said. "Sure. I don't know when I'll see her next, but I'll give it to her."

I nestled the heavy orb into my bag. It wasn't the first time that Evita had done something I didn't immediately understand, and it wouldn't be the last. I decided not to worry about it. Like the piece of focaccia that she gave me, that turned out to be for Urb, I was confident everything would become clear soon enough.

When I approached the large brick house, I saw it was packed with bodies. Gathered to discuss the latest disaster to befall the Valley of Christ's Heart Church, I assumed. I slipped inside, part of the crowd.

"…with all these awful things that have happened, what are we supposed to think, Temperance? Why is God punishing us? We haven't done anything to deserve this!" a woman's voice wailed.

Temperance Rex stood at the front of the gathering, head and shoulders above everyone else. She must be standing on a stool or something, I thought, as I watched her scowl down at the questioner.

"Who are you to question the Lord? Is your faith as weak as that, sister?" Temperance asked. "Our hardships are a test sent by God, and the faithful accept those challenges with strength and grace," she said, glowering down at the woman. "And still gather to worship even when this dark, sinful world makes it feel impossible," Temperance intoned, raising her fist proudly, then she looked down at the hapless woman again and added, "I don't recall seeing you on the mountaintop with the faithful, last Sunday, did I, Eugenia? Yet, you dare to stand here and question God's divine plan?"

A low rumble ran through the crowd at this. "God punishes the doubters along with the faithless," I heard someone mutter under their breath.

zrp zrp
all punished

I put a hand to my stomach, rubbing away the strange feeling. Was Temperance really saying that God punishes the faithful as a test? What is the point of faithfulness, then, I wondered, if you're still going to be punished?

zrp zrp
after life

That's right, it was the promise of eternal bliss or eternal torment, after death, that was supposedly on the line. It was easy to forget. Since I hadn't been raised to believe in either Heaven or hell, the whole concept felt incredibly implausible. How would it even be possible to have eternal bliss, I wondered, when you know that other people are experiencing eternal suffering? Is part of the bliss of Heaven supposed to be that you forget?

A touch on my shoulder made me jump, and I whirled to see what had caused the sudden electric jolt. It was Nora, of course. She gestured for me to follow, and I did. We didn't head up the stairs to her room like I expected. Instead, we headed out the back door.

"Can I ask you a question?" I said, as soon as the door closed, cutting off the noise of the crowd in the house. "How can anyone expect to be happy in Heaven, knowing that there are people suffering in hell?"

Nora shrugged, not looking at me. "There are people suffering everywhere. What are we supposed to do about it?"

"Um, your Christian duty, I thought?" I answered indignantly. "Like, try to help them, or something?"

"That's what we are doing!" Nora replied, whirling on me. "Trying to save people from eternal damnation, and give them the glory of Heaven." Her eyes stared daggers at me. "That's the whole point. That's why we do any of this."

"You don't have any empathy for the miserable people here on Earth, huh? Just suffer, then burn?" I retorted, matching her fierce energy. "It makes me sad to imagine it, but then again, I care about people, so…"

"Empathy is a trick of the devil," she snapped back. "And sadness is a sin. If you're obedient and keep a smile on your face, you'll have your eternal reward, and if you don't, you'll burn in hell. That's all there is to it."

"I don't know why I came here," I told her. "You don't sound anything like the girl from last week."

"Last week, the church hadn't fallen into a sinkhole," she spat. "Because of my doubt and disobedience." Her face cracked, but she recovered herself quickly, reigning in the emotion.

"Because of…" I repeated, trying to make sense of what she was saying. "Nora, you didn't make the church collapse! How could you have had anything to do with it?"

She flashed her pale eyes at me, and I noticed that they were rimmed with red, like she had been crying.

"You really want to know?" she asked, and I nodded. We walked in silence until we came to a wooden structure next to a small stream. Nora gestured for me to climb inside, and I did. It must have originally been built for fishing, I thought, as I climbed onto the short bench overhanging the water. She sat next to me, flicking on a set of string lights whose reflection sparkled in the stream below our feet.

"What's going on?" I asked, after a long, silent moment.

She took a deep breath and replied.

"Uncle always says that I'm the backbone of the church," she told me, looking down at her swinging feet as she talked. "After the old Deacon and his son left so suddenly. But, you probably don't know anything about that, do you? Well, Aunt Tempy and I were the ones who held the congregation together until Uncle could get back from Europe."

"Oh yeah?" I replied, keeping my expression carefully blank. I knew quite a bit about what had happened with the Deacon and his son, actually.

"And I started messing with my grandmother's old books, and the church caught fire. I didn't blame myself for it, then, but the more that I keep thinking about it…"

"But, Nora, why——"

"And I've been so focused on my own worldly concerns, like how I don't want to get married, that I've gone and disrespected God, again, and now look what's happened."

"You think the church fell into a sinkhole because you don't want to marry Byron?" I asked. "Nora, you get how ridiculous that sounds, right?"

Our bodies were close together on the small bench, and in the hairsbreadth of space between our shoulders, I felt her shrug. Then we sat in silence for a long moment.

"What, uh…" I considered what to ask her, then finished. "What's so wrong with Byron?" I could think of some solid reasons that I wouldn't want to marry that hot-headed young man, but I wanted Nora to keep talking.

"I don't know," she answered finally. "Nothing really. Father and Uncle both like him, and he's a godly man. And I've heard my Aunt's marriage lessons enough times. I don't expect happiness. I have Jesus's love to hold me and keep me. It's only…" she paused, trying to find the right words. "Women's bodies are just more attractive than men's, right? That's why men can't control themselves, and they teach us to cover ourselves to help with the temptation. I guess I just learned that lesson too well, because whenever I think about Byron touching me…" she paused again, and I felt her shudder. "I just can't imagine letting him do that. It makes me want to throw up, or punch someone, or, I don't know, something worse than that. But…" She shook her head, then swallowed hard, looking resolute. "We can't trust our bodies, so I'm just going to have to figure out how to get over it."

Of course you can't trust your body, in a belief system where sexuality is controlled and sadness and empathy are both sins, I thought angrily. I would hate to live like Nora, fighting against my own impulses like that.

zrp zrp
why tight

Huh? What was that supposed to mean? As I asked myself the question, though, I realized that I was holding every muscle in my body rigid and making myself as small as possible, so that I wouldn't touch Nora any more than I absolutely had to.

Nora was lost in thought, staring down at the twinkling lights reflected in the water. Intentionally, I released my taut muscles, letting my limbs relax until our upper arms touched. The sensation interrupted her silent contemplation, and she glanced over at me.

"Sorry," I said reflexively, pulling my arm back. Why did I do that? I wasn't entirely sure. What's up, body? I asked. There was no answer.

No real surprise. My mom didn't know what to do with all my odd sensitivities, so she taught me to push through and do it anyway, and so I learned to detach from my body when I was young, to cope. This might be a good opportunity to tune back in, I thought, glancing at Nora. She was watching the stream, deep in thought.

I anchored myself using the four closest elements I could find, the fire that buzzed through the electric string lights, the burbling brook, the wood underneath me and the breeze on my face, and I sank into my body to try to figure out what was the matter.

With my eyes closed, I visualized the red blood pumping through my veins, and the tension, like cords of steel, that was holding my arm tight to my side, away from Nora. I followed those cords away from my prickling skin, and deeper inside my body. They led into my heart. No surprise, I suppose. I took a deep breath and dove into my heart center to see what I would find there.

It was me, or at least, a version of me, which shouldn't be a surprise either, I realized. I must have been about eleven years old, adolescent and awkward, with lank brown hair hanging around my shoulders. I held steel cables in my hands, and I was hauling with all my might. As I got closer, I could hear what I was muttering under my breath.

"Don't be gay, don't be gay, don't be gay."

Above my child-self, a giant specter loomed into view. It wore the disapproving face of my mother, and as it towered over us, the muttering increased to a fever pitch. Well, that made sense, at least. Mom had never told me that I couldn't be gay, but she made it clear that it wasn't ideal. I was already lazy and fat and forgetful. There was no way I was going to let myself disappoint her even more by adding that on top.

I took a deep breath, and exhaled, blowing the specter of my mother away. Then, I stepped forward and took the cables in my hand.

"It's okay," I told my younger self, letting the thick cords fall from my hands. "It's okay. We can be gay."

As the tension released, and my body expanded, taking up space, my arm pressed against Nora's again. She leaned into me, and in response, I felt my heart start beating faster. Jaah was right all along, I realized. I really liked Nora.

"I'm sorry," she said. "I shouldn't have snapped at you like that. You're right. I guess I probably didn't make the church fall into the sinkhole. It does sound pretty ridiculous, now that I've said it out loud. It's just that I'm in my own head so much. I don't have anyone to talk to about this stuff." She turned to look at me. "Except for you, Ona."

"Sounds lonely."

"It is," she agreed. "And it's about to get even lonelier. The folks inside don't know it yet, but after what happened last night, Uncle is going to be moving the church down to Eugene. I'll be uprooted again, just when I was starting to feel settled. Thanks for coming out here with me, Ona," she said, turning to look at the water again. "It's my favorite thing about this house, and you're the first person I've ever shown it to. I couldn't bring Byron out here. He'd get the wrong idea."

"Even though you say he's a good, godly man?" I asked.

"You know what they say," said Nora with a shrug. "Men can't help it." Then she shuddered. Remembering her upcoming nuptials, I suspected. She confirmed this a few moments later when she said, "I wonder if it would be easier, with Byron, if I could try it first, maybe."

"Try it?" I repeated.

"Yeah, you know…" she trailed off, then glanced over at me before continuing. "Just, like, the kissing and stuff. You're a girl, like me, so it would be safe, right, because nobody would take things too far? Just to try it, for practice, you know."

"Practice…kissing?" I asked.

"Yeah," said Nora, looking at me with wide, hopeful eyes.

Chapter 37

"Girl!" screeched Pythia, when I told her the story on Monday night. She waved her arms and kicked her legs, balanced precariously on a bar stool. "See, I TOLD you, Brother. You didn't believe me. But I told you!"

"Oh, I believed you," said Jaah, looking irritably over at their sister. "I just wasn't excited about it. I don't trust this, and I don't like it."

"Aw, you're just jealous. But you can't have it both ways, Brother! Freedom is as freedom does."

"But I didn't even do it!" I exclaimed, exasperated.

"You didn't? Girl!" Pythia scolded.

Nora reached over and brushed a strand of hair off my face, tucking it behind my ear. She was looking at me. Really looking. A small pink tongue darted out to moisten the very edge of her lips, and she leaned toward me, dark lashes fluttering closed.

I jerked back.

"I'm sorry, Nora, I can't." I stood up, backing away from her. "This isn't what practice feels like, and I'm not going to lie for you."

She didn't say anything as I walked away, but I felt her eyes on me, like I had on the day the church burned. I wondered if I would ever see her again.

"Aw, really?" Pythia wheedled, "Poor girl's about to get married off to some man. Seems like the least you could have done was send her off with a nice kiss."

I rolled my eyes. "Yeah, I guess I could have, for her sake, but it didn't feel right. I've admitted to myself that I like women. At this point, I've even accepted that I like Nora. If we kiss, I don't want it to be practice, I want her to know that I mean it."

"Whatever you say," said Pythia, sounding unconvinced.

"What is that infernal buzzing?" whined an extraordinarily old fae with large, pendulous ears who sat nearby nursing his drink.

"Oh sorry," I said, realizing that it was my phone vibrating on the bar. I scooped it up and answered it.

"Hello? Mom, what's wrong? Okay, I understand. Alright. I'm coming now. Bye."

"What's up?" Jaah asked, seeing the expression on my face.

"Evita told me that the universe would be teaching me its own lessons about void and spirit," I told Jaah and Pythia. "I guess this is what she meant. I'll be driving back to California tonight. My grandma is dying."

"You want me to come with you?" Jaah asked. "I've got a job scheduled for tomorrow, but I could move it." I shook my head in reply, and they didn't press the matter. "Well, you might as well make a doctor's appointment while you're down there," they suggested. One of our friends, an intermagical seer, warned me that there was something wrong with my blood. I hadn't had the chance to get it checked out yet, but Jaah knew that I still had a doctor down in California.

"Good idea," I agreed.

I drove all night. As the morning sun crested over the trees, I got a text from my mother.

Come straight to the hospital. It won't be long now.

There's nothing that makes spirit more obvious than its absence, I thought to myself as I laid my grandmother's cool hand across her chest. When I arrived, she was sleeping. Now, she was not, and even though her body still looked the same, lying there in the small white hospital bed, I could feel that she was no longer the same. She was no longer anyone at all. She was gone.

It was a good death. Peaceful, with her family gathered around her bedside. My mother was there, and her brother and sister, too. I saw my cousin dab at a tear with a tissue, but she was adopted, like me. Everyone else was dry-eyed. Serious and stoic, like their mother had been.

I'd been learning to be authentic and embrace my own emotions, in Oregon with my birth family. Here, though, surrounded by the people who raised me, it was almost impossible not to put the mask back on.

222

The funeral was the next day. How she pulled that off, I wasn't sure, but Grandma had made all the arrangements herself. There was nothing for my mom to do but to assuage her ever-present anxiety, she had gone to the church hours early, anyway. I followed along a little while later. It had been more than a decade since I'd last set foot in my grandmother's old church, and it felt strange walking through the enormous double doors. I found my mom in the reception hall, poking at a flower arrangement, looking tense.

Mom looked me up and down with a sneer. "You look nice," she lied.

"What's wrong with what I'm wearing?" I asked.

"Nothing. I'm just confused why you would wear that to a funeral." I had put on one of the simpler dresses from my new collection. It had long bell sleeves and a dark floral pattern, and I had thought I looked perfectly appropriate in it. Now, though, I felt ridiculous, and I tugged at the neckline uncomfortably. As I exchanged condolences with my grandmother's friends, I did my best to shake off the oppressive feeling of disapproval, with some success. I'd had a lot of practice weathering my mother's negative opinions about my appearance. It's just the way she is.

I let out a heavy sigh, and smiled tiredly to myself as the last of the reception line tottered off toward the refreshments. I had run my 'condolences' script successfully, saying the right things at the right times. The exercise had been exhausting, but I did well, and I was proud of myself. I felt like I had performed 'humanity' successfully.

A lot of intermagicals hate small-talk. I don't mind it, though. It's like a dance. The steps don't come naturally to me, but I've been working at it for a long time, and I can fake it well enough, especially when I know my role. Today was straightforward. I was the grieving granddaughter, putting on a brave face, with lots of tight, sad smiles and hand clasping. Alone now, I let the mask drop and felt my tired cheek muscles relax out of their performative smile. I wasn't alone, though. Mom was still there.

"One of my friends told me they ran into that old boyfriend of yours the other day," she said, turning toward me.

"Oh yeah?" I replied, replacing my polite mask.

"Yeah, apparently he's wearing skirts and calling himself 'Rose' now."

"Calling herself, Rose," I corrected automatically. I could feel myself react to this news, but I kept my expression carefully blank, tamping the emotion down until I was safely away from my mother.

"Anyway," she said dismissively. "I thought you'd be interested."

"Yeah," I answered, voice carefully level. "Thanks."

"Oh, and one more thing. Remember your old friend Clara, from elementary school?" I nodded. "She died of cancer, I guess. Just a couple of weeks ago. Such a shock. She was so young!"

"Oh," I replied, glad that I was already focusing on keeping my face calm and empty. "Wow. That's awful. Um, sorry Mom, I've gotta pee."

Chapter 38

I turned and walked away from her, not letting the mask drop until I was safely around the corner. Feeling my eyes begin to prick with tears, I looked around for somewhere I could hide. Luckily, I knew this church well, and I took the back stairs up to the choir loft. Alone and finally safe to do so, I collapsed onto a wooden pew and let the tears come, hot and heavy.

Clara was dead? Clara was dead. I repeated the words to myself in my mind, over and over, trying to make sense of them. I kept trying to picture her, with her bright blue eyes and pale blond hair, but all my mind could conjure was an image of Nora.

"They look so similar," I breathed in between sobs. "I didn't even realize." I grew up with Clara and her twin sister. We'd spent summers at the pool together, all three of us. I was the only kid invited to both of their birthday parties, because the twins couldn't decide whose friend I was. I'd always thought it was ironic, because I could have told you in an instant that I was Clara's friend. I'd thought I was just being polite, never saying so, but in this moment, in the wake of everything that just happened with Nora, it was suddenly all so clear. I couldn't have said anything because it would have meant admitting something to myself that I wasn't ready to understand. "I think I was in love with Clara," I whispered, "and now I'll never be able to tell her."

I looked down at the sanctuary below me. The last time I was up in this choir loft had been for a funeral, too. It was also the last time I'd been inside this church. The place was packed, filled to the brim, since the person who died was the church's own beloved pianist. She had been my beloved piano teacher, also. One of the few people I connected with as a child. Who seemed to understand me. "She was a little bit faerie, I bet," I said aloud into the empty room.

I was young when she died. Not even ten yet, probably. Nobody told me how it happened, but they had taken me to the funeral. We sat way up here in the choir loft because everywhere else was full. I listened, young eyes wide with morbid fascination, as one of her loved ones told the gathered crowd how bravely she had tried to run away and how valiantly she fought his knife. I grew up a lot in the moment that I learned she was brutally murdered by her husband, who was diagnosed with schizophrenia.

Looking back now, with my new perspective, I realized that my birth family would probably think of him as an intermagical, rather than a schizophrenic. Both definitions have their own truth, though. His human diagnosis gave him access to the medication that kept him safe and docile. At least, until it didn't. I wondered what sort of intermagical heritage had left him so tortured and so dangerous. What brutal magic had overtaken him and made him kill my friend?

I let the tears fall from my eyes, feeling the ache of that old wound, layered on top of the fresh, fierce grief I felt for Clara, and the pain of losing my grandmother. I didn't push the feelings away, I let them come. When you're already grieving, is an especially good time to grieve. Eventually, I sat up with no more tears to cry. It would come again, I knew, but for now, the pain receded to a subtle background ache, and I dried my swollen eyes.

"Rose, huh?" I said aloud in wonderment. It was a good name. It fit her well. I would know. She had been my first love, after all. The truth of her identity seemed so obvious, now that I knew. I couldn't even think of her as my first 'boyfriend' now, I realized. Since Jaah was non-binary, that would mean that I'd never actually dated a man at all. At least, not seriously. "I guess I really am gay," I said to myself with a chuckle. Seeing Rose's long, graceful lines, and sharp, stark features in my memory, I realized that she must look quite a bit like Calliope, now. "I wonder if she's an elf, too?" I mused.

It was a relief to be back on the highway, a few days later.

"I'm hungry. I should get something to eat before too long," I said, glad to be free to talk to myself aloud again, and to be allowed to listen to my body and give myself what I need. With my mom, meals are strictly scheduled with no flexibility for the weakness of the flesh. Her obsession with rules and doing things the 'right way' reminded me a little of the Christ's Heart Church, even though she was so staunchly unreligious. How did she come to decide that she 'had to' do the things she had to do? I'd been watching her closely, over the past few days, like a social anthropologist, trying to figure out where she was getting her rules from. It was the media, mostly, I concluded. Especially the idea that thin was good and not-thin was unacceptable. Luckily, my intermagical family was teaching me that I could decide for myself what I value, and who I want to be.

zrp zrp
more tacos

The pulse from my lower abdomen brought me back to the matter at hand.

"Tacos are better down here, huh?" I said, smoothing a hand over the roundness of my stomach. It had always been round, but now that shape felt much more momentous and important. Soon, I would be responsible for another intermagical life. And, I concluded, that was an excellent reason to be developing my own moral code and figuring out how to live authentically.

"You're pregnant?" my mother exclaimed, when I came back from my doctor's appointment. It was true. Jaah might not have known the precise ritual, but the magic we made, on the summer solstice, under a full moon and a meteor shower, after reaching a state of total honestly and understanding, and declaring our love for one another, had been enough, apparently. And, I had been thinking about how much I wanted to be a mother, hadn't I? Evita was right. That powerful magic had sparked something I hadn't entirely intended.

"And I'm diabetic!" I added, figuring it would be easier to get it all out at once. I asked the doctor to run a panel of blood tests, because of what my seer friend had told me, and the strange way my body reacts when I get hungry. I was surprised by how quickly the tests came back with an answer. I swallowed hard, trying not to quaver under the intensity of my mother's shocked, judgmental stare. It wouldn't do any good to tell her that I thought the strict no-fat diet she had raised me with had contributed to the problem at least as much as my own intermagical biology had done.

I had considered not telling her anything, but in the end, it was a good thing that I'd had the strength to be honest. To my surprise, Mom hadn't made a snide comment or given me a lecture. Instead, she had given me a one-armed hug, and muttered something about generations, then had gotten on the phone with the lawyer handling my grandmother's estate. I grinned at the shiny new key on my keyring. My bravery had been rewarded.

As I drove, I fingered the spherical necklace that my mother had given me after the funeral. It fell open, revealing a set of thumbnail-sized photos of me as a baby. I remembered my grandmother wearing it when I was young, and I felt tears well behind my eyes. I had arrived in time to hold her hand and look into her wrinkled eyes, full of the love and the memories we shared, from when I was young. That love was gone now, I realized, letting the hot tears spill down my cheeks. I felt the loss like an ache deep in the pit of my stomach.

Grief isn't the absence of love; it's just love without anywhere to go.

The quote drifted across my mind. Who had told me that? That's right. It had been the sweet old Pastor from Grandma's church. He had occasionally led the youth group when I was a kid. I hadn't known him well, but I remembered feeling safe and comfortable with him. I couldn't imagine him ever telling anyone that they had to submit to God as their Master. I didn't remember seeing him at the church, for Grandma's service. He must be gone now, too, and I felt the pang of that loss deep in my chest.

Evita was right. The universe was offering me some very potent lessons on the nature of spirit this week.

It was early Sunday morning when I crossed the border back into Oregon. Almost exactly one week since I'd left. I'd made the drive down in one long night, but my mom insisted on paying for a hotel room for the drive back. "It's not healthy to be sitting so long, in your condition," she admonished, tainting the nice gesture with her signature flavor of judgmental condemnation.

"Two hundred miles to Eugene," I said, reading a road sign. "I could just about make it to church on time, if I wanted to. Which I don't, of course." I added with a roll of my eyes. That idea got me thinking about Nora, though, and then about Clara, whose bright eyes and pale hair reminded me so much of my new friend. My eyes pricked with tears again, thinking about the adult life that she would never get to live. Maybe that was better than the bleak future Nora faced, engaged to a man she didn't love, at the mercy of a church she never agreed to join. No, I decided, with a decisive shake of my head, it was not better. Nora still had the opportunity to make choices and change her own destiny, even if it felt impossible.

I drove on, letting my thoughts wander. Even with all the other things I had to think about, my mind kept finding its way back to Nora. I passed another road sign. "Only fifty miles to Eugene now," I mused. "Maybe I will stop by, after all. Only because I'll be in the area," I said, defending myself needlessly to the empty van. "Just one more time."

Part 9 - Escape

Chapter 39

It was a few minutes after the hour when I arrived, and I slipped into the back of the chapel with the service already underway.

"And I want to thank you all for your warm welcome. In return, I am so pleased to have the privilege of welcoming you all into the Christ's Heart family," said Reverend Rex, from the pulpit. "There are more people here than you're used to, and I'm sure you have questions. You'll find some answers in this week's program. I know change can be scary, but not everything is changing. As usual, let's welcome your youth choir to lead us in the opening hymn."

As a line of young people filed up the center aisle, I unfolded the pamphlet I was handed. *Welcome to the new Christ's Heart Church*, it read, in large, friendly letters. This church, it explained, was now part of the Christ's Heart Organization, and was being rebranded, effective immediately.

"Interesting," I muttered, setting the program back down. I wasn't the only one. A low rumble spread through the crowd, audible over the chorus of children singing. I could pick out a few phrases that I'd read in the pamphlet, like 'recent acquisition' and 'major remodel.'

"Now, first things first," said Reverend Rex, stepping back up to the pulpit. "I'd like to apologize to you all for the abruptness of this change. I know you love this church, and I don't want to take that away from you. In fact, I want to help this congregation grow into the powerful body of worship that the Christ's Heart Organization knows it can be, rather than dwindling into insignificance, like it has been doing over the last several years."

The perturbed rumbling started again at this. Other heads, though, were nodding in agreement.

"You'll notice some new faces already," the Reverend continued. Some of the congregation of the Valley of Christ's Heart, although certainly not all, had made the hour-long drive to follow the Reverend to the new church. "And you'll want to get used to that. We love converts, and the Christ's Heart Organization expects to see significant growth, year over year. But you didn't come here for a business meeting. You're here for a sermon, so let's get to it!"

I certainly hadn't come here for the sermon. I looked around, but there was still no sign of Nora. Resigned, I tuned back in on what the Reverend was saying.

"Why do bad things happen to good people? I know a lot of you must be asking yourself that question, after everything that's happened. Why did our church catch fire? Why did it collapse entirely? Is this God's retribution? Is he judging us and punishing us for our sins?"

The Reverend looked around, performatively, as though waiting for one of the sea of congregants to answer him.

"No, my friends," he continued, "this is not a punishment. It is a test of our faith! Trusting God means accepting that he has a plan for us, even when we don't understand His reasons. What is a little suffering here on Earth, compared to an eternity of torment? It's not hard to forego a little earthly pleasure, for the promise of eternal bliss, is it?"

He continued on in that vein, and my mind wandered until something he said caught my attention.

"…when the Deacon of the Valley of Christ's Heart was unjustly imprisoned, this spring. That's what happens when lay people try to take the law into their own hands, instead of leaving it to God to sort things out. In fact, that's why I was recalled from Europe. Without the Deacon's sacrifice, I would still be overseas, reviewing CCC statutes and imagining what could be. Instead, his hardship has given me the opportunity to put some of my best ideas into practice by forming the Morality Police to share God's righteousness and defend His holy law."

zrp zrp
own hands

"Good point," I whispered, wondering if I might actually be talking to the tiny life growing inside me. The Reverend was condemning people for 'taking the law into their own hands,' then using the very same breath to pat himself on the back for doing exactly that, except, of course, that he claimed to be doing it with God's authority, instead of his own. Up at the podium, the Reverend was still talking.

"You don't know me well yet, but let me ask you this one thing, okay? If you ever start to question your faith, don't do it alone, okay? Come to me, and we'll talk it out. I'll help you back onto the path of salvation."

My phone buzzed in my pocket, and I pulled it out, glad to be sitting in the back where no one would see me. It was a text from Azalea.

Fionaaaaaa. Pythia won't go out to the park with us. When are you gonna be back? How many new Wylds did you get in California? Can you take me with you next time?

I promised the twins I'd play WyldSight on my trip, and I hadn't thought to open the app a single time. But there was still enough time to sight a few new Wylds before I saw the girls again. Remembering the enormous amount of points I scored the last time I claimed a territory in church, I opened the app. A sea of red dots appeared on the screen. Just more local owl-fox-deers, or squirrel-hawk-bears, likely. Nothing the girls would be interested in. One dot blinked by itself, out in front of the mob. The Reverend mentioned being in Europe recently, hadn't he? Maybe his Wyld would be interesting enough to satisfy Azalea.

"Oh," I murmured, my face falling slightly as the Reverend's Wyld opened without the flashy New Wyld banner. I had already seen this one. "Oh!" I exclaimed in shock when I realized what I was looking at.

The pale, long-horned Wyld reared, pawing the air. It was the Ibex. The blood drained from my face as I looked up at the man behind the podium.

It was him. The one that Jaah and Pythia had been searching for all summer. The man responsible for all those disappearances and for hurting Sylvie and the other girls. The Ibex was Reverend Rex. He had been right in front of me this whole time.

My vision swam, and my heart pounded in my ears, as I fled through the double doors at the back of the sanctuary.

"Oomph." The breath left me as I slammed into Nora, standing right outside the big doors.

"Ona!" she exclaimed, taking hold of my shoulders to steady me. "What are you doing here? What's wrong?"

"He's the Ibex," I panted, nonsensically. "It's him, the one that we've been looking for. He's the one. The Ibex."

"Huh?"

"I have to get out of here, okay? I have to tell someone."

"Tell them what? Ona, can you just breathe for a second? What's going on? Who's the one? The one what? And what on Earth," she asked, voice tinged with exasperation, "is an Ibex?"

"It's-he's-Nora, can we get out of here? There are things I need to tell you, but it's not safe to talk here."

Nora nodded, her large eyes wide. "It's not like I'm not allowed to leave the church," she said, not sounding entirely convinced. As we walked across the parking lot together, she looked from side to side, nervously, like a fugitive, and once she climbed into the front seat of my old van, she let out a sigh of relief.

"Are you going on a trip?" she asked, eyeing the pile of bags in the back.

"Coming back from one," I answered. I told her about my trip to California and the reason I went. It was easier than trying to figure out how to tell her about her Uncle, I thought to myself, turning and pulling out of the parking lot without any idea where I was going to go.

"I'm sorry for your loss," she said, her condolences sounding sincere, although somewhat practiced. "After last time, I wasn't sure if I would ever see you again."

"Me either," I said, "but I'm glad I came today."

I could feel Nora's gaze on me, her eyes a silent question. Why did I come today? But, she didn't say anything aloud, and I kept silent also, driving until I found a city park with picnic tables that would give us a clear view of anyone who might be approaching.

"I don't know where to start," I said, as we sat across from one another under the clear August sky.

"How about at the beginning?" she suggested, and I nodded. That would work.

So, I told her about the Pirate Carnival, my first big revel. And about how the Reverend and the Morality Police had rolled in and stated their intentions to shut down the rest of the summer's festivals.

"That's how I ended up at the Tent Revival," I said. "At the picnic, I mean. Where we met." She nodded, and I continued. "Urb and I decided to investigate the church, posing as boyfriend and girlfriend."

"So he's not your real boyfriend?" she asked, and I shook my head no. "And I thought…" She trailed off, then muttered to herself. "All these things happening, right under my nose."

"Yeah," I said. "I'm sorry. It never feels good to find out that someone has been lying to you. That's, uh, kind of what I wanted to talk about, actually. There's been other stuff going on this summer that you should know about."

I told her about Sylvie, the first trans woman who ended up in the hospital, and the six other victims we had identified, who had all been hurt by the same violent predator.

"So he hires them so that he can get them alone, and then he hurts them?" Nora asked, aghast. "That's evil!"

"That's not the only reason," I told her. "He, um, enjoys their services first. And we think he's feeling guilty about it. There's this other thing that's been going on, and we think it's got to be related." I told her about the disappearances that were happening alongside the violence. "It's almost like he's trying to make up for what he's doing to the trans girls by trying to save those other working girls. We've managed to track a couple of them to Eastern Oregon. My, uh…" I paused, not wanting to explain Jaah at this moment, along with everything else. "My friend is out there right now, trying to track them down." I told her the name of the town, and her eyes lit up.

"Oh! I know that place. Uncle's been out there a few times this summer, scouting locations for a new Christ's Heart Church. He might have some connections out there who would know something."

"Yeah," I agreed. She was more right than she could possibly know. "Um, Nora, have you heard of a game called WyldSight?"

Chapter 40

"That's not possible," said Nora, shaking her head. "There's no way."

"I could be wrong," I told her apologetically. "But I don't think I am." I opened the app and showed her the pale, rearing creature. "Everything fits, when you think about it. This all started after he moved back. And now, you're telling me that he has a connection to the place where these women are ending up, too."

She nodded, handing the phone back to me.

"Uncle would say that you're the devil, using your worldly knowledge to try to trick me into sin, but…" She shook her head, her pale face even whiter than usual. "What if he's the devil who's been lying to me this whole time?"

"Or," I pressed, "what if he's just a man who told you about the devil so that you'd be scared enough to do what he tells you to do, without asking questions?"

She sat frozen for a long moment, considering this, until the sound of church bells cut through the silence.

"Oh no, church is almost over. I have to get back," she exclaimed, then, "But, I can't go back! Ona, what am I supposed to do now?"

"I'm not sure," I told her, then added, "And, uh, it's Fiona, actually."

"Fiona," she repeated, as though tasting the new name. "That fits you better." Then she looked at me, like she was working up the nerve. "Where are you going now?" she asked. "Can I come with you?"

"Yeah," I agreed, after a brief moment of hesitation. "Okay."

When I turned onto the main road, heading away from the church, I could feel Nora's energy next to me. She radiated with uncontained excitement, nearly buzzing, in the passenger seat. When we rolled to a stop at the on-ramp to the highway, the drop in her energy startled me, and I glanced over at her. Her pale head was turned away from me, staring out the window, and I looked too, but I didn't see anything noteworthy. Just some pylons and a man with a panhandler's sign, standing on the sidewalk.

"How're you doing?" I asked. I didn't want to startle her by telling her what I was picking up on. I'd always been good at reading other people's emotions, and I'd learned early how unsettling people find it when you know things about their inner world that you don't have any business knowing.

My gentle probing worked, and Nora turned to me and spoke her thoughts aloud, "What am I going to do, out in the world without anyone to look out for me? There are dangerous, godless people everywhere. I'm going to get gobbled right up."

Behind her shoulder, the pandhandler wrapped on the window, and she turned and shrieked in fright. He must have been summoned by her attention, I realized, and I rolled the window down and reached across Nora to hand him a dollar, while she shrank back against the seat. He accepted the bill with a sad smile and mumbled, "God bless you."

"Doesn't sound godless to me," I retorted, once the window was rolled up and we were on the move again. Her reaction embarrassed me, and my tone was sharper than I intended, when I added, "and just so you know, I've been out in the godless world for a while now, and the only men I've had a real reason to be afraid of were the supposedly 'godly' men of the Christ's Heart Church."

That wasn't entirely true, but it was true enough that I didn't feel a need to correct myself. We sat in silence for a long moment.

"I don't…" Nora started, then paused and considered before continuing. "I don't think I know anything."

My breath burst out of me in a surprised chuckle. "You know what? I said that to someone once, and I'll tell you what they told me." I took my eyes off the road to meet her gaze. "It's not a bad place to start."

"What you said, about bad men at Christ's Heart, was it just Uncle Rex that you meant, or did something else happen?" she asked, voice small and nervous.

"Yeah," I answered. "A few things happened, actually. I guess you could say that I'm the reason your Uncle had to move back to town." I told her about what happened this spring, when I crashed my car into the middle of a plot spearheaded by the former leader of the Christ's Heart Church, and his son, Brandon, to build an enormous water bottling plant and ruin a local ecosystem.

"That was you?" she asked, mouth open in astonishment. "The girl whose evil trickery sent the Deacon to prison? But—" She clapped a hand over her mouth, realizing what she just said.

"That's me," I agreed with a laugh. "The evil trickster girl. Makes you wonder what they'd say if they found out you were with me right now, huh?"

I glanced at Nora again and saw that her face was tight with worry. "I won't tell," she promised, with more intensity than I expected. Her scared expression sent a chill down my spine. "Where are you taking me, anyway?"

"Wherever you want," I told her with a shrug. "But, I was headed home. I live up in Portal Land. Portland, I mean…"

"The big city," she breathed. "I've only ever been there for church conventions, and they always warned us never to go anywhere except the hotel and the convention center, unless we wanted to get shot. Or worse," she added with a shudder.

"Well, I hear about everything that happens in my neighborhood," I told her confidently, grateful for the insight that Jaah and Pythia offered me, "and I haven't heard about anybody getting shot. In fact, the only terrible things happening this summer are the, um…" I trailed off. I didn't want to rub it in.

"The terrible things my Uncle did," she finished, realizing what my silence must mean. I nodded. "Really?" She shook her head in exasperated disbelief. "All my life, I've been told how wicked men are. What evil things they hold in their heart. What their fear of God will convince them not to do."

"Yeah," I agreed. "And how did that make you feel? Kind of makes you wonder how it would make a man feel, to have someone they trust tell them how wicked they are, and how much they need to resist their baser instincts, week after week, and year after year."

"What do you mean?"

"If you tell somebody something enough times, eventually they're going to start to believe it."

"Well, Christ's Heart tells men to be our protectors," Nora argued.

"Yeah, that's one of the things that Brandon and the Deacon offered me when I met them this spring. And it's not a bad thing to have the biggest, scariest monster as your protector, but what happens when you're alone with him? Who protects you from the protector?"

She considered this for a moment, then shuddered. I wondered if she was thinking about Byron. "Yeah," she agreed. "I guess I've never thought about it like that before. You really think some men aren't like that?"

"Absolutely," I said. I thought about Jaah, then remembered how they felt about being called a man. I told her about the play parties I'd been attending, instead, and the extraordinary levels of respect and decency they demanded from everyone in attendance.

"You really feel safe doing all that, as a woman?" Nora asked, astonished.

"I mean, I haven't done all that much of it, yet, actually," I admitted, "but yeah. It feels totally safe. Nobody thinks less of you because of what you're wearing or assumes that you'll be okay with something, just because you said yes to something else. It's been really empowering, actually."

"Empowering," Nora repeated. "I think that was probably my grandma's favorite word. I don't know how many times she wrote it in her journals. That reminds me, could we make a quick stop, actually?"

"Sure," I agreed. Taking the next exit off the highway, I pulled up to the large brick house, and a few minutes later, Nora was back, holding a cardboard box and a duffle bag.

"I forgot this bag here when we left for Eugene," she said, slinging it into the back, "and I was so upset because it's got all my best clothes in it. Auntie said she would send someone to get it, but she never did. Pretty lucky, huh?"

"It's that faerie luck," I said with a shrug, as she climbed back into the passenger's seat.

"It's the what?" she asked.

"Oh, um…" I paused, realizing what I said and to whom. "Nora, have you ever heard the term 'intermagical' before?" She shook her head. "Well," I said, steeling myself for the conversation ahead. "Remember when you said you didn't know anything?"

Chapter 41

Nora looked at me expectantly from the passenger seat.

"I'm sorry," I said after a long moment. "I'm not sure where to start."

"At the beginning?" she suggested. "I just ran away from everything I've ever know, and I'm honestly just trying not to freak out right now. Listening to you talk is helping, so tell me everything, okay?"

"Yeah," I agreed. "Okay. I'm adopted, did you know that?" She shook her head. "I didn't know anything about my birth family when I was a kid," I told her about how I came to Oregon to look for them. "Some, uh, bad stuff happened when I first got to the valley," I told her. "That's when I met the Deacon, and started to form an opinion about Christ's Heart."

"What happened?" she pressed.

I shivered, remembering my first days in Oregon. Slogging, lost and wet, through the woods, and being saved by the sermonizing Deacon, and then later, running naked and freezing into the terrifying heat of a bonfire full of frat boys, before being rescued a second time by the Deacon's son, Brandon.

How could I tell Nora about that without telling her about how the wicked-minded Velia had orchestrated the whole thing, to try to keep me from my birth mother? And, how could I tell her that before she understood about the magic? I ignored her question.

"You know in folklore, how there are faeries and elves and stuff like that?" I asked.

"Sure, I guess," she said. "Aunt Tempy never liked those kinds of stories. She told me that fairy is just another word for demon."

"Well, that's one way to look at it," I said, remembering the demon women I'd met at the play party. "We're all intermagicals, anyway."

"Intermagicals?" Nora repeated.

"Yeah, intermagicals," I agreed. "It's my cousin Faeryn's word, actually. She was the first one to really explain all this to me. About the New World Fae and the intermixing declaration."

"Well, can you explain it to me?" Nora asked, exasperated.

"Yeah, sorry," I apologized. "I'm trying." I took a deep breath and told her what I knew about how the faeries and the other magicals had heard about an empty land of milk and honey across the sea. How they ventured here to the New World, only to discover that it was already filled with land spirits and groups of local humans.

The magicals that found their way here had done their best to make a place for themselves, and decided that a New World deserved a new plan. And so they made an 'intermixing declaration,' and started purposefully mixing with humans, creating the first intentional intermagicals.

"That's where all this human progress has come from, in these last few hundred years," I told her. "The Industrial Revolution and the technology boom? That's the power of intermagical ingenuity."

"Faeries," she asked. "Seriously?"

"Yeah," I nodded. "And elves, and all sorts of things. Every culture has stories of magical beings that date back into prehistory. They weren't making things up. They were making observations about their magical world, and they were talking about us."

"Us?" she echoed.

"Yeah," I agreed. "I'm an intermagical. My birth mother is a faerie."

"Oh," she said, her face falling. "I thought you meant…never mind."

"Huh?" I glanced over at her, but she was looking out the window. Her pale hair glowed in the sunlight, and I reminded myself to keep my eyes on the road. "I don't know what kind of intermagical you are," I told her after a long moment. "But my cousin Faeryn would probably be able to tell. She's an expert at that kind of thing."

"What kind I am?" she asked. "You think I'm an intermagical, too?"

"Yeah," I told her. "Probably. At least, I hope so. We're headed to the Fair Isle, so I certainly hope you're at least a little magical or else you won't be able to get in the front door." I glanced over again, and this time I met her wide-eyed gaze. "I'm not worried, though. I'm sure you'll be fine." She flashed me a tight smile, then turned back to the window. We drove in silence for a few minutes before I noticed an odd sound coming from the seat next to me. "What's up, Nora? Are you okay?"

"Mmhmm," she murmured, wiping her eyes and straightening in her seat. She looked like a child caught in wrongdoing. "Sorry. I'm fine."

"Hey, that's not…" I started. "Nora, you're allowed to cry! You don't have to put on a brave face. I'd be shocked if you were actually fine with the kind of day you're having."

"Yeah," she agreed with a sniffle. "I guess you're right." With that, the dam broke, and she poured her worries into the empty space between us. Horror at what her Uncle had done, and grief for the man she had been raised to believe him to be. Fear of leaving behind everything she knew, and an anticipatory dread of whatever the future might hold. "I'm terrified of what I'll find if you take me to the Fair Isle, but I'm even more scared that I won't be able to get inside the door at all," she confessed, thin fingers picking at the hem of her skirt.

"I hear you," I assured her, wishing there was something I could do to help.

zrp zrp
do magic

That was certainly an idea. My first introduction to my family's particular brand of magic had been a glamour ritual to give me confidence when I needed it. With everything I had learned this summer, it would be simple enough to come up with something similar for Nora. I told her what I was thinking, and felt the tension rise between us, as she considered the suggestion.

"Like something your grandma might have done," I added, and felt her relax a little with that thought.

"Yeah, okay," she agreed. "Sure. Let's try it."

"We should only do magic for a good reason," I told her, once we pulled off the highway and into a secluded patch of trees. I settled my spell case on a conveniently placed rock and opened the lid. "And this ritual is to help you, so what do you want it to do?"

"Um," she answered. "I have no clue."

"Well," I considered, and tried another tactic. "What would you pray for?"

"Oh," she said. "Okay. Well, I guess I would pray for the confidence to be open to these new experiences, and I'd pray for protection from all the scary things out here in the big, wide world. And, I would pray for the ability to see the truth of what's in front of me, and not be deceived by liars." Her eyes flashed with cold fire, and she added, "Again."

"Confidence, open-mindedness, protection, and clarity?" I repeated. "Sounds great. But, instead of asking for those things from an all-powerful guy in the sky, we're going to make it happen for ourselves, using the energy of the world around us, okay?"

"How do we do that?" She asked, sounding skeptical, but curious enough to try.

"There are a lot of different ways, but I can show you the kind of ritual magic that my family taught me."

"Okay," she agreed. "What do we do?"

"Well, that's the fun part," I told her with a grin. "That's entirely up to you." It was fun to step into the role of teacher, after spending the summer as a student, I thought to myself, as Nora looked at me with confusion. I set her the task of looking through her grandmother's things for objects that could represent her four goals, while I rummaged through the spell case.

"How about this for clarity?" she asked, holding up the box that held her grandmother's crystal ball. "Oh, ick. A spider got inside and made it all webby."

"Leave it," I told her, before she could brush it clean. "And you can wipe away the cobwebs as part of the ritual, okay?" She nodded and kept digging through the box.

"I don't know how I could help but feel confident, wearing this," she said, showing me a large black witch's hat with a long fringe around the brim. It wasn't my style, but she looked at it rapturously, and I nodded my agreement. Next, Nora pulled out her grandmother's deck of Tarot cards.

"Look," I said, pointing to the bottom of the deck. "The Fool. That's the perfect card to represent new experiences. I've been reading about it, and apparently the

Tarot tells the story of the Fool's journey through life. This card shows the moment he sets out on his great adventure."

"Just like me," she agreed, taking the card and setting the rest of the deck aside. "That's three. I don't know what to pick for protection, though," she said, pawing listlessly through the box. "None of this stuff feels right."

"Well, what makes you feel safe?" I asked, thinking about the eggshell I used in my own protection ritual, and eyeing a decorative dagger at the bottom of my spell case, speculatively. There are a lot of different ways to protect yourself.

"I don't know," she said, fingering her crucifix necklace. "I always looked to Jesus to keep me safe, before, but now, I'm not sure."

"Well, how about your cross, then?" I asked. "You're leaving the rest of your life behind, but I don't see why you'd have to leave Jesus. He seems like a pretty neat guy with some cool, forward thinking ideas."

"Yeah, okay," she agreed, and her mouth turned up in a small smile as she unclasped the necklace and set it with the other objects.

I drew a circle in the dirt with my toe. Nora stood in the center of it, holding her four objects nervously, while I walked around her, setting out the items I collected. "This smoke represents the element of air," I told her, setting my portable incense burner at the northernmost point of the circle. "And that seems like it could represent openness. What do you think?" She agreed, and I continued my journey around the circle, setting out clear water for clarity, a candle for confidence, and finally a small dish of earth for protection.

"Okay, I've called the elements to help us. The next part is up to you. What do you think you should do with this stuff?" I asked. "What feels magical to you?"

"I guess I could put it on," she said. "Does that work?"

"Sure," I told her, and she placed the dark hat on her pale head and tucked the crystal ball under her arm so that she could re-clasp the necklace. She tucked the fool card into the front pocket of her modest skirt and looked up at me expectantly. "Okay, now what?" I prompted.

"Um, maybe spin around?" she asked.

"Sure," I said again. She made three slow rotations, then stopped. "Did it work?" I asked, then saw her expression and rephrased the question. "Does it feel like it worked?"

"No," she said. "Maybe I'd better do it some more." She spun in a quick circle, making the hem of her skirt float up above her ankles, and kept spinning, until the fringe at the brim of the hat stuck straight out to the side and dust started to rise in whorls around her feet. As I watched, magical motes of light sparkled all around her, although they might have been specks of mica flashing in the bright summer sun, I realized. The effect was mesmerizing, either way.

Eventually, she slowed to a stop. Her eyes were closed, and she took a deep breath before opening them and smiling at me. "How about now?" I asked, and she nodded, expression pleased.

"And I could really feel it, the power all around me," Nora told Pythia, later that evening, leaning over the bar at the Fair Isle in her excitement. "And now, when I wear this, it's like I can't help but feel confident," she finished, peering out happily from underneath the hat's long fringe.

"Seems like that girl really likes it here," Pythia said, after Nora wandered off to chat with a nearby table of fae folk. "I'm glad. I think the Fair Isle likes her, too."

"Any word from your brother?" I asked her.

"Yeah, they'll be back from Eastern Oregon late tomorrow, or maybe the next day," she said, drying a glass meditatively. "They didn't want to say too much over the phone, but I get the impression they found plenty. Oh, and they wanted me to give this to you, in case they don't make it back in time." She handed me a slip of paper printed in a decorative looping script. "Sounds like Fredbeard's figured out a way around all the Morality Police restrictions."

"You are invited to the Buccaneer's Bacchanal," I read aloud. I scanned the invitation once, and then again, before pointing at the date and asking Pythia. "Wait, is this right?"

"Mmhmm," she agreed. "The Buccaneer's Bacchanal is tomorrow!"

Part 10 - Transformation

Chapter 42

I'd decided not to tell Jaah my big news over the phone, but unable to resist, I scribbled a quick note and left it with Pythia before I drove away from the Fair Isle, headed for the Bacchanal. I glanced at the pretty girl in the seat next to me, white hair fluttering in the breeze. With the open road ahead of us, all of the tension of yesterday felt like it melted away in the summer sunshine. I had been so fixated on Nora all summer, but that had just been my intuition pushing me to save her from the oppression of the church. Now that I had done that, and introduced her to my world, there was no need for any more inner turmoil. Which was ideal, I thought, I don't need that kind of stress in my life. Maybe I can be like a big sister to her?

She must have felt me looking, because she turned and met my gaze, smiling slowly.

Gulp. Or maybe not.

"I think my grandma must have lived around here," she told me, looking back out the window. "I recognize the names of some of these little towns from her journals. I've never been out this far. Why is it all the way out here, anyway?"

"For the same reason it's on a Monday, I'd expect," I told her, turning onto a gravel road marked with a pirate flag. "Because they don't want it to get broken up by the Morality Police."

"You really think that might happen?" Nora asked, and I shrugged in answer. I had no idea what Fredbeard had done to safeguard this revel from the Reverend's local militia. Next to me, Nora squirmed in her seat uncomfortably. "Uncle said that the places he would take his boys were 'filthy, sin-infested Sodom and Gomorrahs' and I believed him, but now I don't know what to think."

"You'll get to form your own opinions, soon enough," I told her, which was true. I wished I could tell her more, but the fact was that I had only been at the Pirate Carnival for one day, and most of what I knew about fae revels was hearsay. Instead, I told her more about the play parties I'd been attending all summer and the different ways I had seen people entertain themselves, and each other, with their bodies.

"And it's not just women there?" she asked, eyes wide as saucers. "Men, too?" I nodded. "Aren't they worried that all that temptation will make them stumble?"

"No, not really. It's not like the church, where people almost expect you to sin, and then forgive you over and over again. This community sets high expectations for people, and they meet them, and if they don't, they get educated. And if that doesn't work," I shrugged and waved. "Then bye-bye. They have to leave." I told her what Jaah had told me about consent and making sure not to touch anyone without asking. "Even pretty girls like you," I warned her. "It's up to all of us to keep the community safe."

She blushed and smiled at the compliment, then sobered and nodded. "I understand. I wouldn't want to make anybody uncomfortable." She considered for a minute, then asked. "Do you really think there will be stuff like that going on at this party?"

"I don't know," I told her. "But they're calling it a Bacchanal, so I wouldn't be surprised."

Another pirate flag marked the entrance, and we turned into a bumpy field full of parked cars. There were a lot more than I expected.

"Are you sure I look alright?" Nora asked, fussing with the fringe of her witch's hat.

"You look great," I told her honestly. We both did, I thought, smoothing down the skirts of a ruffled dress that never made it out of my trunk at the Pirate Carnival. I felt the flutter of nerves in my stomach and steeled myself. This was only my second fae revel, after all. "Nervous to be walking into something like this?" I asked, and beside me, Nora nodded. "Me too," I confessed, reaching out and taking her hand. The intensity of the tingling sensation almost made me drop it, but I was getting used to the feeling of magic, and I squeezed her hand instead. "I'm with you. We've got this."

A familiar face greeted us at the gate, and I smiled in recognition.

"Ahoy!" said Fredbeard the Red, grinning from beneath an enormous feathered pirate hat. "Welcome to the Buccaneer's Bacchanal! Do you have your invitation?" I nodded and held out the piece of paper. He snatched it with an exaggerated flourish, then cleared his throat and addressed a video camera that I hadn't noticed before. "Quite right. All official and ship-shape. Before you go inside, there are a few things I have to tell you about this…" he paused to wink at us and then turned back to the camera. "Private, invitation-only, historical re-enactment event. Please note that nudity and sensation play are permitted in designated areas only. All alcohol is being served by licensed bartenders, and use of illegal substances is expressly prohibited by the event coordinators. If you want to spend the night, you can sleep in your car, or use one of the old cabins. This used to be a summer camp back in the day. But no tents, okay? And one last thing. By choosing to participate in this event, you are acknowledging that you understand that any apparent occult activity is part of the historical re-enactment, and nothing more."

"Got it," I said, and beside me, Nora nodded.

"Now, go enjoy this beautiful Monday evening, and have a pi-radical time, you crazy kids!"

The summer sun was still high in the sky when we stepped through the gate into the Buccaneer's Bacchanal. The field was transformed into a charming seaport village, and we stood at the center of a courtyard ringed with small shops, and, surprisingly, a two-story tavern. How they managed to drag the enormous structure out into the middle of this remote field, I had no clue, but I recognized the shape of it from the Pirate's Carnival, so there must be some way of moving it around. Groups of intermagicals in pirate finery socialized in small clumps, greeting old friends with shouts and tight hugs.

"There must have been a whole lot of invitations to this thing," said Nora, looking around at the throngs of pirates surrounding us.

"Yeah, sure seems like it." I wasn't surprised to see so many intermagicals here, though. This was the first revel since the beginning of the season, and folks had jumped at this opportunity to gather.

"Well, what do you want to—" I started, but before I could finish the sentence, Nora interrupted me.

"What do you think they meant by designated areas?" she asked, looking left and right speculatively.

"No clue," I said, giving her a sideways glance. Her nervousness had evaporated now that we were inside, and she was peering out from under her fringed hat curiously. "But, we can check it out, if you'd like."

It wasn't difficult to find what we were looking for, and a few minutes later, we were standing at the entrance to a dilapidated barn. Above the door was a sign reading "The Brig" and, in the way of fae illusion, it looked much more menacing to me than I expected it would have to an unmagical human. From the expression on her face, Nora had enough magic to experience the full effect of the illusion.

"We don't have to go in," I told her. "Totally up to you."

"No," she said, taking hold of her enchanted necklace and steeling herself. "I want to. If the people who taught me about good are actually evil, and the things they told me are evil are really okay, I want to see it for myself, and make my own decisions."

I remembered how I had felt when I had first encountered real magic. The only thing that convinced me was seeing it with my own two eyes.

"Alright," I told her, taking her small hand in mine again. "I'll be with you every step of the way." I used my other hand to push open the door.

I was impressed with the illusion that cloaked the outside of the barn, but it was nothing compared to what was waiting for us inside. When the door clicked shut behind us, it was almost impossible to tell that we weren't below decks in an enormous pirate ship. Flickering lanterns lit the coiled rope and fishing net that hung from long shipboard walls. Chains clanked menacingly the high beams of the barn's ceiling, which managed not to detract from the illusion, and I felt as though I could almost feel the sway of waves beneath my feet.

CRACK!

The sound of leather hitting flesh rang out, reverberating off the boards of the walls. A groan of pain followed, and I heard Nora gasp beside me. We turned our attention to a young man who was kneeling on a folded blanket, on top of an old-fashioned trunk. His white backside was exposed and shone brightly in the lantern light.

"Please sir," he said, looking over his shoulder at the dark-skinned young man standing behind him, holding a leather strap. "May I have another?" Noticing us watching, he gave us a wink before burying his face in the blanket again and arching his back.

"Is he really okay, do you think?" Nora whispered, as the sound of a second crack echoed from the walls.

"That hard enough for you?" asked the man with the strap.

"No, but thanks for trying," the youth on the bench replied.

"Sure sounds like it," I said to Nora. "Want to go a little further in?"

A small crowd gathered at the back corner of the barn, and we joined them, curious to see the spectacle that was drawing so many people. Two women were strung up with rope, and hung upside down, legs bent and tied into a cross-legged position. An older woman with the features of East Asia, and a snow-white pouf of hair atop her head, let out a cackle and heaved on another rope. I watched her sinewy arms bulge as a third girl was hoisted from her seat and into the air, flipping upside down to match her neighbors on either side.

She looked a little different, I noticed, and after a moment I realized that it was because her hands had been tied to the side of her head, unlike the other two girls, whose hands covered their face.

"Magnificent!" Cried the ancient woman, clapping her hands in glee as she admired her work. "I have wanted to do this for so long. See no evil, hear no evil, speak no evil. You are resplendent. Thank you, my darlings."

"Did you get the photos yet, Mistress?" asked one of the girls, lifting her hand off her face, so that she could see.

"Not quite yet, my love. Can you hold on for one more minute?"

"Of course, Mistress," said the girl, readjusting her ropes so that her hands covered her face again. That surprised me. She appeared to be completely immobilized, hanging there, but clearly she wasn't. Beside me, Nora watched the suspended girls with open-mouthed fascination.

Chapter 43

"See?" I told Nora with a chuckle, as we blinked our eyes against the late afternoon sun. "No evil."

"Hear no evil, speak no evil!" she agreed with a laugh, but then she sobered. "The people in there seemed like they were having a pretty good time, but that doesn't mean it isn't sinning. I just—"

"Nora? Is that you?" A voice from behind us interrupted her thought, and we turned to see who it was. It was Urb, of course, and he pulled us both into a warm hug, then stepped back and gave me a quizzical look. "Seriously, Fiona?" he asked. "The Reverend's daughter? Here?"

"It's a long story," I told him with a shrug. "I'll tell you later. At the moment, our friend Nora is having a bit of a crisis of faith."

"Somehow, I'm not surprised," Urb said wryly. "What's on your mind, friend?" Nora explained, and Urb nodded sagely. "You know what? Come with me. There's someone I'd like you to meet who might be able to help."

Urb led us down a tree-lined path into another part of the Bacchanal, where a ring of small wooden cabins surrounded a large campfire with logs for seating.

"Nora, Fiona? This is Sage," said Urb, introducing us to a small person with short, dark hair and an intelligent expression. Was this who Urb went out on a date with the other week? I shot Urb a questioning look, and he nodded with a sheepish grin.

"Nora, here, has some of that good old religious trauma," Urb confessed. "And she's feeling a certain kind of way, after checking out The Brig. I thought you might have something to say that could help."

"Hey, I get it, shame's a bitch," said Sage with a kind smile. "I was a little girl in Catholic School, once. I know how it is."

Little girl? I met Nora's eyes and saw the same question mirrored in her face.

"We had confession once a week," Sage continued, "and they made me feel so scared and guilty that I wouldn't ever actually do anything naughty, but I had to say something, so I'd tell them a lie, and then I'd feel guilty for lying." She shook her head ruefully, remembering it.

A gaggle of goblins sat down on a log on the other side of the campfire, and I watched as they unearthed shiny trinkets from pockets and pouches and cooed over them, exclaiming about what good trades they were making, here at the revel.

"Shame if you're bad, shame if you're good," Sage continued, "there's no escaping it, when everyone tells you it's your nature to be a sinner."

"Huh," said Nora, considering that idea. She stared into the crackling fire, or maybe across at the group of goblins, crowing about their prized baubles.

I took the opportunity to confirm Sage's pronouns.

"She, her," the handsome individual answered, then chuckled at my look of confusion. "Surprised? I don't look like it, do I?" She ran a hand through her short, dark hair rakishly, and gave me a wink. "I stand at the end of an unbroken chain of mothers that stretches back to the dawn of humanity, and I hold the miracle of life inside my body. I'm not about to let society's limited definition of femininity take that away from me. You can say 'they,' though, if it makes you more comfortable."

"No, I hear you. I get it. I'm not exactly society's ideal woman either."

I was thinking about the roundness of my belly, self-conscious after spending so much time with my mother, and I was surprised when Nora nodded in agreement.

"Yeah, you're way too opinionated," she said with a grin.

"Yep. Can't be having any of that. Opinions mean you're thinking. Considering the outcome of your actions, and forming your own ideas about right and wrong." Sage stood up, pacing back and forth in front of the fire. "And they can't stand for any of that. They want you broken and ashamed, so that you have to look up to them as your moral superiors, and they can tell you what to do."

"I'm not sure I follow," said Nora, brow furrowed.

"Then let me say it like this. Shame doesn't make you a better person, and the church knows that. But, when you're ashamed, you don't trust yourself, and that makes you easier to control. If your own thoughts and body aren't trustworthy, you're going to need an authority to tell you what to do, right? That's called Vertical Morality, where someone above you tells you what's right and wrong."

"As opposed to what?" Nora asked, curious but skeptical.

"Horizontal morality," Sage explained. "That's what it's called when you make your own judgments about what's right and wrong, based on how your actions affect other people, instead of trying to figure out what God does or doesn't like. And believe me, I've heard plenty about what God doesn't like, but let me ask you this. Was there anything going on in The Brig that was actually hurting anybody?"

"Well…" Nora started, but Sage interrupted.

"Hurting anybody in a way that they were not enjoying or specifically asking for?"

"No, I guess not."

"And are these religious nutjobs who have been going out of their way to ruin our revels all summer by running folk down with their cars actually hurting anyone?"

"They're hurting me and my family plenty," Urb grumbled.

"And the rest of us, too. But it doesn't matter, because they believe that God is on their side, and they're using that good old Vertical Morality," Sage concluded, smiling grimly.

A pirate with an enormous feathered hat strode into view, with a mallet over one shoulder. She bent nearly in half, white orbs threatening to escape from the top of her corset, and with a mighty crack, sent a croquet ball my way. I lifted my feet, narrowly avoiding the thing, and it bounced off the log underneath me. With a horrified expression, she hurried over and swept her impressive hat off her head in a bow.

"Apologies, didn't see you there, but all's fair in hand-shoes, and horse-grenades, you know? A kiss for your ransom, perchance? I'll be needing that ball back from you, now, if I don't want to fall behind."

"Um," I said, utterly perplexed by the interaction. I bent down and picked up the ball, handing it to her. "Here you go?"

"Excellent," she said, taking it from me with a flourish and pressing her cheek against mine in the European style, then whirling in her skirts and hurrying off again.

I turned to Nora to get her thoughts on the unusual occurrence, but she didn't seem to notice, lost in her own contemplation.

"What's on your mind, Nora?" Urb asked, noticing the same thing I had.

"But what if you look up to somebody with good morals?" Nora asked. "What if they say to take care of other people, and not to hurt them? What about that?"

"Are you thinking about someone in particular?" Sage asked her.

"Well, yeah," she answered, looking down at her knees instead of meeting our inquisitive looks. "What about Jesus? I accepted him into my heart when I was little, and I've been walking with him for a long time. When I need to make a hard decision, I ask him what I should do, and when I make good choices, I can feel how proud he is of me." She smiled warmly, thinking about it, then became serious again, looking up at Sage nervously. "And now you're going to tell me that's a bad thing, huh?"

"Not really," said Sage with an apologetic shrug. "That's beautiful, and I would never want to take that away from you. All I'm going to say is that it's an awfully round-about way of getting to self-love, that's all. Because it's just you, you know? It's always been you. You're the one noticing and appreciating all those little things about you, who is proud when you do the right thing, and ashamed when you don't. You don't have to look for that validation outside yourself, because you're already doing it. Just, with extra steps."

"But on the other hand, that also means that you have to take responsibility if you do end up doing bad things. You can't blame it on demons infiltrating your mind." Urb interjected.

"Taking responsibility for your own demons is an important part of personal accountability," Sage agreed. "That is true."

"Well, I'm alright with that," said Nora, looking relieved. "I was worried you were going to say that there's something wrong with Jesus."

"Not at all," said Sage. "I think he's a pretty cool guy who brought some important Eastern philosophies into the Western world. I understand why the church likes him so much, though. He was such an apocalyptic preacher."

"He was what?" I asked. Beside me, Nora's eyebrows shot upward in surprise.

"An apocalyptic preacher," Sage repeated. "Don't you think it's weird that he was such a champion for the poor and the downtrodden, but never once actually told them to rise up against their oppressors? Why would he tell them to turn the other cheek and accept their treatment?" Sage looked at each of us expectantly before continuing. "It's all that Kingdom of God stuff! He thought Daddy was going to come down and do vengeance. And what's the point of demanding better treatment in the here and now, if God is going to take care of it for you, soon enough, anyway?"

"That's how they justify destroying the environment, too," said Urb. "What's the value of preserving anything, if the world is going to end soon, anyway?"

"But, hasn't anybody noticed that the world hasn't ended in the last two thousand years?" I asked.

"No. They're so worn down and distracted by all the shame and the poor treatment that they don't have the energy to notice very much at all. Or, they're the ones doing the oppressing."

Nora was looking pretty worn down, herself, by this point. She was slumped forward, with her head in her hands. She rocked slowly from side to side for quite a while, then she looked up at me with those wide, pale eyes.

"I just don't know what to believe anymore," she said, forlornly.

"I'm sorry," Sage said, with a look of genuine concern for the girl. "But for what it's worth, I tend to agree with the Gnostics."

"The ones who think it's all unknowable? Really?" I asked, confused.

"Not agnostics, the Gnostics," Sage corrected. "They had some pretty slanderous things to say about the Old Testament God. That's why the early Christians decided to get rid of them."

"Alright, you've piqued my interest," I told her. "Who were the Gnostics?"

"Well, if you listen to the mainstream media, the Gnostics believe that the Earth is a corrupt prison planet, and we're all trapped here to suffer."

"Interesting take," I commented wryly, eyeing the beautiful forest glade surrounding us.

"But, of course, that's not actually what the Gnostics believed," Sage explained. "That's all a Psy Op. A cover-up by the church. Because once you see it like the Gnostics do, you can't really unsee it." Sage paused for dramatic effect while we looked at her expectantly. "Okay. What's the one big, obvious thing that's missing from the Christian creation story?" She looked at each of us in turn. Nora shook her head, as confused as I was.

Urb shrugged and said, "I've already heard it."

"I don't know," I answered, finally. "What is missing?"

"The mother!" Sage announced triumphantly, slapping her thighs for emphasis. "Sure, a man might think that all you need to create life is one big cosmic bang, but women understand that you've got to carry a child and birth it, and sometimes you've got to make sacrifices for your children."

"What are you saying?" I asked. Sage's ranting was entertaining but I wasn't entirely sure I was following her logic.

"I'm saying that the Gnostics tell us the story of what happened to our mother. How she sacrificed herself and made her own body into the planet Earth. Her ultimate act of sacrifice gave us the opportunity to exist. We are her beloved children."

"Oh." The ring of truth in Sage's words rocked me back on the log where I sat. "Of course. Mother Earth. How did I not notice that before?"

Beside me, Nora sat in silence, and I watched micro-expressions flit across her face as she considered this idea. That must totally challenge everything she had been taught about God, I thought, contemplatively. Or, does it?

"But wait, if she's the mother, that still leaves room for a sky daddy, doesn't it? 'Our Father Who Art In Heaven,' and all that?" I asked.

"Sure does," Sage agreed with a chuckle. "Here's how the Gnostics tell it. After our mother laid down her body and gave us life, sky daddy opened his eyes, also. He stood alone, beholding her creation, and in his ignorance, he thought he had created it. And, he hated it. All he could see were the ways that the world was unlike Him, and he thought it was disgusting. Life is messy, you know? Not like the cold, empty vacuum of space."

"He hated us?" Nora asked. "What are you talking about? God loves us. That's one of the first things Christians learn."

"Ever heard the phrase, 'There's no hate like Christian love?'" Sage asked, with a sad smile. "God loves us, as long as we admit that we're sinful creatures, hate our bodies, and deny our human nature, so we can follow all of his rules. That's not love, that's abuse."

"Even as a kid, I thought the idea of a loving God drowning the whole world seemed a little suspicious. You know, with the ark and the animals and all that," Urb interjected.

"Oh yeah," Sage agreed. "The way God is described in the Old Testament makes him sound like a textbook narcissist, doesn't it? With the love bombing and the fits of divine rage. The way he's so disgusted by humanity that he can't even look at us? It all fits the personality profile."

"I don't know so much about the Old Testament," said Nora. "But that doesn't sound like God to me."

"Well, I do," Sage replied. "And I've got some theories about God, or, at least, about the entity that the Gnostics call the Demiurge. And, they just might make you feel better. Or..." She shrugged. "They might not."

"Okay," Nora agreed, hesitantly.

"I don't think the narcissist described in the Old Testament is actually God at all. I think it's his son. No," she said, seeing the expression on Nora's face and raising her hands defensively. "I don't mean Jesus, either. Hear me out, okay?"

Nora nodded, looking skeptical.

"Three thousand years ago," Sage explained. "People used to worship El and Asherah, the father and mother of the gods, and they had seventy children. In the Bible, in the book of Genesis, the world had seventy nations."

"Coincidence? I think not," interjected Urb, and Sage smiled at him before continuing.

"Definitely not. This whole theory is basically confirmed in the Dead Sea Scrolls, by the way. The main character of the Old Testament, this Demiurge guy? He wasn't supposed to be the God of the whole world. He was just the God of the Isrealites. We know that because at one point he does a favor for this guy Naaman, and then Naaman has to carry around two cartloads of dirt, so that he can worship his god on the soil of his own land."

"I don't remember that part," Nora told her.

"You said the Old Testament isn't your strong suit," Sage replied with a shrug. "I'm not surprised. How about Psalms, though? They're still pretty popular. Psalm 82?" Nora shook her head. "Well, that's one of my favorites. It's where God stands before the Divine Council, made up of his brother and sister gods, and condemns them for defending the poor, weak, sinful humans. And it ends with this barn burner." Sage bounced up onto her feet again and raised one fist as she intoned. "'Rise up, O God, judge the Earth, for all the nations are your inheritance."

This exclamation caught the attention of a group of women who stood in a cluster on the other side of the fire. They raised colorful fans in front of their faces and tittered behind them. The motion of it made their opulent outfits sparkle and jingle with tiny bells. One of the women met my gaze, and I felt myself start to rise out of my seat, without meaning to. With a shake of my head, I wrenched my eyes away from the bevy of sirens, and turned back to the conversation at hand.

"I thought the Bible was a pretty monotheistic affair," I mused. "I didn't realize there were any other gods in it."

"Oh yeah, definitely," Sage replied. "The Bible mentions a 'Divine Council' a few times. The Demiurge isn't claiming to be the only god, he's just jealous and thinks you should only worship him."

"And that you definitely shouldn't try to be like him," Urb added.

"Mmm hmm," Sage agreed. "He gets so defensive whenever humans get anything close to divine power. He lies to Adam and Eve, saying that the apple will kill them instead of giving them knowledge. And he destroys the Tower of Babel, instead of letting all of humanity talk to each other, and—"

The end of Sage's sentence was drowned out by a group of enormous men who had just wandered into the clearing, singing a sea shanty at the top of their powerful lungs. The giants had thick beards and barrel chests, and they swayed together, arms over each other's mighty shoulders, red-faced and merry. Soon enough, though, their massive strides took them past the bonfire, and away again.

"And," Sage continued, picking up where she left off, "of course, he sent the great flood to wipe out the Nephilim, the children of humans and angels."

"Angels and humans?" I asked. "You mean, like intermagicals?"

"Absolutely," Sage agreed. "We've been a problem for the Demiurge since the very beginning. And for the people who use him for their own purposes. Personal power is dangerous to him, and we've always had too much of it, for his liking. Too deep of a connection with our mother's divinity, and the god inside of us. Our mother wants to see us to reach our full potential. She's not jealous. She wants what's best for us."

"And it's not like he's really our father anyway, is he?" asked Urb. "If he's a child of El and Asherah, and we're children of Mother Earth."

"More like our step-father," Sage agreed. "Or maybe our cousin."

"God is our cousin?" Nora exclaimed, aghast. "That's blasphemy!"

"Oh, absolutely," said Sage, nodding. "Definitely blasphemy. But that's what it's all about, isn't it? When you're so scared of doing the wrong thing or being disrespectful of authority that you won't put a toe out of line. That's what keeps people on the straight and narrow. A mother's love doesn't control you. It makes you comfortable enough to grow into your whole authentic self."

"A mother's love," echoed Nora, thoughtfully. "Yeah, that makes sense."

I watched as she considered this, wearing a haunted expression under her dark fringed hat. Nora's mother died when she was very young, I knew. I wondered if Nora had any memories of her mother's love, from before she was turned over to the harsh control of the church.

"We carry our mother's wisdom deep inside our bodies," Sage said quietly, watching her. "But we have to find a way to love and trust ourselves enough to be able to access it."

"Yeah," said Nora. "I'm trying, but it's hard, growing up like I did."

"Sure is," said Sage. "Believe me, I know. Why do you think I'm so interested in this stuff? You'll figure it out, just like I did."

"Really?" Nora asked.

"Absolutely," Sage assured her. "The Demiurge is a storm god. A war god. He teaches us that we're allowed to kill anyone who doesn't bow down to our authority. Following his path damages your psyche. It allows you to justify committing atrocities in his name. That's why he is so often the patron God of the colonizer. But, the damage isn't irreversible."

"It's not?" asked Nora.

"No, it's not. Our mother's love is unconditional. She loves us for our whole, authentic self. Finding your way back to that love is like coming home, comfortable and warm. You can still hear the rain beating on the roof, but it can't hurt you, because you know, in your very soul, that you are your mother's perfect divine creation, just like everyone else."

She reached out and took Nora's hand in her own, looking into the other girl's eyes. I watched the subtle shifts of expression that told me that Nora was thinking hard about what Sage had just said.

"Do you ever wonder—" Nora started to ask, but she was interrupted by a commotion near the front gate. We all scrambled to our feet, alarmed by the angry shouting.

Chapter 44

A pirate came tearing through the trees toward us, with a long red belt scarf trailing behind him.

"What's going on?" Urb shouted.

"It's the Morality Police and they're pissed," he shouted back. "Get armed or get outta here!"

"What do we do?" Nora asked, clutching my arm.

Before I could open my mouth to tell her that I didn't know, my body, or possibly my unborn baby, or maybe my newfound mother's intuition answered for me.

zrp zrp
high ground

"We should find the high ground," I repeated, taking her hand and pulling her with me. We ran toward the hill that rose up behind the circle of cabins.

zrp zrp
through here

We ducked through a gap in the underbrush and found a trail that wound through the trees and up to the top of the hill. Before too long, the sounds of the festival faded into the distance, but our adrenaline kept us moving until we reached a little wooden house right at the top.

I turned and looked back the way we came, and realized that from this vantage point, I could see all the way down to the parking lot and the front gate of the Bacchanal. Huge white trucks, like the ones we saw at the Pirate Carnival, were parked haphazardly in front of it.

Another car turned in from the road and headed for the front gate. I recognized the boxy shape and the matte black paint job. It was Jaah's old diesel wagon, the one they took to Eastern Oregon. I watched as they rolled to a stop and threw open the door, then strode purposefully toward the gate with a thick wooden staff in one hand and their large black cloak billowing out behind them.

Grinning from ear to ear, I turned to Nora to tell her what I saw, but before I could, I was interrupted by a voice from behind us.

"Eleanora?"

I whirled, and beside me, Nora did the same. The speaker was a wizened old man, framed in the doorway of the little cabin.

"Having you show up on my doorstep like this is hardly the surprise it might be," he said with a wry smile. "Of all my dead friends, you'd be the most likely to manage a ghostly visit, I'd expect."

"Oh," I started, realizing that the old man must be crazy. "She's not a—" But, before I could say the word 'ghost,' Nora interrupted me.

"I can't remember the last time somebody called me Eleanora," she said, pale eyes wide.

"Well, come on in, old friend, and tell me what you're haunting me for."

Nora followed the old man into the cabin, and I followed also, curious. He motioned for us to sit, then busied himself at the stove. He turned back around with three steaming mugs of tea and set them down on a low table in front of us. Nora leaned forward and picked hers up, blowing away the steam, and he raised a quizzical eyebrow.

"You're not actually Eleanora, are you?" he said, eyeing my friend quizzically.

Nora shrugged, setting the fringe of her hat swinging to and fro. "People call me Nora, or Ellie. Or…" She shot a sheepish glance my way. "Sometimes Lena. But, my name is Eleanora, actually."

"Is it really?" the old man asked, settling himself into an overstuffed armchair across from us.

"Uh-huh," Nora said. "I'm named after my grandmother."

At this, our host's expression split into a wide grin, and he nodded enthusiastically. "Oh yes. That explains it. You share an extraordinary resemblance with your grandmother. Did you know that?" Nora shook her head, making the fringe bounce around again. "And," he continued, "if I'm not mistaken, I believe you're wearing her hat."

"Oh!" Nora exclaimed, snatching the thing off her head. "Yes! You're right, I am! Did you know her well?"

"She was one of my dearest friends," the old man said, reaching out to take the pointed black hat from Nora and holding it reverently. "It is wonderful to meet you, young Eleanora. You can call me Rainbow."

"This is my friend Fiona," Nora said, and Rainbow clutched my hand warmly in greeting.

"What brings you two ladies all the way up here?" he asked. "The party's down below."

"The Morality Police," I said, and watched his expression darken instantly.

"What makes those authoritarian asshats think they have any right to come onto my property and tell my guests anything about anything, I'm sure I don't know."

"Your guests?" I repeated, surprised.

Rainbow nodded. "When my nephew Fred told me about the trouble those square-headed morality meatballs have been cooking up all summer, I told him, of course, he could use the old summer camp. Not like I have much use for it anymore, all alone out here. It feels good to have young blood running through the place, again."

It wasn't always so lonely out here, Rainbow told us. Decades ago, there had been a small but lively community living together, way out here in the wilderness. Nora's grandmother was a part of that group.

"We just wanted the freedom to be ourselves," Rainbow told us, eyes misty with remembering. "The way they tell the story, the Puritans came to America to be free to practice their own religion. It's not true, though! They came to be free to persecute people who don't practice it, and don't want to follow their rules. So, we made our own community way out here, where we could be who we wanted to be, and I'm pleased to say that our way of thinking is catching on. You young people have managed to build such an open and free-thinking culture in these parts that the church had to call one of their big dogs back from Europe to try to put a stop to it. Or, that's how my boy Fred tells it, anyway."

"Are you talking about the intermagical revels?" I asked.

"Intermagical," Rainbow repeated. "That's the new term you young folks are using, isn't it? We used to say odd or different, or 'touched.' But, that was short for 'fae-touched' so we're all saying the same thing, really."

"Are you fae-touched?" Nora asked. "Do you know what kind?" She was fascinated by the concept of magical heritage ever since I introduced her to the idea on the drive to the Fair Isle yesterday. She must have asked almost every single patron at the bar about their fae heritage last night.

"Oh, me? I'm a magical muddle myself. Different kinds of folk scattered all through my family tree, but not enough of any one thing to be significant. Your grandmother, though, was a powerful hedge walker. A mist maiden. An undine." He smiled, thinking about her, then grew serious. "Maybe more like a mist mother, by the end. It doesn't feel quite right calling Eleanora the First, a maiden."

"An undine," said Nora, tasting the unfamiliar word. "Is that what I am?"

"With the way you take after your grandmother? I'd expect so," Rainbow replied. "You both have that look about you, like you're maybe half ghost already. It's no wonder they'd take a liking to you."

"I wish I could have seen what your grandmother looked like," I said.

Rainbow's eyes sparkled, and he sprang out of his seat, sprightly for such an aged individual.

"I'll get some of the old photos." He rummaged in a closet and emerged a few moments later with a dusty box. "Here's one from when she was just about your age, see?" Rainbow handed Nora a black and white photograph of a thin young woman who could have been her twin. "And look, here's one where she's wearing that very same hat." He handed us a second photograph. A slightly older Eleanora, in the same fringed hat that Nora was wearing now, sat holding a blond toddler in her lap. The little boy was frowning and staring straight into the camera in an unsettling way.

"Who is that?" I asked, holding out the photo.

"Oh, that'd be Birdie, her son. One of the twins. Odd little boy, he was. It's funny how that happens sometimes. Perfectly nice family, wonderful mother, sweet sister, but he was always a nasty child. We'd catch him hurting things, sometimes. Cruel, you know. Never listened to anyone, either, except his mother. She never saw the worst of him, of course. For one thing, you can't. Not when it's your own child.

And, for another thing, he kept it from her, seeing as he was afraid of her." Rainbow looked at the old photograph thoughtfully. "I'd say it's because he respected her, but I don't think Birdie ever respected anything. Not really. I haven't thought about him in years. He ran away from us when he was about fourteen. I wonder what became of him."

"Birdie," I said. "You mean like Bertrand?" Beside me, I felt Nora stiffen.

"Yes, that must have been his proper name. We always called him Birdie."

"Well, I can tell you where he ended up," I said. "He's the head of the Morality Police. He might be down there fighting with pirates right now."

"No," Nora interjected, voice small but confident. "Uncle doesn't go with them when they break up the sin festivals anymore."

"Leader of the Morality Police? Is that so? Well, I guess I can't be too surprised. Fred said the man had grown up around these parts. He's been digging into their organization all summer. Trying to figure out what they're up to, so he can beat them at their own game."

"It's a shame this didn't go as well as he hoped," I said, remembering the speech Fredbeard had given us at the front gate. "All that planning, and the Morality Police showed up anyway."

A cell phone buzzed. Rainbow retrieved it from his pocket and read the message. "Maybe," he told me. "And maybe not. Fred says it's all taken care of, and there's nothing to worry about. And he apologizes for the disturbance. Such a sweet boy. You know he was wearing a skirt when he came to visit me?"

Nora didn't seem to be listening. She was curled into herself, at the corner of the couch, lost in thought.

"Oh yeah?" I answered, holding up our end of the conversation.

"I asked him whether he was feeling a little more feminine these days, but he said no. It's a protest against these patriarchal types. They want to say that it's the natural order for men to be superior to women, and when big, powerful men like Fred show that they don't think it's shameful to act feminine, it contradicts their worldview and threatens the whole system. Or, at least, that's what Fred says."

"Uncle calls trans women an abomination," Nora said quietly, surprising me. Apparently, she was still listening.

"I guess I can almost see it, from his perspective," I said, thinking out loud. "They were born to be the next best thing to God, and now they want to be less? They want to choose to move down in the hierarchy? And what about trans men? If people can choose to move up or down on the ladder, that makes the idea of one being superior to the other, fall apart pretty quickly, doesn't it?" I thought about Urb, who had spent all summer being accepted as a man, without question, in the eyes of the church. If they only knew that he was ripping apart the very fabric of their patriarchy, right under their noses.

"You weren't carved from my rib," said Rainbow. "I was born from your womb." Then he caught my eye and added, "Motherhood is a beautiful thing."

"I guess it's safe to go back now, huh?" I asked. "Fred said it's all taken care of?"

"Yes, that's right," Rainbow agreed. "Get back down to the party, you two. No need to dilly-dally with an old man like me. I am just tickled that you found your way up here, though." He opened the door for us and bent low in a sweeping bow to my friend. "It was a special kind of treat to meet you, young Eleanora."

We were halfway down the hill before Nora spoke. "Can we stop here for a bit?" she asked. "I'm not ready to be back in the crowds yet."

"Sure," I agreed, and followed her as she climbed onto a big, flat rock. It made a comfortable seat, and we sat there in silence for a long moment.

"I just don't know what I believe anymore," she said, voice small and tentative. "I used to be so solid in my conviction, but now I feel like I don't know anything." She hugged her knees to her chest, making herself small.

I chuckled, and her red-rimmed eyes shot daggers at me over the tops of her knees.

"Sorry," I said. "I didn't mean to laugh, it's just that I said almost the exact same thing when I first came to Oregon, and learned about intermagicals and everything. And that was just," I counted. "April, May, June, July, August. About five months ago."

"Seriously?" she asked, and I nodded.

"Oh yeah. Up until this spring, I was just a normal, run-of-the-mill human. Or, at least, I was living like one. It wasn't until I moved up here, and met my birth family and learned about magic, that everything changed for me. I didn't have as much to unlearn as you do, though," I said. "Don't get me wrong, there were some tough moments, but when the smokescreen fell away for me, it was mostly all discovery and wonderment."

"And not the destruction of your entire world, and everything you thought you knew?" asked Nora with a wry smile.

"Yeah," I agreed. "Not as much of that."

"It wouldn't be so bad," she continued, "if it was just me who was wrong about everything. But it's not just me. It's everyone I know. Everyone I grew up with. My whole church family. They all believe that Uncle Rex and Christ's Heart are the path of righteousness. I just keep wondering what they would think if they got the chance to walk this same path I'm walking with you. Would it change their minds?"

"I don't know," I said with a shrug. "Maybe. Or maybe not." I thought back to my own first lessons about the nature of magic. "Ordinary humans tend to be stuck in their ways. They do things the same way their ancestors did them, and don't think too hard about it. You and I have that spark of magic running through our veins that lets us look beyond what's right in front of us, and see what is actually there."

"And Christ's Heart is made up of a bunch of ordinary humans, huh?" she asked, voice tinged with bitterness.

"Not necessarily. Not all of them," I replied. "But they probably all believe they're human. And they're doing their best to pretend to be human, just like you and I were, before we learned the truth. Before anyone told us that we had another option. There are a lot more intermagicals around than you'd expect. Or at least, more than I expected, anyway."

She nodded at that, looking somewhat mollified, then sat thinking for another long moment, eyes flicking busily underneath the fringe of her hat, back straight, and expression thoughtful. I couldn't help but admire the sight of her.

"Thanks for sitting with me," she said, finally. "I'm sorry for keeping you away from the party like this."

"No worries," I told her. "Honestly, I'm impressed you're still upright. If I were you, I think I'd be curled up in a corner crying, by now."

She laughed, and the high, fierce sound surprised me. "Want to know something I've noticed about this party, way out in the woods?" she asked with a roll of her wide blue eyes. "There aren't very many corners for curling up and crying in. But this rock is working okay." She patted the gray stone she sat upon, gratefully. "There are so many thoughts racing through my mind right now, though. Can I just tell you what I'm thinking, and you tell me if I sound crazy?"

"Yeah," I told her. "Sure. Okay."

"I haven't been able to stop thinking about my mother, after everything Sage was saying earlier. I don't like to think about her too much, usually, because it makes me cry, and crying is a—" She stopped and corrected herself. "And Aunt Tempest always told me that crying was a sin. And of course, I've been thinking about my grandmother, too," she said, stroking the fringe of her hat contemplatively.

"What have you been thinking?" I pressed after another long stretch of silence.

"They died on the same day, did I ever tell you that?" she said, finally.

"Who did?" I asked.

"My mother and my grandmother. I was really young. I can just barely remember them. Or, at least, I like to think I can. I remember my mother's..." she trailed off, then said, "Never mind. I don't want to cry right now. Not if I can help it. The point is, they died on the same day, at the same time. Out in the woods. There was an accident. These things happen. That's what Auntie would always say."

"I'm so sorry, Nora," I said, reaching out and taking her hand. With all the condolences I had received in the last week, the gesture felt natural and genuine. Her fingers were cool in mine, and I squeezed them, like so many old ladies had done, at the funeral last week. It was helpful to have had the practice. Otherwise, I'd be sitting awkwardly on the other side of the rock, with no idea what to do in this situation. She squeezed back, then pulled her hand away, wrapping her arms around her knees again.

"Auntie always said it was a miracle that they happened to be nearby. She and Uncle were doing ministry work in the area and decided to drop in for a visit, just a few days after Mom and Grandma died. They found my grieving father all alone, with me to take care of, and no idea what he should do."

"That was lucky," I said.

"Was it?" she asked, flashing bright eyes at me. I was startled by her fiery expression.

"What are you thinking, Nora?"

"Aunt Tempy couldn't have babies," Nora said quietly. "And Uncle always said that I was God's gift to her. That God's hand chose to save me from damnation and give me to Auntie for a proper upbringing."

"Oh yeah?" I asked, once the silence had become unbearable.

"I didn't know any of the stuff that old man Rainbow told us, about how Uncle was when he was little, or how he ran away from home when he was young. But the person he was describing sounded a whole lot more like that Ibex you were telling me about than the man Uncle says he is when he preaches on Sunday. But…" she paused again, and this time I waited quietly, letting her collect herself. "But, I've heard Uncle call himself the hand of God plenty of times, and I'm starting to think he didn't just happen to get lucky."

Had it been mere chance, or something more sinister that had put Reverend Rex in just the right position to swoop in and 'save' little Nora and her grieving father? He had the motive and the opportunity. If Jaah and Pythia were right, and the Reverend really was the Ibex, the man who had been hurting and kidnapping people all summer, the idea started to make a horrifying kind of sense.

"You really think that your Uncle could have…" I trailed off, unable to give voice to the terrible thought.

"I don't know," Nora answered, then buried her face in her hands. "I don't know what to think anymore."

I moved so that I was beside her and reached an arm around her thin shoulder. She was shaking, and I pulled her to me, wrapping myself around her protectively. Her shuddering gave way to great heaving sobs, and I held her to my chest, feeling the wetness of her tears soak through the fabric of my dress.

"He's a wilderness expert. Not just a mountaineer, but an alpinist. That's what he always says. And I always thought, if only he had been in the woods with Mama and Grandma, he would have been able to save them. But, what if he was there? Does he really think God told him to do it? Does he believe the things he says? Or, is he just a fraud and a liar?"

"I don't know," I told her, pulling her even tighter to my chest. "I don't know if there's any way to know."

"A week ago, I would have said he'd get his punishment in hell, but now I'm starting to wonder if that's what he wants us to think, so that he can just do whatever he wants and get away with it. And…" she added fiercely, "I don't know that I believe in hell anymore."

"What are you thinking, Nora?" I asked, seeing the wild expression in her eyes.

"I'm thinking that I don't want to wait and trust in God to deliver justice," she said. "Fiona, will you help me?"

"Of course," I told her. "Why, do you have an idea?" She nodded. "Okay. Yeah, let's make a plan."

"I think that might just work, don't you?" she asked, once we hashed out the details.

"You are absolutely brilliant, do you know that, Nora?" I told her. She shrugged, expression turning glum in sharp contrast to the fierce intensity of a few moments ago. "Hey, what's the matter? What's going on?" I asked.

"I'm feeling guilty for even thinking about doing something like that," she said, looking away and not meeting my eyes. "And now that I'm saying it out loud to you, I'm feeling ashamed and embarrassed for feeling that way. It's like my brain and my body are fighting with each other. These new ideas make sense. Really, they do. And I'm doing my best to hold them all in my mind," she told me. "But then my body betrays me and I get sucked back down into this deep, horrible well of shame. You didn't grow up religious. You don't know what it's like."

"Actually, I kind of do," I said, and she looked up at me, surprised. "You're right, I wasn't ever religious, but growing up with my mom left me with a whole mess of shame to deal with, anyway." As a child, I was reprimanded constantly for being messy, forgetful, and disorganized, all traits that came from my faerie nature. Mom shamed me for having curves and rounded features like my faerie family, too. Like the Demiurge, my adopted mother had seen all the ways her child was unlike her, and she hated those differences and made me hate them too. "Constant shame was one strategy for keeping me in line, I guess, but it sure did a number on my self-esteem. I've gotten some distance from it since moving away, but I was just visiting her last week, and I'm still working on shaking it off."

270

"Really?" she asked.

"Really," I agreed. "I get it, I do. That gnawing pit in your stomach, and the way it makes you feel, like a tiny worthless little worm?" She met my gaze, looking vulnerable and small. "It's not the same as what you're going through, but I've been close enough to know how tough it is. I'm amazed by how much work you've done, in such a short amount of time, and I'm awed by everything you've overcome. I'm so excited to get to know the incredible person you're becoming."

"You are?" she asked, turning her face up to mine, with eyes so deep I could almost dive into them. I opened my mouth to answer, but before I could, she was kissing me, and it was not practice.

It wasn't hard to find our way back to the ring of logs and the campfire, and we stepped out of the trees together, hand in hand. I scanned the tree line looking for any signs of life, but there was no one in sight. Beside me, I felt Nora stiffen, and I turned to see what she was looking at. A dark silhouette was approaching us, shadowy in the close-packed trees. I squeezed Nora's hand in mine, trying to reassure her, even as I felt my own heartbeat quicken.

"Hey, who are you?" I yelled, trying not to sound like I was scared.

At the sound of my voice, the dark figure picked up the pace, loping toward us with a cloak billowing behind. I recognized that silhouette. As usual, Jaah had come to find me.

I dropped Nora's hand and ran toward them. At the edge of the tree line, we met and they swept me up into a tight hug, swinging me around, just like they had swung Zinnia and Azalea, at the Pirate Carnival. Except, this time, I wasn't looking on in horror as my world fell apart; I was the one in their arms.

zrp zrp
we are

"Fiona, are we really pregnant?" Jaah asked, voice full of wonderment. They must have gotten my note. Eyes squeezed shut, I nodded into their shoulder, and their arms wrapped even tighter around me. I relished in the tingling feeling of their joyful energy pouring into me and filling me to the brim. Eventually, Jaah set me down, and when I opened my eyes, my stomach dropped.

"Nora?" I said, seeing her horrified expression over Jaah's shoulder. "Nora! Wait, please! I can explain!" I called after her, but it was too late. Her eyes were as cold as ice when she spun around and disappeared back into the trees.

Chapter 45

"She'll be alright, she's an adult," Jaah repeated, stroking my back comfortingly. "She probably just went back up to that cabin and that guy you were telling me about. You said he knew her grandmother, right?"

"Mmhm," I agreed, miserable. They were probably right, but it didn't make me feel any better. Why did I put Nora in that position, and surprised her like that? Why didn't I tell her about Jaah earlier?

"Look, I want to get back out there, now that I've found you," Jaah said, doing their best to control their impatience. "Will you come with me?" I nodded and gave one last glance over my shoulder at the place where Nora disappeared, before following them out of the clearing and back toward the front gate. While we walked, Jaah told me how they had arrived right after the Morality Police.

"I saw you, actually," I told them. "From way up on the hill."

"Nice," they said with a grin. "It was perfect timing, actually. For me, anyway. For one thing, I didn't have a ticket, since you took mine, and for another, I ended up in just the right position to watch the pirates pour out of the woods on top of these guys and hear their affordable blades go snicker-snack."

"Don't you mean vorpal blades?" I asked, with a laugh.

"On these pirates' budgets?" Jaah replied. "Doubtful. Real cool to watch, though. Did you know your brother Egan fights with flaming nun-chucks?"

"Flaming nunchucks?" I repeated, nonplussed. "I know he spins fire at festivals sometimes, but those are called poi, I think."

"Nah, you start hitting people with 'em like that, they're flaming nunchuks, I'm pretty sure."

We rounded the corner where Fredbeard stood, at the center of a ring of pirates, wearing high-heeled boots and a flounced skirt underneath his Admiral's jacket. He was stepping nimbly over the legs of the dozen or so men who sat at the center of the crowd, hands tied behind their backs. Their off-brand military fatigues and short-cropped hairstyles were a stark contrast to the colorfully dressed pirates celebrating cheerfully, all around them.

"Bet you're enjoying having us tied up like this, aren't you, you degenerate fairy."

"Quite the contrary," said Fredbeard, high-stepping his way around the circle of legs until he could loom over the man who spoke. "Now, I'm queer certainly, but I'm sure the fairies would be more than happy to tell you that I'm not one. And anyway, I'm not enjoying this particularly. I'm into consent, and nothing about you being here is consensual. We did everything we could to make sure that you stayed away. But, here you are, tied up in the middle of my festival, and I promise you absolutely no one is happy about that."

"Yeah, right," growled another captive. "I know what you weirdos do with good Christian men. You tie them up and you, and you…" He trailed off, unable to finish the thought.

"And we do what?" Fred retorted. "Smack their cute little bottoms? Only if they ask us nicely, and you've all been so rude today. And we wouldn't want to make you excited," he said, leaning over and winking at another one of the men, before he added, "I mean, uncomfortable."

Fred spun away, his skirts flying out around his ankles. He continued to lecture the captives, but I only had eyes for the man Fred winked at. He squirmed uncomfortably in his seat, and looked like he was struggling with something.

"…acting like a moral authority and making us out to be predators. Saying we're the ones indoctrinating people, when it's you telling children that they'll be punished eternally for trusting their own bodies and minds. For—"

The squirming man could take it no longer and sprang to his feet, an impressive feat, considering his hands were tied behind his back. With an awkward hop, he spun to face the other captives.

"I can't do this anymore," he said, voice heavy with emotion. "I know some of these guys. I've hung out with them, tried some stuff. They're not evil, alright? Fred's a good guy. I didn't know he was the one we were going after."

"It's okay, baby," said Fredbeard, as he untied the ropes at the man's back "These nasty men can't hurt you."

"Who are you calling nasty?" one of the men on the ground shouted.

"You," said Fred decisively. "You're a bunch of nasty bullies who have been brainwashed by powerful people into doing their dirty work. Those big church leaders are so scared of all of us liberated young folk, out here making our own magic and living our truth, that they had to send you in to try to scare us off. It's not going to work, though. They're losing their grip and they know it. They've spent all summer trying to shut us down, and we're still here."

"And so are we!" the same loud-mouthed captive retorted.

"Indeed, you are, but you have no legal reason to be. We're following all of your rules. We've jumped through every one of your nonsensical hoops, and you're here anyway."

"Nuh uh!" said another one of the men. "New rules. Effective this morning!"

"Oh, you've got to be kidding me," Fred groaned. The man he had untied held out a piece of paper, and Fred snatched it irritably. "Straight from Rev. Rex himself, huh? I swear, Christ's Heart sent him back from Europe specifically to be a thorn in my side. What's the new stuff? This here?" He snapped the paper dramatically and read aloud. "No flogging or whipping, no homosexual behavior, and no drug use of any kind, regardless of whether it's sanctioned by the organizers. How are we supposed to control that?"

"Just follow God and act righteously," spat one of the captives.

"Christianity is a white supremacist cult that has raped and pillaged its way through history," Fred replied coldly. "The idea that you have some kind of moral high ground is ridiculous."

"And your parties sound lame," called one of the pirates in the crowd.

"That's true," Fred agreed. "You have to follow all your own rules, too, don't you? You fellows sure have painted yourself into a corner with all these morality statutes you've come up with. Sure, we've got to follow them, but so do you, or else you're cooked, aren't you?"

Murmurs of denial rose from the circle of captives. Some looked resolute, I saw, but others wore shifty expressions and kept their eyes on the ground. Next to me, I felt Jaah stiffen. Then, to my surprise, they squeezed my hand and stepped forward into the open space at the center of the circle of revelers surrounding the captives.

"Hey friend," said Fred, raising a quizzical eyebrow at Jaah's approach. "What can I do for you?"

"It's what I can do for you, actually," Jaah replied. "Are you telling me that these Morality nutsacks would be dead in the water, if they were caught on video passing out drugs, and whipping themselves? Oh, and maybe a little gay propositioning, too, just for good measure."

The gathered crowd was silent. They held out their hand and let something drop from it. My necklace, the crystal point Jaah gave me, swung from their hand, catching the light and sparkling.

"What?" Fred and I both asked in unison.

"Oh yeah, that would be real bad," said the former captive that Fred untied.

My mind was spinning. Was Jaah talking about the church parties I had gone to? They must be, I realized. Who had I seen passing out drugs? I thought back and remembered the woman on the front porch before the Women's Group who had been offering to share her prescription medication with her friend. And, I recollected, there was that quick glimpse I'd gotten through the crack of the door, of the woman holding a leather strap over her bare thighs. But, what about the gay propositioning? I puzzled for a moment, then reddened, remembering how Nora had suggested we try kissing, just for practice.

"This is a camera? Really?" Fred asked, holding my necklace up to the light and examining it curiously.

"Yep," Jaah agreed. "Brand new tech I've been working on. Crystal clear picture."

"Wonderful," said Fred, eyes alight with gleeful menace. "That will work excellently."

"You don't think that's going to stop us, do you?" one of the captives growled.

"A little something like the law, you mean?" Fred asked, and the man scowled in what was clearly agreement. "No, I don't imagine the law is going to stop you. But guess what? The law has been stopping us. If you don't have legal jurisdiction as the Morality Police, you're just regular old Corpsos, and a fair fight means open season, right, friends?"

The sound of swords being drawn from sheaths sent a shiver down my spine, as I watched Fred's face split in an enormous grin.

Part 11 - Home

Chapter 46

"So, what's the other big surprise?" Jaah asked as I turned my van onto the road heading away from the Bacchanal.

"Oh, right," I said, coming back to the present moment. I had been thinking about Nora again. After I told them everything that happened, Jaah went up to Rainbow's cabin, to check for Nora. She was there, Rainbow confirmed, but she didn't want to speak with anyone. There were so many people in her life who wanted to control her and get her to do things she didn't want to do. If she didn't want to talk to me, I would respect her choice. It didn't put me in the mood for a revel, though, and Jaah offered to leave with me, and have one of their friends drive their car back to the Fair Isle later.

"Well?" Jaah prompted after a long moment.

"Sorry," I replied. "It's complicated, and I'm trying to figure out the best way to say it."

My great-aunt, my grandmother's sister, had died when I was young. I didn't remember her, but I knew she had lived up here in Oregon, and helped arrange my adoption. She was an eccentric old lady, and never married. When she died, she arranged for her house to be left in trust, as an inheritance for the next grandchild born to the family. I explained all this to Jaah.

"Fiona, didn't you tell me that you were the youngest, out of all your cousins?"
"Uh huh. I'm the youngest member of my whole extended family. And this baby will be the first new grandchild, since me."

"Wait, what are you saying? Are you inheriting somebody's house?"

zrp zrp
we are

"Yeah," I told them, cheeks splitting in a wide grin. "We are."

"A whole house?" Pythia crowed when I told her the news, later that night, at the Fair Isle. "Girl, that faerie luck just won't quit, will it? A whole house, would you believe that? That's the dream, finding out you have some long-lost ancestor with money. But it makes sense, for you, doesn't it? If that fantasy's gonna come true for anyone, it'd be for an adopted white kid, wouldn't it? At least one side of the family's gonna have some money."

"I guess," I said with a shrug. When I told her my news, a moment ago, I was excited, but now I just felt overwhelmed by it all. A house? A baby of my own? Was I really ready for all of that?

"What's wrong?" Pythia asked.

"Nothing," I lied, then backpedaled, and said, "Nothing really. I'm just tired, I guess. I've had a crazy week."

"For real! You drove all the way to California and back, and your grandmother died, and you found out you were pregnant, and you inherited a whole house. That's enough to make anybody's head spin."

"Yeah," I agreed with a strangled little chuckle. "It sure is!" In truth, my mind had been tangled up in thoughts about my first boyfriend actually being my first girlfriend, and the fact that my childhood friend had died before I'd realized I'd been in love with her. And then, I'd remember how much her big blue eyes looked like Nora's, and about how it had felt, kissing her, and then I'd remember the terrible expression on Nora's face, before she turned and walked away. It looked so much like the expression she'd made when she realized her Uncle was—

"Pythia!" I exclaimed, interrupting my own cascading thoughts. "There's something else I need to tell you!" I filled her in on what I'd learned at church about the Ibex.

"The Reverend?" Pythia shrieked, thumping her fists on the bar. "The Reverend! You're sure? Ooh you have got to be kidding me. But it figures, huh? It just figures!" Her face fell. "But, what are we supposed to do about it, if it's somebody like that? People like him get away with worse than this all the time. It's gonna be tough to make anything stick."

"Well," Jaah interjected. "Luckily for us, that girl of Fiona's came up with something to try." They took a long sip of their drink and sat back, waiting for me to tell Pythia about Nora's plan.

"Oh, um, yeah. Nora did have an idea," I said evasively. "And I want to be down in the valley on Saturday so I can help her with it." If she even wants me there, I added, silently, to myself. But this was about her Uncle, and not what had happened between the two of us. And, I still had her clothes and the box of her grandmother's things that she left in my van. Pythia eyed me, as though sensing that there was more to the story than I was telling. I felt a little guilty keeping things from her, but I could only imagine how she would screech when I told her about the kiss, and I didn't think I could bear listening to her commentary on everything else that happened. Not with the way I left things with Nora. I would tell her eventually, just not tonight. "I think we should drive down to the valley after work on Friday to see the new house," I said to Jaah, changing the subject. "And then we can stay the night at Mom's hill."

"Or we can sleep at the new place!" Jaah suggested hopefully.

"Yeah, maybe."

The rest of the week felt like an eternity, but eventually it was Friday and time for us to drive down to the valley and see the new house. Evita's hill was on the way, and when we pulled up the driveway, she was already standing there, ready to leave.

"Oh, it's you," she said when I stepped out of the van. "It's wonderful to see you, honey. How's your mother doing?"

"She's good, Mom. Or, as good as can be expected," I said, bending slightly to return my faerie mother's embrace. Warmth flowed into me, and I smiled into her shoulder. "It's good to be back."

"It's good to have you back," she replied, giving my arm a squeeze. "Now, tell me where we're going already! I've been buzzing with excitement all day, and I don't have a single idea why." She squealed with excitement when I told her about the house I inherited, and even louder, when she heard the reason why I was inheriting it. "I'm not really surprised," she told me conspiratorially after she had caught her breath. "I've got a sense for these things, but I kept it to myself until you could tell me."

"Well, you might have given me a heads up," I said. "I didn't have any clue until the doctor told me, a couple of days ago."

zrp zrp
some clues

I giggled, putting a hand to my belly. There were some signs, it was true.

Less than an hour later, the three of us arrived. We would have gotten here sooner, but Evita insisted that we stop at a garage sale, and, as was her faerie nature, she had to pick through every little thing before we could get back on the road.

The sound of the gravel crunching under my van's tires, and the feeling of stepping out into the tree-shaded front yard of the large gray house gave me an odd feeling of déjà vu. I had never been here before, but at the same time, it looked extraordinarily familiar. And, I realized, with a shiver that ran all the way down my spine, it felt like home.

The house was set a ways back, but the garage jutted forward nearly to the road. The two dark windows over the open garage door looked like a mouth opened in an 'o' of happy surprise at our arrival, which made me smile.

A glint in one of the windows caught my attention. It was a pair of unusually large, dark eyes that blinked at me, and then disappeared. There was motion inside the garage, and a hatch swung open, followed by a rope ladder. A moment later, a pair of stout little legs appeared, followed by a very round lower half.

In my periphery, I saw Jaah's eyes widen until they were nearly as round as the little person herself.

Beside me, Evita's eyes flicked between the girl's dangling legs and Jaah's slack-jawed expression. She arched an eyebrow at me questioningly. I shrugged a shoulder in answer. The way she wrinkled her brow and nodded hesitantly made me unsure what exactly I just communicated.

The girl made it down the first few rungs without issue, but then her right foot began a quiver that spread to her knee, and then to her left foot, until the whole ladder was jouncing to and fro.

"Hey, do you need any help there?" Jaah called.

"No, that's okay, I'll be alright, I—" the girl called back, leaning around the ladder to talk. This made the unstable structure twist and swing alarmingly. "Woah there! Okay, yeah, maybe."

Now I had the chance to get a better look at her, I realized why her eyes looked so large. She wore extraordinarily thick glass lenses which made her pupils enormous. They bulged comically as she swung on the ladder. Jaah hurried over to the girl and stabilized her as she finished her climb and she hopped down the last few rungs and onto the packed dirt floor with a satisfying plop.

"Sorry," she said, "I got excited when I saw you and thought it would be easier than going all the way around. Guess not!" She turned a pink-cheeked smile on me and Evita. "I just heard the good news! Come on in, cousin! I'm Lucy Brown." She bent down and hooked the bottom of the rope ladder to some anchor points on the floor. "I only ever go up this way," she said, motioning for us to follow her. "I didn't think about the issues with going down!"

Jaah waved me ahead, and I followed Lucy up the ladder. We emerged into a cozy little room filled top to bottom with bumble bees. Not actual bees, of course, but the effect was startling even so, with every cushion and tea towel festooned with little spots of black and yellow.

"Buzz buzz," said Jaah, head and shoulders poking out of the hatch in the middle of the living room floor.

"That's me, Lucy Bee!" said Lucy, flushing a bright pink again. "People just love to give me presents."

"Oh!" I exclaimed, with a sudden spark of insight. "You know what, I think this is for you!" I said, reaching into my shoulder bag and drawing out a charming bee-covered apron. I grabbed on a whim for a dollar at the yard sale Evita insisted we stop at. Now, I handed the pretty yellow thing to Lucy, who cooed over it admiringly and clutched it tightly to her chest.

"You like bees, then?" Jaah asked. "I've always thought I'd like to have a hive or two, if I ever have the space."

"Oh, not particularly," said Lucy. "Creepy crawly little things," she added with a shudder, as she hung the apron I just gifted her proudly on a peg.

"You don't? But, then, why do you…" I asked, gesturing at the charmingly crowded little space.

"Well, people just love to give me presents, and I couldn't ever get rid of a present, could I?"

Horrified, I looked from her cheerful smiling face to the new bee-festooned item I had just added to her collection, unsure of what to do, until I felt the gentle pressure of Evita's touch on my arm. With it came the words, *It's alright, it's her nature. What is done is done.*

"You'll want to see the rest of it!" Lucy exclaimed, seizing my hand and leading me down a narrow back staircase. She stepped aside, gesturing toward the closed door in front of us. "Welcome!"

I felt Jaah's warm presence behind me and reached back to take their hand. They squeezed it as we stepped forward toward the door.

zrp zrp
we're home

Another shiver ran down my spine as I pushed open the door and stepped through.

"Oh, that's beautiful," said Evita, behind me. I stepped aside to let her past, speechless, but in complete agreement. We entered into an elegant witch's kitchen, high ceiling hung with bundles of herbs and shelves lined with all sorts of crocks and jars. The wide window over the sink was draped with hanging plants in a way that reminded me pleasantly of Evita's.

"This is the only room I really use," said Lucy, somewhat apologetically. "But I've got a kitchenette upstairs, and I can keep myself to myself, now that you're here."

"Oh, Lucy, no," I said, finding my voice at last. "This is your home, too. I don't want to do anything to take that away from you."

After my mother explained the situation to my grandmother's lawyer, she handed the phone to me so he could tell me the details of this unusual inheritance. The house was held in trust all these years, but it had not been unoccupied. Instead, it was left in the care of my great-aunt's close friend and caregiver. After her death, it passed to her daughter, who, the Will stipulated, was to be allowed to live at the Garden Home for as long as she chose to stay. Lucy Bee came with the house, a package deal.

She beamed at this, bouncing gently on the balls of her feet. "You want to see the rest of it? It'll be fun to see what all's in this house. It's been packed away since the old lady died. Um, I mean—" she interrupted herself. "I shouldn't call her 'Old Lady,' that doesn't sound very nice. Although, it's true, she was quite old. But she used to be the lady, and now you're the lady. You know what I mean?"

I wasn't entirely sure I did know what she meant, actually, but, remembering how Calliope had called Faeryn her lady, I found I didn't mind it, and returned the girl's bright smile. I was Evita's daughter, after all. The child of a faerie queen. Why shouldn't I be the Lady of the House? But, I hadn't inherited this place from the faerie side of my family, had I? I furrowed my brow, confused, but Lucy was already on the move, and I followed her, resolving to ask her more about my great-aunt, this mysterious Old Lady.

She led us into a large room off the kitchen which had a fireplace and several rugs rolled up in a stack, in the middle of the dark wood floor. I looked forward to unfurling them and seeing what sort of style my great-aunt liked to decorate in.

"We could put my big couch in the corner, and mount a few big screens up on the wall right here, don't you think?" said Jaah, eyeing the sizable space critically. I nodded. A technomage would need a place for their tech, and this was Jaah's home too. The new living space wasn't the only sizable thing that Jaah was eyeing, I noted, as Lucy led us back out into the kitchen and up a curved staircase. I noticed the way that Lucy's cute round shape bounced up the steps too, but my eyes weren't goggling out of my head like Jaah's were.

These would surely be the bedrooms, I thought as I stepped onto the upstairs landing lined with several unmarked doors. Instinctively, I chose one and opened it, stepping into a large Master suite. A large wooden bedframe dominated the space, the headboard decorated with two dragon heads, mouths open, ready to roar fire. Jaah tugged at the corner of a large white sheet, revealing an enormous floor mirror, decorated with shining brass filigree and topped with another ornate dragon.

"Dragons, huh?" Jaah remarked, taking a step back to admire the decorative item.

"Dragons," Evita agreed, following us into the space. "I met her once, arranging your adoption, Fiona. I had forgotten. I remember thinking she was very noble, and that you would be safe with a family of dragons."

"A family of dragons? What are you saying, Evita?" I asked, nonplussed. Looking again at the roaring faces carved into the bedframe, I remembered the research I'd done on dragons earlier this summer. I learned that dragons are deeply magical and cold-blooded. They have a fierce bite and an even more powerful force of will, and you can rely on a dragon to be sitting on top of a great pile of material wealth. I considered this, feeling the puzzle pieces fall into place. "Wait, Mom, is my mother actually a dragon?"

"That makes sense, with everything you've told me about her," said Jaah, flopping down onto the sheet-covered bed and sending up a cloud of fine white dust. "Nothing like a dragon to make you feel like a tiny, worthless worm just by existing. But man, do they give nice presents when they feel like it. This place is amazing," they said, smacking the mattress and sending up another puff of dust.

"Yeah," I agreed with a sigh, looking around at the large, well-appointed room. "This is all we need. More than enough, really."

"But let's check out the rest anyway, huh?" Jaah said, hopping up from the bed and heading back out into the hallway. "Hey! Weren't there a few more doors out here?"

I followed them out onto the landing, where they were tugging on the handle of the door directly across from the bedroom we just explored. It seemed to be stuck, and they wiggled and tugged at it ineffectually. I hadn't taken the time to count the doors I saw when we first mounted the stairs, but my impression was certainly that there had been more than two. The bedroom was plenty large enough for Jaah and me, but it sure would be nice to have another room we could start getting ready for the baby.

"Ope!" Jaah exclaimed, as the door came unstuck, swinging inward. "Oh hey, check this out, Fiona. It's a nursery. There's a little crib in here, and everything."

"Jaah," I said, voice quiet and intense. "Come back out here, please." My whole body tingled as I waited for them to join me.

"Fiona, what is it?" Jaah asked. I pointed, and watched their eyes widen. "Wait, is that—"

"Yep," I answered. Where there had once been a flat, blank wall there was now a third door.

"And why not?" said Lucy Bee cheerfully. Seeing our blank expressions, she added, "It's only natural that the Garden Home would grow for you!"

Chapter 47

That night, we cooked dinner together. Lucy and Evita chopped carrots on the kitchen's large island, while I washed lettuce at the sink behind them, and Jaah busied themselves looking through drawers and cupboards to see what was there.

"We're not really cousins, I don't think," I heard Lucy tell Evita. "But Mama always said that Brownies were a kind of faerie, and I figure that makes us sort of like family."

"Oh, to be sure, dear," Evita agreed. "Fiona will be lucky to have a house Brownie here. Your kind are just so helpful. I know it's custom that I'm not supposed to thank you for it, but I've never been one for following rules, and good help deserves appreciation, so let me just say thank you so much for being here, darling."

"Oh, um, well, how about that?" said Lucy, looking uncomfortable. She gave a little wiggle like she was shaking off the bad feeling, and re-assumed her bright smile. "It's awfully nice to have a family here again," said Lucy. "After the Old Lady died, my Mom met Mama D, and she just loved collecting strays, so the house was always full to bursting. Animals and foster kids, and my two mamas and me."

"That's a lot of mothers for just one person," Evita said, with a glance over her shoulder at me.

"Yeah," Lucy agreed. "I was lucky that way. Nothing like a mother's love, you know? It's been pretty quiet around here these past few years. It sure feels great to have people to cook with again. I could get used to this! It sure is nice that you're so close, too. Fiona can just give you a ring, and you can pop over and help out, any time!"

"Oh," said Evita, taking her own turn to look uncomfortable. "Yes. I'm sure that will be fine. I am quite busy with my own affairs. I have my own little realm to manage, you know. But, of course. Of course, I'll be here whenever Fiona needs me…" she paused and gathered herself before choking out the next thought, "I have a duty to my family, and will do whatever they ask of me."

I turned away and swallowed the chuckle bubbling up inside me, so Evita wouldn't see. I was certain that Evita would be an exceptionally magical and special part of her grandchild's life, but it would be on her own terms. I knew, even if Lucy Bee did not, that calling Evita for help would be asking her to behave in a way that was contrary to her nature, and no good would come of that.

After dinner, Evita took her leave. "I'm so glad everything's working out, honey," she told me, giving me a hug as we said our goodbyes at the front door. "I've been worried about you. You're so young. Barely even stepping out into the world, and already with such big shoes to fill. But…" She gripped my shoulders and leaned back, looking at me. "You can do it. Look how everything is falling into place, just like it should. And, if you need anything, I'm just ten minutes away."

"Yeah," I said, plastering on a smile. "Absolutely. Good night, Mom."

I headed back into the living room, where we unrolled some of the oriental rugs to sit on, until we could get Jaah's big sofa moved down from the city. Jaah and Lucy were sitting together, heads bent in close conversation. When I stepped through the doorway, they jumped apart, startled.

"Oh," I said, stomach dropping. I whirled around and headed back into the kitchen. Seeing my steaming cup of tea on the counter, I picked it up and took several slow breaths to let my heart rate slow back down. I surprised them. It was a natural reaction. They were't doing anything wrong. Even if Jaah was interested in Lucy, there was nothing wrong with that, was there? That was our arrangement, wasn't it? I took a sip from the steaming mug, and another calming lungful of air before heading back through the doorway.

"Everything okay?" Lucy asked, seeing me.

"Yeah," I said. "I just forgot my tea in the kitchen."

"Okay," she said, sounding unconvinced. "If you say so."

"It's nothing, really," I assured her, taking another step into the room. "I'm fine. I'm just tired. Maybe a little hormonal, too, I'd figure. What with the pregnancy, and everything?"

"Oh!" she exclaimed, bouncing to her feet. "You're pregnant! Oh, that's wonderful! It all makes sense. I feel a little silly! Of course, I should have realized. You're pregnant, and it's the baby that's inheriting the house! I thought maybe you were a long-lost granddaughter or something. I'm so excited! A baby, here? Oh, Fiona!" She hurried over and flung her arms around me in a tight hug. "I just can't wait to hold him, and rock him, and rub his little back to sleep. And warm his little bottles. Oh, but you'll probably want to breastfeed, won't you? Have you thought about names yet? And are you considering cloth diapers at all? Mama D always said they were so much nicer, but an awful lot of work to keep up with. But, I'll be here to help, of course!"

"Oh, I…" I gulped, unable to find any words to answer her barrage of questions. "I'm not feeling so well. I'm going to lie down."

Turning on my heel, I fled up the stairs and into the dark bedroom, throwing myself down onto the dragon-headed bed and curling up in a little ball, wrapping my arms around my knees. Hot tears trickled down my face, and my breath caught in my chest. "I'm not ready," I whispered. "For any of this." The darkness swallowed my words, and I felt incredibly small. How am I supposed to raise a baby when I feel like a child myself? I've only just graduated college and started my first real job. A job I was going to need to quit, if I was moving down to the valley to live here. Here, in this enormous, overwhelming, magical house. Here, with Jaah, the father of my unborn child, who I had only known for a few months, and Lucy Bee, who I had just met today, and who was already proving herself to be more capable of caring for this baby than I was.

I felt myself beginning to spiral. "I don't know anything about babies," I confessed. I was still the youngest person in my whole adopted family, until this baby was born. I hadn't grown up around little kids. I couldn't even remember the last time I held a baby. I'd seen some in college, doing observational case studies at the university daycare, but one childhood psychology class didn't make me fit to be a parent. I certainly didn't want to use my own cold, rigid childhood as my model. And, while certainly wonderful, in many ways, the better I got to know Evita and her defiant faerie nature, the more I realized that I didn't want to parent like she did, either.

"How am I supposed to do this?" I asked.

zrp zrp
just do

The pulse came from the very center of me, and I realized, in my misery, that I'd wrapped myself around the tiny life growing inside my belly. Maybe I did have some maternal instincts, I thought, the idea bubbling warmly inside of me, safe and secure like the child I carried.

But, in just a few short months, this baby would be outside the protection of my body, thrust into a world full of dangerous people like the Reverend and predatory organizations like Christ's Heart. Born vulnerable and small, into the world of the Demiurge and his followers, with only me to protect them from that darkness. And who was I, in the face of that power? They had put me in prison once already. I shuddered at the memory of that long, cold night, unsure whether I would ever get out of that terrible place. And here I was, planning to go up against them again tomorrow. Putting myself back in the line of fire, to stand beside Nora and help her with her plan. And not only that, I was the one filming the footage Fredbeard was going to use to take down the Morality Police.

Was I really hoping that they wouldn't realize it was the same girl who got the Deacon arrested last spring? I had put an enormous target on my back, and that realization was all the more horrifying when I considered the vulnerable little life I was now responsible for. I was worried about being ready to raise this baby. Should I be more worried that I wouldn't be allowed to raise them at all, because I'd be rotting away in jail?

Nora might be there right now, telling them all about me. I told her everything. For the millionth time, I saw her look of betrayal behind my eyes, the one Nora gave me before she disappeared into the trees. It was all my fault. I should have told her about Jaah. Of course, I should have. How could I have been so careless? So callous with her feelings? How could I be ready to be a mother when I didn't even have the emotional maturity to keep Nora's heart safe? How could I live with myself if I did something to make my own child look at me the way Nora had?

"I can't do this," I whispered into the night. "I need more time. I'm not ready for this. I'm not good enough. I don't know enough. I just wish I had a little more time." But, when would I feel ready? How much life experience would be enough? Questions floated in the empty space above my bed. How much more time did I need? "A lifetime, maybe?" I answered with a breathy chuckle.

The bedroom door swung open with a long whine of old hinges, and I wrapped myself in the blanket, pretending to be asleep.

"Are you alright in there, Fiona?" Jaah whispered from the doorway. They paused for a while, then asked, "Are you sleeping?"

I lay still and silent, waiting for them to shut the door.

Chapter 48

I woke up before the sun.

My pretend sleep must have slipped into real slumber, I realized, as I listened to Jaah snoring softly next to me. Going to bed when I did, it made sense that I was up so early, and feeling so well-rested. The darkness I felt last night had faded somewhat in the morning light, and I found myself feeling quite a bit better. It might also be this ridiculously comfortable bed, I thought, as I sat up and stretched.

It was early morning, and I didn't need to meet Nora until the afternoon. And, I reminded myself, putting a hand on my stomach, there was still some time before the baby would be here. There was plenty to think about, it was true, but I didn't need to worry about it all, right now.

Wrapping myself in a flowery silk robe that Evita found for me, I headed down to the kitchen and put the kettle on to make tea. Out the kitchen window, I could see the first blush of morning light beginning to illuminate the garden. It looked so inviting that I decided to take a quick stroll outside while I waited for the kettle to boil.

"Garden home, indeed," I breathed, as I stepped off the back porch and onto the soft lawn. It was beautiful back here, overgrown with late summer flowers and bumbling with bees. I picked a snap pea off a vine as I made my way deeper into the garden. After a while, the flower beds gave way to a more natural undergrowth of nettles and ferns, and tall trees towered overhead. "How far back does it go?" I wondered aloud. There might be no back fence at all, I realized, and I was now walking barefoot in the forest.

Eventually, I found a charming little step bridge spanning a burbling brook. Up until now, the ground was carpeted with soft clover, but once I left the footbridge, I would have stepped out onto pine needles and sharp rocks, which didn't look nearly as pleasant. Reaching the far side, I decided to turn around and pivoted on the smooth wood. As I turned, I saw something slither out from under the bridge.

The troll was long and lean, with skin like smooth gray rock and mesmerizing eyes, like river stones underwater.

"Ah, ah, ah," they said, wagging one long finger at me. "It still counts. You crossed my bridge, even if you never stepped off the other side. That's a clever trick, I'll admit, but across is across, and I'll have what's owed me. Your toll now, miss."

"My, uh…" I started to speak, then stopped, pausing to collect myself before I said the wrong thing to the wrong sort of fae. "I'm sorry, friend troll," I answered, finally. "But you've caught me in an unfortunate circumstance. I don't have anything to offer you. Not even the shoes off my feet." I raised one bare foot and shook it, in demonstration. The truth was, the only thing I had with me was the robe on my back, and I wasn't about to give them that. "I would be more than happy to go back to the house and find something shiny for you." I smiled in a friendly fashion, doing my level best not to cause offense, and added, "I'll be right back!"

"No," they replied, fixing me with their strange watery gaze. "That won't do. You have to pay the toll before you go. That's the rule. Perhaps," they mused, laying a long finger along their jaw thoughtfully. "You could tell me a story, and sit with me for a while."

"Alright," I agreed, tugging my robe more tightly closed around me. "Sure." The troll extended their hand to me, and when I touched it, I slithered underneath the bridge, alongside them.

It was surprisingly cozy and colorful, in the troll's hole. The uneven walls were covered with beautiful, soft tapestries, and the effect was mesmerizing. The troll found me a comfortable place to sit, nestled in among their shelves of books, near a small window where I could watch the hypnotic shadows of the water dancing on the smooth earthen floor.

"What story do you want to hear?" I asked them once I was settled.

"The story inside of you," they replied, taking my hands in their long, cool fingers and looking deeply into my eyes. "Tell me the story of how you came to be."

"The story of me?" I considered this for a moment. "I guess you could say that my story began when I learned my own true name. Or, maybe just a few hours before that." They nodded expectantly, and I took a deep breath and began. "Once upon a time, there was a girl driving through the rain down a lonely stretch of highway in her mom's old minivan."

"What a wonderful story," they said, once I had finished. "Have you considered writing it down? I would love to have a copy for my collection." They gestured to the bookshelves beside me, crammed with all sorts of papers and curiosities alongside the countless books. "But that is more than you owe me. What if I tell you a story, in return?"

I nodded, taking the sheaf of papers they handed me, and settling in to listen as they constructed an entire universe in the space between us. It was a beautiful story, and when they finished telling it, they asked if I would like to hear another.

It was in that way that I passed my first year in the troll's hole, telling stories and writing them down for each other. Exchanging truths about ourselves in the form of prose and fiction. The more they talked, the more deeply I fell, and the more deeply I fell, the more beautiful they looked until I could not imagine anything more exquisite than their smooth gray skin and fathomless eyes.

In my second year in the troll's hole, I studied the reflection of my face in their cool gray eyes, until I forgot the self-loathing I learned as a child and began to accept, and then to love, and eventually to even like what I saw there. And, in my third year, we asked each other deep, probing questions until we didn't know our own minds anymore. Then we reconstructed them out of the rubble, and understood ourselves better for it, and when they were troubled by the cruel voices in their head, in the way that I learned it was a troll's nature to be troubled, I would hold them to my breast and whisper sweet nothings into their soft curls and promise that I would never leave them.

In my fourth year in the troll's hole, we debated about morality, long into the night, pulling sources down from the overstuffed bookshelves to argue our points, honing my reasoning ability until it felt razor sharp. In my fifth year, we examined the concepts of man and woman, masculine and feminine, and with my newly honed reasoning ability, found that those ideas didn't make very much sense at all, if you really look at them. And, I felt my own attachment to being a woman drift away into irrelevance. And then we talked about the idea of being a parent and the experience of being a child until there wasn't anything more for either of us to say on the subject.

Eventually, I felt hungry, and having detached from the shame I took on in childhood as part of my identity as a woman and having fallen deeply in love with the version of myself I saw reflected in the troll's eyes, I told them of my hunger, without guilt or apology. And so it was that in my sixth year, I picked up more books from the shelves and taught myself to cook. And, while we ate what I cooked, we made up our own language until we were completely unintelligible, then went back to English and started over and did it again.

In my seventh year in the troll's hole, we lay together, bodies entwined, and held each other in blissful stillness. I rested, deeply and well, in a way that I had never been allowed to do, in a way that I had never allowed myself to do, until I felt well and whole. Until I felt ready.

zrp zrp
it's time

I jolted upright in surprise.

"What is it?" my love asked me, disturbed by the sudden motion. "What happened?"

"I have no idea," I told them, but even as I said the words, memories started flooding my mind. Images of a life I forgot, and a whole world outside this troll hole.

zrp zrp
remember me

"Oh!" I exclaimed, putting a hand to my midsection. "My love, I think I'm pregnant!"

In that moment, everything changed. The cozy, familiar sight of the troll's hole melted around me, and my love, the troll, rose up to a terrible height above me.

"YOU'RE PREGNANT?" they roared, looming over me like a great gray mountain. "GET OUT!"

And then I was alone, in my flowery robe, sitting on a carpet of soft clover. I cried out for my love, but they were not there, and I felt my heart break, and I wept. I had lived an entire lifetime in their arms. I had grown and changed and become myself, and now the only person who knew me, the only other person I had spoken to in years, was gone.

zrp zrp
what years

My heart, lying broken in my chest, now fell into my stomach with a sickening plummet. How long had I been lost in faerieland? Who had I left behind? What must they have thought when I disappeared without a trace? Distant memories of people I once knew bubbled up to the surface of my mind. Evita, whose eyes look so much like mine. Jaah's dark face and bright white smile. Nora's pale blond—

"Nora!" I cried out in horrified realization. "Oh no! I never went to help Nora!" The thought of her, and the memory of her face when she walked away from me was still painful, but not like it once had been. Now, it was like a well-scabbed wound, tender but nearly healed. I had wondered if she would even want me there to help her, but now, with the clarity of time and distance, I realized that it didn't matter.

Her plan wouldn't have worked without the items I was supposed to bring for her. My own ego was irrelevant. She had a plan to take control of her life. To make meaningful change in the world and do real good by stopping a bad man. And I didn't show up for her. I'd let her down. I had failed her.

Sobbing even harder, I curled up into a ball and let my tears flow onto the earth beneath me, ignoring the tiny rocks and sticks that needled at my bare legs. I cried until I didn't have any more tears left, and then I lay there, in horrified silence, for a long time. How long it had been, I wasn't sure, but after seven years in faerieland, it hardly seemed like it would matter.

"Fiona? Fiona!" A voice called out, and I heard footsteps approaching. Slowly, I disentangled my limbs and sat up, blinking against the bright sun. "Fiona! There you are. We've been looking everywhere for you."

It was Lucy Bee bouncing toward me, with a look of concerned relief on her face.

"Oh, Lucy, is that really you?" I asked, reaching out for her. "It feels like it's been a lifetime since I last saw you."

"You okay, honey?" she asked, looking at me critically and extending a hand to help me off the ground. "Seemed like you weren't feeling too well last night."

"Last night?" I repeated. "Lucy, what are you saying?"

"I'm saying you've been missing since this morning, hon. Did you hit your head or something?"

"Since this morning? What time is it?"

"Almost one o'clock, by now, I'd think. Come on inside and we'll get some lunch together, okay?"

"One o'clock?" I repeated, welling excitement replacing my despondent gloom. "I can still make it! There's still time!"

Chapter 49

Good girl. So calm and focused.

The thought drifted through my mind in a voice that was not my own, as I gripped the steering wheel and sped down the highway toward my goal, doing my best not to let the speedometer drift too high, in my anxiety.

Mind so clear that you can even hear me? My, my. That is an improvement, isn't it?

The voice sounded comforting and familiar. It stirred up a memory of a time that I was scared and alone, and the ghost of one of my ancestors visited me. Or, not a ghost exactly, more like a copy of my ancestor that I carry inside myself.

"Mama Jo?" I asked aloud.

Yes, dear. Feels like it's been a lifetime since we last spoke, doesn't it? It's just amazing what a little rest and contemplation will do to clear out some of that idle chatter. Your head is usually so noisy, you know.

"A lifetime," I repeated. "Mama Jo, what just happened to me? I spent years with that troll. I know I did. I remember everything. Or, at least, I did remember. Now I'm not so sure. But I feel different. I am different," I let the words tumble out of me. "But everything else is the same. Did I make it up? Did I hit my head or something?"

You didn't make it up, dear. You're right, you are different. You've grown up, and a good thing, too, to be the kind of mother this child deserves. And you will be, of course. It's what you were born to do.

"Because I'm a woman?" I asked, frowning at the thought.

No, because you're a faerie godmother, like your mother before you and her mother before her. Though I hear she's styling herself as 'Queen' these days. But, there's no real difference, just a matter of scale.

"I'm a…what? A faerie godmother? What is that supposed to mean?"

Yes, child. You are. And it means that you're going to keep doing exactly what you're doing now. Finding people who need what you can give them, and giving them what they need.

"That sounds exhausting," I replied with a tinge of bitterness. "No wonder Evita is tired all the time."

Your mother has overextended herself. Focus on the work that feeds your soul and let everything else go, child. Are you exhausted now? How does your body feel?

How did I feel? My knuckles were white where they gripped the steering wheel. My whole body felt energized and ready. My heart wasn't racing, but I could feel its powerful beat in my chest.

"I feel really good, actually," I told her.

As you should, because you are standing in your power, and acting in alignment with yourself. You have understood this girl to be one of your own, and you are giving her what she needs to succeed in her aims.

"Is that why I've been so drawn to her all summer? Because I'm her faerie godmother?" I considered the implications of that, and added, "Wait, what about that kiss? Is it ethical for me to be kissing godchildren?"

Yes, dear. Sometimes what our people need from us is our love or our affection. You wouldn't be the first one to get caught up on the 'mother' aspect, but you'll only be a parent to that little one you're carrying.

"Good to know," I said with a little sigh of relief. "That's very helpful, actually. But why are you talking to me like this? Did I level up, and now you get to give me all this info about my new powers, or something?"

No, child. I'm always *talking to you. You've just managed to quiet your mind enough to be able to hear me. Before you took that time to grow up a little, the only one who could cut through the chatter was that baby.*

"So, it's just a coincidence that I happen to be learning all of this right now?"

A lucky coincidence, certainly. And luck is a significant part of our magic, you know. For instance, this will be an excellent reminder that our ancestors live inside our bodies. Now, don't miss your turn!

"Oh!"

I swerved into the off-ramp at the last possible moment, grateful there weren't any other cars nearby. In just a few minutes, I was pulling into the alleyway behind the sinkhole that used to be the Valley of Christ's Heart Church. The whole area was cordoned off with caution tape and temporary fencing, but I could see that there were still some buildings standing at the edges of the collapse. There were 'No Trespassing' signs everywhere, but Nora assured me that Reverend Rex would pay those no mind. It was his church, after all.

I stepped out of the van, unsure of what to do. I'd brought the things Nora asked for, but she left before we could iron out the finer details.

"Hey," said a quiet voice. It was Nora, of course. She stepped out of the shadows where she was waiting, and gave me a sad little smile. "Thanks for coming."

"Of course," I said. "It's good to see you. I was worried."

"I'm sorry," she said, voice flat and expressionless. "I didn't mean to worry you. I just needed to figure some stuff out by myself. And you have a family to focus on. I'm not going to get in the way of that."

"Nora, I'm so sorry I didn't tell you about Jaah. I just-we…" I paused, then tried again. "I didn't know how to tell you. But Jaah and I, we're not exclusive. It doesn't mean that you and I couldn't…" I stopped, seeing the expression on her face.

"You told me to listen to my intuition, and I believed you. My intuition tells me that family is sacred. Motherhood is sacred. I'm not going to complicate things between a little baby and its parents."

"Okay," I told her, glad to have the distance and maturity that my time with the troll gave me. "I understand. Now, how can I help you with your plan? Do you really think the Reverend is going to be here today?"

"I know he is," she replied. "He's in the little chapel, now. I drove up with him this morning."

"You went back?" I exclaimed, aghast, then clapped my hand to my mouth, embarrassed by my outburst.

"Of course I did," she shot back, eyes flashing. "Where was I supposed to go? I know what happens to girls like me, out on the streets. No," she said, seeing the expression on my face. "I appreciate everything you did for me, but I can't rely on your charity forever. I need to make my own way and figure out how to take responsibility for myself. Now that I know how much of my power they're stealing, there's no way I'm going to let them keep doing it, but I need some time to make a plan and figure out my next move."

"Okay," I said. "I can see that. But, aren't you scared, now you know the truth about your Uncle?"

"Petrified," she agreed. "But that's better than powerless, and that's how I felt before. You know, they didn't even ask any questions when I came back? Just welcomed me back into the fold with open arms. I've never been the one who needed to be forgiven before. It's like they expected me to be a sinner, and didn't even care. Like the rules don't even really matter, as long as I keep my head down, and stay with the flock."

"Really? All those rules, and they don't even care?" That was such a stark contrast to the play parties and revels, where the rules were there to keep everyone safe, and if you broke them, you had to learn from your mistakes, or you had to leave. I said as much to Nora.

"Yeah," she agreed with a dark little laugh. "And the ones who don't learn end up in places like Christ's Heart, where they can do evil and be forgiven over and over again. Like my Uncle. I like the sound of your community better. I think that's how my grandmother's was, too, from what Mr. Rainbow told me, and what it says in her journals."

The mention of her grandmother reminded both of us of the task at hand.

"So, how do you want to do this?" I asked her.

"Well, my grandmother was the only one he was ever afraid of, right?" I nodded in agreement. "And you've got her séance stuff, don't you?" I nodded again. "I'm supposed to be good with ghosts, I guess. I was thinking I could, um, call out to her spirit and see, uh, whether she can help?" Nora's voice quavered, much more tentative than it was, up on the side of the mountain, when we first discussed this plan. "I'm just hoping that it's really her, and not one of those trickster spirits I read about in her journals."

"Yeah," I agreed with a little shudder. "That wouldn't be ideal."

zrp zrp
her body

"You know what, I might have a better idea," I said, and told Nora about my experience on the drive this morning, and about the time when I first came to town, in the spring, when Mama Jo had appeared outside my body, to help me through a particularly difficult night. "What if we call on the part of your grandmother that lives inside you?"

"I've been talking to her, actually, in my head," Nora confessed. "After everything Sage told me about Jesus, I started talking to my grandmother instead. She and Jesus say mostly the same things, but she sounds a little different than he did. Do you think it's actually her?"

"If this works, we can ask her. Should we give it a try?"

We gathered ingredients for the ritual from my spell case, selecting a plain white candle, a feather, some moon water, and uncorking a little bottle labeled 'grave dirt' that I hadn't noticed before. Next, Nora opened her grandmother's boxes, handing me a long black dress and veil, and a decorative bottle.

"Anointing oil," Nora told me, as I examined the beautiful object. "That's what her journals call it. She used to put a drop of it between her eyes." Next, she pulled out the scarf-wrapped card deck. "Oh, whoops," she muttered, as the scarf fell open and one of the cards slipped out.

"Judgment," I read, picking it up and handing it back to her. "Sounds about right. Birdie's Judgment Day."

"And this," said Nora, ducking back into the shadows and emerging with her grandmother's pointed hat. "That's everything I can think of. Now, follow me." She ducked underneath the caution tape and behind the temporary fence. She didn't look back until she reached a courtyard tucked between two of the smaller buildings that had not been destroyed. It was surprisingly peaceful, with a spiral of rocks at the center of it, and ferns growing in the shady corners. "My Uncle is in this chapel, right here," she told me, indicating one of the buildings with her chin. "I thought this would be an alright place for the ritual."

"Yeah," I agreed. "It'll be great."

We set out our elements, with the candle in the South, the moon water in the West, the feather toward the East, and the grave dirt in the North. Nora stood at the center of the spiral and placed a drop of oil between her eyebrows. Then she put on her grandmother's black dress, and her long, dark veil and finally the fringed witches hat.

"What am I supposed to do now?" she asked, but I didn't have any more of an idea than she did. Probably less, since it wasn't my spell. I shrugged noncommittally, giving her time to consider. Finally, she cleared her throat and made an invocation.

"Grandmother, please come help me."

"That's all you needed to say, young Eleanora," my friend said, in a voice that was not her own. She smoothed her long skirts and straightened her hat, then strode purposefully toward me. "Thank you for helping my granddaughter bring me here. Now, please excuse me, I have some business to attend to."

I sat down on a decorative bench to wait. Within a minute or two, a high, keening wail rose up from behind the wall that Nora had disappeared behind. This was followed by some muffled sounds of shouting and crying, but I couldn't make out any of the words. Eventually, there was silence, and finally, the door swung open again, and the black-shrouded figure swept back around the corner.

"We need to get away from here. Take my granddaughter home, now, please."

"Okay," I agreed, walking with Eleanora back the way we came. "Did it work?"

"I believe so, yes," said the curt voice of the woman beside me. She sounded so different from her granddaughter. It was strange to think that two such different voices could come out of the same mouth. "Thank you again for this opportunity to come back and take care of some unfinished business. I wasn't a perfect mother, and none of us are. But, it just wouldn't do to leave behind that monster as my legacy."

"What did you do to him?" I asked.

"I scared him. Quite badly, I think. He's a frightened boy. Always was. That's where his cruelty comes from, I think. His fear of being powerless, and the desire to prove that he's not."

"You think you scared him straight?" I asked, trying not to let any hint of skepticism sneak into my tone.

"No, of course not. If I could have done that, I would have managed it when he was a child. No, his fear will not be his saving grace."

"So, what, then?" I asked, and to my surprise, she laughed.

"Well, I told him that I would be haunting him for the rest of his days, and that it didn't matter what powerful ghost wards he found in the church's occult archives and tried to raise against me. I would always find a way to break through them, to plague him with nightmares, as punishment for his evil acts."

"Is that true?" I asked, and she shook her head in reply.

"Of course not. I live inside my granddaughter's body. I can't haunt anyone. But, knowing my son, he'll be like a dog with a bone, sure that he can find some arcane spell to stop me. The church has enormous stockpiles of ancient texts that they keep safeguarded from the likes of you or little Nora, but a big important man like my son would be able to keep himself busy with obsessive research for the rest of his unpleasant days. And, of course, I know that my Birdie has always been tortured by his nightmares."

"So, whenever he has a nightmare, he'll think you've broken through his ghost wards to haunt him, and have to start again?"

"That's the idea. I also told him that I would be helping the police solve my own murder, so if he wanted to stay out of jail, he'd better get outside the local jurisdiction before they arrest him. I said it like a mother who cares about his well-being, too," she added with a wry chuckle. "Which is pretty rich, considering he killed me. But, I expect he'll be on the next flight back to Europe, which will give my sweet granddaughter some breathing room, at least."

"Why is he like this?" I asked, unable to help myself. That was the question that had been eating at me, since I had first discovered that Reverend Rex was the evil Ibex we were searching for.

"I am not sure," said Eleanora. "But I do know that he is a powerful Archon of the Demiurge. One of the tools that the CCC uses to spread darkness over the world. Now, it is possible that the Demiurge saw his potential and recruited him after he ran away from home, but I don't think so. There is a lot of magic in the hills where I raised my children, and there's been something wrong with Birdie since he was small. I have to wonder if maybe something got to him and burrowed itself deep inside. So deep that nothing I did, as his mother, could ever really reach him. It's hard to believe that there's darkness in your own child, and it took me longer than I'd like to admit to truly see him for what he is."

Back at my van, the girl had shivered then stripped off the veil and dress, stuffing them back into their box, clearly Nora, once again. We didn't talk much on the drive back to the big brick house.

"Good luck," I said, as I slowed to a stop. "With everything."

"Yeah," she replied in a small voice. "Thanks." She hefted her box awkwardly and headed toward the door, then paused and turned back to me. "I hope I'll get to see you again, some day."

"If you're ever looking for me, you can always ask at the Fair Isle," I told her, forcing my mouth into a smile that didn't reach my eyes. She nodded, then turned to go. She made it clear she didn't want to be my responsibility, so I didn't wait until she reached the front door before driving away.

When I got home, Pythia sprang out from around a corner and launched herself at me with an exclamation of. "Nice place!" and questions about Nora and the Reverend. Ever the helpful hostess, Lucy Bee had ushered us into seats on the back patio.

"And what? that's all there is to it?" Pythia crowed, one I told her the way Nora and I left things. "Girl, you are gonna be the death of me!"

"What am I supposed to do?" I asked, accepting the cool glass of iced tea Lucy Bee handed me.

"Now you've gotten that story out of the way," said Jaah, with a pointed look at their excitable sister. "I'd like to know what happened this morning. I got woken up by a screaming teapot, with no Fiona to be found. Care to explain yourself?"

"I'm sorry," I said sheepishly. "I just meant to get a breath of fresh air. I didn't mean to spend seven years in a troll's hole."

"Seven years?" Jaah echoed, eyebrows knitting as they considered this.

"Apparently, it was actually only seven hours, but it felt like seven years to me."

"You do look older," said Lucy Bee, and we all turned to look at her in confusion. "Well, I guess you don't actually look different, really, but when I met you, it felt like we were about the same age, and now it doesn't."

"Well, I want to see this troll bridge," said Jaah, who stood up and strode purposefully off the porch. Lucy, Pythia, and I followed them into the garden and through the trees until we reached the little creek.

"There's no bridge here," said Jaah, looking left and right along the burbling brook. They were right, of course. The bank was bare and empty. I scanned along it, looking for any sign of the troll I had loved.

"Oh!" I exclaimed, bending and retrieving a small rectangular package that was tucked between two rocks, right at the edge of the streambank. I tore the brown paper wrapping off, revealing a sheaf of paper with a symbol drawn on the top.

"What's that?" Jaah asked, as I sank to the ground, unsure whether I was about to laugh or cry.

"It's my manuscript," I told them, tears pricking at the corners of my eyes. I had worked on it for ages, practicing the art of turning expansive thought into storytelling, and reading chapters to my love, the troll, in front of their cozy fire. "It's my story. The story of what happened when I first came to town. Of how I saved Faeryn." I hugged the bundle to my chest, tears starting to fall in earnest. "I thought it was gone, forever."

"Intermagical," said Jaah, bending close to read. "That's the title, huh? Makes sense. But, what's this symbol here?"

I turned the bundle over to look. "Oh!" I exclaimed with a little giggle. "It's a joke."

"What do you mean?"

"Well, we made it up. It represents reclaiming your magic," I explained. "Because it's a little sparkle star, right? Like a magical mote?"

"Okay," Jaah agreed. "I get that, but what's the joke?"

"Well, first you draw a cross, right?" I said, using my toe to draw the shape in the dirt by the riverbank. "And then you put a big X right on top. Cross that cross right out."

"Nice," Jaah agreed. "Magic without religion. Is this the icon for, what do you call it, Logical Mysticism?"

"Oh," I said, considering the idea. "Yeah, maybe."

A symbol for the ideology of Logical Mysticism? I hadn't ever really considered that. But, I remembered how it felt when I first learned about intermagicals and the truth about our magical world, and how it had been, sharing that knowledge with Nora. If I really was a faerie godmother, there was a good chance I would be called to share that knowledge, again and again, when I found people who needed it. It wouldn't be a bad thing to have an emblem. And, I thought, with a wry smile for the crossed cross in the dirt, it did fit.

Back inside the Garden Home, I drifted from room to room, unsure what to do with myself, now that everything with Nora was over and done with. There was nothing ahead of me, except months of waiting for this baby to grow. Time in the troll hole had just flown by, but now it dragged. Probably because each month with the troll had only lasted about five minutes, I realized, staring out the kitchen window moodily.

Something caught my eye, and I turned my head, glad for the distraction. It was Lucy Bee, coming around the corner. My glance must have surprised her because she jumped and skittered off out of the kitchen, then slowly leaned her owlishly magnified eyes back around the corner to peer at me.

"Hey Lucy, you alright?" I asked her.

"Yeah, sorry about that," she replied, stepping back through the doorway. "I'm not used to having other people in the house yet, and you surprised me. You've got a real strong aura, you know that, Fiona? Makes me a little nervous sometimes," she added with an anxious giggle.

"It'll be an adjustment for all of us," I agreed.

"That's true. And hey, speaking of me being startled, I wanted to apologize about last night. After you went to bed, Jaah told me about how you two are polyamorous, and with the way I was startled, maybe it looked like something was going on, but I just want to let you know that there is no danger of that, from my side. That's your family, and I'm just going to make sure I keep myself at an appropriate distance, and remind myself that that kind, considerate, extraordinarily good-looking man is attached and off limits, okay? I'll just—"

"Well, for one thing," I said, interrupting her, "they're not exactly a man. And you're right, I did have a pretty strong reaction, seeing you and Jaah together, but I've had some time to process that since last night," I told her. "I really like you, Lucy. I know we just met, but I have a sense about people, and I have a really good feeling about you. I'd like you to be a part of this family, too, and that means being authentically yourself."

"Aw, Fiona!" said Lucy, wrapping me up in a tight hug.

"So, if you and Jaah like each other, you should explore that, okay?" I told her. "Just go slow and be careful. We're building something to last, right?"

"Really?" she asked, eyes like saucers behind her lenses. "Do you really mean it? I was so worried that I'd upset you, and I really like you, too, and I really want us to be friends. Friends? Oh, I forgot!" She rifled in her pocket and came up with a folded slip of paper, which she handed to me. "Your friend stopped by. Big, charming fellow. He gave me this for you."

Hey Fiona, guess what? Fredbeard just called my mom and told her that he'd gotten the legal stuff all sorted. We get to have our fair this year, after all! We never gave up hope, so we're not starting from scratch, but there's a lot to do if we're going to be ready to open on Saturday. We'd be happy for the extra hands, if you want to come out and help.

Tomorrow, I would head out to the fairgrounds and help Urb, I decided, and a wave of serenity washed over me, a sharp contrast from the despondent moroseness of a few moments ago. Urb must be one of mine, I realized, remembering what Mama Jo had said. Maybe I really was a faerie godmother after all.

Chapter 50

Saturday morning, I stood next to Urb and waved to fairgoers as they passed through the faux castle that served as a front gate for the Shrewsborough Renaissance Faire.

"Hey, don't I recognize that group from Christ's Heart?" I asked, as a gang of college-aged men and women walked past, including the exceptionally beautiful girl I watched being baptized. "What are they doing here? They aren't allowed to do this kind of stuff. It's an evil revel."

"Well, the church has been closed for over a month now," Urb said with a shrug. "It's not like the college kids are going to drive down to Eugene every weekend. With the weekly reminders gone, the rhetoric probably dried up pretty quick."

"Well, isn't that great?" I said with a smile. "I'm really happy for them."

"Ren! You got this?" called a woman in a motorized wheelchair, carrying an overstuffed clipboard that matched Urb's. He turned his head and gestured with his own clipboard.

"Ren?" I asked, confused.

"It's the name she gave me, so I don't mind if she uses it," Urb said in his characteristically sheepish way. "It's short for Serenity. Plus, Mom never found the name 'Urb' as funny as Dad and I did."

At my questioning look, he added, "It's short for Disturbance. You know, since Serenity didn't fit?"

"Disturbance, really?" I asked.

"Yeah," he said with a laugh. "What can I say, I appreciate a good shake-up. I know you guys didn't really mean to, but personally, I thought all that stuff with the church this summer was freaking cool. That sinkhole was one of the best things that could have happened to this town."

zrp zrp
me too

"Well, it's nice to be appreciated," I said with another chuckle. "If we really did have something to do with it, and there is still plenty of room for doubt about that."

"If you say so," Urb replied, with a shake of his head. "Next, you're going to say that you didn't actually do anything to fix my luck, either."

"Well, are you having any more luck getting what you want at the bakery in the morning?" I asked, and Urb shrugged in reply.

"Sometimes, yes, sometimes no. But, if I'm really in the mood for something, I'll ask real nicely, over my left shoulder, and sometimes it seems like that helps," he said with a laugh. "But, Sage says she'll stop by the fair later today, and we have another date planned for next week, so I'd say things are going alright."

"Well, luck is in the eye of the beholder, I guess," I said, happy for my friend.

"Fiona!" a cry rang out in the crowd, and I turned to look.

It was Faeryn, smiling at me with rosy cheeks and eyes brighter than I'd ever seen them.

"You look great!" I told her, giving her a hug over the new life-preserver-shaped device that she wore, to circulate her spring water. "It's so good to see you."

I hadn't seen my cousin since she returned to her mother's city a few weeks ago, and I realized how much I missed her passion and her fire. Faeryn was like a hot stove. She'd burn you if you touched her wrong, but she could heat a whole household with her warmth, and I basked in it. It was easy to see why her subjects held their princess in such high regard, and I was sure they were overjoyed to have her back home with them.

"What a beautiful revel," she breathed, spinning in a slow circle. Pennant-topped tents were filled with all manner of colorful frippery, and patrons in various states of costume watched a juggler gamboling on stilts. She sighed happily, taking it all in. "Shrewsborough has always been my favorite fair."

"What do you want to do first?" I asked her.

"Eat everything," she said with a grin. "I've finally managed to get my appetite back, and I want a turkey leg."

"It's wonderful to see you eat like that, my love," said Arlee, watching Faeryn devour the enormous drumstick with gusto. I had to agree. After a summer of watching her pick at her food, this was a beautiful sight.

"Seems like your research is going well," I said.

"Yes, and no," she said, taking another bite of the leg. "I've managed to block the worst of it, and I am feeling much better, but Velia's curse is drawing on some awfully dark forces, and there are still some pieces I'm struggling to untangle. That woman is a piece of work. You've got to have some real nastiness inside of you to make magic like that."

"Well, let me know if there's anything I can do to help. The three of us were throwing around quite a bit of power this summer, protecting the valley. Can we do some kind of ritual for it?"

"Maybe," said Faeryn. "I'll let you know. The trick is figuring out what she's doing, so I know what we should do to counteract it, you know what I mean? And there's still the question of why our magic was so strong."

"Oh, well, I might have a clue about that," I said, cheeks flushing.

"You're pregnant! Of course!" she exclaimed, once I told her my news. "That makes perfect sense, actually."

"It does?" I asked. "Care to fill me in? I could use another magic lesson."

"Well, we were calling on the power of the triple goddess, weren't we? The triskelion. I poured one when we did that divination in my bath, do you remember? I should have realized it then, but that curse had my brain so foggy I could hardly put one thought in front of the other."

"That was on the summer solstice, wasn't it?" I asked, furrowing my brow in recollection, and she nodded. "Yep, that was the night I got pregnant. Must have been."

"I remember the way the energy was flying around. And there was a full moon and a meteor shower too, wasn't there? You two certainly made something powerful that night."

"Yeah," I said, putting a hand to my stomach. "I think we did."

"Oh, there you are," said Evita, coming up behind me and giving my shoulders a squeeze. "I've been looking for you two. I've got a little spell, and I'd like you to help me energize it."

"Sure," I agreed, following Evita back to the front of the fair. "What are we doing, Mom?"

"Just a blessing," she replied, leading us toward the beautiful display of garden flowers that she gifted to Shrewsborough. Now that I looked more closely, I could see that the bouquet was also a piece of spellwork, and I joined hands with Evita and Faeryn, forming a circle around it. "I thought the three of us might want to make it a tradition."

"I love that," I said, smiling, but I saw a dark shadow cross Faeryn's face beside me. "What is it?" I asked, giving her hand a squeeze. She shook her head, replacing the troubled expression with a tight smile.

"Well, if Fiona has a little girl, she can take my place as the maiden, if I'm not here next year."

"What do you mean, dear?" asked Evita. "Of course you'll be here next year. Where else would you want to be?"

"Nowhere," answered Faeryn, looking beyond us and out at the fair.

More of our family had arrived without my noticing. There were Jaah and Pythia, and Zinnia and Azalea, too. I watched as Azalea tickled her sister with a long peacock feather and then dashed off, with Zinnia in fierce pursuit. And Lucy Bee, bobbling along behind them. Egan and Zelai were there, too, perusing a stall selling handcrafted weapons. I continued to scan the crowd, until I found Calliope, eyes closed, swaying to the music of bards playing the lute. I had never seen her look so relaxed and content, I thought, resolving to invite her to the Garden Home for a visit, some time soon.

I couldn't remember a time when I was more relaxed or content, either, I thought, squeezing the hands on either side of me. I'd helped to give our community back our festivals. I had given Nora what she needed to set herself free. And, I had grown up into someone who was ready to be the mother my child deserved, with a loving family and community to support me, and a beautiful place to call home. At that very moment, everything was right in my world.

Inspired, I spoke. "Yesterday is in the past, and tomorrow is never guaranteed, but right now, we are all here, together at the fair. If all we have is this season, this one beautiful moment, let us be grateful for this time and enjoy it."

"Blessings on this beautiful day," Evita cried, and we released our clasped hands, sending our intentions out into the clear summer sky.

Author's Note

Thank you for coming on this journey with me. If you haven't read it yet, this would be an excellent time to pick up Intermagical, and see where all the trouble started, you know? And you do know, now. The broad strokes, at least. And that's the best way to look at a story like this: from a distance, for the impression of it all. This is a work of fiction, but there is a lot of truth woven throughout the story. Truth about the world we live in, and about my own life, also.

Fiona takes up the mantle of her true name and unlocks her magic at the extraordinarily young age of 22. I did have the opportunity to follow that path myself, but instead I found my way (essentially) into a troll's hole and didn't step through that particular door until after the transformative process of having a child and becoming a mother, at age 30.

Now, five years later, I'm editing this novel while my son snuggles me on the couch, home sick in his first month of kindergarten. It took me a long time to unpack the trauma of my competent yet cold upbringing and discover my own guiding light and personal truth.

The book's Fiona managed to unlock her magic in one fell swoop. (Or swell foop, as I'm fond of saying.) Sometimes I wish I'd done it faster, like she did, or otherwise done things differently, but generally, I'm glad to have taken things slow, and unpacked my trauma carefully, at my own pace. My own journey to personal understanding has come with the comfortability of being an adult who has had sufficient practice at being myself.

All this to say, if you have finished this book feeling a bit behind in your own journey, or perhaps even jealous of the leaps-and-bounds progress of our young heroine (or looking askance at her tender age, in the face of her impeding motherhood) please know that I, the author, am standing right beside you, having that self-same experience.

I like to call the New World Fae series 'fam fiction', idealizing and romanticizing reality, with a dazzling of fae illusion, into something that might have been. Writing is a uniquely human magic, after all.

This series was inspired by the magic I discovered when I moved to Oregon to get to know my birth family, and especially my cousin, whom you know as Faeryn and Visc. In Festival Season we meet more of the important people who make up my own magical world.

The characters of Calliope and Urb are inspired by members of my found family, both of whom are trans, and thusly, so are their characters. The inspiration for Nora was a girl from the Renaissance faire, who did remind me a lot of a childhood friend of mine who died young, but, as far as I know, neither of them were ever members of a predatory evangelical church. My second boyfriend was, though. The sweet kid I dated for a while, after breaking up with my first love, the elven redhead. I held his hand as he battled with the demons of his upbringing, ultimately deciding to leave his family's high-control religion.

I was raised by atheists, and have always felt an undeniable pull toward the magical and the mystical. My lifelong fascination with comparative religion and deeply logical neurodivergent brain has left me with a lot of thoughts and opinions about religion and mysticism. I look at Evangelical Christianity from an outsiders perspective, just like Fiona does in the story, and marvel at the evils that are perpetrated by its infection of the Western World.

Like Intermagical, this book flowed out of me like water, the first draft completed within the calendar month of November 2022. It feels as though these stories are coming from something outside of myself, like I am stepping into the stream of inspiration and receiving them as gifts, almost fully formed. Although, my background and life experiences are so interwoven into the story that it certainly feels like I am the right person to deliver this message.

If I had to guess, I'd say that the stories of the New World Fae are a gift from those hidden folk, for all of us, to share this important message in these dark times. But, specifically, these books are a gift for my cousin, the real faerie princess, who died less than a month before the release of Intermagical, knowing that she would get to live on in fiction, in the hearts and minds of all of you. She had a fierce love for Intermagical. Festival Season, though, she was less fond of. I can understand why. It captures more of the difficult truths of her experience living with chronic illness, and of her own fiery faerie nature. She didn't tell me not to, though, and I think that's because she understood, like I do, that people will know her better, this way, and to know her is to love her.

Thank you to everyone who has helped bring the New World Fae to life. My nuclear found-family, who are already honored here as Jaah, Calliope, Urb and Lucy Bee, and the other important members of Team Intermagical: Holly, the Admiral, my editor Mekhala Spencer, my friends who have been beta readers and gifted me their attention and their opinions, and all my parents, who have done the hard work and made the necessary transformations for us to have a relationship, in adulthood. None of this would be possible without you, and you have my unending gratitude for your gifts of time and resources and for allowing me the space to let this all-encompassing mission take over my life so completely.

There is a third, and perhaps final, installment in the tale of my family and the New World Fae, that is sitting in draft on a shelf somewhere. I expect I'll get that odd, itchy feeling when it's time to take it back down and polish it into something ready for all of you, just like I did with Festival Season. But, I have the sense that I have a little more living and experiencing to do, myself, before it will be time for that.

I hope this book gives you what you need, whatever that is. A launching-off point for new thought, a good laugh, a feeling of community and solidarity, or something else entirely, as long as it's helpful and moves you forward on your personal path. I am a faerie godmother after all.

As for me, I'll continue tripping gayly forward along my own path, preparing to release this book on the summer solstice, at the return of Brig-a-doom, the latest incarnation of the Pirate Carnival. Then, on into a summer of festivals, neurodivergent community, queer joy and magical revelry.

43

316

About the Author

The author, who grew up with the uncomfortable initials 'TS' and now lives much more happily as Fiona, moved to Oregon after college to get to know her birth family. At that point, fiction and reality diverge, but much of this work of fiction was inspired by the real people and experiences of the author's magical life with her husband, young son, bonus children, polyamorous loves, and an ever-expanding neurodivergent community in the mystically beautiful Pacific Northwest.

Fiona never set out to be a writer, but she did live with one for most of her twenties, a highly intelligent and deeply magical bridge troll who inadvertently gifted her with the knack of turning expansive thought into storytelling. She started her career in the field of mental health to satisfy her desire to understand why people are the way they are and provided care to adults with severe mental illness for several years before burning out and transitioning to the field of technology.

After resigning from a highly anticipated, but ultimately ill-fated start-up for whom she had been the acting CTO, she decided to take an easy administrator role for a year, to give herself a much-needed break. Without the intensive technological problem-solving to take up her intellectual bandwidth, the novel Intermagical flowed out of her like water from an underground spring, with a second installment following shortly after the first.

She looks forward to a long, green summer full of fun, festivals, and building a greater intermagical community.